the Huntress

This is a work of fiction. The characters, incidents, and dialogues in this book are of the author's imagination and are not to be construed as real. Any resemblance to actual events or persons, living or dead, is completely coincidental.

Also by Sevannah Storm

The Blood of Legends Series

The Huntress

The Healer

*

The Gifting Series

Soul Forged

Fate Forged

Sun Forged

War Forged

Star Forged

Shadow Forged

Earth Forged

Lust Forged

Fire Forged

*

The Qaldreth Warriors

Sol Survivor

*

The Space Hunter Chronicles

The Shikari

*

Standalones

Xiaxan Fox

Ire of Silver

*

Plump Playwright Series

Plump Jane

Seducing Amelia

Loving Finley

Keeping Tessa

Kissing Navy

*

COMING SOON

Inkoded

The Justisaar

Dark Survivor

CHAPTER ONE

BRAVERY VS. STUPIDITY

CALLIE TREMBLED IN THE darkness, unable to hide, not when they could hear her heart pound and scent her fear on this blustery night, not when she clung to the side of a building twenty levels up. Focusing on her breathing, keeping it shallow and as silent as possible, she tried not to hyperventilate. To them, she had to sound like a wheezing geriatric. She should have stayed away, but stubbornness was one of her *many* faults.

On top of it, she'd lost her gun when she'd first stepped onto the building's ledge. Her purse as well. Shoving the gun down the front of her gown to nestle between her breasts might have been a better option. The image of her captain lambasting her for losing her weapon *again* was enough to consider suicide. Thoughts of impending doom niggled her, tempting her to leap onto the moonlit balcony, throw herself at their feet and demand they end her life now.

She shrugged. Despite the paperwork losing her gun would entail, it didn't matter. Not at the moment. Therein lay her fear.

Balancing on her bare heels on a narrow ledge to eavesdrop? Insanity at its finest. She inched toward the balcony, rethinking her *genius* plan to climb onto the ledge and cling to the glass façade as if her fingertips were octopus tentacles. She wasn't *that* desperate for leads, was she?

Something suspicious was happening tonight, which explained why she was at Mayor Duhamel's ball, dressed like a sequined mannequin with enough make-up on to disguise a rhino. She stared at her manicured toes hanging over the edge. The chilly wind plucked at her burgundy gown, trying to rip her away from the building's embrace. She tightened her grip on the glass as if she could resist the wind's incessant nagging. Her cheeks stung, and if these bastards didn't hurry, she'd suffer from frostbite, or at the very least, she'd look like a happy cherub for days. Typical selfish suckbloods. Her fellow officers would show her no mercy. She grimaced—they'd torture her for sure.

"The drop-off is happening tomorrow evening," a sexy voice rumbled.

It was smooth like decadent dark chocolate. So sex-on-a-stick sexy he had to be a suckblood.

Drop-off?

"I want no surprises," said the suckblood.

"I don't expect any. They know better than to disappoint you," yet another sexy male voice reached her.

Shit! How many were there? She could take one, and only if she was properly armed, which she wasn't. The dagger strapped to her thigh was all this disguise allowed. Much good a single weapon would do her now.

"Good," said Suckblood One.

"Are you sure you want to do this alone? It doesn't sit right with me." Concern was clear in Suckblood Two's voice.

"I'll take a few guards with me, but I need you to hold the fort, so to speak." The first one's chuckle was deep, husky…alluring. "It's not as if I can't defend myself."

Callie nodded. They were excellent fighters, able to resist human weapons with ease. She'd developed her personal arsenal after years of dealing with suckbloods and beasts. The boys at the precinct mocked her for it but, in truth, her battle-readiness had spared many lives, including her own.

If Dad saw her now, though. She winced, imagining the shake of his head and the silly smile he donned when she'd done something brave or idiotic.

"Fine. Should I assist the woman off the ledge?" asked Suckblood Two.

She snorted at his question, confirming their awareness of her presence, and she didn't like the eagerness in his voice. He sounded ravenous.

"Her scent is delicious, but I need a drink, not nourishment. Do as you see fit."

"She does smell good," said Suckblood Two, as if the bouquet of her blood mattered.

Oh, fuck!

Suckblood Two's appearance at the balcony's railing made her grip on the glass slip. Tall, at least six-foot-four, with blond locks falling below his collar gave off a Viking-of-old vibe. His broad shoulders with matching biceps strained his sleeves in his expensive-but-struggling tux barely containing the visceral magnetism pouring off him.

His face was another matter—square jaw to a pointy chin with a dimple for added effect. An unnecessary effect. He was a stunner without it. How did they recruit converts? One look at him made her believe they trawled the fashion runways. To be beautiful forever would tempt Narcissus himself.

"Admiring the view?" he said.

A smirk curled his upper lip, yet she sensed no hostility, leaving her to stare into his entrancing blue eyes.

The wind whipped at her again, snatching her from the mesmerizing depths of his seductive eyes. She hadn't admired the view until now.

"Yes, stunning," she said, proud of herself for managing to string two words together.

"I could join you...?"

"It's a free world last time I checked," she said, her hair blowing around her face.

She wouldn't flick it out of her eyes, unwilling to remove her fingers from the glass.

"Or you could join me?" His voice cut through the wind.

Unable to see him, she huffed like an asthmatic hippo, trying to shift her hair. With the help of another gust of wind, she cleared her vision.

"For a scotch?"

She scowled. How did he know her preferred drink? She hadn't indulged tonight, so the scent of it didn't cling to her.

"Have we met?" She snorted at the naïve question.

Such a face wasn't easy to forget.

Said face burst into a charming smile she didn't appreciate. He offered his manicured hand as if beckoning her to trust him. Since the jig was up, she should accept his assistance. Besides, he might—and that was a humongous might—reveal more about this drop-off.

She slid her bare feet from heel to heel until her fingertips could brush his. He extended his arm and grasped her hand, his grip warm, firm. With a sharp tug, she tumbled into his arms.

Sprawled across the front of him, with her fingers curled over his tuxedoed shoulders, she drew in a shuddering breath. Despite having her feet back on something solid, she wasn't grateful. Concern furrowed her brow, instead. Her responses to men were never this instantaneous, but she expected it from a suckblood. She hoped he wasn't one. It would be nice to meet an attractive *human* man for a change. One who couldn't manipulate her with his pheromones.

"Your name?" He glided his hands up her bare back, drawing her into the warmth he emanated.

She shivered, goosebumps rippling from her spine to her thighs. After burrowing his nose in her neck, he inhaled her scent, shameless in his appreciation.

"Callista," she said.

"Ah, beautiful beloved huntress of Zeus." He chuckled.

Of course he knew what her name meant. Damn suckbloods. Overeducated arrogant bastards. Was that supposed to impress her? Okay, it did! But that didn't mean she had to *succumb* to his seductive ways.

"Yes." Her instincts screamed, demanding she flee.

She ignored them for now. This man had information about the package. Not that she had any idea what *it* was.

Disappointment dampened her mood. She should've known crashing this event wouldn't garner evidence—only raise more questions and create new crimes to investigate. Her compiled files on the various patrons attending tonight needed a few secrets to unlock the investigations further. She was desperate for closure.

He gathered her hand in his distracting her from her thoughts and brushed his lips across the pulse at her inner wrist. The sensation was too good to be natural.

His head shot up. He scowled, but it didn't detract from his dazzling handsomeness—it made him brooding, which was downright breathtaking.

"I must abandon you, sweet Callista. Rest assured, I will find you."

"Why?" She claimed her hand back.

She fought the urge to rub her wrist along her outer thigh to erase the memory of his kiss. He was too close for her senses or her instincts to handle, not to mention for her peace of mind.

Smothered by his presence, she raised her hands palm up, placed them on his chest, and pushed. He didn't budge, but she did, stumbling backward from the force she applied. She suspected she'd surprised him and thus gained her freedom. She'd felt his strength—iron-like and indomitable—beneath his tuxedo. He could have held her against him for as long as he pleased, and there wouldn't have been a damn thing she could do about it.

"Because you smell delicious." He smiled.

What had she expected? Typical suckblood, thinking with his stomach. The poor man was hungry, like she gave a damn. "So?"

He blinked, tilting his head to the side. "Don't I smell good too?"

She arched a brow, her suspicions confirmed. He *was* using his pheromones on her. His sheer beauty swayed her more than his cologne. Since he waited for her to respond, she leaned in to sniff him, her nose brushing along his Adam's apple, which bobbed at the contact. Citrus, bonfire, and earthy undertones combined to form a mind-numbing enticement, yet her knees remained unaffected.

She stepped back, resisting the temptation to place an open-mouthed kiss to his throat. Her knees were fine, but her lips weren't. They tingled, made demands of her, needing his skin's warmth. She forced a shrug, and his horrified expression was worth it. But when it morphed into a fascinated one, she sighed. It was official. Her evening wasn't going as planned. She should leave now and chalk it up as bad luck.

"You smell good. Your cologne suits you. Now, if you'll excuse me, I see scotch in my future."

Spinning on her bare toes, she made a beeline for her pumps she'd left in the back corner of the balcony. If only she'd thought to leave her purse there. What the hell had she been thinking? Climbing the side of a building while clutching her purse—idiotic. Not to mention, she couldn't bring herself to leave her gun unattended. Well, it sure lay unattended now, wherever it had landed. Hopefully, it hadn't hit someone on the head when it fell.

She sensed his gaze caressing her as she slipped on each shoe. At least he missed her wince as she squished her toes into unnatural shapes. Nerves had her fluffing her hair and sliding her damp palms down her velvet-covered thighs before entering the crowded, unbearably hot hall, vowing never to do something so stupid again. She hadn't gotten much for her crazy death-defying balancing trick.

There was a drop-off tomorrow? Hell, there was always a drop-off. What she needed was a location. Inner City was huge, so she'd appreciate any clue. This wasn't the movies. This was real life where information didn't magically fall into her eager hands—she had to fight for every morsel, every titillating secret.

Her targets had taken their champagne glasses to the balcony's seductive privacy. She'd raced here in the hopes of hiding behind a potted plant or in the shadows. There'd been neither with the balcony illuminated by Chinese lanterns. No one would speak of sensitive matters with her leaning against the railing admiring the cityscape. Now, while she hesitated at the door, a few men assessed her. None were panty-dropping gorgeous enough to match the first suckblood's voice.

Not that she could sweet-talk *him* into revealing the drop-off's location. If she guessed his current position, he was amid a group of desperate women, their body language blatant with intention. Lust's stench emanated from that side of the hall—oily, wicked...tempting.

Callie spun on her steel-tipped heels to weave through the dancing couples to the bar. She claimed a barstool with a deep groan, relief instant with her weight off her toes. Her killer heels were doing just that, killing her. Smothering a borderline hysterical giggle, she flicked her hair off her face, hating the frustration that pounded at her patience. Disappointment ate at her, at the disastrous outcome of a promising evening.

"Scotch, neat," she said to the bartender, not bothering to meet his gaze.

A tumbler of the burnished liquid glided across the glass counter and into her line of vision. She scooped it up and threw back the finest malt she'd tasted in a while. Peppery, smoky, and smooth, it flowed down her throat, bursting her innards into flames of false courage. She should've started the evening with this.

"Are you acquainted with Leonardo?" a gentleman asked. "You seemed cozy."

She stiffened, assessing the man...Devlin Carter. Needing the time to compose her thoughts and a poker face, she took a careful sip from her refilled glass.

He was tall, cresting six feet, and filled out a tux like no forty-year-old should be able to. Gray streaked his temples, adding to his distinguished appearance and his sensual appeal. Not that he tempted her—his nefarious deeds were well documented. Okay, only by her, and she never made it official. The very-much-human senator had a thick case file of his own. She'd been investigating him for years.

"Leonardo, Senator?" She opted for ignorance, arching a brow in query.

"That answers my question." He grinned.

His cold blue gaze traveled her bared leg and settled on her adorned foot. Oh, yes, the foot fetish. She fought the urge to twitch her toes under his unashamed depravity.

"You don't strike me as his type."

"Their type is human." She twirled the amber liquid in her glass before raising it to her lips again.

"Touché. Does he know you're in law enforcement?"

Knowing who she was, or at least, what she did, didn't bode well. Her instincts skittered along her nerves, worse than when she'd stepped onto the ledge. Something about Carter had her skin crawling. That something was slimy and dangerous.

"He didn't ask. I didn't offer." Her reply was sharp.

She sighed. Her miserable mood called forth her worst manners. Not to mention, he had her at a disadvantage. Somehow he had known she was police. She must have given herself away. Maybe her shifty gaze, distrusting everyone, her stiff shoulders and over-vigilant stance screaming she didn't belong here. She'd ruined the evening with her subconscious behavior.

She tried not to grimace at his delighted smile. He was enjoying their conversation, very much aware of how he put her on the defensive.

"So why crash James's party?" Carter gestured to the bartender, who served him a tall blonde beer with a thick head.

Beer? An interesting choice at a ball.

"I felt like dressing up." She tapped her unpolished fingernails on the glass countertop. "Listen, Senator, you're not one to waste time, nor to beat around the bush. Mind telling me the purpose of this conversation?"

Her bluntness made him chuckle. Thankfully she hadn't pissed him off. If that happened and her captain found out, she would be issuing parking tickets for a year.

"He's enamored with you," Carter said, not answering her question.

She shook her head. "Ah, so if we were on a first-name basis, I could spy for you?"

"Spy is such a nasty word, and I didn't ask you to," he said, licking the beer foam off his lips.

"My apologies, Senator." She flicked her hair back in an exaggerated manner and giggled, batting her eyelashes hard enough to hurt. "What I meant to say was that we could discuss over coffee the merits of suckblood-feeder relationships and the impact of this on the psyche."

If he found her sass offensive, he didn't show it. A consummate diplomat, he gave a deep belly laugh that sounded authentic. "Yes, something like that. I've heard horrendous stories of their sexual prowess. It's enough to harm my ego."

"Yours?" She admired his form, stopping to study the pin on his lapel—a large, winged bird embedded in flames.

It was solid gold and crafted by a master jeweler, she didn't doubt. She couldn't imagine him shopping at the local stores.

"Can anything harm your ego, Senator?"

"He's interested, mark my words, my girl." Carter shifted closer as if intending to share something for her ears only. "When he comes for you, pay attention to anything unusual. I don't trust these...suckbloods. Never have and never will." He flicked his two fingers, his business card pinched between them. "Here's my private number. Call me if you find anything useful."

She took the card and slipped it into her cleavage. She didn't want to accept it, but she sensed he'd stay with her until she did. He sauntered away to bombard other guests with his bombastic personality. Goosebumps prickled her skin in an instinctual warning that he wasn't a man to trust.

She didn't intend to have another scotch, but the interlude with Carter and his false happiness highlighted the sadness staining her heart. No matter the circumstances, the distractions, the environment, or the company, her sister's terminal illness circled the edges of her mind. Scotch wouldn't solve her problems, despite its aged smoothness. Her bed beckoned, and she planned on flopping onto it in a most unladylike manner.

Facing the hall, she caught a glimpse of her scowling captain bearing down on her.

So much for her best-laid plans...

Chapter Two

Forming an Attachment

Leo strode away from the balcony, his feet tingling like lead. An odd sensation for a vampire. Never had he regretted leaving a morsel as tempting as her. But Syl had summoned him, so he obeyed. Not that he feared his king, but he'd given a vow of loyalty, one that went deeper than blood.

"How was she?" Syl asked when Leo re-joined the party.

Beneath Syl's jovial demeanor lay a heart of gold. Most only saw what he portrayed—a charmer and a decadent vampire. His ability to assess a person's character was a gift Leo admired.

The overly perfumed women crowding his king irritated Leo tonight, his usual serenity absent. Shock and disappointment immobilized him—two emotions he hadn't experienced in a long time.

The bounty within Callista's veins had called to him, rumbling his stomach and moistening his tongue. He'd been too distracted to bother reading her thoughts, and now he wished he'd taken the time.

Glancing around the hall, he frowned at not spotting her. Had she left? He doubted Duhamel knew her. She wasn't his usual preferred guest, meaning Leo couldn't syphon any information from him. He sighed, not that he enjoyed trawling a human's mind. It felt...dirty, as if a thousand baths could not cleanse him.

"You called me back, so I didn't find out. Strangest thing, Syl. She didn't succumb to my pheromones" Leo rubbed his nape before dropping his hand with a drawn-out sigh.

To earn his loyalty, all Syl had done was kill Leo's sire, the bastard who'd massacred his family. The vampire forced him to watch as the blood ran freely from their sliced throats. His parents fought the hardest, wanting to protect their two children. He drained Leo's younger brother, tossing his corpse like a discarded rag, then licked his lips in absolute delight. Even as a young man, Leo hadn't been strong enough to fight off an ancient determined to *father* a son.

"Off your game tonight?" Syl teased.

It happened. Not taking offense at the implication, Leo spun to the closest woman, a brunette, and smiled, releasing the same amount of attraction he'd used on Callista. The woman gasped. Her cheeks flushed as her nipples pebbled, tenting the silk of her cocktail dress. Her pupils dilated with her mouth parting on a throaty moan. As she reached for him, Leo switched it off and stepped back, leaving her disoriented. He didn't allow her to stumble. It wasn't her fault he'd found better prey that evening.

"Game is fine." He scowled at a blonde distracting Syl. "She complimented my cologne and walked away, unaffected."

"Intriguing." Syl slipped a hand up the woman's dress, baring her thighs in full view of the hall.

No one noticed. She could've given him head. Hell, he could've fucked her on the buffet table and remain unseen if he chose to hide his antics. Their existence might be public knowledge now, but the full extent of their powers they kept hidden, for the most part.

"To say the least," Leo said.

"Her thoughts?" Syl nuzzled the woman's neck as his fingers stroked her core.

She released a breathless moan, and the scent of her arousal—like budding roses, thick and heady—permeated the air to tease Leo's nostrils.

"Snippets. Nothing solid."

At Leo's disgruntled tone, Syl's head shot up. His gray eyes met Leo's, and he arched a brow, but his fingers didn't cease their sweet torment.

"What I could pick up was her desire for a scotch, her self-directed anger over a lost pistol, and a woman called Valerie."

Mourning the missed opportunity, Leo did another slow turn, hoping to catch her auburn hair at a bar counter. The heads of the crowded hall hindered his line of sight.

"I'll do a walk around."

"If you find her, bring her to meet me." Syl glanced down when another woman unzipped his black tailored trousers.

Leo grunted, acknowledging the command and strode to the center of the dance floor. No one bumped into him, as expected. The mentors taught such a skill to younglings. Vampires secreted specific scents which triggered a human's flight response. Wherever he stood or walked, they'd avoid him without realizing it.

He closed his eyes, drew in a deep breath, and opened his mind. Images and thoughts bombarded him. Greed, lust, murder...the usual. He discarded each one as if he flicked dominoes across a table's wooden surface. Until...Captain Johanna Metcalfe. He located her with ease, a woman with a perpetual frown. Callista's name flitted across her mind, stained with disbelief and anger. Callista Devereaux, a detective at the Inner City Precinct. He had her full name. At last. A sweet burst of satisfaction sang along his veins. She was at a bar. He knew that already. Her final words stated her intention, but which bar?

He followed the mental link and couldn't prevent the smile denting his cheeks when he found Callista seated on a bar stool, with a tumbler of scotch in one hand. He strode toward her, his vision tunneling as if a spotlight illuminated her glorious mane of flaming hair. She'd crossed her legs at the knees, leading his gaze to travel along their length to her delicate feet then back to her cinched-in waist and bountiful breasts straining a gown not made for her.

She raised the glass and sipped, then licked her lips to savor every drop. An appreciative hum vibrated up her throat, and Leo had to admit—it was a sensual sound. Her eyelashes fluttered in ecstasy. Her expression snagged his focus, and his heart paused.

"Devereaux, what the hell are you doing here?" her captain asked, anger pitching her voice.

Callista opened her eyes, and an impatient expression crossed her delicate features. She didn't look guilty, even though he'd suspected she hadn't received a formal invitation. As he closed the distance between them, her focus fixed on him, her eyes widening, before her narrowed gaze settled on her captain.

"Callista's my guest," Leo said, but he didn't glance at Metcalfe.

He remained focused on Callista's emerald-green eyes. Her ruby lips parted, and she flashed him a grateful look.

"Oh, Mr. Travisano. I didn't know you two were acquaintances." Metcalfe's tone turned respectful, but a hint of suspicion remained.

"We met under serendipitous circumstances." He stood behind Callista's chair to slide a hand around her waist.

She stiffened before relaxing against his chest, playing the part he wanted her to.

"Yes, it was." A smile curled her lips.

He blinked, dazed by her white teeth dimpling her lip. His heart skipped a few beats as he lingered on the curve of her upper lip and the tempting plumpness of her bottom lip. He sucked in a shuddering breath, inhaling her unusual scent. An essence in her scent eluded him. No matter how deeply he inhaled, he was unable to trap it within his lungs. His body cried out for that elusive fragrance, needing to saturate himself in it. He coiled his trembling fingers into fists, forcing his sharp nails to recede.

Gathering Metcalfe's hand in his, he peered into her eyes. He placed a single thought there...to leave these two lovebirds alone. She blushed, the splash of color taking years off her complexion. After flashing a parting look at Callista, she scurried away.

"Weird, but whatever you did, I thank you." Callista unfolded and refolded her legs, revealing a silky toned thigh and the tip of a dagger.

Leo's fingers twitched as he fought the urge to stroke her skin along the scabbard.

"My pleasure. How do you know Johanna?" He went through the motions even as he drew in a deep breath, trying again to inhale as much of her essence as possible.

He couldn't explain its addictive quality. It had the same effect on his senses as if she'd released pheromones. No otherworld undercurrents clung to her, implying she was pure human.

His mind reeled. Arousal would deepen, darken, and intensify her scent, making it more potent. Despite his pheromones, she remained unaffected. He amped the amount he used, testing her resistance.

"I'm a detective. She's my captain," she said, wrapping her lips over the rim of the glass.

He lingered there, wondering what she'd taste like with or without scotch.

"Ah, not a suicide attempt?" he teased. He focused his gift, staring into the emerald depths of her eyes with a delight he hadn't expected.

"I'm investigating someone," she replied.

Illicit images of the mayor with a young blond man entered his mind, although she made no internal comment or judgment on the salaciousness of the photographs. Determined, he intensified his search, delving deeper. As he broke through her mental barriers, he found himself swimming in dark murky waters, thick and cloying. Random memories floated on the surface, like discarded advertisement flyers and abandoned photographs.

He lunged for one, and it dissolved through his fingers to reform blurry and illegible on the surface. Growling, he grasped for another floating nearby. It too disintegrated and reformed just out of his reach. He snapped back to the present, furrowing his brow.

What was she?

"You don't have to answer," she said.

His frown deepened into a scowl. He could pull a question from a person's mind as it formed. Deep within her mind, he hadn't sensed her thoughts.

"Long day?"

"Yes." He sighed.

Longer after he'd met her. She did pose a dilemma, though. An unpredictable detective, one he couldn't read, would complicate things. Perhaps Syl could add enlightenment. Leo checked on his king's status and found the woman's mouth on his cock.

Now wasn't the time, judging by Callista's disdain as she followed his distracted glance.

"Your...friend is somewhere in there under those bobbing women?" she asked. "You should rescue him. Those women could gift him with more than what he asked for." She paused and arched a brow. "Are your kind even susceptible to our human diseases? Never mind, don't answer that. It's mean of him to imply he can sexually satisfy them all. I don't care how much of a stud he thinks he is." She stepped off her stool, crowding Leo.

He didn't move aside, needing the heat of her skin as she shuffled past him, eager to smell her for a little longer. Exhaustion pounded off her, darkening the shadows under her eyes. He shifted closer to bury his nose in her hair, to inhale her essence then jerked back, discerning another female's scent clinging to her. One infinitely sweeter than Callie's.

"Whose gown are you wearing tonight?" he asked. Reacting like this to one woman was possible, but to two?

"My sister, Valerie's." Curiosity flitted across her features. "Thank you for being my knight, Mr. Travisano."

For the second time that evening, and certainly in the last century of his life, a woman walked away. He admired a mole on her bare back where it rested above her left hip undulating with her strides. The realization she was about to leave him had him bolting forward. He caught her wrist and spun her into his arms...and landed on his back, with her elbow at his throat.

Too startled by her speed, he hadn't shrouded them in time. The crowd responded with alarmed murmurs. Sprawled across him, she had placed a bare knee at his waist. He raised his fingers to brush over her hips, finding traction there.

He squeezed as he whispered, "My name is Leo."

She peeled herself off him, not in the least bit sorry. With an admirable tolerance, she endured her captain's chastisement, dutifully apologized as if her boss was her mother, and made a hasty retreat before he could stop her. She didn't spare him a backward glance.

Why she twisted his insides, he couldn't explain. The entire time Metcalfe reprimanded her, he'd stared at Callista, dazed, forgetting to blink. Her scent was delicious, but not as intriguing as her sister's.

Grumbling over the twist to the evening, he faced Syl and sighed. The image of his debauchery shimmered—a tell he held a glamour in place for any would-be voyeurs. His lips were on the blonde's neck, blood trickling and staining her white gown, as another female sucked him off. Leo squeezed the bridge of his nose, attempting to halt the headache forming. Another rare experience for a vampire.

His life was dull. There lay the crux of the matter. A situation he'd pondered more of late. He was tired of whoring his way through his time, from a fuck to a feed too many. After dropping into the seat Callista vacated, he imagined the residual heat from her backside remained. He gestured to the bartender to refill her tumbler. The rich scent of scotch intensified, but the smoothness of it didn't compare to the taste of her lingering on the glass.

He tugged out his cellphone and dialed. "Callista and Valerie Devereaux. I need our best man on it."

Chapter Three
PERMISSION GRANTED

Gabriel lifted his face, taking a deep breath, imagining the cool caress of the silver moon's light. The air was crisp with a hint of pine. Just the way he liked it. That is, when, and *if*, he left his home. The usual guards stood alert at their posts, and the Italian architecture of their stronghold in pale sandstone glimmered under the moon's glow. He was here to visit his brother, and the sooner he did, the sooner he could return to his haven.

His long legs made short work of crossing the hall. He bounded up the spiraling stone stairs with fake enthusiasm. He couldn't recall when he'd last found anything exciting. After entering without knocking, he spun and closed the door on a whisper. That the room was opulent by vampire standards twisted his lips into a wry smile. As vampires, wealth was par for the course having amassed properties and other investments over the centuries. Managing their affairs was simpler now that they no longer had to hide their existence. He'd hated changing his name every eighty years or so.

Facing his brother, he sighed at him sprawled nonchalantly in a leather chair. "Your summons is pointless," Gabriel said. "You're insane to tempt the human laws like this, Sylvester. Your luck will run out, bringing the irritating yet futile human police down on us," he growled at his younger brother. Frustration tensed his shoulders and clenched his fists.

He forced himself to relax, uncurling his fingers before running them through his hair. He didn't like to reveal many emotions around Syl. With Leonardo, his advisor, sure. That was unavoidable when Leo was a telepath.

Gabriel nodded a greeting at Leo, who leaned his bulk against a wall, before he said, "Pissing off the humans isn't going to solidify our alliances. You know this better than most."

"We need fresh meat and soldiers." Syl bounded out of the chair to pace, revealing his agitation.

"Are the clubs not providing?" Gabriel wasn't in the least concerned.

The de Winter Hold owned various nightclubs—all depraved, appeasing sexual appetites no matter the preference. These establishments kept them well-funded and well-stocked. He shook his head...and well-satiated. He often visited Elixir when he was in an amorous mood. Lyssa, the club's manager, kept a few blondes just for his enjoyment. Heat surged through his loins, and an unexpected arousal strained against his jeans. Perhaps it was time he relieved his growing tension.

"There are only so many humans in this city," Syl said as he sipped his meal from a wine glass. "Our reputation has preceded us, and recruitment has stagnated. Those bastard shifters are taking half of the recruiting pool as well."

"Yet you trust them with this formula?" Gabriel arched a brow. Hearing about the supposed cure bored him, but he endured hours of discussions because it altered Syl's countenance to that of his youth. Seeing him so carefree like when they were children always brought Gabriel pleasure. Those moments were as if centuries of vampirism hadn't marred his brother's soul.

"We're close to freedom," Syl said with conviction.

"Freedom? Is that what you're telling yourself?" Gabriel said in a softer tone. He loved his brother—which was why he'd followed him and begged Syl's sire to convert him as well. They had to sweet talk the old vampire, but Gabriel couldn't regret his decision; too many centuries had passed for remorse to play a role.

"This will be the last festival for the year, Gabriel. We need new blood, and increasing the frequency of these festivals from once a year to every second month hasn't helped. The shifters are killing our people faster than we can convert." There was a pleading note to Syl's voice. "We are losing this war, brother."

"That tells me we're sending them to their deaths untrained," Gabriel said.

"Told you." Leo chuckled, receiving a glare from Syl for his interjection.

"If you distrust our trainers, perhaps you could revive your long-dormant fighting skills for a lesson or two?" Syl gave him a pointed look.

Gabriel grunted at having his bluff called. Yes, he could fight. Lacking his sire's favor meant he'd had to fight to feed, for privileges, for mercy. Everything he owned, he'd earned, so he valued his privacy above all things. Now, however, the thought of fighting bored him. The initial rush had diminished into distaste. It was cyclical: the battles, the killing, the sex, and the feeding. Endless life had to have more purpose than this. Hope was once the sustenance he'd lived on, a warmth in his heart like the sun's touch on his upturned face. Hope had rested with one woman—Abigail. Centuries ago, she'd torn his heart out with her words and disgust.

He released a slow breath, thrusting any thoughts and memories of her deep down, away from Leo's prying mind.

"Fine. Then why so close to the Hold?" Gabriel leaned against the rough-hewn stone wall of his brother's chambers.

Syl ruled the four vampire quarters in this city with diplomacy, which was unheard of for vampires. They weren't the oldest, but due to Syl's popularity and generous approach to ruling, he had loyal followers. They stood united against any older vampire wishing to usurp the throne. The added advantage of Leo made Syl's reign nigh unshakeable. The quarter leaders liked and respected Syl. He didn't demand obeisance nor tribute from them. He treated them as equals, as if they belonged to an elite club. Inspiring loyalty in his leaders meant no uprisings from any quarter, creating a united front.

"The police are monitoring the other sites, and since we've never used this location, it would mean a smoother festival. The marketing team is on it already. It promises to be an exceptional turnout." Syl collapsed into his brown leather chair, resting his face in his hands with his elbows on his knees. The exhaustion rippled off him in almost tangible waves.

Gabriel frowned, concern rising to the fore. For a vampire to show this level of exhaustion meant he hadn't slept for at least a month, or his feedings were irregular.

"How was the ball?" he asked.

"The usual. Although, it's a pity you didn't attend. A moment or two were entertaining." Syl glanced at Leo with a smirk curling his upper lip.

Gabriel trailed his stare and frowned. What was that about? He wouldn't outright ask Leo though, knowing how much he valued his privacy. Oh, the irony wasn't lost on him.

"Regardless, I'm collecting the formula tonight," Syl said. "We'll need to plan accordingly."

"I'll make sure your subjects don't realize you're delayed," Leo said.

At Leo's statement, Syl turned his gray gaze on Gabriel. Shit. He knew what the pleading look meant, having succumbed to it on many occasions.

"No, I'm not participating. You know how I feel about these festivals, Syl." Gabriel ground his teeth, fighting the roiling fury rising to choke him.

He hated how these events turned vampires into the predators of old, wild beasts without control. None of that was necessary, not with blood banks and the nightclubs, yet Syl insisted they continue.

"Damn it, Gabriel. These festivals keep you in supply." Syl shot Leo a desperate glance.

But Leo couldn't convince Gabriel to participate. Or could he? He arched a brow at his friend and received a shrug in reply.

"It's not our only source, and I can hunt old school so don't throw that at me. It's a no, and I promise you, if anyone disturbs my sanctuary, I'll retaliate," Gabriel said.

Burning fire tightened his muscles as anger coursed through him. Each festival recycled the same discussion, and yet Syl refused to give up. Pushing away from the wall, he was more than ready to end this argument.

"Typical," Syl muttered, glaring at Gabriel.

Syl's anger and disappointment didn't move him. It ceased to do that at least a century ago. "Be content with your victory, Syl." His tone was as gentle as he could make it. "I'm letting you hold the festival on my land."

"True." Syl flashed an unexpected smile that made Gabriel's heart swell with nostalgia.

His brother had always been the fun, charming one. Everyone around their farm knew who Sylvester was. The best de Winter son, according to them. Gabriel's brooding countenance hadn't endeared him to anyone. Still didn't. He couldn't complain though. It meant they left him alone, human, and otherworldly.

Chapter Four

AS EXPECTED

C allie shoved the last bite of her hot dog into her mouth and grabbed her can of soda. She shrugged, hoping to convey her frustration but failing.

Mike's expression remained blank. He pursed his lips, took a long draw from his can before crushing it in his meaty fist. "Nothing? You hookered up for no new leads?"

Since he was her partner, she wouldn't take offense at the hooker part of his question. She *had* felt out of place in the gown and setting.

"You don't have to rub it in." She pouted. "Carter wants me to spy on the suckbloods, like that would ever happen. Says one of them thinks I'm *purty*." She fluttered her eyelashes at Mike with a fake giggle. "The idiot didn't realize I dolled up for him, Duhamel, and Hawkins."

"I can't get over what a waste last night was." Mike ran a hand over his rugged face. "Those fancy idiots tossed something off the balcony. Damn thing bounced off the sidewalk and over my car."

Callie gasped and grabbed his arm. "Tell me you investigated?"

"Hell, no. Whatever it was, it looked lethal."

"Honestly. You're the twice-decorated homicide detective Mike Barrows, and you couldn't bother to leave the damn car?" Her jaw dropped. "I lost my piece when I climbed off the balc—" She bit her lip and flicked him a glance, hoping his sharp gaze missed her slip.

"Whoa." He grabbed her empty can and crushed it, tossing it into the trashcan with too much force. "Tell me you didn't take your skinny ass out on the building's ledge, Callista? Tell me you're not suicidal?"

"I had nowhere to hide so I took a chance. Besides, I realized my stupidity soon enough." She relaxed when he did nothing more but grumble.

"I'm failing your father with Val's illness. I can't lose you because of your damn tomfoolery."

Memories flashed—years of knowing Mike. He'd been her father's partner until the day Dad died. All her birthday parties and school events had been under Mike's supervision, and he was the *only* one to step forward after her last partner quit on her.

She bit her lip hard enough to draw blood, the taste bold and metallic overpowering the plastic flavor of the hotdog. She'd have preferred a rant over a guilt trip. His look of despair was harder to bear. The weight of the situation settled on her shoulders, reminding her there was more to living than chasing clues and taking reckless chances. More to life was time spent with Val as she wasted away. More life, in this case, meant years added to Val's life.

Mike engulfed her in a warm hug against his massive body, and she softened, accepting his offer of comfort. He stepped away and handed her a napkin.

"What?" She wiped her chin and mouth with it.

"I got mustard on your uniform." He chuckled.

She cried out and dabbed her chest with frantic swipes. "Let's recap. Duhamel?"

"Mayor James Duhamel—charismatic, overeager, and arrogant. Large contributions to his campaign raise my hackles. Taking money from Hawkins, but why? What's the connection between Carter and Duhamel? There's something sinister going on. I just can't find out what."

"We still have those dirty pictures I took."

"Yeah, they're in the file." He pursed his lips at yet another argument he'd lost. Her skinnier ass had chosen her to be the one to climb into Duhamel's heating ducts to take those photos. "That just makes him a liar and a man-whore."

"Alan Hawkins?"

"Nothing's changed. He's the CEO of Floges Corporation. His fingers are everywhere, his coffers overflowing. He has companies in too many industries to bother counting. He also has biotics and research labs doing who knows what. I can't get in there to investigate. Their security is tighter than Captain's ass. Every damn newspaper has his face on the front page." Mike huffed and leaned his elbows on the roof of the police vehicle. "There must be...*something*. Perfect people make me nervous."

"First, use the tablet I bought you for your birthday. No one buys newspapers anymore, Mike. Second, if you must tell me again the how's and why's perfect people make your ass twitch, I'm calling a taxi."

"Are you sassing me after I bought you lunch? Your father didn't raise a disrespectful, ungrateful lady." He climbed into the car, ducking his head as he folded his great bulk into the small confines.

"Are you confusing me with Val again? I'm the boy he never had."

She clambered into the passenger's seat because he didn't let her drive. He was old school which meant men drove. She let him because it kept the peace.

"Your father *loved* you, Callista," he said, *sotto voce,* and gave her a long stare until she nodded, acknowledging he was right to remind her. "That leaves Carter." He clicked on his seatbelt and started the engine.

"State Senator Devlin Carter. That man's slimier than a snake. I can't pin him down with anything. He dodges evidence, leaving barely a trace of his involvement. He's stinking rich, which is why he can gift generous contributions without feeling it. Maybe I should take him up on his offer?"

"Hussy for him?" Mike's sausage-fingers gripped the steering wheel until it creaked under the abuse. He shot her a warning glance, taking a corner fast. "Oh, hell no."

"To spy on the suckbloods. Why would he ask me to do that? 'Look for something extraordinary,' he said." A burst of joy spread through her like a belly full of hot cocoa on a chilly night. "He doesn't like them. That's not the image he portrays to the media. Could that be the angle?"

"Sounds like you got a lead, after all."

Chapter Five

A Dunk in the Bay

They lived among us. Not aliens. Shifters, vampires, and probably the fey.

It made a huge difference to Callie. She was law enforcement, and every damn day she had to take down some crook. Suckbloods, the beasts, and stupid humans. The same crimes plagued each species: corruption, greed, lust, anger, and now racial tensions. Who did what didn't matter to her. The law was the law, and she was the enforcer.

Not that she was one hundred percent human either, not according to her gramps. Being of Irish descent meant she had a bit of fey in her. She snorted. No one would hear her from where she was hiding in the shadows of a crate. Her partner was somewhere behind her, sneaking with those enormous feet of his, so she was on her own, as per friggin' usual.

The whole there-are-other-creatures-in-the-world drama unfolded due to a threatening war between shifters and vampires. People-monitoring in this technological age also played a part. Amateur footage was freely available, revealing these creatures to the human populace. Of course, humans couldn't lose their minds over this revelation. They were so outgunned, it was ludicrous. The go-to reaction would've been to nuke the bastards, but since they couldn't be tracked, it would be like throwing a grenade into a room and praying it would hit selected targets only.

Wars were normal between the beasts and the suckbloods. History could attest to it—the Crusades, the Inquisition, the Salem Witches. As the suckbloods tell it, all the worst of humanity's war-torn history was due to them. Well, if they were stupid enough to claim responsibility for it, who was she to correct them? People were people, regardless of their genetic makeup, and in her experience, evil came in all forms.

With the existence of supernatural creatures in the open, some things were starting to make sense. Her connection with her sister was otherworldly. She knew when Val was worried, or sad, and lately, sick enough to die.

Callie wiped away her messy thoughts. She was on duty and needed her wits about her. Something was going down at the docks—so cliché. Like they couldn't choose a nice family restaurant to conduct business? She activated her smartwatch and messaged Mike. He was, unfortunately, one hundred and fifty percent human—big, heavy on his feet, and made a bull in a china shop look like a ballerina. He was hers though, hers to guide and protect. Again. For some strange reason, she went through partners like folks chewed gum. It wasn't her fault they were shot at.

This brought her right back to the fey part. She sensed where the criminals were, what was coming, when to duck, when to fire. She crept forward, placing her feet with care. If she announced her arrival, they'd shoot at Barrows again. He didn't deal well with people trying to kill him.

Hushed sounds ahead paused her steps, and she listened, not only with her ears but with her instincts. Her heart pounded, a deafening and annoying distraction. There were two men chatting up ahead. Their sinewy bodies were typical of beasts. Their sculpted jawlines and broad foreheads were definite giveaways. Not to mention the lifting of their heads to sniff the air like a poodle would.

Crap. *Werewolves.* Why couldn't these beasts morph into domestic creatures like tabby cats?

She didn't respect those dogs. They worked in packs, so finding two alone was worrying. She assessed her surroundings, relying on her instincts and senses, since her human eyesight and hearing were useless. Sweat slid down the nape of her neck, tickling her, which was never good. It meant shit was about to hit the proverbial fan. What worried her was their agitation with their hands twitching and their shifty side glances, as if they expected trouble.

Well, here she was—trouble. According to Captain and Barrows, Trouble was her middle name.

She took a mental inventory of her bag of tricks. Gun, check—a new, standard-issue handgun with two refill cartridges—so she couldn't lose this one. If she did, Captain would have her cleaning guns at the range for months. Grenades, check—three stun and one explosive—not standard-issue, but she would rather die than say who her supplier was. The explosives were a last resort, when death was on the horizon or poking her with his bony finger. That happened more often than she cared to admit. Next, poison tipped blades, check. The silver throwing blades she'd sheathed in her boots. It wouldn't kill a suckblood, but it would slow them down. Their speed was preternatural, so slipping cytotoxin in their blood sure evened the odds. And the cytotoxins plus silver—double the damage on beasts.

She drew in a deep yet silent breath. Who was she kidding? Since she was human, they scented her, both beast and suckblood. They must've been aware of her presence for a while now. But then again, what kind of threat was she? They had to at least pick up Barrows, who reeked on the best of days. She had spoken to him about his use of cologne, but he insisted he stank worse without it.

She snorted. Stinking of garbage was preferable to a perfume factory. His vanity would get him killed, and of course, he'd blame her.

One of the men glanced up, catching her spying. He didn't bolt, didn't reach for a weapon, just lifted his chin in greeting. She scowled. Oh, this was bad. So very, very bad. They feared her and the law the least. Whoever they were meeting was a mean son of a bitch, one who frightened them more than her badge did.

A solid black SUV pulled up, making the two perps twitch, their anxiety intensifying. She fought the urge to snort again. What did they do, buy their getaway vehicles from Crooks-R-Us? She sighed, holstered her gun, and climbed two stacks of crates until she could clamber up the side of a cargo container. She sprawled onto her stomach, ignoring the soot and grime lining the corrugated metal. She removed her handgun again and aimed.

The tuxedoed man who slid out of the vehicle made her breath catch. No man should be that handsome. She scowled as she studied his perfectly coiffed dark locks. His broad shoulders barely fit in the tux, which seemed ill-suited for one so muscled. He was the suckblood from the mayor's ball, the one Leo had guarded. *Sylvester.* Was he tied to Carter somehow? No, with her covered in grease and sweat, she couldn't see the connection.

Suckbloods had the ability to alter their appearance, to make themselves irresistible to either sex. Damn it, she must've been losing her touch, since it was freakin' working on her libido. Her panties drenched as his pheromones reached her. She mouthed a curse while wiping her damp palms on the sides of her police uniform. Sucking in deep breaths, she willed her ovaries to cease their enthusiastic applause, but it was too late. She'd rather do the werewolves than plastic Sylvester. She fake-gagged.

"Devereaux?" The man froze mid-stride to glance at her hiding spot.

A delicious smile lit his face as if her presence entertained him. What the hell? She was aware humans were the weaker species, but despite him doing something illegal in the shadows of the docks, her presence didn't concern him.

To top it off, his voice was sex-on-a-stick. Wait. He was Suckblood One from the balcony. But of course, Leo was Suckblood Two...shit. She banged her forehead on her clasped hands gripping the gun. Had Leo told him about her? Damn it, this made her vulnerable to an attack...made Val vulnerable. Callie tightened her sweaty palms around her gun.

When she didn't respond, he shook his head and faced the two men. "Do you have it?"

"Of course, my king."

King? Shit. Suckblood royalty? No effing way. It explained Leo's obedience to the man.

The dog held out a silver canister with no other demarcations on it—not that she could rely on her human vision. Her instincts screamed that it held something worse than the Inquisition.

She couldn't shout, *Freeze,* like in the movies. It would announce her intention to intrude on their little tea party. Instead she withdrew a blade from her boot, hoping the cytotoxin would work swiftly on Sylvester. She threw it, hitting him on the hand as he accepted the canister from the dog. He dropped it. Then hell broke loose. Her kind of hell.

She launched off the shipping container, breaking her fall with a roll before stopping on her haunches. Where had the canister fallen? She shot both dogs in the head, expecting it to incapacitate them for a few minutes. Bullets didn't kill suckbloods or beasts, but their bodies still needed time to heal.

Sylvester reached for the canister as she rose to face him with a blade in hand. She released it, her aim true, yet he spun last minute and caught it out of the air. Fucking suckblood. She glowered at him while palming the stun grenade. Sunlight drained them, making them mortal enough for a bullet to wound them. It didn't kill them—they'd heal soon enough. Neither did the sun, like the legends said. She didn't know what *could* kill them, having never witnessed one dying, nor seen a dead suckblood. Thankfully they were susceptible to bright light and sound, as were they all—human and anti-human.

She tossed the grenade at him. He caught it as she dived forward and scooped up the canister lying between his feet. Nice shoes. She smirked as she burst into a run. It was futile to do so, but instinct had kicked in, and her legs pumped her away from the scene.

She wasn't certain, with the grenade's explosion ringing in her ears, but she thought she heard, '*Don't shake it,*' roared from behind her. She doubted the explosive would stop him from coming after her. She crushed the canister to her chest, trying not to shake it, taking his warning to heart. There had been fear in his voice, and a scared suckblood required her full attention.

Rounding the corner, and instead of running more, she dove into the bay waters, grimacing at the filth coating the surface. Surviving this toxic dunk would require a few full treatments. When the force of the icy water rushed past her, the canister slipped out of her fingers. She grappled but managed to close one hand around it, taking it down with her to the depths of the bay. Water messed with anti-human's senses, so a dunk in the bay had been inevitable.

She swam along the bottom until the need for air drove her to the surface. She broke through the water under a pier and listened. Above the lapping waves, sirens sounded, confirming Barrows's call for backup. Scanning the edge of the dock, she searched for a tall, handsome suckblood. Her vision was human and it was nighttime, so her chances of spotting him were low.

What the hell was in this canister? Should she even open it? She tightened her fingers around it, tension tearing through her as exhaustion stung her eyelids and burned her nostrils. Why couldn't it have been a simple drug run? She assumed he'd recognized her scent from the balcony. He wasn't a hundred percent sure, though. His voice had held a questioning lilt. She shuddered from both the cold and the stench of the water creeping up on her. Police-issue uniforms weren't waterproof and certainly not sludge proof.

She activated her smartwatch and messaged Barrows, informing him she was fine and heading home. His response was immediate—she was an idiot for jumping in the water in the first place.

He had also scheduled treatments for her at the local clinic, since the bay water was a chemical weapon of its own from eons of human disregard. She shoved the four-inch-diameter canister down the back of her pants and yanked herself out of the water. The nearest clinic was two blocks south. She'd go there first, receive her meds, and head for the safest place she knew—her sister's apartment.

Chapter Six

NOT A SAFE HAVEN

Callie winced as she counted down another block to Val's. Eleven down, one more to go.

The night air made her shiver, yet the exertion kept her sweating like an expired stick of dynamite. She cursed the suckblood who'd stumbled into her territory. Callie always checked on that area since regular drop-offs happened there often. She hadn't expected for the drop-off from the ball to occur there. Lucky her.

Tightening her uniform jacket around her, she hoped the drenched fabric would prevent the wind's icy fingers from seeking a bare patch of skin. It also gave her an opportunity to hide the canister in a mundane gesture. As evenings went, it wasn't the best shift she'd lived through, but it wasn't the worst one—that went, hands-down, to the bodies they'd discovered in a disused sewer. Decomposing bodies in stagnant shit didn't improve with age.

At last, she reached her sister's apartment block and entered the foyer, flashing the guard on-duty an apologetic smile. "Sorry about the mess, Eddie. It's been one of those nights."

The retired-ex-cop-now-turned-guard grinned, jumping up to call the elevator for her. "I can smell so. Did you get the bastards, Miss Callie?" he asked, and the joy of the chase echoed in his myopic eyes.

"Do we ever truly get them, Eddie?"

"Another rises to take his place." He held the elevator door for her and let her pass.

Eddie had the right of it. Although, if she took down Carter and his cronies, how long would it take for someone to assume the void he left?

"Don't you worry about the mess, Miss Callie. It's a small price to pay for all you sacrifice for our safety."

"Ah, Eddie...you be sure to give Meredith my regards." Callie smiled, pressing Val's floor number, all misty-eyed from his kind words.

Not one to cry, but thinking they were tears was preferable than some sort of eye disease thanks to the sludge also known as bay water.

"Same to Miss Valerie. She had a bit of color on her cheeks this afternoon."

"Oh, I hope it stays, Eddie. I could do with good news." The elevator doors closed on her, and Callie slumped, but not enough to lean against the mirrored interior.

It would mean more cleaning for Eddie when his arthritic knees couldn't take it. After entering Val's apartment, not bothering to knock, she sought her sister, hoping she wasn't in the bathroom losing what food she'd managed to consume.

"You stink," Val said from the comfort of her couch.

She'd burrowed into multiple blankets, which meant she was recovering from the last set of chemo she'd endured. Her body's reaction to the treatments was the same every time, with no improvements. A fact Callie abhorred.

Callie surveyed her sister's slight figure, desperate for a sign she wasn't deteriorating. Cervical cancer, third stage. She grimaced, trying not to recall the day they'd received the news.

"How're you feeling?" Callie asked as she tugged the canister out of her pants and balanced it on the kitchen counter.

She stroked the tiny triangle carved into the metal. It was thicker on one side, like the Greek symbol for delta.

"The usual," her sister said, the dark circles under her eyes taking on death's mask. Her short auburn hair stood out like she'd stuck her finger in a power socket.

"No change?" Callie peeled off her sodden uniform.

This one would need incineration. The clinic had offered, but the thought of running around the city in a hospital gown hadn't sat well with her. Besides, where would she have hidden the canister, in her disposable panties? No taxi had wanted her as their fare in her sodden uniform, which meant she walked the twelve blocks to get to Val's.

Her shirt came off with ease, but her armored pants made sucking noises as she tugged them off. She was grateful she'd chosen to wear her uniform and not civilian clothing.

The force replaced uniforms damaged in the line of duty, after making her jump through various red-tape loops, of course.

A yellow flyer on the kitchen counter caught Callie's attention. It advertised one of those suckblood festivals where a human could convert to a suckblood if she survived.

She was so livid she struggled to form words. "What the fuck is this?"

Snapping her head to meet her sister's eyes, her vision tainted with fury. She snatched the paper off the counter with trembling fingers, the wave generating enough wind to further cool her chilled skin. A shiver coursed through her, but she didn't look away from Val's face, needing to gauge her reaction.

"The neighbors are trying to be helpful," Val said.

Callie studied her, attentive to every expression or facial twitch. Judging by her sister's downcast eyes, she *had* considered it. Callie couldn't fault her for dreaming of being healthy, but this came at high cost.

"I want you to kick this cancer in the backside, Val, but not as a suckblood. I couldn't bear to have to hunt down my own sister."

To convert was frowned upon. The government figured it didn't help their cause if humans joined the suckblood forces. Yet the suckblood conversion festivals remained popular despite attempts to shut them down. Callie blamed the movie industry for romanticizing vampires.

"I wouldn't even survive the run." Valerie's mumble disappeared into the blankets.

Callie nodded and left the conversation to use her sister's shower for a good long wash.

Chatter reached her ears as she stepped out of the shower. She wrapped a towel around her head and body before padding through to the lounge.

"Devereaux." Sylvester leaned his tall frame against the kitchen counter, the canister now firmly in his grasp. Right by his elbow sat her gun and her remaining arsenal, minus one dagger and stun grenade. Too close to him to do her any good.

"Shit," Callie muttered, anger burning through her, setting her cooling skin ablaze.

She was unarmed, wrapped in a towel and—with her sister now involved—at his mercy. She should've known he wouldn't let her keep the damn canister, that he'd tail her. She should've known coming here would endanger Val. Idiot! She must not have taken her smart vitamins this morning.

"First the ball, now here? You consistently surprise me," he said in his smoky voice.

His lids lowered over his gray eyes as he scanned the length of her, making her shiver with revulsion and desire. The urge to cover herself warred with her protective instincts. Fucking suckblood. He had no damn right to look this good, not after the last few hours of hell he'd put her through.

"Take the canister and go!" Her self-directed anger hardened her voice, and she smothered a wince.

Pissing off a suckblood wasn't wise, but he had to know she was prepared to fight to the death to save her sister. She twisted off her head towel and tossed it onto a nearby chair. If she needed to fight, it would get in the way. After tightening the knot on her towel and between her cleavage, maintaining her modesty, she shifted her feet into a fighting stance, ready for anything he might throw at her.

"How gracious of you," he said in a bored tone. A small smile played across his sensual lips. "I shan't be seeing you again, now that I have this."

"Giving up a life of crime so easily?"

Her sister gasped at her sarcastic words, but Callie ignored her. The bastard was taking her canister. If he left them alone, she'd be happy with that. Yet it went against her genetics to allow him to leave. Allow? There was no allow with a suckblood. He'd do what he wanted, regardless of her opinion.

"What's in the canister, anyway? Schrodinger's cat?"

He chuckled, and warmth spread through her chest at his smile. Could he stop oozing pheromones for one frigging minute?

"Our future." He glanced at Val, who nodded at him as if they had made some sort of arrangement.

Callie's blood boiled underneath her skin. Not knowing and imagining the worst was killing her. As swiftly as he arrived, he was gone, closing the door behind him without a sound.

"What the hell, Val?" She glared at her sister.

"He walked through the door like he knew you were here." Val gave her a pointed look.

"He must have waited for me to arrive, the bastard."

"Regardless, he could've killed me. I wouldn't have put up much of a fight."

At those words, Callie scowled. Yes, they were both petite, but she liked to think she had a core of steel running through her. Val even more so, having endured chemo after chemo.

"Did you see the size of his hands?" she said, running a trembling hand through her red spikes. "No matter how much I struggle, he'd snap my neck like a twig."

Okay, so Val wouldn't have let the suckblood kill her to end her lot in life. That had been Callie's biggest fear—suicide. She bit her bottom lip to still the sorrow pressing on her control. It threatened to erupt on a constant basis, but she couldn't release it. She needed to be strong for Val.

"A wasted evening," Callie murmured, shaking her head.

She'd have to go in and explain to her captain what the hell happened. Despite being an ox, Barrows had her back. She liked that about him. At least her captain wouldn't be in the dark, for the most part. She only had to mention suckblood royalty, a silver canister, a dunk in the river, and voila, they'd assign her to a psychiatrist for her overactive imagination. Of course, trying to keep Barrows alive meant he hadn't witnessed the action firsthand.

"Not really. He was nice eye candy." Val giggled, and the sound surprised Callie enough to draw her attention.

"You know they use pheromones, right?" She blessed Val with a huge smile. Warmth burrowed into her chest at her sister's good humor.

"Sure. Doesn't mean we can't look. After all, it would be a waste of good pheromones if we didn't at least *enjoy* their efforts."

The smile dimpling Val's cheeks made Callie's heart ache. She rubbed at it, wishing for a time when the cancer hadn't hung over their heads like a death knell.

"Going into the office, dear?" Val asked as she tugged her blankets up and under her chin.

"I have to. Captain will want a full report."

"Good. Pick up a pizza on the way back with loads and loads of raw onions."

The fact her sister suffered from strange cravings wasn't unusual for someone in her condition. Currently it was raw onions, and by the tub load.

Callie slipped back into Val's bedroom to don the spare uniform she kept there. "I'll order in for you. I don't know how long I'll be."

"Suits me. Just eat something. You're looking skinnier than me, and that's saying a lot."

Val's observation had Callie nodding. She needed something else to focus on than the nausea roiling within her.

Callie jerked to meet her sister's green-eyed gaze. "I get enough food—Mike makes sure of it. So don't worry about me. You focus on you."

She blew her a kiss and beat a hasty retreat, not willing to let Val see the tears forming on her eyelashes. What Callie wanted to do was to trap her sister within her embrace as if doing so would hold off death's impending march.

She leaned against the closed apartment door, clasping her hand across her mouth, and stifled a sob. Searing pain lanced through her, crippling her. With her knees buckling, she slid down the door to land on her backside as something squeezed her chest, crushing her heart, threatening her ability to breathe. Tears bathed her face, dripping onto her fresh uniform. The pain, the helplessness, was at such an intensity it paralyzed her.

"Callie?"

Mike's voice through the speaker on her watch jolted her, and she sucked in a much-needed breath. Wiping the tears from her cheeks with rushed movements, she released her breath in one shuddering exhale before answering.

"What is it, Mike?" She held her smartwatch close to her lips in the hopes he'd hear her clearly and make this call a short one.

"Captain's up-to-date, and if you walk into the precinct before our next shift, I will take you over my knee, young lady."

Callie forced a chuckle as her chaotic emotions pulled her apart.

"Got it," she said. With a sigh, she followed it with, "I love you, just saying."

"Holy cow, it's worse than I thought," Mike said after a small, significant pause. "Love you too, my girl. Now off to bed with you."

She climbed to her feet, using the wall to pull herself up. She drew in another breath, pressed her palm to Val's door, dipped her head and sent up a silent prayer. She stepped away, trailing her fingertips down the door's smooth surface as if she was reluctant to leave it in God's hands. Dropping her hand to her side, she turned and squelched down the corridor, heading home.

Chapter Seven

CHECKING IN

"Leo, I'm pissed...pissed enough to rip her fuckin' head off."

Leo winced at Syl's words coming through his cell. What happened? He glanced around the crowded hall, keeping his mind ajar for insidious thoughts.

"Your detective took it. Moon above, she's good."

Warmth flooded Leo's chest, and he smiled. "You didn't kill her?" Leo's voice darkened.

If Syl had, he didn't know how he'd react. The tension across his shoulder implied something lethal.

"No...I didn't, but I need to get my property back. If she fights me, I'll hurt her...just a little. That will teach her not to take what doesn't belong to her." The call ended on Syl's chuckle, as if he relished a skirmish with a human.

Leo grumbled, not liking that. Casting instructions at the guards, he threw caution to the wind, bolted out of the hall, and launched himself skyward. Molding the wind to his bidding, it propelled him to his destination. The air flitted by him, and the sense of freedom that only flying could offer him filled his entire being. When he arrived at her apartment, her unlit windows announced she wasn't home yet.

After landing on her balcony, he manipulated matter to unlock and open her sliding door, then meandered around her sparse apartment. Essentials dotted the room. A large brown leather-bound chair called to him, and as he ran his fingers across its back, he assessed the seat indented with the shape of her backside. He lowered himself into it to study the view. No television, no entertainment system, only a bookshelf filled with vampiric romance novels, weapon instruction manuals, and books on biochemistry. No pictures adorned her walls, no dust-collecting mementos. He bolted out of the chair and slipped into her bedroom. The scent of her lingered. He paused to inhale. It wasn't enough to saturate his senses, but it would do. She'd made her bed crisp, almost military—the sheets in dark blues and grays with a single cream-colored stuffed teddy bear nestling against the pillows. It was the softest thing in the room. The evening gown from last night draped over a chair in the corner. Her heels peeked out from under the dress's fabric pooling on the tiled floor.

He approached the nightstand that held a compact alarm. All seemed innocent, but this was Callista. He lifted the pillow and broke into a bright smile. A dagger rested there. He sniffed and buried his face in her pillow, inhaling again.

What was it about her scent? Her sensuality aroused him, and her strength of will was sheer poetry.

He replaced her pillow and wandered back to her brown chair to slide into it, prepared to await her return. His phone vibrated, and he frowned at the caller ID.

"I have it." Syl's voice came through, his excitement clear.

Leo tensed. "Callista?"

"Unharmed."

An eager tone to Syl's voice made Leo wary. What solidified Syl's reign was his ability to inflict pain in such a way the victim begged to die. He found their weaknesses. Few were aware of this particular trait of his, but knowing secrets was Leo's forte.

"She has a sister," Syl said.

"Valerie," Leo said, having received that information hours ago. He planned to visit her tomorrow to find out why her scent made his blood sing.

"She's dying. I convinced her to attend the festival." Syl chuckled, a pleased-with-him-self sound Leo recognized. "*If* she survives, she'll be an excellent addition to our family."

Leo scowled. Oh, she'd survive. He'd make certain of it. "But if she doesn't?"

"She won't suffer anymore." Syl's logic was sound.

Though his points were valid, Leo suspected Callista wouldn't agree. Moon above, he didn't agree.

"Where are you?" Syl asked.

"Running an errand. I needed fresh air."

"Don't be long. The trials must start." Syl's clipped tones conveyed his impatience.

"You know who is fully vetted and chosen so start the trials now." Leo tamped down the hope the results would be conclusive. He knew better than to allow hope free reign.

As footsteps approached, his pulse leaped with unexpected excitement. "I'll be there as soon as I can."

"Enjoy." Syl's wicked smile was discernible across the connection.

Leo slid his phone into his jacket pocket and waited. Callista entered her apartment, shutting the door behind her before bolting it. While running her hands over her body, her movements were methodical, hypnotic. She placed her weaponry in a precise arrangement on the kitchen counter. After unraveling her braided hair, she bent to undo her boots. They squelched as she did so.

"Damn suckbloods," she muttered. "I'm talking to you, Leo." She rose to face him, shook her head, then slipped into her bedroom.

How had she known he was there? He hadn't made a sound. Had held his breath the entire time.

She banged around her room. A whisper of fabric and the soft fall of her footsteps came before she returned with a brush in her hand.

"Your *sire* said the future was in the canister. What's inside? Can *you* at least give me a straight answer?" She ran the bristles through her locks in slow, practiced strokes.

Leo shifted his attention to her gray tights and baggy T-shirt, baring a smooth shoulder. She was beautiful. He wondered if Valerie had the same features. He sucked in a deep breath, catching their combined scents.

"He didn't sire me, and his name is Sylvester. The canister holds some sort of chemical."

"Shit. A weapon?"

Great. I assumed it contained a chemical. No wonder I couldn't shake it. I sure hope I haven't allowed a maniac full access to a biochemical weapon—capable of untold violence. Perhaps even catastrophic? I would so lose my badge over that.

He chuckled, for once reading her thoughts before the gates to her mind sealed shut. He slid the brush out of her hand to run it through her locks, his hand stroking behind the brush's path. "It's not a weapon. Why would we jeopardize our harvest?"

"Good point." Her shoulders slumped, exhaustion pounding at her, tightening her shoulders.

"I smell Valerie on you again," he said.

"I saw her earlier with *Sylvester*. Do you smell the chemo medication on her? She used to smell like strawberries on a rainy day."

"I'm sorry, Callista." Leo handed her the brush.

She shrugged, but it was stiff, revealing her anger, vulnerability, helplessness. Using his other senses was incredible, not relying on his telepathy for every assessment. Although, he suspected the novelty of it would wear thin.

"The cancer's killing her. You know, she's tempted to throw herself in with your stupid suck-fests. I can't blame her if she does. I'm not ready…to lose her now."

"We all have to die, Callista." He winced as he said it, wishing he could console her in some way.

"Says the ancient vampire?" She stepped away from him. "You can call me Callie. Planning on staying long, or are you done stalking me?"

"Stalking?"

"You're in my apartment without invitation, and you've had me investigated. You could've just asked, Leo." She stomped to her kitchen, slamming cupboards as she searched for something. "You're probably the reason your *Sylvester* found me at Val's. Did I thank you for that?"

"You took his canister, Callie." Leo gripped the counter, slowing his heartbeat to listen in on her thoughts…nothing. Her mind remained sealed. Was she aware she could do this?

"Now it's my fault your asshat king is having clandestine meetings in my neighborhood? Shit, you suckbloods sure are arrogant."

"Suckbloods?" His lips twitched, and before he could stop himself, he chuckled. "What's wrong with the word *vampire*?" he asked, a smile lingering in his voice. He allowed it—for once not having to guard every reaction or expression he made.

"Vampires are so sexy. Like, I've-gotta-bag-me-one-of-those-totes-hot-babes," Callie said, mimicking a schoolgirl's speech patterns. "I've seen your kind kill, hunt, and feed, Leo, as I've seen my kind do the same…Well, maybe not the blood drinking. But who knows? Weird things happen all the time." She opened a new bottle of scotch and poured a healthy portion into a chipped coffee mug before downing it. "I'm tired, disappointed, and overall miserable, so if there's a point to you being here…can you get to it?"

"How do you resist my pheromones?"

"That's the question you're here to ask me? I guess I should be happy you're not here to kill me." She placed the mug in the sink and stashed the closed bottle in a cupboard she hadn't found it in. "I just can. They say officers have undergone extensive training since the Great Reveal, but that's bullshit. We can't resist your kind. They hypnotize us into believing we can. Such arrogance. Many on our force have died under that misapprehension."

He shoved his hands in his pockets. "You know this how?"

"Val and I don't do well with hypnotism. Found out during her college days. I faked the going under part when it came to my turn. Wasn't hard."

"What were you doing on the ledge?"

She grimaced. "I snuck into the Duhamel's ball to investigate a few men. Thanks for covering for me. The next day, Captain chewed me out for taking you to the floor. Sorry about that. Oh, and I may have implied...just a little, that you touched me indecently. Oops." She headed for her front door, unbolted, then opened it, her expectation clear.

Leo grinned, pleased by her behavior and indifference to him. He couldn't recall the last time a woman had kicked him out. This was a new experience, and it felt human, as if life-giving blood pumped through his veins. Or it was the way she treated him, like he was a person and didn't fear him.

"Very well, Callie. I bid you goodnight." He strolled through the door and turned at the threshold to meet her tired-eye gaze.

"Night will do. There wasn't anything good about it." She slammed the door in his face.

He laughed, shaking his head as he meandered out of her apartment block and onto the moon-swathed street. Taking to flight, he was too energized to return to the Hold. He found himself knocking on a cellar door in a field in the middle of nowhere.

"Leo?" Gabriel banged his door open and revealed his displeasure at the intrusion. He grunted and gestured to Leo to enter. "Coffee?"

"Something stronger, because moon above, do I have a story to tell you."

Leo had unburdened the Callista saga—his perceptions, his unexpected emotions, everything—onto Gabriel's wise and capable shoulders.

"Intriguing." He swirled his brandy in his tumbler.

The glint of amber caught Leo's eye, so he raised his own glass to his lips. It always looked better than it tasted. He could recall, before he converted, how sweet, smoky, and intense brandy had been on his tongue. Now, only bitterness burned a path down his throat to pool in his belly.

"You say she's beautiful?"

"Yes. A wealth of auburn locks. I wish you could read my mind, Gabriel."

"It's her sister's scent you find addictive?"

"Yes, like a spicy fragrance luring me. It tugs here." Leo tapped his chest, wishing he could describe the strange sensation.

Gabriel nodded as if understood where Leo didn't. "Have you sought her out? I suppose not, unless you have and aren't sharing the encounter with me?"

"No, I haven't had a chance. Too late to prevent the fondness from forming for Callie though. Dawn's near, so it will have to wait until after the festival."

"Oh, yes...that cursed festival. Thanks for the reminder." Gabriel downed his brandy with a grimace.

"I suspect Valerie might be participating. If Callie hears about it..." Leo chuckled. "Now *that* would be entertaining. I can't get over that she kicked me out." He threw a smirk at Gabriel. "It felt...good."

"I can imagine." A smile twitched Gabriel's lips but didn't fully form.

Leo couldn't recall the last time his friend had been happy. "Next time I visit either of the Devereaux sisters, you will be accompanying me. For the entertainment value, of course."

"Will I?" Gabriel arched a brow, but there was a stubborn tilt to his chin.

"You owe me, so I'm calling in the favor."

"Over this? It's a waste of a favor, but I accept. I was more concerned you'd ask me to challenge for the right to rule."

"I know." Leo vanished his glass to the ether from whence he'd summoned it, the magic taking no more than mere thought. He had long since learned this power like all young vamps did.

After saluting Gabriel with two fingers to his forehead, Leo dissolved into molecules, easily carried on gentle breezes. This unique gift wasn't as quick to learn. Some vampires never mastered it, but he was powerful.

He sped across the planes and into the Hold to reform in his chambers. With a flick of a finger, the lamps lit, and the fire blazed in the hearth. He ran a palm over his chest and met smooth skin, vanishing his suit as he readied for bed. A smile lingered when he slid between crisp, sun-kissed Egyptian cotton sheets.

A good day. The best he'd had in a while.

Chapter Eight

DESPERATION AND INSANITY

CALLIE NEEDED SUNLIGHT—HER PASTY skin attested to it. A coffee break on her balcony would've sufficed. Not out in the wild, one hundred miles from civilization, where human women competed against each other for the ultimate prize—conversion.

She was here for Val, who'd tossed in her chips. She wouldn't survive in her weakened state, which meant a swift and painful death. Fuck. Callie could kill Syl for this. For inspiring Val to get off her couch for suicide. For sending Callie into the disease-riddled bay and for distracting her from her actual investigation on Carter.

As a suckblood, Valerie would be cancer free. Either way, she died today. Callie had used her police siren to get here, which would cost her a few merits if Captain found out. She didn't care. This was an emergency. She should've sensed something was up when Sylvester had nodded at Val. She should've listened to her instincts. Instead, she'd been more upset over the loss of that damn canister.

She sighed as she pushed against the crowd of eager women, searching for her sister. The sweaty, overly perfumed bodies nauseated her. Or was that fear coiling in her stomach like a cobra about to strike? Her heart pounded in her ears, but she ignored it, keeping her focus on the various women around her.

They came in all shapes and sizes, but all with either lust or greed on their faces. The suckbloods bussed them in so no vehicles remained abandoned on the land. And of course, all had signed a waiver. Just as she had. She was here to find her sister to talk her out of this stupid idea but couldn't go in until she'd signed that silly thing. With panic overruling her innate distrust of everything, she'd signed it unread. So she assumed it was a waiver of liability.

Her badge and gun had no effect on them. In fact, as soon as she flashed them, she lost both. Bastards. More demerits coming her way. Captain would have her ass for this, again. She'd *just* received her replacement gun. Not to mention, her stranded police vehicle would draw unwanted attention from her fellow officers. Everyone would clear out when this festival ended, with no evidence of anything having happened. No bodies, no blood, no signs whatsoever except for her police vehicle. It would look as if she drove to the middle of nowhere for no reason. Shit. She hadn't even disabled the tracker.

Her focus returned to her surroundings, to the eager chatter of the participants. As far as she'd overheard, it was an obstacle course. If the suckbloods caught you, they'd drain the blood from your body and leave you to die. The women who made it through to the finish line would suffer the conversion, and only a handful survived that process. This was mortifying. By her calculations, Val had a thirty-three percent chance of survival, even less since mathematics had never been Callie's strong point. The cancer had drained Val of her energy and personality but not her will to survive.

"Val," Callie yelled into the crowd, drawing attention from a few women. None deigned to help her. *Bitches.*

They faced the front where a tall man waited. The head suckblood. She didn't spare him a glance. Why would she care that he was gorgeous, so well-built, and any other description the women whispered?

"Val!" she called again. She scanned these pitiful women, searching for a redhead.

How many were participating? Two hundred, three? How many would make it through? The air hung with desperation and aggression. How many would kill each other to reach the finish line? She shuddered and doubled her efforts to find her sister, fearing more than the possible conversion.

There! She spotted short-cropped auburn hair at five-foot-seven—the right height for her sister.

"Val," she screamed. In slow motion, she faced Callie with at least five rows of women between them.

Val's green eyes widened in recognition, then angry determination, before she whipped away from her.

"Val!" Callie's voice cracked. She tried to push through the women between them. They held firm, making her realize she was close to the front line. They refused to give. "If you get out of my effing way, I can grab my sister and get her away from here. Two fewer women to worry about." She tried to negotiate with the women, but their lack of compassion cemented their features.

"You lie," a woman snarled.

"I do not," Callie said, shocked someone would imply she'd do such a thing.

"You'll die like the rest of them, bitch," said the stocky woman next to her.

Callie gaped, stunned—not by the insults—but by the sheer stupidity emanating from the women. What was wrong with them?

She blinked at the healed bite marks on their exposed skin, shoulders, necks, arms.

They were feeders.

Her lips curled in distaste. You couldn't talk to feeders. They only saw the ecstasy they received when they volunteered for suckbloods to feed from them. Rumors said a vampire's saliva could heal, but repeated feedings from the same spot left their mark.

She shuddered and shuffled to the side, trying to go around. After another few frustrating minutes, the packed bodies made it hopeless too, and she elbowed her way back until she had Val in her sights again.

The hollow blast of a starting pistol silenced the incessant chatter, and the women burst forward. The crowd carried Callie toward the trees, ignoring her screams. She pushed forward, trying to reach Val, who sprinted surprisingly well for a cancer patient. Callie wanted to stop her before they breached the dense forest forming part of the course.

She was little over five feet from her now when the path split, but the women shoved her to the left, away from Val.

"No!" She twisted to go back, but the crowd wouldn't let her. "Get the fuck out of the way." Callie's booming shout shredded her throat, but it didn't matter when they ignored her.

Val's disappearing bobbing redhead had panic gripping Callie, tensing her muscles, and driving logic to the far edges of her mind. She wished she had her gun—she'd kill these stupid women where they ran. They were dead anyway once the suckbloods joined the feeding frenzy.

She jumped off the path and out of the way of the charging women. From this vantage point, the stampeding masses raced down the two paths. She had a bird's eye view of the suckbloods descending as if from the sky. They helped themselves to the stragglers.

It disgusted and fascinated her as female and male suckbloods drained woman after woman—the abused, slaughtered, or sacrificed bodies lay abandoned afterward. She never saw the act of it happening, and if she had, she'd learned many years ago to cordon off the part of her mind that cared. Corpses were clues and puzzles needing solving, nothing more.

One suckblood paused and tilted his head at her, his black eyes menacing, his interest clear as he drew in a deep breath. He grinned, his pointed blood-coated teeth denting his bloodied lip. With a cry, she took off, not along any path in use but through the middle, making her own path.

"What the hell were you thinking, Callie?" She gasped. "This was your stupidest idea yet." She grunted, wiping sweat off her temple with a flick of her wrist. "Now you're food. How can you help Val if you're dead?"

She vaulted over tree roots and big boulders, not a stranger to exercise as law enforcement. Her job required she ran, dived, rolled, or ducked. On top of a protruding boulder, she stopped to get her bearings. Women screamed as they stampeded on the left and right of her, so she was sure she was in the middle of both paths. She tried to discern a focus point. A white object lay straight ahead. She would aim for that.

She stumbled forward as soon as something behind her crashed through the branches like an unskilled hunter. He toyed with her—his *food*. It fueled her to run faster, harder, even though he made noises only to spook her.

Argh. How she hated suckbloods.

With branches slapping across her face and bare arms, she sprinted to the white *thing*. Focusing her breathing, she sucked in great gulps of air as sweat dripped into her eyes, stinging and blurring her vision.

She allowed a small smile to form. They'd chosen the wrong prey. Although, she did wish she'd dressed appropriately. Her sneakers were fine, but should she survive until nightfall without crossing the finish line, her cut-off jeans and T-shirt wouldn't keep her warm. A sports bra would've been helpful. Not to mention any number of her throwing blades or grenades—anything other than just her wits.

She stopped short before breaking past the tree line. One suckblood already hunted her, and she couldn't afford to attract another hunter. She studied the white structure in the clearing. It was a skylight—round, with a glass roof, approximately knee-high off the ground. There was something underground that required natural light. She frowned, not seeing an entrance. She'd hoped she could escape here since she wasn't interested in conversion, anyway.

Sighing, she glanced around, accepting that this skylight wasn't her hoped-for refuge. A faded footpath marred the forest floor—one that looked abandoned. She followed it, praying it led her to safety.

At the sound of someone entering the clearing behind her, she careened along the path to dive behind a large bush. She landed on something hard, jabbing her thigh. She yelped. The force knocked the breath from her, and she instinctively bit down on her lip to stop herself from gasping.

With their excellent sense of smell, the bush wouldn't hide her from the suckblood. She stank less than the other women, having forgone deodorant or perfume in her rush to find Val. But she'd washed her hair.

She brushed her hand over something metallic and glanced at a handle to a trap door. Before she could second-guess her decision, she lifted the hatch. It opened on well-oiled hinges, startling her, since it had a rusted and ancient texture.

She grabbed onto the visible part of the ladder and climbed into the hole, pulling the hatch with her. The pitch dark didn't deter her with fear driving her to be bold. She continued down the ladder, feeling for each rung before stepping onto what she hoped was the floor. Using the rock wall behind the ladder, she guided herself around the room, tapping her foot, hoping the floor wouldn't drop off beneath her. Her vision adjusted to the darkness, and she discerned unfamiliar box-like shapes that were useless to her. They wouldn't hide her for long, and they weren't weapons.

The hatch opened, casting a sunlit rectangle on the dirt floor. Throwing caution to the wind, she dived behind one of those shapes, slamming her head against the wall. Dizziness and a piercing pain hit her. She raised her hand to touch the lump forming and winced—her fingers came away wet and sticky.

Great. Now she was bleeding, enticing him like a matador waving his *muleta* at the bull.

"I sense she went down here," the deep voice said. "I can smell her coconut shampoo." An inhalation followed his words. "She's injured."

There was a smirk in his voice, as if he'd been the one to draw her blood. The fucking arrogance.

"It's *his* place. I don't know about you, but I'm not willing to anger him," a woman said, her voice sexy and breathless.

Freakin' predators.

"I want her. She challenged me." The urgency in his voice sounded feral, skittering Callie's heartbeat. So this was what prey endured? She didn't like it.

"You're on your own," the woman said. "I will choose another meal. I doubt you would've shared anyway."

"True." The man chuckled.

"See you later, Darius."

The male suckblood descended the ladder, closing the hatch behind him. What law enforcement was taught about suckbloods wasn't something she would stake her life on. They *could* see in the dark, but was his swift, confident clamber down the ladder due to a familiarity with the hideaway?

Shit. He might have corralled her toward his lair.

"I can smell you, my pretty," he whispered, causing her to shiver at the lethal seduction in his voice.

Like an idiot, she'd trapped herself.

Chapter Nine

SWAPPING A BOY FOR A MAN

Callie strained her ears. His tread reverberated through the dank room, sounding closer, but it was directionless, as if he intended to disorientate her. She breathed through her nose, forcing herself to control the rising panic.

"I will convert you, anyway. You made this fun for me." He sounded pleased with himself. "I can smell your blood. I can hear your heart beating. Why do you hide from me, my sweet?"

Why? She frowned at his unexpected stupidity. Or was she being the obtuse one? After all, to attend a festival was to seek conversion. He had a right to expect she wanted that, and his offer to convert her should've pleased her.

Nope. That wasn't going to happen. No way, no how. He made a slow and deep inhalation, followed by a fast whoosh. It came from the left of her, sounds—she suspected—he'd made on purpose. An elaborate show of sniffing her, not to locate her since he could see her.

Her heart cinched, and before she could control her legs, which had developed a mind of their own, she stood. It startled her to find herself now exposed, with the top of the stacked crates under her fingertips. Her suicidal courage reared its head when she least wanted it to.

He'd convert her? How kind of him. She suppressed a giggle. Now wasn't the time to laugh, although imagining Carter's expression when she told him she was a suckblood almost had her considering it.

Drawing in a shuddering breath and using her remaining willpower, she faced the direction of his voice. "My thanks for your generous offer, but I don't want to be your meal or converted."

She hoped telling him she wasn't here for the festival might convince him to let her go. A futile hope, but she tried anyway.

He laughed, the sound coming not three feet from her left. "Nonsense. Why participate then, mm?"

Lamplight illuminated the room, and she shut her eyes against the brightness. "My sister is here. I wanted to stop her."

She cracked open one eye, wincing as she faced him, his hand on the lamp chord, proving he was familiar with the hideout. He *was* handsome, in a boyish sort of way.

Eyes peered at her from the shadows behind him, snatching a gasp from her. She bit her lip, anger burning her cheeks as fear coursed through her blood. Damn it, she should've controlled herself better and not jeopardized someone else's life.

She could barely discern the person in the shadows. They shifted, and the light revealed a masculine brow over his eyes before darkness consumed him again.

Another man. And the way he glared at the idiot—Darius, wasn't it—was good news for her...she hoped.

Darius preened like he was God's gift to man or suckblood, assuming her gasp meant she found him breathtaking. She smothered a smirk. Typical suckblood arrogance.

"Not running from me now?" he asked.

She focused on his face, searching for any nuance that would indicate he was aware of the man lurking in the darkness. With the preternatural gifts suckbloods had, he should have, but he didn't pause in his determination to reach her. Unless the man was a suckblood too? If he was, she foresaw a Callista Devereaux smorgasbord situation served up for their pleasure.

On the off chance he was friendly, she tried not to look at him so she wouldn't give away his presence, despite her initial faux pas. Her conversion or death at Darius's hands was inevitable. The stranger didn't need to suffer from the same fate.

"What's the point?" She sidled to her right, ensuring Darius didn't glance behind him, keeping his focus on her.

"Yes, indeed, although I enjoyed the hunt."

"I can climb the ladder, and we can continue this for say, another half-hour, but we'll be back to this point. I still don't want you to feed from me, convert or kill me."

"I can't wait another thirty minutes. Your blood smells delicious."

He licked his lips as he grabbed his crotch. She shuddered in disgust. He frowned with his focus narrowing on her face.

"You truly don't want me." Amazement warmed his husky voice.

"No, I don't want you." She fought a snort and kept her voice level. Now wasn't the time for her sass.

Leo was the same—don't I smell good?—what nonsense. Like the taste of blood was all that mattered.

Darius puffed up like a startled pigeon, slicing through his buttoned shirt with a sharp-looking fingernail to expose his rippling muscles and taut stomach. She'd have admired him had he been on the cover of a magazine.

A strange sickly-sweet scent washed over her, forcing her to see him in a more favorable light. She was aware of the change in her, as if she'd taken a weak drug that manipulated her idea of handsome. Still a forced attraction, not enough to tempt her.

"Now?" His voice deepened to gravel.

"What has changed since a minute ago?" Callie asked, her tone bored.

His eyes widened with delight. He was a sick bastard, this suckblood. He toyed with her like a little boy with many diversions. How different would her life have been if they didn't exist?

"Indeed you are a surprise, my pet." He chuckled, stepping closer to her.

The hidden man moved with him, bringing his body into the lamplight. Her mouth fell open. She inhaled a shuddering breath. Now *this* was gorgeous. He was six-foot-six she'd say, with broad shoulders and dark hair slashing across his forehead in thick waves. His ghost-gray eyes were sensual and lethal, dazzling her. He peered down his sharp nose, dragging her stunned gaze to his wide mouth with its fuller bottom lip. He'd pinched them together enough to whiten them. His carved angular jaw dominated his face. His barrel-wide chest tapered into a trim waist, and dark designer denims hugged his tree-trunk thighs.

Her panties dampened in reaction to the unadulterated image of him. He was such a visual delight; she couldn't blame her traitorous hormones for blowing her revered self-control to smithereens. It wasn't often a man devastated her senses. *Oh, sweet justice, don't let him be a suckblood.*

Darius inhaled again, a grin flashing. "Your scent is stronger, more intoxicating. So a delayed reaction, mm?"

The idiot still thought it was him. She dipped her chin, a hysterical giggle bubbling up her throat, but her gaze unerringly returned to the stranger. He mesmerized her like a beautiful marble statue in a museum drew admiration. A statue that depicted the ideal man. Although, if mystery man was nude, she'd need to pick her tongue off the floor.

He looked familiar though, like Sylvester but more virile, if that was possible for a half-dead. What? She pinched her lips against a gasp. He was a suckblood? Fury and disappointment shattered her hopes.

When Darius darted for her, ending her internal pity party, the man lunged for Darius. She dived behind the crates—her previous sanctuary—making sure she didn't bang her head this time. Nothing she did could help the other man. *Coward.*

What could she do? She had no weapons and no way of surviving this.

"Damn it, Gabriel, I followed her down here. I had to trespass to get her," Darius whined, trying to negotiate with his attacker.

That they knew each other didn't surprise her.

Despite her regret, she smiled, loving his name. *Gabriel.* It suited him. Avenging angel? She snorted at her thoughts, blaming them for the stressful situation.

As she peered over the top of the boxes, the altercation continued to play out. Gabriel wrapped his forearm around her hunter's neck. Judging by the whine in Darius's voice, his usual confidence had fled.

A suckblood feared by other suckbloods? A slimy feeling curled in her stomach. They fought over her like a meal. Shit, she was in a heap of trouble now. Had she swapped one hunter for a more lethal one?

"You know better." Gabriel's voice was deep gravel, calling forth a shiver of pleasure from her.

All her senses came alive, as if he had run a hand along her skin. Her panties saturated again. Damn, this was embarrassing. She clenched her thighs tight, praying for help. For the first time, she understood why they were considered sex gods among human women.

"Smell her. She's mouthwatering." Darius tried to break the chokehold.

With a flick of his wrist, Gabriel broke his neck. "Mine."

She thought she heard him growl, but she couldn't be certain. The sound he made was animalistic. He let the body slump to the floor before turning to where she peeped over the crate.

"Is he...dead?" she asked, unable to keep the curiosity or hope from her voice. She'd been shit scared and usually, nothing phased her. She studied the twisted body and released a drawn-out breath to calm her erratic heartbeat.

"Nope, just incapacitated."

Dismay slumped her shoulders. Well, duh. She should've doubted Darius had died since bullets weren't a known weapon to kill suckbloods. Experience had taught her a broken neck meant he had a few minutes before he'd heal himself, and then he'd be angry and arrogant again. She'd prefer not to be around when that happened.

"It'll be a while before he heals." Gabriel offered his hand—long-fingered with a squarish palm. It conveyed safety.

She reviewed her current predicament, wondering what her choices were? He *had* saved her, but she would be stupid to accept his assistance without giving it serious consideration. She chewed on her lip, weighing up her options. Something told her he wouldn't let her climb out of here. Then again, he'd done nothing to alarm her. Her annoyingly vocal instincts weren't screaming to save herself, either.

After sliding out from behind the boxes, she accepted his hand, and the warm calloused fingers wrapped around her small ones.

A bright burst of blood on his T-shirt snagged her attention. He was bleeding from his right side. "Shit, did he hurt you?"

An uncommon emotion rose to cloud her thoughts, one she didn't often experience, not since Val's diagnosis—panic. This had been a panicky sort of day. She searched for a cloth to stem the flow, her braid whipping around as her head did. Ripping off his torn shirt might give him ideas as if he was in a condition to follow through on her eager thoughts. Heat stained her cheeks. She yanked her shirt off, crunching it into a ball to press to his wound. He layered a gentle hand over hers, trapping it against the heated velvet of his skin.

"I can smell your injury." His hoarse voice sent a shiver through her.

Dipping her head to hide her reaction to him, she shrugged off his observation and focused on his wound.

"I'm not as hurt as you. How can you stand? That's a lot of blood." She glanced up at his intense gaze, and as she drowned in ghost gray eyes, her breath hitched. "Lean on me if you need to," she said, grateful her tongue worked under her dazed circumstances, despite the strangled quality of her voice.

He slipped his right arm around her and tugged her to his side. He gave off so much heat she shivered, making her aware of the cold, dark room they were in.

"Where can we go?" She grunted, carrying a little of his weight. He was a heavy bastard. "Are you trapped down here? We need to find help."

"No help." His words were an octave above a growl, causing her to shiver again, with heat of another sort coiling in her core. "There's a door at the back." He gestured to the dark shadows, where the light didn't reach.

She stared at him and smiled like she'd seen medics do. If he didn't want help, she couldn't force the issue. He was too big to drag up the ladder, anyway. Anyone trapped underground had to be hiding from the law. Unfortunately for him, the law had found him.

"No help. Okay." She hobbled to the back of the room with his fingers at her waist, strong and scorching.

His scent surrounded her, and she breathed it in, deep enough to expand her lungs. It was spicy, with hints of forest and grass. Delicious.

Was he using pheromones on her? Damn suckbloods and their supernatural gifts. She needed to get him to safety then leave.

When they reached the door, she leaned forward to open it before helping him through it. As soon as she entered the well-lit room, she moaned at the beauty that greeted her. Lush Persian carpets, wall-to-wall mahogany shelves holding thousands of books—some of them looked ancient—and comfortable leather-bound chairs filled the large room. Various doors led off it.

"You live here?" she asked before facing him.

With a gasp, she rushed to him, replacing his hand clutching her bloodied shirt to his wound. His home had surprised her, and in her stunned delight, she'd forgotten about his wound.

"Sorry," she said before guiding him to a nearby chaise lounge. "Your home is beautiful."

"Thank you." He lay on the chaise, but she got the impression it was more to appease her than from any need on his part.

"What can I do?" Shooting glances around, she wrung her bloodied hands, hoping he'd offer guidance. She didn't have the time to waste on nursing him, not with Val on the verge of dying.

She stood before him in her low-riding jeans and a white lace bra, which did nothing to hide her abundant assets. A sports bra would've. She fought the urge to shield herself, knowing it would draw attention to her sparse coverings. Damn it, why had she offered him her shirt? She'd have to race after Val in just a bra.

"I need blood," he said, his focus intense like he expected her to go bat-shit crazy at the mention of blood. She shouldn't; she wasn't a feeder. Still, the quicker she helped him, the quicker she could leave.

"Of course you do. You're a vampire," she said, trying to confirm her initial assessment. After all, he had handled Darius like a ninja assassin.

"Yes."

"Why don't you participate?" She didn't need to elaborate. by his dismissive expression he'd understood her.

"It's barbaric." He winced as he adjusted his frame in the uncomfortable-looking chair.

She nibbled on her bottom lip. He had saved her, and it was only fair she reciprocated. Not that she wanted to be his feeder, but she needed him healed. He might be able to find Val and save her before she died or stop her conversion if she survived. An ally would be wonderful, right about now.

"Here, take from me." Callie offered her wrist.

It looked delicate and pale, marred with blue veins and scratches from her mad dash. Would he notice them? Gabriel glanced at her wrist then at her face. She must have startled him with her willingness to feed him.

"You offer your lifeblood freely?" His voice was above a whisper, denoting his disbelief.

What the hell? This day was one of her weirdest to date.

He spoke the words in an otherworldly way, formal. He waited for her response; his focus intense as if he required a verbal confirmation from her.

"Yes, I offer my blood *freely.*"

He breathed in, his eyelids fluttering shut, showing his unforgivably long lashes. A deep inhale was a suckblood's way of smelling her. *Thanks, Darius, for that lesson.*

She sniffed her armpit and winced. "I can wash first if I smell...bad."

His eyes flew open, a smile tugging at the corners of his sinful mouth. If he had dimples then life wasn't fair.

"You heard what Darius said. You smell delicious."

Heat stained her cheeks, and she ran a hand over her face, not believing the situation she was in. The urge to bolt overwhelmed her. If she ran, it wouldn't be for fear of her life. She'd be running from him and what he invoked within her. Vulnerable, naïve, and lost in a situation she'd never been in before—there was nothing in her officer handbook on how to handle this.

"Like food?" Her stare was unblinking.

If he said yes, she was leaving his ass on that couch, bleeding or not. He'd heal, but not as quickly without her fresh blood.

"No, like sex."

At his words, silly need coiled in her belly before traveling lower to throb. Well, that was unexpected.

"Pure, unadulterated sex."

"Oh." Heat traveled down her throat to her exposed cleavage. His gaze traced the path of her flush. His blatant interest had her kneeling beside him, conscious of her state of undress, his blatant admiration blasting away her usual confidence.

She pressed her wrist to his soft lips. "Please heal."

He released her shirt, and with the lightest of touches, grasped her hand. He held her still as his fangs grazed her wrist. She trembled but didn't move away. His teeth pierced her skin, but along with the pain came breathtaking pleasure. Like nothing she'd experienced before.

A moan tore from her, and she buried her face into his T-shirt-covered bicep, shivering as rush after rush of exquisite endorphins swept through her.

Chapter Ten

A Mysterious Woman

Gabriel had no intention of rescuing any woman stupid enough to participate in the festivities. Leo had called to him, desperation seeped in his mental voice—a tone he'd never heard from the stoic vampire—begging Gabriel for help. Leo said he picked up not one, but two dark spots in his mental scans of the eager festival participants.

Val had taken the bait as expected, but Callie's presence complicated things. Leo couldn't protect Callie and Val. The need to ensure they were both safe was driving him to panic. That Leo had revealed some of his emotions in the mental conversation said more than his words ever could. Gabriel could not recall seeing his friend so vulnerable, so human with his feelings.

Not understanding how Leo's gift worked, Gabriel assumed he'd compelled Callie to run toward him. When unusual shadows fell across his skylight, along with the beat of running feet, he'd sighed, abandoning an old text on Greek mythology to move into the stock room. He wouldn't leave his sanctuary, but should she venture into his domain, he'd come to her aid. For Leo.

She'd descended the ladder as he had mentally influenced her to. Her enticing backside swayed as she clambered down until her scent hit Gabriel. Fragrances he hadn't experienced in centuries—vanilla, peaches, chocolate, and musk. Sweet flavors and tastes he'd lost upon conversion.

As she fumbled her way deeper into his life, he'd gaped at her in frozen disbelief, not understanding his body's reaction to her. The need to go to her, to hold her, to taste her life's essence...almost brought him to his knees. Was this Leo's doing? He shook his head, having not sensed a compulsion.

When Darius descended, a fierce possessiveness claimed Gabriel. He wouldn't, no, couldn't, share her.

Her courage amazed him. Her ability to resist Darius's pheromones intrigued him—as Leo had mentioned—though he hadn't believed him at the time. When she'd spotted him, her arousal's scent only for him, had his instincts reacting, his control non-existent. He clenched his fists to rein in his volatile emotions, and he barely succeeded.

Darius wouldn't have her.

He'd clawed Gabriel's torso a second before Gabriel had pinned the male in a choke-hold. The fact he'd allowed the younger vampire to wound him was beyond acceptable, but worth it when she insisted on helping him.

Who was this woman?

He knew her name and what Leo told him, but she was nothing like the crazies who toyed with vampirism. With her desire not to be food, to die, or convert, it confirmed his impression of her.

As gentle as he could, Gabriel bit into her wrist. He didn't need her blood. He said he did to observe her reaction. He found her determination to help admirable, and the temptation to taste her was more than he could bear. That was a surprise, especially when his control was legendary.

The taste of her blood made him growl. The sound tearing from his throat was one he hadn't released in years. Sheer ecstasy.

Peaches. She tasted like peaches.

At her throaty moan, he hardened to his full length, having been in a state of semi-arousal since she'd intruded. The scent of her desire hit him at the same time her blood altered to taste like...chocolate? He tightened his grip on her wrist. He moaned and drank deeply.

Damn. A human woman not enamored with vamps. Someone who tried to save him and even offered her blood. One whose blood was sweet... Who was this intriguing woman?

Gabriel stared at the heavy auburn braid falling across his right arm. She'd moaned and clung to him, experiencing the thrill his saliva bestowed upon his prey—and for the first time, by the looks of it. Her emerald eyes widened in surprise before narrowing into a heated expression he yearned to see again. Her reactions were pure, impulsive, and instinctive. Desire and need rolled through him, parting his lips on a soft gasp. Pounding in his ears, his heart leapt and danced in excitement. Every instinct within him demanded he learn all he can about her. What an enticing creature she was.

When she slumped to the floor, he ran his tongue over the puncture wounds to heal them.

His heart lodged in his throat with an unfamiliar fear squeezing his lungs. Gabriel drew in a long calming breath. Fool. He'd drunk too much. It had been centuries since he'd lost control.

With an angry growl, he sat up and scooped her onto his lap. He listened to her faint heartbeat as panic descended upon him. Vampires didn't panic. He cursed himself even as he fought for breath with his eyes squeezed shut. It seemed as if the Devereaux sisters had a talent for inducing panic in ancient and battle-honed vampires.

After slicing his wrist with a sharpened fingernail, he pressed it to her parted mouth, compelling her to swallow. She did. Her throat working was a sensual delight. After licking his wound closed, he ran his tongue over her lips, cleaning her of his blood droplets. Moon above, the taste of her ripped through him. He jerked away, studying her upturned face before gathering her close to him.

He sat there in a state of unbelievable bliss, with tears dewing his lower lashes. Just holding her close to him gave him indescribable joy, an emotion he rarely experienced. In fact, the warm and pleasant sensation solidifying in his chest required focus to identify. He fought the urge to crush her to him, as if keeping her there would freeze time.

With trembling fingers, he traced the curve of her jaw, to clasp her chin between reverent fingers. Her unconsciousness allowed him the luxury of admiring her features without the distraction of her emerald eyes. Long, dark red eyelashes brushed alabaster skin marred by shadows. Concern? Fear? What could've caused her sleepless nights? Valerie's sickness?

His vision blurred as he blinked at her—dazzled. Amazement coursed through him at his interest, at his dislike that she suffered. When last had he cared for a human? Abigail? He dismissed her image before it formed, clinging to the woman in his arms instead. Fondness, Leo had called it. To feel such emotion so swiftly worried him. He was not one to act in an irrational manner. Nor was he one to form an immediate attachment.

Witchcraft. It had to be. He'd seen much in his centuries of existence, so it was plausible.

If Valerie's sickness and impending death was real, then Callista as a detective had to be real as well. If she used witchcraft to entice him, she must not be aware of it. He hadn't changed his vendors or his routine, so it wasn't potions or tainted blood. Nor had he met any witches of late, taken one to bed, or suffered their companionship otherwise, so charms were also a no.

Only once had he misread the signs and succumbed to an unpleasant lust spell. For decades Sylvester had never let him forget how he'd saved his older brother. Gabriel had learned to be cautious after that.

He brushed his fingers over her delicate nose and across her petal-soft pink lips, the heat of her breath warming them. The urge to kiss her, to taste her again, shuddered through him. It tempted him beyond his current level of control.

He drew in a ragged breath. With a gentleness he hadn't known he was capable of, he placed her on the chaise, making certain she was comfortable. Thankfully his overindulgence wasn't enough to kill her. His blood would help her heal, rest, and recover.

Gabriel searched her scalp for her wound, his touch featherlight. When his fingers found the lump, he tugged her forward to lick it. That tiny taste of her life's essence had him shivering with need, even though he'd had a fair share a minute ago. With a flick of his tongue across her pale skin, he healed the scratches marring her.

He rose but paused to stare at her, a question between his brows, wondering what would happen next.

Could he let her leave? Could he keep her? Would she mind? The idea of enslaving her didn't sit well, no matter how much she tempted him.

With a start, he jerked back to the present. How long had he regarded her? He left to take a shower—the running water would give him a respite from her enticing scent.

CHAPTER ELEVEN

A LIFE ALTERED

CALLIE JERKED AWAKE WITH Gabriel's name on her lips.

How long had she been asleep?

Asleep? She snorted. She had fainted, good and proper. Throwing a hand to her head, she searched for the lump but didn't find it. There wasn't any pain, either. If it wasn't for her blood-matted hair, she would have doubted the memory.

Swinging her legs over the side of the chaise, she blinked at her surroundings. What was she doing when she passed out?

Oh, yes.

She lifted her wrist to study it, seeing no marks or scars. Ignoring the blood smears, hers and his, pleasure zinged through her at the memory of his lips on her skin. She rubbed where he'd bitten her, trying to erase the erotic sensation that lingered.

Damn suckbloods, using their unnatural gifts so willy-nilly. There should be a law for that. She snorted—who would enforce it? Law enforcement was understaffed as it was, which was why she investigated Carter in her private time.

"Gabriel?" she called, standing up and stretching. It had been a while since she had slept so well. With a gasp, she remembered her sister. Idiot. How could she forget?

"Gabe, damn it!" Panic dominated her voice.

Her heart leaped and bounced, affecting her breathing. On trembling legs, she rushed to where the door used to be, but there was no seam, no handle. There had to be a mechanism somewhere, anywhere. Her heartbeat hammered in her ears. She rubbed her hand along the doorframe, searching for a dent, a button...hell, she'd be happy with a crack.

"What is it?" Gabriel asked, leaning against another doorway.

She paused. Clothed, he was gorgeous, but with a towel wrapped low around his hips, his chest bare, his black hair damp...he was devastating.

Focus, Callie.

"Wh-what is the time? Is the race finished? Do you know who crossed the finish line? Have the conversions taken place yet?"

He strode across to her, grasping her shaking hands in his damp ones. "Tell me everything."

She fought his hold, the fire of his touch. "I don't have time to explain it. Crap, I shouldn't have stayed. Val needs me."

He held firm, peace pouring off him as if time was at his beck and call. "Spare me a few minutes."

His gaze snared hers, and she nodded, pinching her lips.

After guiding her back to the chaise, he sat next to her. She tried to concentrate, to gather her thoughts in some sort of order, but he smelled so damn good, and heat emanated from him. She trailed his ripped torso with her fingertips where his wound had been. The skin was smooth—there wasn't even a scar.

His stomach trembled, and he grabbed her hand in his, stilling her stroking fingers. "Start with your name." His voice was hoarse.

The sound of it had her ovaries sparking velvet butterflies in her core.

She hesitated, fighting to calm her breathing—her heartbeat—and to squelch the lump forming in her throat. "My name is Callista Devereaux. My sister is Valerie. She has cancer, and the chemo isn't working. In absolute stupidity, she signed up to participate in this." She fluttered her hand, indicating the race above ground. "I rushed here to stop her, but she wouldn't talk to me."

A tear slipped out the corner of her right eye and traveled down her cheek as she remembered Val's expression, one of determination.

"I won't survive losing her." She wiped at her tears with her free hand, realizing she was smearing old blood across her face but didn't care.

Argh. She hated to cry, but she had to admit it had been a long time coming. "I'm selfish to want her to live one more day for me."

He stood, taking her with him toward a bookshelf in the corner. With a forefinger, he tugged on a red book, and the bookshelves separated, exposing an expensive screen. A keyboard slid out with a mouse, and the screen switched on. He clicked on an icon, and the screen lit up like a sports results panel. Names of the dead ticker taped along the bottom. A presenter gestured with animated flamboyance, but Gabe muted the sound. On the righthand side, a mini screen showed the highlights, and on the top right was a scrolling panel with the names of those who'd survived conversion.

"You treat festivals like a sports event?" She scanned the names of the dead, dreading finding Val's name.

"There." He pointed to the top corner. "Your sister survived the conversion."

Air whooshed out of Callie in relief as she read Val's name for herself.

"She survived?" she asked in disbelief, glancing between Gabriel and the panel.

She squealed and hugged him, laughing and crying at the same time as sweet and intense joy burst through her—it was uncontainable. His arms wrapped around her, firm yet comforting, and she allowed herself the enjoyment of his embrace.

"I'm so happy." Her laughter dwindled into a grin.

"Her conversion would've been difficult. It can kill a healthy human. Her blood would've been unpleasant for her sire." He grimaced, the action not marring his attractiveness. "I'm pleased you're happy."

"Don't humans taste like each other?" Callie asked in surprise, having not given the taste of O positive versus AB negative much thought. It made sense that Val wouldn't taste good with all those chemicals in her system. "She doesn't taste like me?"

"No one tastes like you," he growled, his arms tightening around her, trapping her to his bare chest. Heat and his spicy scent radiated off him.

She blushed and glanced down, a surge of shyness constricting her throat, then wished she hadn't. His nipples were hard, and his skin looked like molten caramel. She had the unbearable desire to kiss and lick him. The urge was ludicrous for her. Besides, what would the poor man think? Unless he was using his pheromones on her?

Relief slumped her shoulders, and she smiled at her silliness. Of course he was. This wasn't normal behavior for her, and he *was* a suckblood. Then why did she succumb to his scent, but not Darius's or Leo's?

She frowned. Time to focus on the matter at hand and not her sudden overactive libido.

"Can I see her?" She drew in a shuddering breath, fighting to keep her attention on his chin. She didn't want to meet his gorgeous eyes or linger on any part of his anatomy lower than his collarbone.

"No. We keep new converts or younglings away from the Hold until they quench their voracious thirst."

"I'm supposed to take your word for it?" She scowled, glancing around the underground home, anywhere but at his sculpted chest.

Sighing, he flicked a button. An image appeared on the screen, one with metal bars and screaming women. He switched between security cameras until pausing at a single cell holding Valerie. She sat on a bed looking none the worse, swinging her feet like she used to when they were little.

"She's in her own cell, which is good."

A private cell was still imprisonment. Callie's nostrils flared, and she bit down on her bottom lip, halting the barrage of curse words burning her tongue. "A prisoner? How long until she quenches her thirst?"

She didn't like seeing Val in jail, as if she were a criminal. What galled her the most was his blasé attitude, like imprisoning people, even his own kind, was an acceptable thing to do.

They'd placed Val in isolation as if being alone was good? The other younglings were rabid, clawing at the walls and bars. It was a stark contrast to Val's serene expression.

"When can I see her?" Callie glanced at him, then lowered her gaze. Could he please put on a damn shirt? "When will *you* release her?" She placed emphasis on "you," blaming Gabe and his kind for this nonsense.

"In a few days. Conversion affects humans in different ways."

"Holy crap. I can't just go home, then come back for a visit?" She ran a hand over her face, fighting the need to scream. At least Val was alive...sort of.

"Go home?" He arched a brow as a smirk curled his upper lip.

Her breath caught, and she shot glances at the doors. One of them had to lead out of here.

"Gabe?" She stiffened, preparing to struggle at the possibility she was as trapped as Val. "Am I a prisoner too?"

He frowned before he pinned her against him to nuzzle her hair. The gesture was so unexpected she could do nothing but grab onto his forearms for stability. "You are mine, Callista."

Shit, that didn't sound good. Like she was his pet. An animal. She'd heard of a few suckbloods who *owned* humans. The fucking balls on this sexy...um, *annoying* man. Part of her exploded in tingles at his dominant nature. The detective part wanted to shoot him where he stood.

She'd have lost her virginity years ago if any man had shown such audacity. That it was him left her torn. A suckblood as hot as this one, with the capability to seduce her with his scent alone? How could she stand against that? Did she want to? Damn it, yes. She hadn't survived this long to succumb with such ease.

She lowered her gaze, tracing a water droplet's path down to where their bodies met.

"By *mine*, do you mean your *feeder*?" she asked. Images rose of those women with the bite marks, and she gulped.

Heat burned her cheeks, sudden and intense. Not from fear, but embarrassment. She didn't mind in the least if Gabe fed from her. Oh, how the judgmental have fallen, but she could do it with her freedom intact, thank you very much.

"No," he said, his tone hard, almost brutal. "You fed me your blood to heal me, and that was an admirable thing you did."

She bit her lip as she searched his face. "Not a prisoner and not a feeder. Then what? Can I leave? Will you hurt me if I try?"

His gray eyes darkened, and the shadow crawling across his face reminded her that he was a predator.

There was no fear, and her instincts stayed silent. Odd. He was a suckblood. Yet...

"I'd like you to stay, as my guest." He brushed escaped curls off her temple, his touch gentle. "You're a mystery, Callista. One I need to solve."

Mysteries she understood. How they delved into one's psyche, demanding resolution and often becoming obsessions. Saving lives and sharing blood had bypassed formality, but she had to admit the way his name or nickname rolled off her tongue felt sinful. *Great. So much for her impartiality, and all it had taken was a pair of gray eyes.*

She avoided suckbloods and beasts because of their innate sensuality. This was dangerous territory. Sleeping with either meant she'd pick a side, and the law had to remain neutral. She smothered a snort. One sensual look from him and she became a blushing sixteen-year-old girl, all aflutter.

She was still a detective, and someone who'd resented, feared—if not hated—suckbloods for over a decade. Trust didn't come easy to her, and she wouldn't change just because her dormant ovaries had broken into applause.

"You can call me Callie," she said. "I'd like to see Val now...please." She met his gaze with hers. Stubborn, demanding, expectant. The same one she used on her fellow officers. "I don't know you, so I have no reason to trust you."

He nodded, and his hold tightened, raising her suspicions as if he had something to hide. At this point, she needed him to find Val whatever his agenda was.

"I like when you call me Gabe." His deep voice rumbled as he pressed his mouth to her temple, his breath hot.

She gasped when he buried his face in her neck, pressing his lips to her pulse. She clenched her thighs together, fighting a throbbing, growing need. He stiffened, his breathing deepened, and a hoarse sound tore from him. Her body's reaction ought to embarrass her. If that had been his intent, to embarrass her, then it only proved she was susceptible to him, which was a new experience for her.

"Are you using your pheromones on me?" she asked.

He leaned back to meet her gaze. His eyes widened before he laughed. The sound of his humor was rich, enticing...unexpected.

Oh, scales of justice, please say yes. She'd like something to blame for the weakness in her knees and the loss of her mental processes.

"No. Do you want me to?"

She stared, chewing on her bottom lip. If he wasn't enticing her, then all of him was for real? Her reactions were her own and not some chemical-induced lust tainted with shame? She'd liked to succumb to pheromones at least once, though, out of curiosity.

"Yes, please. I need to know the difference."

She fought a snort. What she wanted was to prove him a liar. All suckbloods were. If she succumbed to him, then none of what she felt was her fault or within her control. She needed to know—something in her soul demanded she make certain.

"Very well."

He drew in a deep breath, his chest expanding enough to close the distance between them. Her fingers itched to touch him, to learn his every ridge of muscle, to follow the trail of hair that dipped below his towel.

She licked her lips. She'd never encountered a man this sexy.

His cologne called to her, and yet, even as he spread his pheromones, she only wanted to nibble on every inch of his skin. But there was no crazed lust, no desperate need to eat him up. Well, not more than there already had been. What the hell?

"So?" he asked as he tugged her closer to him.

She let him. The heat of him was enticement enough.

"You smell as good as before. I want to lick you, just not in a way that jeopardizes my sanity. I expected your pheromones to make me go fuck-you-crazy." She didn't avert her gaze despite her burning cheeks.

He had to know she found him attractive. What was the point of hiding it? Suckbloods were masters of seduction, and she was an unskilled student eager for a sharp learning curve. Not that he had to be the teacher. If this incident had taught her anything, it was time to find a lover. It wasn't as if he'd complain though, not with this you're-mine nonsense. Still she'd play it cautious with hopes of an escape, because making a fool of herself was out of the question.

"Fuck me crazy?" His gray eyes darkened, his voice roughened with the rapid rise and fall of his chest. He grumbled, his arms crushing her against him.

So he liked that? Shit, the way he looked at her had her second guessing her plans for freedom.

If he continued to hold her, she knew where that would lead. She *did* want him, anyway he would have her, and that's what scared her. Succumbing to these needs would start her down a path she couldn't envision the consequences of.

Well, maybe she could envision some of the consequences. Losing her job for one.

Her stomach twisted then gurgled. Right, food then Val. Why hadn't she snatched a protein bar on her mad dash to get here? "Gabe? Perhaps you should put clothes on...and feed *me* for a change?"

Anything for a distraction. Besides, with Val converted, Callie had time to lull him into a false sense of security. She could slip out after seeing her sister and escape his mesmerizing presence. Freakin' addictive, seductive suckblood.

He chuckled into her neck, sending pleasure shooting through her again. Her nipples peaked against her lacy bra. She suspected he didn't laugh often. Just like that, the virginal whore in her wanted to stay. Something felt different with him. It defied logic.

"Typical woman. Only thinking of *her* needs," he teased as he drew away from her, and damn it, there were the dimples she'd dreaded.

Her mouth fell open in awe, mesmerized by the beauty of him. He looked better than cunning Sylvester the bastard, even better than Leo the stalker, and that was saying a lot. The image of Gabe in a tux made her breath catch.

"What...what needs do you have?" She couldn't prevent herself from asking, something primitive compelling her. Her heart paused, time stretched, and an unquenchable thirst assailed her. She licked her parched lips.

"Callie." His gray eyes swirled into molten silver. "Please don't look at me like that."

Tingles at her nape sent fiery shivers down her spine. She didn't appreciate his chastisement, as if she was at fault for looking at him in a particular way.

She straightened her shoulders but glanced away, trying to tamp down her guilt and self-disgust. She hated suckbloods, something she needed to remember.

Smelling delicious to him didn't mean he liked her, after all. It might be better if he wanted nothing more to do with her.

"I'm sorry." She yanked away from him. Not touching him might help her gain perspective. Might break the hold his sensuality had over her.

"Don't be." He slid his hand up her neck to grasp her chin, guiding her gaze to meet his. He feathered his lips across hers, so soft she thought she had imagined the caress.

He nudged her to yet another door. "The kitchen is through there."

He disappeared through the open doorway that must have led to his bathroom.

If she knew where the damn doors were, she could bolt now. Wait, not without seeing Val first. Videos were easy to manipulate. She needed to see her sister with her eyes, touch her face, speak to her. Callie sighed before entering the impressive kitchen constructed of light wood and stainless steel. There were the usual appliances, all looking brand-new, and the sink was small, suitable for one person's needs. A large industrial fridge dominated the room, with a glass front revealing the fridge's contents. There were bags of blood placed in meticulous rows and a lone carton of milk.

She frowned.

So he'd lied about needing blood? Strike one. Arrogant effing suckbloods. She'd *freely* offered, so she wasn't angry with him for feeding from her, but Dad hadn't raised a fool. If he lied to her again, then she was out—O.U.T.

Shivering from the remembered euphoria skittering across her sensitive nerves, she rubbed her wrist again where the feel of his lips lingered. Her reaction belied her conviction. Damn.

With a deep sigh, she washed her hands at the sink, splashing water onto her face in the process. She opened the fridge to take the milk before searching the cupboards, hoping to find real food. Breakfast cereal? After placing it on the table, she went in search of the bowl and spoon she'd seen in passing.

Minutes later, she sat at the kitchen table, munching on cereal for dinner, but she didn't mind. The aching coil in the pit of her stomach had to mean she was starving. That explanation was better than the alternative. Besides, finding cereal in a vampire's home was a Godsend.

She pondered her volatile reaction to him.

The need to spread her thighs was new for her. She didn't know how long she had—whether she'd survive today—and meeting a man hot enough to melt her socks had certain thoughts claiming her focus. Before she died, she wanted to do it at least once, and it would be glorious if it was with him. She could even squeeze in a few more times before her death, if he was willing. He'd had years to master his *technique*.

Her breath caught, and she choked on a mouthful of cereal.

Her face burned as she planned how to proposition the man. For the first time in years, she wished she'd taken one of the many offers thrown her way. If she managed to resist the temptation now, she'd find one of those offers. Better a human man than a suckblood. No matter how devastating Gabe was to her senses.

Under Dad's watch, both her and Val had struggled to find men not scared of him. After his death, Mike had assumed the role of cock-blocker. She sighed, chastising herself for feeling embarrassed at her inexperience. She couldn't do someone at her precinct, so it had to be a fireman or a bodyguard. She shrugged. If he wasn't interested, she'd walk away. No harm, no foul.

Gabriel strolled into the kitchen, dressed in low-riding jeans and a tight black T-shirt. In an instant, her mouth dried, and the cereal turned into sawdust. He prepared a pot of coffee as she swallowed the now tasteless cereal because she needed the nourishment.

"You found the cereal." He flashed her a small smile, enough to curl a lip.

"It's strange food for a vampire to have," she said between mouthfuls. "You like coffee?"

"Cereal doesn't nourish me, but I enjoy the texture regardless. Vampires can only taste bitter flavors. During the conversion, we lose the ability to taste salty or sweet human foods. Only when feeding might we encounter other flavors, and those are on the savory side."

He took out two mugs and placed them on the table in front of her. He added several packets of sugar and two teaspoons. The coffee aroma permeated the room. She breathed in its tantalizing scent. He placed a filled mug in front of her, to which she added milk and sugar. Taking a sip, she moaned in pleasure when the caramel sweetness coated her tongue.

"I hope they have coffee in heaven," she said, aware he sat there with his unwavering stare on her. It made her feel awkward. She gripped the cup to hide her trembling fingers. She wondered what he thought when he looked at her like that.

"I hope they have you in heaven." His chest rose as he fought for breath.

She whipped up her head then glanced away, unable to deal with that much intensity. Heat hurried from her cheeks down her neck, and shyness struck again. She jumped up to take her empty bowl and cup to the sink to hide her awkwardness. While there, she started on the dishes, desperate to hide her reaction but aware of his stare boring into her back.

"You should take a shower while I find you something less provocative to wear."

How kind of him to offer. She couldn't visit Val in her bra. Sure, she felt vulnerable, exposed, but more so without her weapons.

She smiled her thanks, hearing the amusement in his voice as she placed the cup on the drying rack. At the sight of his full smile, the cup slipped from her hand. With a curse, she lunged to catch it and sliced her hand on the knife in the drying rack. The sharp burn of the wound had her crying out.

"Callie, it's okay," he said, her bleeding hand now cradled in his. He'd used his preternatural speed to reach her—a blur she'd seen from the corner of her eye. "It's just a mug."

He leaned forward and licked her cut, dragging his rasping tongue across her palm. Her senses were alight, her nerves on high alert, so much so that his touch curled her toes.

He moaned, and his eyelids fluttered shut—his facial expression was one of pure bliss. He was beautiful to look upon, like an angel raising his face to God's loving gaze.

"Your blood tastes like caramel," he rasped in amazement. "From the coffee?" He opened his eyes to meet hers. "What are you, Callie?" He returned his lips to her hand, tasting, licking until he'd healed her wounded palm.

"Gabe." She drew in a shuddering breath, surprised she'd let him lick her. "Ready to take me to Val?"

He dropped her hand and gestured to her chest. "Perhaps a quick shower?"

She huffed, tugging her hand back to rest on her hips. Sure, her palm tingled as if she held fizzing pop rocks, but he didn't need to know how he affected her.

"You're stalling." She narrowed her gaze as scenarios played out in her mind. Could she take him? That was a hard no. Could she outrun him? To where, the lounge? So, also a no.

She folded her arms across her chest, hoping to hide her nipples tenting her silk bra.

"I'm not." He scowled. "I don't want others to see you like this and if you use the soap in the green bottle, it will mask some of your scent. Let's not create a feeding frenzy when you visit Val."

All valid points, damn it. She nodded then stilled when he grimaced.

"What?" she asked as he stepped away from her.

"We have visitors." He brushed a curl off her temple. "I'll get rid of them. You go shower." He pushed her toward the kitchen door.

She hesitated, needing to see where the door was. But he waited, watching, and she stumbled to the bathroom before closing its door behind her.

Visitors? She assumed that meant more suckbloods. Trying to eavesdrop, she pressed her ear to the door.

Despite his allure, she would leave after Val. *Argh.* Callie was so out of her depth it was laughable. His sensuality was off the charts. She should escape and find a safe human man for her first time. Now that she'd had a sample of lust, she wouldn't shy away from men.

If she stayed and succumbed, Gabe would rock her world. Could a normal man ever compare? But could she walk away without experiencing his expertise?

Giving up on hearing anything, she opened the bathroom door. The living room was empty with no sounds to guide her, so she closed the door. A shower, a visit to Val, then she'd leave.

CHAPTER TWELVE

A MYTH

GABE PAUSED AT THE front door, trying to control his breathing and his heart rate. He willed his erection to subside, but it was a foolish hope. Not that he wanted it to go, when everything within him longed to bury it in her softness and have her scent drench him.

His mind's eye lingered on where he'd rather be, what he'd rather be doing, with the vision of Callie in the throes of passion with her blood dribbling over a taut nipple. He shuddered, his erection throbbing with his heartbeat. The need for her was painful, and he relished the burn, the novelty of it.

Drawing in a deep breath, he acknowledged the reason behind Syl's minions intruding. Darius. Not that it made dealing with them easier. He could smell them—their fear. They had a right to fear him. Now more than ever. They had interrupted what would have been a treasured experience.

His mind drifted to Callie again, unable to cease returning to the temptation of her. Her hooded green eyes, her parted lips, the rise and fall of her lace-encased breasts... Leo had been right to find her fascinating, to form a fondness for her. She was beautiful—her auburn hair against her creamy skin was its own enticement.

Her taste. How was it possible? Gabe shook his head. He suspected her blood changed with what she consumed. She was a myth. In all his centuries, he'd never met one such as her.

Goosebumps rippled along his sensitized skin. Yet another sensation he hadn't felt in centuries. Eagerness, need, pleasure, pain, fury, frustration—too many emotions to experience in one day.

He sensed the impatience of his visitors, but he didn't care. If it wasn't for their intrusion, he'd have her pinned to the wall, tasting her and her delicious blood as she orgasmed.

With a grunt, he wrenched the door open. This entrance was one of three—two known, one secret.

"What?" he demanded of the two vampires—a tall woman and a stocky blond man. Gabe didn't know either and didn't care to.

"Lord Sylvester requests you bring your captive," said the tall brunette woman, her skin glistening, and her lips pouting.

He didn't pay attention to her lure. Their kind used their physical wiles to attract dinner, for the most part. Turbulent, selfish, vain, vampire women were far more trouble than they were worth.

He rested his forehead on the hand that held the door open. "Did Darius complain?" When had his life become so complicated? Fragrant Callie arrived to torment him, yet her stubbornness was a barrier he looked forward to breaching. Now he had visits from his brother's sycophants.

The blond man nodded.

"I'll be there." Gabe slammed the door in their faces and strode to the bathroom.

The shower was running. A vision flashed before him, burning into his retinae. Callie rubbing her body with the soap dancing down and over her curves in rivulets. Her breasts upright, her hips curved, her thighs strong and firm.

He groaned and again rested his head on the doorframe as dizziness assailed him. To not follow orders tempted him. The urge to defy Syl, his authority, hissed across his mind. Delicious and sinful as the thought was, it would bring many vamps down on Gabe, perhaps harming Callie in the ensuing battle. No, he had to obey. The sooner the better. A tiny lie or an innocent secret became monstrous over time. Revealing who she was, how special her blood was, should be done now.

He cursed, thumping his forehead on the doorframe. Once they knew how precious she was, they'd hunt her, challenge him for the right to her. Worse, enslave her. He sucked in a sharp breath. Not on his bedraggled soul would he allow harm to befall his untamed Callie.

He opened the door and walked into the spacious bathroom. Steam filled the room, adding to the romance of it.

She cried out, slamming her body against the tiled wall as if to hide her nudity. "Gabe?"

"Yes." Moving the high-back chair closer to the shower, he sat, spreading his knees to accommodate his arousal.

"What the hell? There are boundaries. A shower means privacy." She waited, as if he would leave. When he didn't, her shoulders slumped, and she continued to soap her body.

Despite the misty glass obscuring her, his gaze trailed her hands as they traveled over her body. The reality was better than his vision. A flick of his wrist cleared the glass to reveal her nudity in pure clarity. His mouth watered in anticipation.

"Who was it? What did they want?" She stepped under the water to rinse off.

"They want you." He opted for honesty.

The squeak from her showed she hadn't expected that. She switched the water off. The shower door slid open, and she popped her head out, a breast pressed against the now transparent glass.

He groaned and studied her. Did she know what she did to him? How sexy he found her? How her every move aroused him? Was she sent to torment him, to deceive him? He didn't have any enemies he could think of, though vampires did have extensive memories, carrying grudges far longer than they should.

Her brow furrowed. "Because of Darius, or because I didn't die or convert?"

"A little of both."

She was smart. He admired that.

Fear darkened the green of her eyes. Her expressive face twisted his insides something fierce. "Will they harm me?" she asked. "I'm out of my depth here. No weapons, no badge."

"Badge?" He remembered she was a detective, but having her admit it meant she wasn't here to deceive him.

"Detective Callista Devereaux, at your service," she said as she twisted the water from her hair.

The fact she was law enforcement explained so much about her. Her courage under fire, her ability to resist their pheromones, her muscled yet supple body, and the inner core of strength running through her.

"They won't harm you," he said. "I'll be there with you."

Her smile of gratitude pierced him with the startling revelation that she didn't—and perhaps never had—feared him. He, the most formidable vampire in the region, feared by vampires and shifters alike, didn't scare this human woman.

"Good." She flashed him another smile, and hooked the towel, pulling it into the shower to dry off. She didn't close the door, and that left an unhindered slivered view of her.

Air rushed from his lungs. Naked, glistening with water droplets trickling off her, disappeared behind the thick terry cloth.

"You did mention dressing me in something less provocative." She paused. "Do I want to know whose clothes I'll be wearing?"

"Yours." His voice was gravel incarnate, scratching his throat as he spoke.

"Mine?" She slid the door open and stepped out with the towel wrapped around her body.

"This *is* less provocative." He bolted from his chair and pinned her to the bathroom wall. "What are you doing to me?" he asked, burying his face in her neck, licking the water droplets, tasting her skin, scraping his fangs across the pulse there.

She shivered, and he smiled, pleased at her reaction. He crushed his lips across hers, conquering her mouth—a desperate attempt to bury himself in her and consume her very essence.

"We don't have time for this now." He cupped a towel-covered breast, massaging it, teasing the nipple with the pad of his thumb. Her breathless moans threatened his self-control. "Your first time with me should be slow and thorough."

"My very first time with anyone should be quick and painless." She gripped his shoulders, and he didn't know if she meant to pull him closer or push him away.

She was a virgin? His erection throbbed in eagerness.

The word *pain* ricocheted through his mind. He never wanted to cause her pain.

"You deserve slow and thorough." He trailed his hand over a breast to her belly button. "A shirt with your jeans should be okay for now?" His gaze returned to hers, and he growled.

Her hooded eyes were intense with a longing that mirrored the need pounding at his control.

"Callie." He wanted to kiss her, to ravage her mouth again with a desperation he'd never experienced before. He peeled himself away from her, his hands shaking with restraint. "We need to go." He cursed his brother under his breath.

"Very well." She released a slow sigh. "A shirt like this?" She fingered the sleeve of the black T-shirt he wore, meeting his gaze with boldness. She waited, as if he would leave and return with the items.

At her expectation, he snapped out of his daze and opened a wooden panel. He tossed her a towel for her hair before choosing another black T-shirt, offering it to her.

"So that's where you hide these? I thought those panels were decoration." As she rubbed her hair, she flicked her gaze to the door, a silent command for him to leave. But he pinched his lips, folding his arms across his chest as if to say he wasn't budging.

She huffed. "This is unusual, rude, and all kinds of messed up." She pulled on her jeans under her towel. "You'd think you haven't seen your share of naked women."

"Somehow, with you, it's different." He scowled, not wanting to admit she impacted his emotions, his control. She was right though. They didn't know each other well enough for him to assume certain liberties.

Sighing, he gave her his back, wishing he could watch her yank on the shirt, with her breasts bouncing. The shirt might have caught on her nipples on the way down. Just the idea of it froze the air in his lungs. Only after the slap of a wet towel hitting the rack did he turn around. When she bent to slip on her sneakers, her wet hair had darkened the shirt's fabric.

"Ready." She rubbed her hair with a hand towel. It was darker when wet and made her skin glow. She pursed her lips when he didn't move, instead stood there, watching.

"Fuck." He needed to get her back here ASAP and start his seduction because she wasn't leaving him until he had her beneath him. He grabbed her hand and led her out of the bathroom. The hand towel dropped in his haste.

"My hair. It'll be a wreck."

He narrowed his gaze on her temple for a second before dragging her toward the front door. He didn't need towels. Vampires had power over some of the elements, including air.

He glanced at her vibrant auburn hair, tempting him to linger. But he couldn't afford to. Syl first, then Val, then maybe, by then, Callie might trust him a little.

Fuck.

Chapter Thirteen

Her Big Mouth

"Your hair is beautiful," Gabe muttered as he ushered her out the door.

Callie touched her hair, amazed to find it dry. How had he done that? She ran behind him, struggling to match his long strides as he led her through a hidden door, down a tunnel, and out into the night.

"Gabe," she pleaded, her calves burning as she did double the effort to match his gait.

"No more, Callie. Do not tempt me now. We must see my brother or else."

She wanted to snort despite the joy bursting like fireworks in her chest. She tempted him? Was he insane? "I know, but I can't keep up."

He paused, and his gaze roved over her as if studying her flushed face before sweeping her into his arms and breaking into a super-fast run. She squealed in surprise and grabbed his shoulders for stability.

After a few minutes, she relaxed and admired the night sky sparkling with stars, the cool breeze refreshing on her flustered face. "You said your brother. What should I expect?"

"He's my younger brother. We converted together." His voice had a faraway sound to it, as if he was remembering that day. "I am stronger than he is, and he leads because I won't challenge him for the position."

"Does he fear that one day you might?" Why weren't suckbloods involved in human politics? With their uber-powers, they could ascend to presidency. Syl would give Carter a run for his money. Perhaps it was for the best. She didn't need to investigate yet another power-crazed maniac.

Gabe sliced a glance at her, and a smile teased his lips. "Yes." He looked away. "We are almost there." He stopped, jarring her, then lowered his gaze to hers. "I need you to agree to everything I say. You're in my world now. In Val's too. If they discover your unique flavor, your ability to resist pheromones…I might not be strong enough to save you." He grimaced, whatever his imagination conjured, it didn't look pleasant.

"All right, then Val afterward?"

"Yes. As you saw, younglings remain separate. Their monstrous thirst is the reason why vampires have a bloody history." He broke into a run again.

"No pun intended?" she teased.

He grinned, but didn't dip his head to look at her. "Callie, perhaps you shouldn't mention your sister for now. Your scent and blood are unusual. I would prefer we don't share this in case it endangers her. Let her grow stronger first."

She didn't know what conversion did to a cancer patient, so if he believed Val needed time, then Callie had to agree with him. She didn't have to like it, though. Like letting Val go to chemo on her own. The first few times Callie had accompanied her, she'd sobbed in the bathroom stall. She hadn't been strong for Val at all.

"I defer to you on this." She had to trust him, trust that Val could survive this. Burying her face in his neck, Callie inhaled, relishing the masculine scent of him.

Hot damn. What the hell happened? She went from "the law is neutral" to sniffing a suckblood. There were men she'd given a second glance, but life had distracted her, and she'd let it, not having the energy to thwart Mike's cockblocking. Therein lay the crux of the matter. He wasn't here, and even if he was, she wanted Gabe, wanted to know him better in more ways than carnal. Although, that played a major role in her reactions, decisions, and behavior. She wouldn't lie to herself about that. Adding his consideration, thoughtfulness, and kindness, he'd done everything to negate her skewed opinion on suckbloods.

Having always considered herself impartial, she grimaced. She'd deceived herself for so long. Had Dad known? Her fellow officers? How long had she hated suckbloods and beasts? Racism in its purest form. Each species had their rotten apples, yet she'd painted them with the same brush, judging them on their worst examples. Call it hatred, fear, or distrust, but she didn't socialize with any, and didn't speak to non-humans other than to mete out justice. She buried her face deeper as if it could hide her shame. Within one day, she'd learned much about her own character, and it wasn't pleasant. Could she face a suckblood without her preconceived notions and expectations?

Gabe halted, and she studied their surroundings, tightening her grip around his neck. They were at an entrance to a building that was unusual for this part of the country. Italian design, with vaulted arches, sandstone, and wall-mounted candelabras casting rippling gold flames and ebony shadows.

He lowered her to her feet, and she clung to his dry shirt. The run hadn't drawn a drop of perspiration from him. "Thank you," she said, her ingrained manners coming to the forefront.

"Always *my* pleasure," he said, his voice husky. It skittered along her senses like velvet on her skin.

"Lord Sylvester awaits you in the hall," a man said, surprising her.

She hadn't noticed his appearance. Why? She shook her head to clear her lust-fogged mind.

"Of course he does." Gabe tugged her behind him, his fingers laced with hers.

He had the right of it. She was in his world now. Even though, as a tough detective, having dealt with all manner of criminals no matter their species, she had to trust him. Him, a suckblood. Who was to say he would survive this meeting with his brother? She studied his broad shoulders and confident stride. Maybe he'd risk his life to save hers.

Or not.

If he decided to kill her, it would be like swatting a bug for him. She'd seen how easily the suckbloods killed, draining and tossing women as if they weighed nothing. Not one suckblood had walked away with defensive wounds. Without her arsenal, she couldn't defend herself, which left her at Gabe's mercy.

She shivered, not liking being vulnerable, and as she fought back the panic rising like a lump of lead in her throat, she reminded herself she didn't have many choices here. She could succumb to this attraction and pray Gabe was an honorable man. A suckblood honorable? Okay, so trusting him might take longer, but it came back to her choices. Trust him and see where his intentions lay or run from him. Would he hunt her? Her instincts welled up, pressing on her chest and speeding her heartbeat. *Yes.* Would he hurt her? Butterflies exploded into a crescendo, freezing her lungs. *No.* So escape wasn't the best solution, according to her instincts.

"Should I be submissive?" she asked, her voice soft. She wished she'd thought to discuss strategy or expected behavior for a human amid a suckblood's stronghold.

His chuckle was delicious and wicked as if he loved the idea of her being submissive. He arched a brow at her, his gaze roaming her body.

"Gabe," she moaned, blushing at where his thoughts must have gone. The idea of using her handcuffs on him had her butterflies pooling in the pit of her stomach.

"Be yourself, Callie." His broad smile dimpled his cheeks. "You've watched too many vampire movies."

Despite her burning cheeks, she chuckled and trailed him as he pushed through a hefty wooden door. It opened into a massive hall with a vaulted ceiling painted like a cathedral. Its immense size snatched her breath, the colors vibrant and depicting naked bodies like the Greek paintings of old.

She returned the curiosity of the many vampires studying them. They had her at a disadvantage, and their numbers forced her to trust the man holding her hand. One or two, she could take on, but an entire hall? She flashed a smile. If only they knew she went commando. Someone up front on the dais chuckled, causing Gabe to glance at her, a question in his eyes. Shit, did these people have unique gifts? Could they read her thoughts?

Yes, to the gifts, but only I have this talent. I'm surprised I can read you.

Callie stiffened as the voice flitted through her mind. How the hell had she not known about this? That there was one who could read minds was alarming, but not as daunting as the possibility of hundreds. She grinned, content to settle for one mind reader than a roomful.

Upon a dais sat a man in a throne-like chair. *Holy shit...Sylvester?* He resembled Gabe. What she'd seen of Syl made her sneer. All those women circling him, his confident stride through the docks, enticing Val to attempt suicide. He was selfish and arrogant—all the traits she'd painted suckbloods with. How could he be Gabe's brother when they were so vastly different?

He can be selfish and arrogant, but he has his reasons. The voice floated through her mind again.

Who are you? She studied the faces before her, trying to determine—in vain—who could read her mind as if there would be an outward, physical characteristic. Yet another thing not in her officer's handbook. God only knew what else they didn't know. If their knowledge on suckbloods was lacking, their knowledge on beasts was as suspect.

You know me, Callista. I'm strangely disappointed to see you so intimate with Gabriel.

"Syl," Gabe said, drawing her attention as he addressed his brother.

"Devereaux, what a surprise."

She focused on the vampire before her. He was tall and as well-built as Gabe, with the same hair and eyes. His nostrils flared as if he scented the air. She didn't like him, or anyone other than Gabe, doing that. It made her feel violated. Cold slithered along her nerve endings with a sense of filth coating her soul.

"Of all the detectives, you are by far my favorite."

She scowled. She didn't want to be *his* anything. Fury tore through her, and she trembled with restraint. She gripped Gabe's hand like a lifeline. Attacking his brother might not go well with the spectators or with Gabe. Not to mention, she'd lose and die.

"You set my sister up to this, asshole," she said, the words coming from behind clenched teeth. She was furious with him, but more with herself. After all, it was *her* fault Val had met the bastard in the first place. She might have ignored the flyer. And for all Callie knew, when they met, Syl could've offered Val a guarantee of sorts. "You had the canister, but no, you had to fuck with my life."

He appeared indifferent to her accusation, which riled her further. Red circled her vision. She sucked in gulps of air.

"Entertaining, as usual, Devereaux. What happened to the woman who liked the look and scent of me?" He stepped forward as if to touch her.

She bristled—if he laid a hand on her, she'd take a piece of him. She wasn't completely helpless. Gabe laced his fingers through hers and tugged her back.

Syl studied her, then Gabe before chuckling, surprise softening his features. "Never mind, I see you've made a champion of my brother."

"Your brother has a will of his own," she snarled. If the suckbloods thought she'd show this idiot any respect, they were sadly mistaken.

"She defends you, Gabriel? This is too delightful for words." Syl raised a hand to touch her hair, but she jerked away from him. "Darius?" Sighing, he lowered his hand before tilting his head toward Darius who stood to the side.

"Yes, it is her, Lord Sylvester." The damn whine hadn't left his voice.

Coward. She smirked.

Shifting her focus between Syl and Darius, she wondered what the point was of this meeting. Darius's annoying presence had her thinking he was at the core of it.

With a telepath in the room, her thoughts weren't her own. She pictured a wall, building it around her mind like she'd read about in her paranormal romance novels.

Much to her chagrin, she'd fantasized about suckbloods and beasts, but the fictional ones weren't as disagreeable as the real ones.

She didn't want her mental intruder to hear her thoughts about Syl and Darius, or worse, Val. She wasn't certain the wall would work, but she tried it anyway. Doing something was better than standing idly by and allowing someone to mind-fuck her.

Mind-fuck? the voice whispered. There was a familiar quality to it. She shook her head and focused on strengthening her wall and her musings.

What the hell was this royal suckblood doing wandering around the docks in the middle of the night? In a tux, too? He'd said the canister held their future. Leo had said it wasn't a weapon, but how well did she know Leo? Could she trust he hadn't lied to her?

It's not a weapon.

Get out of my head! she shot back.

"You've upset Darius by taking his toy." Syl addressed their audience as if this was a theater performance.

She tightened her hand on Gabe's while she added a thick layer of concrete to her mental wall.

If this idiot thinks I will choose Darius—

He's my king, but yes, he does sometimes do idiotic things.

Like have a woman blow him in the middle of a ballroom. She searched the crowd for Leo. If Syl was here, where was his shadow?

You saw that? How did you see that, Callista?

She didn't answer him.

"I don't give a shit about Darius. If the fool hadn't intruded…" Gabe's voice resonated with anger. "Regardless, I speak the Rite of *Adsumo* over Callista, as you now bear witness to."

The crowd gasped, followed by shocked murmurs. She glanced at Gabe then at the surrounding suckbloods. Was this what he'd asked her to agree to? Okay…*Adsumo*. It sounded ancient, like something tribal and best left in a dark cave miles beneath the earth's surface. Not knowing what it was, she reserved judgment. For all she knew, it could mean sex for a while, or keeping her as his pet or as his personal feeder, although he'd denied the latter. Judging the crowd's reaction, claiming her was something not done lightly. Regardless, she didn't want to agree to any of them.

"She'll weaken you." Syl's eyes widened with a mixture of surprise and anger. "You haven't announced the rights over anyone, not in centuries."

Whoa. What Syl said made her instincts leap again. First, centuries? Gabe was that old? They had longevity, but she hadn't realized it spanned hundreds of years. Second, how could keeping a feeder weaken him?

She scowled, not liking the idea of causing anyone harm, not after the countless partners injured in the line of duty because of her.

You have chosen your champion wisely, Callista.

"He cannot have her. She's mine," Darius whined.

Syl flicked his hand at him to be quiet.

Darius stilled, his blatant obedience lowering her opinion of him, not that he had far to go.

"Devereaux, have you bewitched my brother as you have tempted my advisor?" Syl asked her with honest interest on his face. Gone was the annoying smirk, the pseudo-charm in his voice. Instead, he arched a brow and peered into her eyes with unwavering curiosity.

She suspected genuine expressions were rare for him. "What the hell are you talking about?" she asked. He was a blithering idiot.

He means me. You have tempted me...

I don't know you! Why isn't my wall working?

Syl tutted. "I suppose I'm being an idiot. You're human, are you not?"

"Yes," she said. "You're being an idiot."

She smirked, ignoring the discontent that rippled through their audience. She was being a smartass, but he did irritate her. Then again, his twinkling gray eyes denoting his peaked humor didn't please her, either. She hated him with the passion of a thousand suns. This level of hatred surprised her. He took the canister from her, made her endure two full treatments, and still managed to convince her sister to attempt suicide. If he'd cost her Val, then she supposed her hatred was justifiable. She wasn't one to blindly hate, though. Or so she'd thought.

"Has she agreed?" Syl faced Gabe even though he addressed the crowd.

"Yes." Callie raised her chin to project her voice. Time to step out on faith. Gabe had asked her to agree, and if it wasn't to her liking, whatever this rights nonsense was, she'd give him more than a piece of her mind.

She wouldn't humiliate Gabe by debating this in front of his people, specifically in front of his too-cocky-by-far asshat brother. Syl winning so much as an argument was unacceptable. Besides, how bad could claiming be?

Honorable.

Is there any way I can get you to shut up? She huffed.

Syl approached her. "Come forward, Devereaux."

Gabe guided her to the front but kept her pressed to the length of him. Her back rested against his solid chest, the heated strength of him warming her. As she stood before Syl, she added a layer of reinforced steel bars to her mental wall. It wasn't working since the telepath wouldn't shut up, but she was stubborn.

She held Syl's gaze, determined to be strong for Gabe, for her survival. Syl puffed up as Darius had done, mesmerizing her.

A scent surrounded her, one that was like Gabe's—forest, grass, and masculinity, but with hints of grapefruit. The scent wasn't one she liked or disliked. It simply wasn't preferable.

Gabe's hold on her arms tightened, and she assumed what Syl was doing wasn't to his liking, either. She studied Syl, her focus unwavering. Yes, he was handsome, but he lacked...muchness.

She giggled...*muchness?* She did feel as if she'd fallen down a rabbit hole.

Syl's eyes widened at her laugh. A chuckle came from the side, a sound familiar to her. Before she could search for the man, Syl's voice drew her attention.

"What, pray tell, do you find amusing?"

"That you puff up your chest and expect me to swoon at your feet." Her laughter rose from her belly, deep and joyful.

It felt good to laugh, the warmth unexpected and freeing. Val's impending death had dampened any joy she found, but now she had a second chance at life.

"It's as I suspected, I didn't affect you at the docks either," Syl said. "Nor in your sister's apartment."

"I don't ally myself with criminals." Callie glared.

"Criminals? I like her, Gabriel," he said to his brother. "May I?" he asked permission, something which was unheard of, judging by the audience's strangled gasps or barks of outrage.

Get a television, for fuck's sake.

"If she allows it," Gabe said, placing the decision upon her.

Had he not, she might have become belligerent. She nodded, the quicker she did whatever, the quicker she could see Val.

"Callie, would you allow me to scent and taste you?"

That Syl *was* asking made an impression on her. He could take what he wanted, and she would be helpless against him.

She looked to Gabe for guidance. His nod was slight.

"If it ends this farce." She stepped forward, her left hand still clasping Gabe's, the touch of his fingers a safety anchor.

The realization she was the only doe amid a hall filled with hunters had her heart skittering and her cinched lungs limiting her ability to breathe. If the shit hit the fan, she needed to be close to Gabe.

The crowd watched in breathless silence. She frowned. These people were weird. What did it matter if the suckblood-sire tasted her? There wasn't enough blood in her body for them all to sample her. And damn it, Gabe better make sure that didn't happen.

Syl met her halfway and buried his face in her neck. He moaned, the sound deep and penetrating, reverberating through her. It was too appreciative for her liking.

"She *does* smell good." He searched for someone behind him before leaning back to study her, taking her right hand into his.

He pricked a finger with his sharp teeth, squeezing to draw a drop of blood. He licked it and gaped. "Caramel."

A rumble ran through the crowd, and with it came betrayal. She was Gabe's ready-meal and fuckbuddy. Pain constricted her chest, piercing her heart with unerring accuracy.

Syl glanced at Gabe, and the expression had her panicking. "Do you think...?"

Gabe had said they couldn't taste salt or sweet from other foods and only savory from blood. She leaned into him to whisper. He dipped his head to her level, and her lips brushed his earlobe. A tremor raked through him, but she ignored it when anger consumed her current mood. No one liked to be used.

"Is that why you want me? You said I wasn't your feeder." She grimaced, her voice revealing her turmoil.

She couldn't school her features, hurt and angry with herself he'd lied to her, and she'd lapped it up. She'd trusted him, believed every seductive word dripping from his sensual mouth. How naïve could she be? So gullible?

Like someone as good-looking at Gabe would like *her* for something more than food? A detective? A human? She complicated his life just by being who she was. Why would he take on such a nuisance?

He didn't answer her. Instead, he studied her face. What he saw she didn't know. A feeling of entrapment swirled in the pit of her stomach, overriding the peace she'd experienced seconds ago.

Could she run from him, find Val, and escape this place? Were there side effects to conversion, like losing one's memories? The idea of Val seeing Callie as food gripped her. Shit, she was *so* in trouble here.

Valerie is safe, the voice said.

Get. Out. Of. My. Head. She added enough anger in her mental voice to bring heat to her cheeks. She searched the hall for exits. There were a few unguarded, as if they'd never needed to consider preventing someone from leaving.

"No, you mean more to me than the flavor of your blood. Everything in my being wants you."

Gabe brushed his arousal across her hip, dispelling any doubts about his desire for her. He felt hard, hot, but it could be a ruse. After seeing Syl's spectacular sexcapade at the mayor's ball... She shot Gabe a look, implying they'd talk about this later. Once he escorted her to Val, she might make a run for it, especially if his explanation was weak.

She faced Syl again. He offered her a large strawberry. Where he'd gotten it, she didn't know. With a shrug, she took it and bit into it. She *was* hungry. Everyone watched her eat, making her self-conscious as she chewed. After swallowing, she extended her hand to Syl, assuming this was like the coffee incident. He pricked her finger and licked it again. His groan of pleasure was genuine.

"Strawberry! It's been years..." His hold on her tightened as his gray-eyed gaze traveled her face in delight and confusion.

Oh, shit. Her focus shifted from Syl to Gabe. What now? Why the hell did it matter if she tasted like strawberries?

You smelled delicious that night we met.

Wait. She recognized that voice, that phrase.

Leo? You're here? Damn it, you suckblood. I could've done with a friendly face. So you watched me squirm out of boredom?

She didn't want to entertain these sycophants. She was here for Val and only Val. Yet now she'd gone and agreed to Gabe claiming her. Fuck. If only she could blame Gabe's pheromones, she could've at least had that excuse. Could she plead insanity?

Syl grinned and released her to slap his brother on the back. "I second your Rite of *Adsumo*, Gabriel. She's worthy of you."

Gabe's shoulders relaxed, and she almost followed suit, wanting to burrow into the safety of his arms. Instead, she stiffened her spine and tried to pull her hand out of his. Her word and honor trapped her, but that didn't mean she had to agree to everything he said and did. She still had free will, didn't she?

You're beautiful, Callista. Your honor is precious.

"I don't approve." Darius stepped toward them. "I saw her first."

"Callie, do you accept Darius?" Syl sighed.

She sensed he asked as a formality. "No," she said, her tone firm.

"There's your answer, Darius."

Darius lunged for her. Before he could take a step though, an unseen force snapped his neck. She gasped, her hold tightening on Gabe's waist. Holy shit! She'd never seen anything like that before. How naïve had she been to go into fights with just her dipped daggers?

"Thank you, Leo," Syl said as a tall blond-haired man stepped over Darius's slumped form, a man she recognized.

Leo crossed to Syl and acknowledged his thanks with a nod. "Callie, this is Leo, my advisor. You've met before, I believe."

Leo stopped in front of her, and as she studied his familiar features, the tension between her shoulders eased. He could have killed her three times already. Would he be her ally if she needed one?

Yes, but you don't need me, Callista.

"Leo," she said, by way of greeting.

His bow was formal as he flashed a grin. Gabe frowned, his expression intense. She gave him a look that said she'd explain later.

"No more suicide attempts?" Leo teased.

She shook her head. He held out a hand, palm upward, and out of nowhere, a tumbler of burnished gold liquid appeared. She gasped and accepted it from him, a little dazzled. She raised it to her lips and sipped the best scotch she'd ever tasted. The intensity of it warmed her stomach, swirling like a voracious lion. She downed it and gave him back his glass. It disappeared before her eyes. Right, yet another talent she didn't know about.

"And?" Syl asked Leo.

With a chuckle, the tall man shook his head, his pale-gold hair brushed his shoulders in the process. "Snippets, as usual."

"Nothing?" Syl asked. "As per the ball?"

"There was something when she entered, but once she realized I was there..." Leo shrugged. "She has compartmentalized her thoughts. I can share in a few, and only those she deems acceptable."

"Well, well, Devereaux. A fountain of surprises." Syl grinned, shaking his head in disbelief. "Could you train her, Leo?"

It's a pity you belong to Gabriel now.

I belong to me. She felt like thumping her chest. This was the 21st century. You'd think suckbloods would move with the times.

Not anymore, Callista. "Yes, I could train her," he said, his lips twisting. Sadness flitted across his face then nothing, no expression, just serenity. *I wanted to taste every inch of you.*

She gasped, surprised he'd liked her in that way.

"Are we done?" Gabe asked as he yanked Callie against him.

She scowled at him. What was she, a chew toy?

"Yes, by all means, go." Syl dismissed them.

With a nod, Gabe tightened his fingers clasping hers and tugged her through a side door.

"You know Leo," he said, as she studied the silver moonlight caressing his features. He led her through a courtyard, crossing cobblestones that looked ancient.

"We met at the mayor's ball." She shrugged.

"He told me he didn't touch...?"

Leo told him? They'd discussed her at some point, or did Leo talk to him telepathically? Wasn't that the same thing? It took a while for Gabe to voice that question. She wondered why it mattered. He was hundreds of years old—it wasn't as if she was asking him about his past lovers. Not that she and Leo had ventured in that direction.

"No. He was a gentleman. Okay, spell it out. What does *Adsumo* mean?" She admired the starlit sky spread above them, not wanting his handsomeness to sway her determination. She needed answers.

"Thank you," he said.

Without a doubt, she understood he thanked her for agreeing to this publicly.

She reached up to stroke his cheek, caught herself, and shoved her hands into her back pockets. "My pleasure. What did I agree to?"

Part of her wanted to rant at his audacity, at placing her in such a situation. As if her being here, at the festival, in his home, now in this stronghold, was his fault. But she'd agreed to chase after Val, vulnerable with no weapons, and she'd chosen to descend through the trapdoor. It was on her when she helped him to the chair. She could've returned to the race. She might have made it, saved Val, or she could've died and found herself sitting alongside Val as a suckblood.

Part of Callie wanted to run and never look back. She wasn't a quitter, but the panic, the overwhelming circumstances, her illogical intense attraction to him drove her to consider it. So much was happening too fast. It left her head spinning and herself second-guessing her decisions.

He shifted closer to her, bringing a little of his warmth and his intoxicating cologne. The moon illuminated his face with enough light to reveal his troubled expression, as if he measured his words with care.

"Faced with your unique blood, I had to help you. *Adsumo* means no one would dare to drink from you without your permission or enslave you."

"Enslave me? Help me why?" She scowled, imagining hordes of suckbloods popping in for a quick drink, at her home or at the precinct. "I'm trapped here?"

Shit, shit, shit!

Her blood had placed a target on her back. Why hadn't it ever before? Her heart hammered against her chest. "Nowhere else is safe? Another city, maybe?"

He shook his head. "Your existence is on everyone's lips, and vamps live for gossip. Darius taking his request to Syl ended your life as a human."

She gaped at Gabriel, disbelief warring with anger and helplessness. "M-my life as a human?" The question came out high-pitched as she shifted her weight from foot to foot.

Part of her had known, her soul ringing with the truth in his words. With Val as a suckblood, how long would she have remained neutral anyway? She clenched her jaw, fighting that the decision was out of her hands. Gabe's announcement had sounded formal, as if he'd staked his claim to her and her remarkable blood.

"You own me?" She kept her gaze locked on his, desperate for him to say no.

A shiver ripped through her, and she squeezed her backside through the denim.

"No. You're not my feeder, Callie, nor my slave."

"Right," she said, releasing a pent-up breath. "Okay, explain what this *Adsumo* thing entails."

"Announcing the Rite of *Adsumo* before so many witnesses means you agreed to be my wife so to speak, agreed to conversion...to spending many lifetimes with me."

She sucked in a sharp breath. She stared then shook her head in disbelief. Had he said wife? Holy shit! They'd just met, and yes, she wanted to lick every delicious inch of him, but marriage? The things she got herself into...but he had agreed to it. Why sacrifice himself if what he said was true?

"You committed yourself to me to help me? You could've let me die. This makes no sense, Gabe. I've known you for a day!"

She paced before him, running her hands over her face. No longer was the moonlight beautiful. Where she was and with whom she was, toyed with her sanity. "I didn't hope for anything more than temporary. Maybe a wild affair on the dark side for me."

He chuckled, pulling her closer with a gentle grasp of her wrist. "We'll have an affair that will last for an eternity."

Her breath caught in her throat. "You want me for more than short-term?"

The men she met, and sometimes dated, thought only of the now, maybe up till tomorrow night if pressed. She'd done the same with Gabe, expecting sex and goodbye. Well, mostly sex, sex, and more sex.

Commitment? No, no, no.

She bent over, fighting for air. Gripping her thighs added stability to her trembling knees. She straightened, arching her back to suck in breaths.

"I want you more than I can convey at present." He cupped her jaw and chin, brushing his thumb over her bottom lip, making her knees weaker with that one touch.

"We just met. How could you possibly decide in that time if you want—?"

"I do." He searched her face. "Trust me to know my own mind, Callie."

"I'm not saying you're insane, Gabe." A hysterical giggle escaped her, and she choked it back, fighting for calm and to maintain what integrity she had left. "No, actually, I am. You're insane. We just met."

"You said that already." He grinned, joy dancing across his face, softening his expression to one of tenderness.

How could she trust his sincerity? He was a madman to believe the nonsense he spouted.

"Yeah, well, it's a pretty important factor." She tugged her hand free and stepped away from him, resuming her pacing. "Humans don't marry after a day of meeting, Gabe. Ever."

"I know, but vamps do."

"I'm not a suckblood." She tossed her hands into the air, gesturing wildly as she struggled to accept this. How could she explain this to Mike or Metcalfe? *Oh, by the way, I met and married someone yesterday. Could you pass the ketchup?* This was insane, a nightmare—maybe she died at the suckblood festival, and this was hell for her.

"You don't like me?" His charming smile curled his sensual lips as he scooped her into his arms and burst into a run.

"Of course, I like you. But marriage and taking a wife implies love, doesn't it? Liking someone isn't enough to base a commitment on." She watched him and waited, ignoring the wind-whipped tendrils obscuring her line of sight.

"Do you want...love?" He hesitated when he asked her, his voice almost hoarse as if her response mattered to him.

"Yes, I do. Unless you're thinking to death us do part? Marry me until you kill me?" She arched a brow, then wanted to hit him when he chuckled.

"We don't marry, we claim, and when we form that bond, you become as strong as me. I can't kill you, Callie. A part of me will reside in you, and to harm you would harm me."

"Shit." She tightened her fingers on his forearms. "I'd be your kryptonite. I'd weaken you, like Syl said. Your enemies could get to you through me."

Killing her would be far easier than killing someone as experienced as him. That he was a great predator wasn't in doubt. How he'd handled Darius said much about his skills. So why take the chance? Why tie himself to her when it wasn't in his best interest?

Pent-up energy zinged through her blood, and she shuddered, wishing they would reach Val's cell. She needed time away from his intense eyes, his mesmerizing scent, and this strange new world she'd stumbled into.

"Yes." Unfazed, he grinned and opened a massive door in front of them. Stairs descended along a well-lit passage, and she stepped back at the cacophony of screams echoing off the stone walls.

Sucking in a deep breath, she skipped down. Gabe followed her. She would never admit how grateful she was for his company. Iron bars filled the vast room, swinging light bulbs shifting shadows off the bare stone walls. In each cell, a few women paced, slept, sat, or clung to the bars. Blood dried on their contorted faces, new fangs piercing their bottom lips, and their clothes hung on them in tatters.

"She's with me," Gabe said to the hulking guard in a crisp suit.

Callie hadn't seen him with her interest fixed on the women's faces. Mounted cameras flickered red lights from the corners. The footage Gabe had shown her was real. Score one for the suckblood.

"Callie?" Val's voice cut through the din.

Her sister was alone in a cell. The rumpled clothing she wore showed no sign of abuse. Her skin was paler than usual, but there were no shadows under her eyes, and her irises glowed, switching between green and red. More surprising was the long wavy auburn hair she had prior to the chemo.

"Val, what have you gotten us into?" She hurried to the cell tucked into a corner.

Gabe leaped in front of her, throwing an arm across her chest as if Val would hurt her.

Callie elbowed him in the ribs, slipped around him, and gripped the bars.

Val didn't move from the bed but raised her nose to sniff the air. "You shouldn't be here, Callie. You smell...human."

"Damn it, I'm with suckbloods because of your death wish." She closed her eyes, trying to forget this was all her fault.

"I didn't ask you to follow."

If it wasn't for the shimmer of a blood-red tear on her eyelashes, Callie would've thought Val was possessed or drugged. "I promised Dad, Val, you know I did."

"Since I won't be dying for many more years, I would say you've fulfilled your promise." She raised sad eyes to Callie. "Thank you for coming. I thought you'd died." She sniffed and dipped her face as if the lighting hadn't picked up on the crimson tears scouring her cheeks.

"It was touch and go for a bit." Callie smiled. "Gabe says you stay down here for a few days. What happens after that?"

"We've had the siring ceremony where vamps request to mentor the younglings." Val unfolded her legs and rose off the bed, as graceful as a gazelle. "Leo is my mentor. I assume training follows." She shrugged.

Getting Leo as a mentor was good. "Will you let me know when I can visit?" Callie glanced at Gabe. "That's possible, right?"

He shook his head. "Not alone."

"She's my sister." She glared at him. How dare he imply Val would harm her.

"I'm not referring to Val. Alone, you are vulnerable to an attack, Callie."

Val laughed, breaking their staring contest. "I'll visit you, sis."

"I'm glad you made it, Val, even though it was a foolish thing to do." Callie sighed. "Do you need anything? A book, a magazine, a pint of blood?"

"Ha, very funny." Val smiled and nodded at the stairs. "Off you go."

Callie left with a bounce to her step, trailing Gabe. The moonlight was once more beautiful, perhaps because all was well. Gabe had kept his word, and Val lived, sort of.

"Thank you." Callie drew in a deep, satisfying breath of the cool night air.

He scooped her into his arms and broke into a run, reversing their earlier mad dash between his home and the stronghold. She gripped his shoulders, holding on as she worried her bottom lip. How to tell him she wasn't staying?

"Is there a process to this Rite of thing you mentioned?" She closed her eyes, not needing the moonlight to paint his features any handsomer than they were.

"Sex, often." His voice was hoarse, but when she peeked at him, he kept his focus ahead.

There went her heartbeat, dancing the mambo or something with complicated steps.

As soon as he lowered her to her feet outside his front door, she shook her hands to rid herself of restless energy. "I can't talk you out of claiming me?"

He shook his head. "Announced, witnessed, permission received, and if we don't convert you soon, many will try to take you from me."

She huffed. "This is barbaric." She paced in the dark confines of his tunnel, rubbing her damp palms on her denim-encased thighs. "As it is, you've tried to help me and you have my thanks for that. There's no need to embroil yourself further. Gabe, you shouldn't claim me. It's suicide, don't you see that?" She paused, waiting for his response.

His chest froze as if he'd stopped breathing. Did they even need to breathe? She pressed her hand to his temple. He was hot to the touch. So ice-cold suckbloods were a myth. She'd heard they didn't need oxygen. In his continued silence, she fought the urge to press her ear to his chest to make sure there was a heartbeat. Blood flowed through their veins, so it needed pumping somehow.

"So is facing a werewolf at noon," he said, at last with a voice hoarser than grinding gravel against rock. "That doesn't mean I should fear it. I *want* you, Callista."

He surprised her with his soft dry lips caressing hers before he hardened the kiss. She moaned under the onslaught. After all, this suckblood had years to perfect the art of kissing, and under his lips, it was truly an art form. Designed to seduce, he didn't even have to use thirty percent of his tricks on her. She was a disgrace to womankind, to the force, to the Devereaux name.

But to hell with it.

He tasted like sin—hot, wet need, yearning, and love—all in one.

A fang must've nicked her lip since she tasted salt and iron. His tongue slid along the tear, and he growled, his arms trembling. He pulled away, sucking in breaths, his irises swirling silver and dark gray.

"Syl announced it into law," he said, his breath cooling her heated lips.

Just like that? The rest of her life decided for her? She studied his face, wishing she could read his mind. He must know how she felt about all this. In shock, undecided, tempted. She'd been pretty vocal since they'd left the hall. She needed to meditate on it all, to decide what this meant and whether there was an escape. A divorce, of sorts.

"So this means I'm yours for an eternity?"

"As I am yours," he whispered, opening his door and ushering her inside.

Chapter Fourteen

Captain's Conniption

"Callie! Where the hell are you?" Barrows's voice came through her smartwatch.

She yelped, not having expected to hear from him on her day off.

"I'm kind of dealing with a family crisis," she said into the watch.

"Captain's having a conniption," Mike said, in a bored tone.

"No one says conniption anymore, Mike." Callie chuckled.

"From where I'm standing, she's having one. That your police vehicle is at a last-known suck-fest location? There's your problem. Like I said, where the hell are you?"

"Shit, she's here?" Callie faced Gabe, running a caressing gaze up his denim-hugging thighs and T-shirt-encased torso.

He wasn't doing anything illegal, hadn't even participated in the festivities, but fear burned in her chest. She couldn't let any harm befall him. Not on her watch. Not even married an hour, and already her "husband" was in danger. Typical of her.

"Damn straight. Now get your ass here and fix this. Oh, I have your gun and badge. I snagged it before she spotted it lying there on the hood."

Relief flooded her at those words, some of the tension between her shoulders easing. "Thanks, Barrows. I owe you one." She headed for the front door.

"Callie?" Gabe arched a brow.

"Sorry, Gabe. My captain's outside. I gotta deal with this before she summons the SWAT or even worse, the military."

His brow furrowed, and his expression darkened as if something bothered him, but she wasn't sure what. That she wouldn't come back? That shit might reach him down here? She couldn't say.

He sighed, stepping around her to open the door. "Let me take you part of the way. I don't want you lost."

She nodded her thanks at his offer even as she studied his face. Perhaps some other time he'd explain his reticence. For now, she'd deal with Metcalfe, and she did need his help leaving his home. She wasn't sure where she was, having run like a bat out of hell earlier without taking note of her surroundings. Turn left at tree, right at rock, dive around the third bush? She was a city girl—forest foraging wasn't her forte.

"How do I reach you?" She smiled at his sudden exhale. So he had been worried about her return. "I'm a woman of my word, Gabe."

Yes, she was, but despite that, something deep within her commanded her not to walk away from him. She had seen Val, and her sister as a vampire meant Callie's life would change. There was no way she'd abandon her sister because she drank blood for sustenance.

"This pleases me, Callie." He flashed a smile, scattering her thoughts. A dimple appeared, making him look more charming. The seductive bastard. Yet she couldn't deceive herself—he was still a lethal suckblood capable of who knew what.

He strode forward, and her breath hitched. Hot damn. Had she said lethal? Hell yes, he was deadly to her senses.

He scooped her into his arms—a place she was becoming fond of. She locked her hands behind his neck and held on. As if she'd never see him again, she rested her cheek against his chest and inhaled the forest scent of him,.

But a potential consequence haunted her—would she have to give up being a detective when he claimed her? She might have to make the sacrifice to keep Val's conversion a secret so she couldn't blame Gabe for it.

He carried her to the edge of the forest. In the dark, the police lights flashed red and blue. Quite a few vehicles were parked. Hers looked odd without the matching lights flickering—gray, devoid of emotion, unfazed. Barrows—with his great bulk—leaned against the hood.

Gabe lowered her feet to the path, and she spun in his arms to press her body against his warm one. He had no right to be so toasty since he was a suckblood. She loved that he wasn't cold-blooded. That might've been off-putting. Then again, there had to be something she could hate. Otherwise, he'd be perfect, and perfect was bad, because she wasn't, not by a long shot.

"How do I find you, Gabe? It isn't as if you have a street address."

He gathered her wrist in his large hand, and with a fingertip, he drew a symbol on her skin, below her smartwatch. A mark she didn't recognize glowed pale orange. It hadn't hurt, but his reverent touch made her shiver.

"Whisper my name, and it will pulse as you near me." He freed her wrist to bury his fingers in the curls at the nape of her neck. "Smear your blood across it, and I'll find you." His voice deepened, as if he too, felt this was goodbye.

She sighed—it wasn't goodbye. It couldn't be. Who would've imagined stumbling after Val would lead to finding a suckblood this sexy? One who'd claimed her to save her from her own stupidity. Holy tamale, she was in a shit-ton of trouble, as per frigging usual. Before, she'd wanted to survive, to walk away, to have justice served, to spare people's lives. Now, with Val a suckblood, Callie's career would change. What could she do with her life if it wasn't in law enforcement? A scary thought.

She needed distance. Her thoughts circled, blurred, weaved until confusion reigned and she had to rely on her instincts and emotions.

She left his arms and frowned, not wanting to deal with her captain today of all days. She was aware that Gabe had *allowed* her to leave him and his embrace. He could've gone all alpha on her and kept her captive. She chewed her lip as she studied his gray eyes and tempting mouth. Now she'd never know if she'd have loved him being all up-in-her-face macho. Her lady bits would. They hummed with an eagerness that made this feel like Christmas Eve.

"I'll be in touch," she said with a smirk and left. Each step was painful, with something deep inside of her cursing herself for leaving him.

Whoa. Her instincts sure weren't happy.

"Devereaux," her captain bellowed, and she cringed. "You've got some explaining to do, Detective."

Callie fought the snort that promised to get her fired, or at least suspended.

Metcalfe was a woman in her forties with a permanent case of PMS. She managed the precinct by yelling. She was a firm believer that if you wanted her to shut up, you'd do your job and not give her a reason to yell at you. It had worked for her four sons and, therefore, should work for everyone under her command.

It did.

"Nothing to explain, Captain. I'm guarding this spot." With a wild sweep of her arm, Callie gestured to the surrounding fields. "Got a tipoff about a possible suck-fest and staked out this area."

"In plain clothes?" The captain glowered at her attire.

Callie forced herself to appear casual and not to twitch under that steely glare. Metcalfe could sniff a falsehood at ten paces.

"It's my day off, Captain. I had to incinerate my last uniform." *Oh, the perfect excuse.* "I'm short for next week."

"You saw nothing?" Metcalfe flicked her fingers, sending a few vehicles on their way.

Callie tried not to relax her tense shoulders. Any outward sign would tip off Metcalfe. The woman had instincts a beast would've been proud of.

"There were a couple of cars filled with stupid women. I could've shot them to improve the gene pool, but when nothing was happening..." The lie tumbled out of her with ease. With Metcalfe, some deception kept everyone's sanity intact.

Her colleagues shuffled their feet, their impatience to leave adding to the tension of the vehicles pulling out. Callie smothered a snort. They all wanted this over with.

"Good. A few women not drained will have to appease the mayor." Metcalfe twisted her lips in distaste.

"The jackass is on your ass again?" Callie asked, knowing he was. She couldn't count on all her appendages the number of times her captain had cursed out Mayor Duhamel. Not within his hearing, of course.

"When isn't he? Regardless, good job, you two," she said to Barrows, who acknowledged her praise with a wink.

Lazy bastard.

Callie strode to where her partner waited for her. The last police vehicles pulled out, leaving the two of them stranded in the dark.

"Okay, out with it." Mike raised his face to the starlit sky and folded his beefy arms across his massive chest. His stance was clear—he wasn't going anywhere until she spilled the proverbial beans.

She took the time to admire the sky. This far out of the city had the stars shining their brilliance with no light pollution to interfere. The kaleidoscope of stars twinkling mesmerized her. It always had her wondering what was out there. All those planets? There had to be intelligent life because there sure as shit wasn't any on Earth. Then again, if aliens arrived, between the humans, suckbloods, and beasts, this planet would be so fucked.

"Val got converted," she said, the finality of it solidifying in her mind.

Feelings bombarded her, sharp and painful yet hopeful. The hope was the strange part. It had to do with Gabe more than anything else. She debated telling Mike she'd managed to land face down in a pile of manure. Married, claimed, the Rite of something? None of that made sense to her, never mind how to explain it to Mike. Perhaps easing him into the idea was better…after a few shots of whisky.

She shuffled her feet, drawing unseen patterns in the dirt with the toe of her sneaker. "I also met the tuxedoed man from last night."

"Shit and shit." Mike pushed himself off the hood.

She nodded, but Syl wasn't what she wanted to discuss. "I might have to quit the force over this, Barrows." Her voice hitched, and she swallowed the lump forming in her throat. "I can't be on the force and hunt suckbloods. What if she crosses my path, and I have to—"

Mike's head shot up. His face was visible, but she couldn't make out the expressions crossing it.

"You're not quitting the force, Callie, and Val isn't a criminal." He clasped her shoulders, to shake or comfort her, she didn't know.

She cringed. When he crowded her and dipped his head to maintain eye contact, it meant he had a few words to say to her, and she didn't have all night to be his good little partner. She wanted to head home, sort through everything that had happened today, and try and understand why she felt this pull to return to Gabe. The need was bordering on obsession.

"We gotta find out what's so important about that damn canister. Now that Val's converted, I'm pretty sure they're going to keep her busy for a while." He sighed. "She's not gonna die anymore, Devereaux."

She sucked in a sharp breath, struggling to escape from Mike, but he held firm. Damn Neanderthal using his strength against her. "Because she's dead already?" Her voice squeaked, and she cleared her throat. "Not much consolation there, Barrows. How do we explain her miraculous healing when no doctor has survived examining a suckblood? What about family meetings or dinners? Am I on the menu?"

Giving up on freeing herself from his grasp, she cupped his elbows instead.

"Not with Val, Callie. I don't see her changing who she is just because she has to survive on blood now."

Damn, she hated it when he was right. Barrows being right shifted her axis.

"Find anything out about Carter?" Mike released her and shifted away, granting her a little breathing room.

"When was I supposed to do that, Mike? While dodging suckbloods and leaping tall trees in a single bound? Or fighting feeders for their sugar daddies?"

He huffed. "That sass of yours is going to get you into trouble one day, my girl."

"It did, today." She lowered her chin to her chest as she pondered the cluster-fuck she'd triggered.

None of it pertained to the case which she was no closer to solving. She threw her hands up as she paced out her frustrations. "Carter's *distaste* for suckbloods is recent. Something personal must've happened because there are no media records of him snubbing suckbloods or a deal gone sour."

Pausing to rub the back of her neck, she mentally reviewed her files. What stone had she left unturned?

"I *do* have some news for you. Duhamel's received another sizable contribution from Floges. Is the mayor campaigning again?" Mike furrowed his brow in concentration.

If it wasn't on the sports pages of his newspaper, he wouldn't read it. The man on the front page was all he'd notice.

"Does it matter if it's election year or not? He'd never turn down any contributions, no matter how rich he is." She bounced on her toes, eager to finish this conversation.

"Good point. Now what?"

"I'm going home, although, I'd rather head back," she said, excitement burned along her veins to nestle between her thighs. She prided herself on being honest with her partner at least. He had her back in all things, as she had his.

"Why?" he asked, his confusion clear.

"I met a man." She couldn't stop the smile splitting her cheeks.

"A suckblood," Barrows said, anger hardening his voice. "Are you frigging insane?"

She winced. Sudden light blinded her, and she moaned, shielding her eyes. Mike shone a flashlight in her face. The white circle moved across her body. She ground her teeth. He was searching for bite marks.

"I'm not a feeder, Mike. Want me to strip so you can do a more thorough examination? Did you bring your gloves? Might as well do a cavity search while you're at it."

"Don't get sassy with me, Callista Devereaux. I made your father a promise, and I mean to keep it."

"Promise? I'm the one saving your ass, like all the time." She pitched her voice and blessed him with an exaggerated pout.

"Good. As long as I'm taking the bullets, you ain't getting hurt."

"Whatever. I'm not drugged. I'm not on any euphoric high." She winced at the memory of Gabe feeding from her wrist, and she rubbed the skin there, shivering when her nipples pebbled. "I've got a way into the suckblood community, and I'm grabbing this opportunity. It's the only lead I have. I need to find out why Carter has a sudden aversion to suckbloods and what's in that damn canister."

"It's going to get you killed, Callie! Or worse—converted."

"There's been talk of getting suckblood recruits. At least you won't have to retrain a new partner." She paused. That was an option, a way to stay on the force.

She tapped her chin as she imagined Metcalfe's reaction to the suggestion. That wouldn't be a pleasant conversation.

Sadness and disappointment warred within Callie, as if she teetered on the edge of a cliff. She could have companionship, her sister—kind of—or she could uphold Dad's legacy.

"There you go with the sass again. Does this suckblood know what you're really like?" The affection in Mike's voice drew her back from a good cry and reminded her that no matter what she chose, she had him, Val, and now Gabe.

"He'll find out." She flashed him a cheeky grin, one Mike was partial to.

"Who am I kidding? He ain't gonna see you coming, sweetheart." He chuckled.

"Yup, I'm gonna make you proud, Barrows."

"Now what, you just walk into the dark and find him?" The doubt in his voice mirrored her own.

"Not tonight." She released a shudder. "I plan to head home and smash my face into my pillow."

Eager to see Gabe, she was tempted to stumble around in the dark, whispering his name across the orange symbol like an imbecile. Her determination concerned her, and it was for this reason she'd decided to distance herself.

Mike's face fell. "Would you have walked around like a lost fart? Isn't that a little dangerous? Like I said, I made a promise—"

"Like I would leave her alone, unprotected?" Gabe said, stepping from the shadows.

She smiled, torn between believing he didn't trust her and melting into a puddle on the ground. His voice was sex, smoky fires, and the promise of breathless nights.

Damn suckbloods. They could seduce even the most hardened of hearts. With a clicking sound from his fingers, a sconce appeared out of nowhere and illuminated them in a yellow fiery glow.

She studied his long legs in his jeans and the black shirt he'd yanked on earlier, straining across his broad shoulders. She lingered on the dark stray curl that rested on his forehead. His gray eyes were in shadow, but she didn't mind. He was gorgeous—the mere sight of him standing there snatched her breath and kept it.

"Gabriel de Winter. A pleasure to meet you, Mike." He held out his hand toward her partner, looking as if he were a businessman greeting someone for the first time.

Barrows accepted the offered hand for a shake. He didn't squeeze Gabe's hand in a show of bravado. If he had, it would have cost him the bones in his fingers.

"What are your intentions?" Mike's fatherly tone had her scrambling for a distraction.

She groaned at his question before rushing to intercede. "You don't have to answer that, Gabe."

Saying something was meant to delay the inquisition Mike would bore her to death with. He cared. He'd promised Dad. She got that, but now wasn't the time. But like earlier, he had his piece to say, and say it he would.

"I wasn't talking to you, Miss Sass," Mike said, not looking away from Gabriel, waiting for his response.

"She's mine for eternity," Gabe said.

Barrows jerked as if punched. "You plan on converting her?"

"Eventually." Gabe buried his hand in his pocket, tugging the waistband down, drawing her focus to the taut, caramel skin peeking out. "In the most painless way possible."

"Shit." Barrows glanced between Gabe and Callie with horrified awe contorting his features. "I can't save you from this, my girl."

"Save me?" She folded her arms across her chest against the cool night air. "Not all monsters hiding in the dark are bad."

"Monster?" Gabe asked with his lips twitching.

"I'm human, remember." She grinned.

"You're not human," he said, arching her brows upward in surprise.

"I'm not?" she asked, then gave a dismissive shrug. "Gramps said we were fey, but we never believed him."

"You're not fey, either." He tightened his arm, looping her shoulders and pinning her to him.

She liked the comforting weight of it, despite not being used to open affection.

"Crap, this is bad. I'm not beast, am I?" She squeezed her eyes shut as she waited for his response.

Not that beasts were bad. Just that the idea of an animal trapped inside her was hard to wrap her head around.

"Beast?" Gabe asked.

"Shifter."

It took forever for him to shake his head.

"Zombie?"

She grinned, and he chuckled in the same way Mike laughed at her silliness. "Alien? What else is there?"

"Legend." Gabe brushed his lips across her temple and tingled her skin. "You're legend, Callie."

"That doesn't sound bad. My sass is *legend*ary," she said, spotting Mike's I-told-you-so expression, not understanding what he meant and not wanting to know.

Being a legend didn't sound good—like some sort of destiny awaited her.

"Agreed," Barrows said. "As long as you can keep her safe, then I'm happy to have you guard her on her time off, Gabe."

"Keep her safe from herself? Is that even possible?" Gabe grinned, his teeth flashing bright against his shadowed face.

"Hey! I'm right here." She curled her lip in a pout.

She leaned away from Gabe and rested her hands on her hips. She did not need saving or protecting...when would the men in her life realize this?

He reached for her hands and drew her near him again, not letting her off so easy. "I'll always know where you are, and I'll always put you first." His husky voice lowered, like rough velvet caressing her skin.

She swallowed past the lump in her throat. Was he serious?

"That's my cue. I'll wait in the car." Barrows held out his hand, and she sighed, wiggling out of Gabe's embrace to dig in her back pocket for the keys. She took her gun and badge he offered her, then slapped her keys onto his open palm.

She waited until he closed the door, then released a long breath.

"I like him," Gabe said. "Now what's this about heading home?"

"I'm tired, it's been a long day."

He scowled. "Callie, it's not safe."

She huffed. "You haven't claimed me yet so if I die, it won't affect you."

He growled. "You think I'll allow you to die?" He gripped her shoulders, forcing her to meet his narrowed gaze. "I don't announce the Rite of *Adsumo* for any woman. I wanted you since you descended that ladder."

Her breath hitched, not only from the silver in his eyes but by the strength in his voice.

"Thank you for telling me that. Um, I've been on my own for a long time, Gabe. Being in danger is not new to me, but I need time to understand what happened today and what committing to you means to me." She cupped his cheek, sighing as his warmth traveled from her palm down her forearm. "You saved me and I'm grateful, but as handsome as you are, I can't make a decision this serious based on sexual attraction."

"How long will you need?" His voice was hoarse, his shoulders stiff, but his touch on her hips was gentle.

"A few days, maybe more?" She shrugged.

With a flick of his fingers, the sconce disappeared. Plunged into darkness, she didn't expect to feel his lips on hers. Sweet scales of justice, her heartbeat spiked as he teased her bottom lip with his tongue. He looped an arm around her and gathered her against his chest. She gasped and he kissed her, thoroughly. The sheer taste of him was like the finest of scotch with the darkest of chocolates.

She melted into his embrace, attempting to join this exploration. When she swept her tongue across his, he groaned, deepened the kiss, and scattered her thoughts.

Mike switched on the headlights, and she pulled away from Gabe, feeling like a teenager caught necking on the porch.

"Um, I don't know what to say." She inched toward the passenger door. "Call me tomorrow? Leo might have my number."

"I don't like this, Callie." His growl conveyed how much he didn't like her leaving. He followed her, his hand shoved into his front pockets.

"Gabe, you've been without me for centuries, what's a few more days?"

He paused, and the car's lights shone on his hopeful expression. "Then you'll move in with me?"

"Whoa, not so fast. I'll give you my answer then." Didn't he know, couldn't he see how leaving him was tearing her up inside? That alone was reason enough for distance. It wasn't natural and normal to yearn for a man she'd met that day.

He clenched his jaw. "No, not liking this."

"Call me." She climbed into the car and closing the door had a finality to it. Mike reversed the car, shining the headlights on Gabe. She watched him for as long as she could see him, not daring to blink.

Mike didn't speak, and she was grateful for the silence.

If the investigation tied the canister to Carter, that would involve Syl, and arresting Gabe's brother wouldn't bode well for their "marriage." Iced pain wrenched her stomach. The idea that she might have to choose between love and the law had her tightening her hold on the seatbelt.

Hope dawned, melting the dread, warming the cold lump in the center of her chest. What if the canister wasn't tied to anyone in her current case files? She'd walk away as best she could, trusting Leo that it wasn't a weapon.

She needed to talk to Gabe about the politics involved with the shitstorm she was in and the implications for his brother. Arresting him wouldn't be easy, if it came to that.

The damn canister better be harmless, or she might have to kick Syl in the balls. Leo too, for lying to her.

Chapter Fifteen

DISINTEGRATING LIFE

GABRIEL LISTENED TO HER, but her words didn't alarm him. He understood what Callie was thinking, so he didn't take her words to heart.

She was infiltrating the *suckblood* community, knowing she would become a vampire like him. Her priorities would have to shift, but for now, she needed a reason to remain with him, one her partner would understand. She was walking a fine line between both worlds, yet she had no choice but to crossover. The how and when were the unknown factors. He needed her to become his sooner—his throbbing erection wouldn't abide. He ached to hold her, to inhale her scent, to claim her, both body and soul.

There'd been only one time in his history when he'd been this tempted.

Abigail.

He hadn't thought about her in years, and now three times in two days. The dull ache in his chest was less intrusive, as if he needn't mourn her loss anymore. As if, at last, he was free of the guilt. She hadn't chosen him then, preferring to lose her life than be with him. Her rejection had scarred his soul, dropped him in a morass of misery that made his violent conversion pale in comparison.

Yet here, on this day, he had spoken the Rite of *Adsumo* over a woman, one whose honor and internal fire made him breathless. She'd chosen him—repeatedly—having decided he was worthy, and defended him to his brother.

His bold, fearless Callie was worth the centuries of loneliness he'd endured. Despite her blood demanding he save her, he might've claimed her anyway.

Could he afford to grant her a few days to think this over when it was a done deal in his mind? He sighed, vaulting in the air to trail her police vehicle. He swerved and manipulated the air currents to maintain a steady speed.

She would have the illusion of freedom—it was all he could offer her.

When he was younger, he might have held her captive, convincing her to stay after vigorous bouts of sex and copious amounts of pheromones. With Callie, he wanted her to choose him of her own free will. Once he had that, her heart would follow.

His breath caught at the idea of love.

So elusive yet yearned for, and across his long life, he'd experienced many forms of it.

Never had he wanted a woman with this intensity. Should he question it as she did?

She climbed out of the car as soon as Mike pulled up outside an apartment building.

Gabriel shrouded himself to hide from her. She mustn't know he guarded her, not wanting her to misread his actions as a lack of trust. His warning had fallen on deaf ears. She hadn't heard the whispered comments in the hall. Many planned to sample her blood, and along with feedings, came lust. The thought of someone other than him, feeding on her, touching her, fired fury through him. He trembled trying to contain it.

This reaction, as intense and breathtaking as it was, shouldn't occur, not this soon. She had the right to ask for time. The madness of his emotions didn't mean he had to leave her unprotected.

She trudged up the stairs, exhaustion dragging her feet. Locking her door behind her, as if that could keep out a vamp, she threw back a glass of scotch, peeled off her clothes, and slid between the sheets. He caught the curve of her breast and the indent of her waist before shifting shadows beneath her window drew his focus.

"You're being an idiot." Leo appeared beside him, staring out her balcony window.

Gabriel closed his eyes before tilting his head to look at him. "How did you know I'd be here?"

Leo pursed his lips, his eyebrow arched. "I am all-knowing?" He chuckled. "I read Callie's intentions when she left Val."

"She's not taking the Rite seriously."

"What do you expect? She's trained to distrust instant love or lust? She's expecting her future husband to woo her or, at least, date her." Leo shook his head, a smile lingering. "Start with flowers, specialized daggers for her arsenal, maybe the finest bottle of scotch?"

"Buy her love?" Gabriel didn't like that idea. Although, the possibility of her smile when she received something from him made him consider Leo's advice.

Leo sighed as if Gabriel tested his patience. "It keeps you in her thoughts. Have you learned nothing about women?"

Gabriel grunted. "When I have an urge, I see to it."

"You caveman." Leo chuckled as he flicked his fingers and broke the necks of the vamps landing on her balcony. "We don't upskill them as well as we should."

Gabriel grunted. "They don't fear the ancients either."

Leo gestured to the couch behind him. "Her dad's leather chair is quite comfortable." He dissolved into a fine mist and passed through the glass.

With a sweeping glance at the horizon and the streets below, Gabriel ambled into her room to ensure she slept well. His phone vibrated. Leo had texted him Callie's number. He smiled, choosing to slide down a wall until his backside hit the carpet.

He'd guard her from here, and should she awaken, for whatever reason, he could shroud himself. Was this crossing a boundary, intruding on her personal space? Yes, without a doubt, but he couldn't see an alternative short of using witchcraft.

He'd have to consult with someone since his past attempts at charms had backfired. This was the safer option, and sleepless days lay ahead for him.

He kept his gaze on her, finding her soft breathing and her steady heartbeat as she slept peaceful.

A whisper of sound whipped his attention to the balcony. He vaulted to his feet, blurring as he ran. Launching with his arm extended, he caught the vamp by the neck and leaped through the opened sliding door.

"Which part of the Rite did you not understand?" Fury strangled his throat and his fangs extended, dimpling his bottom lip. He dug his nails into the man's throat, fighting his instincts to kill.

The male vamp wheezed-laughed, wrapping his fingers around the grip Gabriel had on his throat. "My part is done."

He snapped the man's neck and released him to tumble hundreds of feet to the road below. Casting a glance at the sprawled body, he shot back, bursting through the door and into her room to find a female vamp leaning over Callie.

He yanked her away, tightening his hold on her shirt so she wouldn't slam into the wall. He spun the vamp, pinning her to his chest with a forearm around her throat. "I'm tempted to kill you, and rid our stronghold of your stupidity." He kept his voice below a whisper, at a level only vampires could hear.

Whispering an incantation, one of the few he knew well, prevented her from misting. He extended his nails until they were as sharp as daggers. Muttering a command, they glowed orange.

He sliced her chest. She screamed, but he muffled it with a hand across her mouth. Hot blood dampened her T-shirt and saturated his senses with the bitter aroma.

"Find Leo and ask him to heal you from my *melios,* or you will scar."

She gasped, writhing within his arms. He released her, and she staggered.

Tension trembled his body and tightened every muscle. "Return here and I *will* kill you, weakling."

Gabriel trailed her to the sliding door, watching as she vaulted down to her accomplice. He closed the door and settled into the leather chair. He leaned his head back, staring at the ceiling as he calmed his ragged breathing. It had been a long time since he'd battled and enjoyed the adrenaline spicing his blood

After the fourth attempt, he risked it and wove an incantation at her doors and windows. If it backfired, anything could happen at any time. He hoped they weren't here when it did.

Callie stretched, sighing at how well she'd slept. With Val no longer at death's door, the constant worry had evaporated. She should've lost sleep over her odd day and looming decision for or against Gabe, but she hadn't.

A shimmer, nothing defined, caught her attention—but she dismissed it as sleep in her eyes. Her instincts weren't warning her and besides, she didn't want to deal with anything before coffee.

Throwing her feet off the bed, she padded naked to the kitchen. She shivered, as a cool breeze disturbed the air around her. Pausing in a pool of sunlight, she allowed its warmth to engulf her. Singing under her breath and shaking her hips, she started a pot of coffee.

In passing, she ran her fingers over the back of Dad's chair as if to say morning, before disappearing into her bathroom. Stepping under the hot spray, thoughts of the day ahead merged with her open case on Carter. Not wanting her lack of progress to dampen her mood, she hurried through her ablutions.

With towels wrapped around her body and hair, she poured a coffee, then curled into the chair.

A familiar cologne teased her nostrils, like Gabe was here with her. She buried her nose in the leather and inhaled, then jerked back. Why did her chair smell like him?

I hope they have you in heaven. His words replayed in her mind. She sighed, sinking deeper into the leather.

As compliments went, it was one of the best she'd heard. Most men tossed out how they'd love for her to handcuff them or asked if she was as good in bed as she was with her gun. Those men were hardened or petty criminals. Not dating material.

She shifted her backside, loving how her body hummed when she thought of Gabe. Shaking her head, she hoped it would dispel the dazzling effect he had on her. This attraction made no sense, and her body's reactions were silly.

Her smartwatch buzzed and she smiled at Mike's message. He was on his way to pick her up and had ordered new uniforms for her. The package would arrive later that day.

Donning jeans, a T-shirt, boots, and a corduroy jacket, she braided her hair, and stashed as much of her arsenal on her person as her outfit would allow. Clambering down the stairs two at a time, she left her apartment building.

A shimmer in her peripheral vision tightened her hold on the balustrade. She would almost say she wasn't alone.

"Hello?" She stared at the corner of the landing, holding her breath even as she pulled a poison-tipped blade from her boot.

The hairs on the back of her neck rippled, and she smothered a shiver. *Never let them know you feel, you bleed, and you're alone.* Dad's words had her snorting and sheathing her dagger in her boot.

"Are you coming?" Mike peered up the stairwell. "I'm double parked, and if I get a ticket, it's coming out of your pay."

Throwing one last glance behind her, she trailed him to the police vehicle.

As soon as she slid into the passenger seat and buckled in, he handed her a coffee. "Ready for today?"

She shrugged. "I feel under armed."

His grin was wicked. "You can spend the day finishing your reports."

She groaned into the coffee cup. As much as she hated paperwork, she agreed he was wise to suggest it. She didn't want to leave the precinct today.

The elephant in the vehicle expanded until she couldn't breathe by the time Mike pulled into the parking lot.

She leaped out of the car, tossed the empty coffee cup, and trailed him up the steps.

"Mike, wait." She stopped, gripping the railing, the cold metal pressing into her palm. "You have nothing to say? Nothing more about Val and...Gabe?" Flipping her braid off her shoulder, she drew in a deep breath. "You've had time to think over my circumstances and you bombard me with your opinion on everything else. Why are you silent now?"

He laughed, skipping down the steps to loom over her. "He wants you, and since he's a suckblood, my girl, I don't see you wheedling your way out of this."

He nudged his head at the double doors. She grumbled, trudging forward.

"With Val on the dark side, it's a matter of time before you cross over." He pinched his lips. "What's bothering me is whether I will follow."

"Devereaux, Captain wants to see you." Martinez, the officer behind the desk, gestured to his counter. "What do you want me to do with these?"

Roses, lilies, and orchids filled the room with their pungent fragrances.

"Did someone die?" She stroked a finger across a white petal.

"Die?" He slammed the cards down on the counter. "I had to read each one to make sure they're all for you. Just say yes to the poor man, for pity's sake."

Her breath caught, and her fingers trembled as she swept up the cards. She shuffled through them, her heart leaping with excitement and joy. Bouncing on her toes, she grinned at Mike, needing to share this with someone.

"Well, what do they say?" Gathering a few vases, Mike nudged her hip with his.

She followed suit, grabbing a few bouquets. "Sweet one-liners and an invitation to dinner tonight."

Clouds rolled out before her, and she felt as if she floated through the precinct to her desk. Her thoughts swirled around his scrawled words.

Thinking of you.

Wish you were here with me.

Dinner tonight?

The messages weren't intimate, and she was grateful for that, not wanting Martinez or anyone else on the force to read anything personalized. A few fellow officers placed the remainder of her flowers around her desk and on Mike's. He grumbled but didn't move them.

"Devereaux." Captain Metcalfe hovered in her doorway. She flicked her finger, and Callie bolted across the open plan. "Close the door."

Ice drenched her from her neck to the base of her spine. To close the door meant her captain had something private to discuss. This was it. She was about to lose her job.

"I just spoke to the mayor." Metcalfe stared out of her window, hiding her expressions from Callie. "He wants me to employ...non-humans to the force, then he mentioned you by name."

She gasped, tightening her fingers gripping the chair. "What? Why?" One name came to mind...Carter. He must have spoken of her to the mayor. The ass sure was determined to make her his spy.

"They need a liaison between vampires and us, said he saw you at the ball talking to one." Metcalfe spun and leveled on her an I-told-you-so expression.

Fuck. Callie clenched her jaw, fighting the curse words burning her tongue. She nodded when Metcalf waited for her response.

"Good. I need frequent reports on your progress. No doubt the mayor will ask often." She tilted her pointed chin at the door. "And Devereaux, keep this between us."

"But Mike—?" Keeping secrets from one's partner who was also a detective was damn hard.

Metcalfe sighed. "Very well, you can include him but no one else."

Dazed, Callie ambled back to her desk, ignoring Mike's arched brow. She'd tell him when they were alone. She slid into her chair, staring at her closed laptop. Beside it, a light flickered on her phone—a text awaited her attention.

Her heart leaped, then sank into the pit of her stomach. She drew in a deep breath and responded to Gabe's dinner invitation. She needed to talk to him about her new duties. Hiding it from him didn't sit well, especially if she chose to believe in this Rite nonsense.

"Devereaux." Martinez's bellow filled the open plan and everyone paused to look at him. "We have a problem. Several walk-ins claim to have performed crimes and have asked for you by name."

"What?" She scowled. What the hell had happened to people?

Martinez shrugged. "Where do you want them?"

"Them? How many?" She threw out a hand. "Never mind, one at a time in the interview room."

Mike grabbed his jacket and tugged it on, trailing her into the sterile room with a metal table and four plastic chairs.

She held the door open for him, ignoring the man handcuffed to the table. A shimmer and Gabe's cologne brushed past her.

She stilled, narrowed on the mirage, and smothered a gasp. How long had Gabe been following her?

She spun on a heel and stepped out of the room, closing the door on Mike's frown. Had Gabe been in her apartment? Seen her naked?

She squeaked, stamping her feet as she tried to contain a scream. Fuck, she'd kill him.

Chapter Sixteen

ABSOLUTION

C‍ALLIE YANKED THE DOOR open and entered the room. The urge to slam the door shuddered up her arm so she shut it on a whisper. Ignoring Mike, she circled the room, searching for that shimmer.

There! In the corner was the shape of a tall man. She rushed toward him and rested her shoulder against the wall beside him. "We need to talk about this, Gabe."

He jerked and straightened.

She nodded and shifted away, pinning her focus on the supposed criminal.

"James Jones?" Mike read off the tablet. "Supposedly killed someone over drugs, wants to rat out his accomplices."

"What did you do?" She narrowed her eyes, running an assessing gaze over Jones's clothes screaming wealth. She shook her head at his pale skin, dark eyes and hair. Suckbloods were smug, expecting to avoid justice for any and all crimes. They had no respect for human law enforcement so one walking into a precinct and offering himself up? Improbable.

Which had to mean he was here for one thing.

She didn't want to believe it—Gabe hadn't lied about her future as a human. Then again, didn't becoming a suckblood mean her blood changed?

She leaned in, almost setting her chin on Jones's shoulder. He stilled, then drew in a deep inhale confirming her suspicions.

"Breathe me in, suckblood." She kept her tone soft and friendly. "This is as close as you'll get."

Snapping the handcuffs, he lunged for her, his fingers wrapping around her throat. "Well spotted."

She dangled a few feet off the floor, unable to reach for the daggers in her boots, and kicking the man went unnoticed by him. She knew better than to struggle against his hold, but she tore at his hands anyway. She was an idiot for taunting him like that.

Mike pulled his gun, screaming at Jones to drop her.

The suckblood laughed, tightening his grip until spots circled her vision.

Mike shot him, the bullets jerking Jones's body but not weakening him.

"Do you need my help?" Gabe's voice teased across her ear, sending shivers of delight across her skin even as her life faded.

She wasn't equipped to handle suckbloods, not in hand-to-hand combat and not without her arsenal. Tears trickled as Jones scraped his teeth along her cheek. He didn't smell bad, like a normal human man. It would've been fitting had he stank of rotting flesh or congealed blood.

He'd pinned Mike to the wall with an unseen force. Her partner and dearest friend's mottled face contorted with fear and horror, as he screamed something she couldn't hear.

She cast her blurred gaze at the shimmer, wishing she could see Gabe's face one last time. Closing her eyes, she accepted the darkness and the lack of breathing scorching fire from her throat to her chest.

She collapsed to the floor and the sweetness of air filled her lungs. Coughs racked her body with breathing spiking painful shards.

Bodies wove around her, fading, merging with one flying across the room. She raised her gaze to where Gabe had Jones pinned to the wall, before snapping his neck as he'd done to Darius.

Mike's roaring filled the room. He fell to his knees.

As Jones slumped to the floor, Gabe sprawled alongside Callie, wrapping her within his embrace. She wanted to snuggle into him and at the same time proclaim she hadn't needed rescuing. But she had, yesterday and today, like a silly damsel in distress.

"What took you so long?" As admonishments went, this one could have been better if her voice hadn't rasped.

He grinned and like the sun casting its golden rays, so did her heart warm.

"Now do you believe you're in danger?"

Cold fingers gripped her spine and squeezed her chest so tight she curled into herself. "You set this up?"

He jerked back like she'd slapped him. His handsome features hardened, and pain flickered across his gray eyes. He pulled away, rising to his feet, and taking her with him. When cool air replaced his warm touch, so did guilt strike her, twisting her stomach into knots.

She swallowed past the nausea and raised her hand to stop him from leaving or to take back her unfair judgment.

"I'm sorry. I didn't mean that. How...how many have tried?"

His shoulders relaxed, and he laced his fingers through hers to tug her against him. "Four while you slept."

Mike dragged himself to his feet, wobbling the metal table. "Do you think the others asking for Callie are also suckbloods?"

Gabe nodded but didn't look at Mike, keeping his gaze on her.

"So you agreed to give me space knowing you couldn't?" She frowned then huffed. "I'm stubborn, I know, but—"

"What would you have done in my place?" Gabel lifted her fingertips to his lips and kissed them. "If Val was in danger and wouldn't see it?"

She stilled, staring at his mouth, wondering why his lips burned her, sending tingles down her arm to her elbow. "The same, I guess."

The door burst open. A few officers rushed in, gaping at Jones on the floor.

Gabe had faded, but his warm hand still held hers. She sighed, closing her eyes against the feeling of safety his presence brought her. Not that she would admit it.

After her explanation and they arrested Jones, her fellow officers lined the walls of the interview room. They stood united and ready should any of the other supposed criminals turn out to be suckbloods. A few confessors hid their species well, so Callie and Mike took their statements, arresting them for the two days it might take to verify their claims.

With each pale face she interviewed—male or female—the truth in Gabe's warning settled like lead in her heart. Was this what lay ahead for her, constant fending off suckbloods wishing to feed on her?

By lunch time, exhaustion hounded her, and she was ready to discuss moving in with him. By five in the afternoon, she was eager for a conversion, anything to save her from the tedious day.

As she and Mike interviewed a suckblood, more arrived, some confessing to decade-old crimes and all asking for her. Flowers, chocolates, and jewelry swallowed her desk as suckbloods tried to buy her favor.

Metcalfe had Martinez clear the precinct, loading the gifts into an armored van. Callie had never been so excited to see the piles of paperwork on her desk, shadowed by one of Gabe's vases.

She'd always wondered what it would feel like if she received flowers from a gentleman. With the bouquets from Gabe, that elation, excitement, and girly giddiness had sent tingles from her scalp to her toes. The other gifts couldn't compare to that, not for her.

"Mike, I'm heading home." She grabbed her corduroy jacket and the package holding her new uniforms. "Got a hot date with my man." She winked at the shimmer.

"Want me to take you home?" Mike rose as well, curling his jacket off the back of his chair.

"I'll take a taxi. I need you to distribute the stuff in the van, pretty please. Widows, orphans, lonely women in payroll." She nudged him in the ribs.

He sighed. "Is he still here?" Mike scanned the open plan area looking for Gabe.

"See you in the morning." She strolled out with a wave, loping down the steps to the curb to call a taxi. Gabe's presence followed her, and she held the taxi's door open just long enough for him to slide in. As soon as her backside touched the seat, he draped his arm across her shoulders, pulling her into the curve of his invisible body.

"Ready for dinner?" His breath across her cheek sent shivers down her neck.

"Let's head to your place. I'm tired and don't feel like dining out." She raised her gaze to where his should be. "I have the one couch so my place isn't ideal for entertaining."

"Are you talking to me, lady?" The taxi driver peered at her in his rearview mirror.

She laughed. "Just muttering to myself."

Chapter Seventeen

Beyond Temptation

Having Callie in his arms was promising. Gabriel hadn't known she could see him shrouded. When she leaned against the wall and whispered to him, he'd gaped. He hadn't been horrified by this, no, pride had puffed out his chest.

Then Antoine had squeezed her throat, and fury tore through Gabriel. The man was a rebel, stirring up discontent, and Syl had yet to deal with him. Wanting Callie to realize the severity of the situation, Gabriel had waited. Each second had passed like a decade until he couldn't stand back anymore.

Endangering her went against every fiber in his being, and if she didn't hurry up, then he'd have to endure this for as long as a week. The way she nestled into him gave him hope that tonight she would choose instead of making him wait days.

Her suggestion to dine at his home had him shifting on the taxi's backseat, trying to ease the ever-present arousal he sported. Anywhere with a bed nearby suited him.

She paid the taxi driver and climbed out.

Gabriel paused on the sidewalk outside her apartment, scanning the sky and the shadows forming in the setting sun. He sniffed the air. No vamps lingered and watched. The sight of his motorcycle, a matte black Ducati, taking up prominence in a parking bay, summoned a grin. As soon as Callie suggested dinner at his place, he'd asked Leo to send over transport. The bike was a nice touch, forcing her to wrap her arms around him. With a wave, two helmets formed on the seat.

Leo was a true romantic, and though Gabe had known this, he hadn't appreciated it as much as he did now. As advised, he'd ordered the flowers in the silence between attacks. She had glowed when she read his cards, proving Leo right again.

She climbed the stairs with more enthusiasm than she had last night, despite the bruises around her neck confirming she'd had a bad day. He hated seeing them, and if he could, he would heal them as he had her head wound.

Releasing a breath on a rush, he shut the apartment door behind them. She'd disappeared into her room, the shower coming on.

"I'll just freshen up then we can leave." She returned, hovering in the doorway with peach staining her cheeks. "You saw me naked this morning, didn't you?" She gasped. "And last night?"

"I won't lie to you, so yes."

Pursing her lips, she nodded. "Do you mind waiting?"

"No." He wished they'd finished the Rite so he could read her thoughts. Was she pissed with him for seeing her naked? What did her nod mean? He sank into her chair, settling in the same spot his backside had occupied for hours last night.

The bathroom door closed, and he gripped the arms, his groin aching, demanding he storm in, and watch her or better, join her. Growling, he pressed the back of his head against the chair. His torturous mind replayed memories of her in his shower, the way the soap clung to her curves, the length of her hair brushing her back as she shampooed it.

Sooner than expected, she saved him from the lust-filled mire, popping her head through her door. His gaze snagged on her pink towel wrapped around her.

"Jeans okay?"

He nodded, not willing to trust his voice. Another few minutes passed with him straining his hearing, guessing what she was doing and wishing he could watch her instead.

"Ready." Jeans hugged her figure, and an off-the-shoulder cream sweater tested his control. "Do that thing with your eyes."

Gesturing to her hair, she gave him her back.

He rose, released a shuddering breath, looped his arm around her waist, and tugged her against his chest. He ran his fingers through her damp hair, vibrating air particles to heat and dry each lock. She'd given him the opportunity to touch her. He could've done it with one glance, but tonight was for seduction.

His control was thinning, but he buried his face in her hair to inhale her scent and the fragrance of her shampoo. If her stomach hadn't gurgled, he might have succumbed and kissed her.

He laced his fingers through hers and led her down the stairs to the bike.

She gaped, circling the bike to admire it, before accepting the helmet he held out to her. She tugged it on and raised her chin so he could do the straps. After pulling his on, he threw a leg over the bike, kicking the stand back. He closed his eyes when she gripped his shoulder, swung her leg across, and nestled her hips against his backside.

Then she hugged him, and contentment settled deep within him. This felt perfect, like a photograph capturing true companionship. He engulfed her with warm air so she wouldn't feel the cold or the wind tearing at her. As he took the corners along a hidden road, she laughed, pulling away from him before pressing her breasts against his back again.

His spirit answered her siren's call of freedom and exhilaration, reminding him what it felt like to be human, to live in the present.

After parking the bike at the top of the tunnel to his home, he waited for her to dismount before he powered off and kicked out the stand.

She fiddled with the clasp, tugged off her helmet, and blessed him with a bright smile. "I loved that."

Flipping up the visor, he smiled at her. "I can see that." He hung their helmets on the bike's bars, held a hand to the base of her spine, and escorted her to his front door. "Are you hungry? I have more than cereal," he teased, seeing her thoughtful expression.

"I'll cook if you keep me company." She opened his door and stepped across his threshold of her own free will.

He loved the ease with which they communicated. She had no idea how precious she was.

"Sounds like a plan," he said, his voice gruff. He trailed her to the kitchen and chose a chair as she familiarized herself with the contents of his cabinets.

"We'll need to go shopping tomorrow."

His breath caught. "We?"

"After today, *us* is a matter of time, isn't it?" She faced him but twirled her foot on the toe of her sneaker. "You were right. This isn't my world. I didn't understand the dangers, and I thought I knew everything about suckbloods." She raised her gaze to his. "Gabe, I'm a little scared to take the leap."

He gasped, rising to reach for her, but she shuffled back.

"I don't want to lose myself as a person, nor do I want you to be my knight, as if I can't stand on my own." She drew in a long breath. "I assume it's safer for me here in your home until we level the playing field."

He froze, then his fingers twitched with the urge to hold her.

"I don't know if I can have sex with you, I'm not skilled, and you make me nervous." She closed the distance between them. "I'm willing to try though."

His chest swelled with warm, consuming joy. He hugged her, crushing her against his chest. At first, she kept her body stiff then she softened, wrapping her arms around him.

"Thank you, Callie." He kissed her temple. "We'll take this step-by-step."

She cleared her throat. "So...um, shopping tomorrow?"

He nodded, visualizing browsing food aisles and tossing items into the trolley, like a couple. The idea pleased him. "I can order in. They *do* deliver." He offered to be respectful, though he hoped she didn't accept his suggestion.

"Where's the fun in that?" She pulled away to pop a pot on to boil. "Do you even own a car?"

"Yes, quite a few." He returned to his chair, resting his elbows on the table.

"And you hide them where?" She glanced around his home with a frown.

"I'll give you the tour tomorrow." He smiled, liking how she showed genuine interest in him, in his life.

"Okay, sounds like a plan." She flashed a grin, echoing his words from earlier as she spooned salt into the near-boiling water.

"What time do you start work?" He refused to ask the real question everything in his body demanded to know—how long would he have to guard her? There was no leaving her unprotected, not when each second passing intensified this attraction and growing affection between them.

"Eight, but I should take time off, don't you think?" She put a saucepan on the stovetop and poured in the pasta sauce to warm. "If I plan on ravishing you, that will need time."

Though she added the pasta to the boiling water with nonchalance, everything in him stood at attention at her words. And he meant *everything*.

"I would like that." He clenched his knees with stiff fingers as he fought lunging for her, taking her right here on the counter, burying himself in her, claiming her as his.

He cleared his throat and adjusted himself in his now too-tight jeans. "Please add garlic to your sauce. I haven't had it in years."

"Parmesan?" She held up the powdered parmesan he kept in the freezer, shaking it for emphasis.

He had no idea how old it was, though.

"Yes, please." A rush of endorphins pumped through him, escalating his heartbeat and ramping his level of affection, formulating one circling thought—he adored her.

She made dinner for herself, knowing he'd drink from her later, taking his wants into consideration. Why had no man snatched her up? Not that he liked the idea of it. He just wondered what was wrong with human men in general.

She was his now, and he wasn't releasing her from her vow, ever.

She served herself, sprinkling parmesan over it, before choosing the chair next to him.

"It smells good," he said, admiring her features as she forked pasta into her enticing mouth.

"It tastes good. I've never tried this brand before. We'll get more of it tomorrow."

"Do you need anything from your home?"

She blinked, her body stilling, as if his question startled her. "My uniforms, a few books but that's about it. I can't sell, though. The apartment was my dad's."

She was willing to trade in everything for him. Moon above, the hold this woman already had on him.

"Tomorrow, we can see if Val can visit." He offered, needing to give her something... Something that could match what she offered him—herself. It felt as if he fell short, though. As if nothing could compare to her worth.

"That would be wonderful, Gabe." She held out her arm, resting it across the table. "Hungry?"

"Starving." He stared at the smooth skin of her wrist.

"I freely give." She smiled and licked her fork.

His gaze rested on her lips, torn. He could feed now and enjoy the taste of garlic, tomatoes, and parmesan. Or he could wait until she was beneath him. At the memory of her aroused, her chocolate flavor burst across his tongue, and he shifted in his chair to ease the throbbing.

He pressed his lips to the soft skin of her inner wrist, scenting the bounty that awaited him. The staccato of her pulse tapped a rhythm on his lips in her excitement. He lingered on her flushed cheeks. The emerald of her eyes sparkled, and her mouth parted, revealing her small white teeth. She fought to breathe with the rapid rise and fall of her chest, her food forgotten.

With a shudder, he brushed his fangs along her skin, teasing her and himself in the process. He spread his thighs to accommodate his erection, ignoring the constant ache. When he bit into her skin, he ensured she endured the least amount of pain. Her eyelids fluttered closed, and a throaty moan tore from her.

Garlic, parmesan, pasta, tomatoes, and oregano overwhelmed his taste buds. He moaned in pleasure. He refused to close his eyes to savor her flavor, though. The last time he did that, he'd lost cognizance of how much he'd taken. He needed her well for when he buried himself deep in her and tasted her again. Dragging his tongue across the tiny wounds he'd made, his saliva sealed them. Licking his lips, relishing every drop, he stared at her with a need that roared at his sanity.

He kissed the now-healed spots. "Thank you."

"Had enough?" she asked, as if she would offer him a second helping.

Not releasing her wrist, he shook his head, doubting he'd quench the craving for her that went deeper than hunger, than sexual. "I don't think I'll ever have enough." He stroked his thumb across her soft skin mesmerized by the flush staining her cheeks again.

"Have you?" He gestured to her almost empty bowl.

"Yes, thanks."

He'd promised to take it one step at a time, but he could kiss her, at least. Jumping forward, scraping his chair backward, he startled a gasp from her. He took full advantage, crashing his mouth across her, plundering without hesitation. A groan rumbled up his throat, and he tightened his hold, needing every inch of her to touch him.

She clung to him, digging her nails into his biceps as she swept her tongue across his.

Fuck, he didn't need her participation, not if he had to go slow.

He pulled away, throwing himself against the wall, adding distance between them.

"Sorry, I promised you slow."

Her lust-filled gaze, her parted lips with the tip of her tongue toying with the fullness of her bottom lip made him thump the back of his head on the wall.

"Woman, you're killing me." He tugged her toward him to wrap his arms around her, crushing her along the length of him.

With his hard edges contrasting against her softer curves, she clung to him. Closing his eyes, he sucked in a shuddering breath then spun and pinned her to the wall, his mouth crashing across hers. He claimed her soft lips, meeting her tongue with bold, masterful strokes. Splaying out his fingers, he embedded them in her braided hair, holding her captive. He loved the taste of her, how she overwhelmed him, and her evocative groaning as she raised her trembling hands to rest on his chest. How she dug her fingernails into his flesh through the fabric of his T-shirt as she sank into him.

"Callie." His voice hoarsened, packed with emotions he couldn't decipher.

"Gabe." She offered her neck as he kissed along her jaw, shivering when he nibbled on her ear. All he could breathe, taste, smell, and feel was her. His senses saturated his thoughts. His will was no longer his own.

"We need to stop." He drew away, resting his elbows on either side of her head. "Any more and I'll take you, Callie."

Her cheeks flushed pink, the glow traveling down her throat. "Then take me."

He stilled, disbelieving his ears. "Are you sure?"

She nodded, her fingers now digging into his shoulders. The sharp delicious pain tightened his nipples.

After scooping her into his arms, he carried her to his bedroom. She laughed—a throaty husky sound that made his balls spasm with need. He tossed her on the bed, and as she squealed in mid-flight, he commanded their clothes gone. The sight of her spread nude across his bed, with her flaming hair as her only adornment, made him still.

"You're beautiful, Callie." His voice was hoarse, but he couldn't control his vocals, didn't even try to.

A few days ago he'd known only his privacy, his need for peace and to be left alone. That was what he thought he wanted. Yet here lay a woman strong enough not to need him, nor to succumb to his pheromones, with the intelligence to know she had to remain with him. For her safety, of course. He was content to let her believe that was it for now when what she invoked was something he hadn't felt for a woman in a long time…infatuation and affection. Deep within him lay the guilt of manipulating his way into her life. He dismissed it, choosing to believe it was for her safety when she meant more to him than a feeder.

He laid himself alongside her, resting a trembling hand on her taut stomach, but he didn't care that he revealed his nervousness. Many lovers—both male and female—had laid beneath him, and the euphoric high of lust and companionship had exploded color into his mundane existence.

With Callie, he wanted more than sex. Something about her summoned his protective instincts urged him to claim her. He did so now, capturing her lips, moaning at the need that drove him. Her mouth parted for his intrusion, and his heart hammered in his chest.

Moon above, she was perfect.

He learned every nuance of her delicious mouth. Her dueling tongue told him more about her. She took what she needed, and she needed him. No matter the danger to herself, she might have walked away from him had she not felt the connection between them.

He paused, losing parts of his soul in the glorious green of her heated gaze. Each second stretched in time and embedded itself in his memory. The softness of her skin, the sweetness of her curls, her eyelashes fluttering shadows as she struggled to contain her responses and with those, came the sexiest sounds. One mewl from her spasmed his balls and skittered goosebumps down his spine.

She buried her fingers in his hair, scraping her nails across his scalp, causing him to shiver—one that rippled through him, heightening his senses. Her rich chocolate-laced scent filled the room, urging him to rush their first union.

He wouldn't, though, not with his Callie.

Tonight would be her first conscious feeding, and he needed it to be perfect. He didn't want her to fear what was going to be a necessary part of her life.

Fluttering his fingers down her neck to brush her breasts, he toyed with her nipples. She writhed beneath him, her need calling to him. She was honest to a fault, honest with her reactions to him—to his touch—hiding nothing from him. Her trust amazed him, calling forth a smile even as his heart blossomed. His breath hitched under that potent warmth of—dare he hope— happiness?

Unable to sift through the emotions she invoked within him, with lust clouding his mind, he rolled over her, pinning her to the bed. She spread her thighs, and his hips slid into a position as old as time. His erection brushed her heated essence, her need drenching him. He shuddered, wishing he could bury himself in her with one thrust.

But he couldn't. This was her first time, and he wanted to make it as pain-free and pleasurable as possible. Relying on his century-honed patience, he held himself back, inching in at an achingly slow pace.

He feathered kisses down her neck, scraping his fangs teasingly. Her throat vibrated on a moan as she arched her back, thrusting her breasts into his adoring hands. Her body flushed, and goosebumps spread across her creamy skin. She tempted him to taste every inch of her, to trace the path down to where she wept for him. He leaned back to trail his fingers to the red curls at the juncture of her thighs, beckoning him to ecstasy.

The whimper that tore from her shook him to his core. He dipped his fingers into her moist lips, marveling at the scent, the heat, and the silkiness of her. She trembled, her breath jarring when he rubbed her swollen nub. Sliding a finger into her, he pumped her, flicking his thumb across the bundle of nerves. Her reaction was instantaneous. Her hips rose off the bed, gyrating hypnotically.

Had he known she was this aroused, this close, he might have eased her discomfort after her shower. It didn't matter now—it meant he would be inside her sooner. Her breath came in gasps as he increased the rhythm, listening to the beat of her heart.

He admired her features, the toss of her head from side-to-side, her mouth parting to allow her tongue to dampen her bottom lip. Then she stilled, frozen on the cusp, and her heartbeat paused. With a single thumb flick from him, she screamed his name, coming apart in his arms, her body twitching, her nipples puckering as she found her release.

She was so beautiful, his Callie.

Surrendering her grip on his bedding, she floated down to reality. She spasmed around his finger as he withdrew it. Her mouth parted on a silent *oh*, but as he positioned himself to thrust into her, she moaned, her excitement echoing his.

He slid into her wet sheath, amazed at the silkiness, at the strength with which she grasped his length and tugged him deeper into her. His nipples tightened, tingles of anticipation traveling along the length of his erection. She grasped his upper arms, even as she wrapped her legs around his hips, urging him on, pulling him into her core.

His orgasm rushed toward him with too much enthusiasm, having not allowed himself the enjoyment of being in her. After what he'd endured the past few days, he didn't want it to end soon. He wanted to savor every one of her unconscious reactions. She incited him to lose his mind, to sacrifice his control. While he sucked her nipple, his control snapped. He pressed an open-mouthed kiss to the swell of her breast, and at the final thrust into her, seconds away from an implosion, he bit her.

Dark chocolate greeted him as he shattered in her. Her channel fluttered around his sensitized nerves and urged him into a second implosion. Her sheath milked him, shooting shivers through him, his body twitching at the subsiding euphoria. Yet it didn't leave him completely, it hovered in anticipation of a third release.

He licked her wound closed and fell to his side, taking her with him. He stayed buried within her, kept her sprawled across his chest. Every move she made burned into his memory—her fingers brushing his skin, her gasps as she tried to catch her breath.

"I'll need you to take some of my blood, Callie, love," he whispered. He couldn't rouse the energy to raise the volume of his voice.

"Okay," she said before she kissed his nipple. Her touch burned him, leaving an invisible imprint on his sensitive skin. "I don't want to hurt you. I don't have your sharp teeth."

His chest swelled at her concern, at her easy acceptance of what he required of her, and at her trust. He held up a finger, extended his fingernail, and sliced at his chest, above his left nipple.

She squeaked at the scarlet fluid that oozed out of him. Without encouraging her further, she dipped her head and licked the cut. She released a throaty moan and latched onto him, sucking. The tug of her mouth reached down to his balls as she toyed with his nipple.

He gripped her hips and pumped into her with a desperation that bordered on insanity. She gasped and released his skin to arch her back, thrusting her hips to meet his. He sat up, wrapped both arms around her, buried his face in her neck and exploded again.

Falling back, he took her with him, keeping her trapped against him.

"Hot damn," She mumbled into his neck. "That was amazing," she said with a sigh.

She dipped a finger into his parted mouth and traced his saliva across his wound. His heart lurched at this gesture. Warmth of another kind flooded his chest, and the ability to breathe escaped him.

"I'm not your prisoner, nor your feeder...how about sex slave?"

He chuckled—the unexpected humor surprised him—merging with the warmth in his chest to form...hope.

She giggled. "I ought to arrest you for having sex with a minor."

"Unavoidable," he said as he kissed her temple. "How old are you, Callie?"

"Almost twenty-nine," she said as she traced a pattern on his shoulder with a fingertip. "You're the sexiest geriatric I've ever met." She grinned before leaning in to brush her lips across his.

He claimed her mouth for his own, deepening the kiss. He couldn't help himself—he adored the taste of her.

Chapter Eighteen

Earth Shattering

Callie kissed Gabe's chest, unable to resist the temptation to do so. Her body hummed with contentment. Lethargy tugged at her, beckoning her to close her eyes and enjoy being in his arms. The euphoria from his previous feedings was enticement enough, and now, with her new knowledge, she could understand why folks went crazy when they weren't getting laid.

As lovers went, she couldn't have asked for a better one. Not that she had any experience to judge, but her deflowering had been less painful than she'd expected. He'd been attentive and gentle, even when he'd bitten her.

She trailed her fingers across his skin,. He twisted to kiss her temple. Something cinched her heart. She drew in a shuddering breath. It felt as if she stood on a cliff, a tempestuous wind pushing her toward the edge.

So much had happened that she struggled to process it. Val's healing was forefront, but a huge part of her couldn't believe she was well, almost as if she needed x-rays to prove it.

And here she lay, in the arms of her *future husband*.

She stilled, shutting her eyes, hoping to hide her inner turmoil from Gabe's observant gaze. She couldn't fall apart. She wasn't ready yet. No, not to face the loss of Dad or what she'd smothered during Val's sickest days.

She drew in a slow, soft, and long breath. Was she accepting her fate too easily? Had there been a way to avoid it all? Had she been impatient to comprehend the ramifications of her decisions?

His arms tightened around her, one hand caressing her back to grip her hip. It felt incredible to have someone hold her, as if she was no longer alone and facing the world with fists raised. Would Dad be proud of her, of her choices? She fought the tears, cursing herself for her weakness. But she couldn't stop them from slipping past her lashes, her defenses.

Sharp pain speared through her, and she gasped. She squeezed her eyes closed, but he shifted. She peeked at him through her lashes. He brushed his fingers along her jaw, then gathered her tears with the pad of his thumb. He said nothing, just engulfed her in his arms. His warmth, and the steady rhythm of his heartbeat beneath her cheek where he trapped her against his chest, offered more comfort than he could ever know.

Since the floodgates opened, she let the tears flow but smothered any sobs welling up her throat. A huge part of her wanted to cry like a toddler, but she was still Callie—still the strong one. His little fortress, Dad had called her.

She threw her arm around Gabe and clung to him. One day she'd thank him for stroking her back, for the sweet kisses he gave her temple and hair.

"I didn't hurt you, did I?" he asked when her tears subsided.

"No, you were wonderful." She twisted to kiss his palm still cupping her cheek. "I didn't mourn my dad's passing, and with Val's illness, I needed to be strong for her."

"I'd tell you that you have me now, but I suspect I'm part of what overwhelms you." He buried his fingers in her hair and tilted her head to meet his gaze.

His gray eyes swirled with an intensity that snatched her breath. He brushed his lips across hers, and she moaned, loving the tingles that spread from his touch, his taste. Trailing kisses down her neck gave her a chance to breathe.

"I won't lie to you, Gabe. I'm drowning here. Why me?" She shook her head, not wanting him to spew platitudes. She didn't expect love confessions or tokens of an affection he shouldn't be feeling. Not yet. "Please, no words of flattery, or promises of devotion. I've committed myself to you, and if love grows between us, I'll be content." She tugged him up to look at her. "As a suckblood, I anticipate many years for us to get to know one another."

"All right, but I will tell you again—I wanted you when I saw you," he said. "Trust me, this is stronger than lust."

"That's good, right?" She flashed a teasing smile before kissing his chin.

"Callie," he said, his voice hoarse. He tightened his fingers on her hip, tugging her closer. "It's better than good."

His lips claiming hers zinged heat through her body, and she succumbed, more now than earlier since she knew what to expect. His arousal rested on her belly, and the promise of it had her meeting his kiss with her own ardor. She scraped her fingernails down his back to cup his tight backside. He growled and flipped her over, pressing the length of his body to hers and trapping her beneath him.

With his hips pinning her in place, he plundered her mouth, his hands stroking across her eager, pebbled nipples. She whimpered, burying her fingers in his hair, clinging to him. Stars shimmered behind her closed eyes, and the scent of him engulfed her. Hot skin, velvet heat, and decadent promises lingered between their needy bodies. He trailed his fingers lower, and as scintillating as his touch was, she needed him inside her. A compelling ache pulsed from her core with an urgency bordering obsession.

"Please," she said, her voice husky. "Gabe, please."

"So greedy," he said with a chuckle, feathering kisses along her throat to her collarbone.

She wriggled until her legs were free to wrap around him, nestling him between her thighs.

He sucked in a sharp breath. "That's playing dirty." He gyrated his pelvis.

"I call it fair play," she said on a breathless moan, gripping his hips with her thighs to yank him closer.

He rose, tilting his hips until his erection pressed at her entrance. With excruciating slowness, he slid in, a smirk curling his top lip upward. "Making demands of me?"

But she didn't care what he said, or thought, as long as he filled her. She gasped in awe. The sensation of him stretching her raked shivers across her skin, sharpening her nipples before settling in her lower belly. Yes, she was tender from her first time, but he felt too good to deny.

"Callie," he said, his voice hoarse, as a pained expression crossed his face.

She scraped her nails over his nipples, and he groaned, his eyes fluttering shut—long ebony lashes brushing his cheeks. He thrust in hard, and she cried out, gyrating her hips until she found the perfect angle. He hooked her leg over one shoulder then pistoned out and in.

She thrashed her head from side-to-side, as wave after wave of intense sensations burst outward. She screamed and arched off the bed, tossed over the orgasmic edge without fanfare. Floating in a sea of languor, she expected to see fireworks and hear a philharmonic orchestra, but none of that compared to the roar of pleasure wrenched out of Gabe as he orgasmed. A fine sheen of sweat coated them. He collapsed on top of her.

She smiled. If she could spend an eternity in this blissful state, she wouldn't complain.

Chapter Nineteen

ON DUTY

"Where the hell are you?" Syl said through Gabe's cell phone.

He removed it from his ear to frown at it, wondering why he'd bothered to answer.

He returned it to his ear. "I'm out."

"Doing what? Are you with Devereaux?" Anger permeated the connection. Syl's voice had a lethal quality to it. An angry Syl was never good. He tended to act rashly and repent later—if he chose to.

"Keeping her alive." Gabe stared at his woman moving from shadow to shadow with her gun drawn. He'd started the conversion and with their numerous sexual antics, she was well on her way to being his wife.

He'd taken her to her apartment this morning to dress for work. As far as he sensed, she had no idea he hovered, watching. Yet, after the first day in the interview room, he knew better. Callie could see him, even if she didn't reveal her awareness by word or deed.

"She's still a detective? Are you insane?" Syl hissed. "I need her off my ass. Convert her already. I don't want to have to kill her if she gets close to the truth."

Rage ripped through Gabe at his brother's threat. The force of it snatched his breath, trembling his hands. If Syl was beside him, he would've gripped his throat and thrown him against a wall, brother or not.

"You will *not* touch her, Syl," he ground, putting all his anger in his voice. Silence met him, followed by a deep sigh. Every muscle in his body clenched.

"I won't harm her, brother, not when she's soon to be my sister. Just talk to her, please."

Gabe's muscles slackened as relief filled him. "Why not try the truth? Knowing Callie, she's imagining all sorts of horrors exist in that canister."

"She implied it was Schrodinger's cat, Gabriel." Syl chuckled. "I like her, I do. I just can't handle her curiosity. Please…"

Syl begging alarmed Gabe. His brother had invested in this, had placed all his hope on the chemical concoction within the canister.

"I'll bring her to you. Tell her the truth," Gabe said, seeing it as the only option that would calm both parties.

"Moon above! Fine, fine! But if she goes to the law with this…"

"Then I'll kill you, and it won't matter," Gabe said, not liking his brother threatening the life of his woman. He sighed when the call ended with Leo's laughter in the background.

Gunshots drew his attention, and his head whipped up as another body hit the ground. He wondered, and not for the first time, why he believed she needed protection. Against humans, she never missed, never hesitated. He respected her skill, her finely honed instincts that kept herself and Barrows alive, day after day.

Gabe sniffed the air. The only scents he discerned were from the dead bodies, Barrows's strong cologne, and Callie…delicious Callie. He levitated down to her and looped his arm around her waist, surprising her from behind. She froze before melting into him. He loved that she did this—it made him tremble with need.

"You've killed them all or chased them away." His words feathered her neck as he dragged his fangs along her pulse. "I sense no more heartbeats."

"Damn it," she mumbled, even as she arched her back, thrusting a breast into the palm of his hand.

"They did drop a container in their haste," he said as he fondled her through her uniform.

He imagined lowering himself to bury his face between her thighs, tasting her as he pleased. She gasped at the sensation he projected.

"Did you just…?" Her voice broke on a throaty moan.

"I have many talents," he mumbled, and she shivered in reaction to a psychic finger sliding into her. With trembling fingers and hasty movements, she holstered her gun before placing a hand on the brick wall.

"Hot damn." Her words came between pants, and her nipple puckered in his palm.

He claimed her mouth then, as he mentally sucked on her nub again. The taste of her, along with her reaction to his bombardment, had his balls spasming with need. He hadn't used psychic seduction on anyone in centuries. It'd been his preferred seduction, his enticement for feeders. The festivals and nightclubs had done away with the necessity to hunt.

With Callie, it was different.

It was more than her blood. He needed her explosive reactions, her orgasms, her breathless sighs. He swallowed her throaty moan as she splintered under his onslaught. Her need drenched her panties, and he inhaled the delicious, alluring scent of her.

"Make your jeans disappear," she said, and he did, eager for whatever she planned.

The lustful expression that hooded her eyes had his erection bobbing. She dropped to her knees and the heat of her mouth wrapping around his arousal ripped a groan from his throat. He shrouded them so that no one—not even clueless Barrows loitering somewhere on the docks—could see or hear them.

Callie rubbing enticing circles on his balls grabbed his full attention as she blessed him with a drawn-out suck. He imagined burying himself in her heat, and at the same time projected it. Her breath stuttered, and she arched her back, giving him access as if he'd buried his physical erection in her.

"I'm going to..."

She released him to lick his balls, while she pumped his length. He roared his orgasm, the real and psychic sensations merging to blur his vision, his senses, his inhibitions. With a flick of his wrist, he vanished her police trousers. He spun her to face the brick wall, and he buried himself in her, thrusting his way to another orgasm, taking her with him, demanding she partake in their glorious union. She screamed his name, clenching around his length. She was the victor and he the conquered with the way she affected him and rattled his control.

He wanted to hold her in his arms, to convey how much she meant to him. Yet the time and place weren't conducive to that.

After withdrawing his ever-present erection, he dressed them both before pinning her to the wall again for a kiss.

"You don't like to swallow?" he asked into her parted mouth.

"I wouldn't know." She grinned, unrepentant. "What? You couldn't wait for me to get home?"

"Home," he whispered, awed at how much emotion that one word invoked within him. He stole another kiss from her. "I had no intention of having you here, against this wall, in this filthy place. Things got out of control," he said before stepping away from her and lowering the shroud.

"What the hell?" Barrows growled in surprise.

Gabe nodded in greeting, acknowledging that their sudden appearance had startled the man. "Keeping her safe, even when she's on duty."

"I wasn't in any danger," Callie said in passing.

"My heart demands I protect you," he said as he faded into the shadows, merging his form with the darkness. "I'll collect you in two hours. She's yours to guard until then, Barrows."

Gabe levitated off, knowing he'd stunned her partner again with his ability to manipulate air. Flying was a standard vampire gift, one easy to master. She would learn to do so after her conversion. By now, she should be enjoying a few enhancements—sight, strength, scent, speed. Why hadn't she mentioned them to him yet?

Hovering meters above her, he hesitated, unable to leave her, not until she was a full vamp. She endured Barrows's chastisements with gracious ease. He loved that about her, the way she brought humor to every situation. Not that she couldn't be serious when called for.

"Dispatch, we've got a few dead criminals. Want to send over the coroner?" She spoke into her smartwatch.

"Again, Devereaux?"

"Yup. These bastards have a death wish. They keep posing in front of my gun. What's a girl to do?" She chuckled before rattling off the address.

"On duty?" Barrows muttered again as soon as she ended the call.

"Yup, the best ever. Hadn't planned it though."

"On duty," her partner grumbled.

"When did you get so old, Mike? Rumor has it you've bent an officer or two over the water cooler."

"Lies." He grinned. "Under the circumstance, I have the right to complain. I didn't see a thing."

"There's the problem, you old pervert."

"It would've made for a good beer story." Barrows shrugged. "I have to live through your sexual exploits, partner."

"That's an *ew,* and you know it." She chuckled as she retrieved the discarded crate.

She carried it back to her police vehicle and stored it in the trunk, strapping it down for safety reasons, Gabe assumed. He couldn't pick up ticking, but then again, bombs were more sophisticated now. A sniff revealed no chemical compounds inside.

"Why aren't you chasing after Anna McCarthy in payroll? She's been throwing you those come-get-it looks for ages."

"Anna is a good woman. She deserves a better man than me."

"That's bullshit. Stop making excuses, Mike, go get the gal."

"I've my hands full with your sassy ass," he said as he squeezed into the driver's seat.

"Still making excuses." Callie climbed in on the passenger side.

They sat in the car in silence and waited for the coroner. As soon as the ambulance pulled up, she jumped out of the car and strode toward the driver. "I got two perps gunned down by my own hands, boys. They left a box behind. I'll have the squad test it first before I send the contents to the lab. I doubt it's an incendiary device the way the perps were shaking it."

"Roger that, Devereaux."

"Need me to stick around?" she asked the coroner as she leaped aside to let them scurry past her.

"Nope. Send your report over when you're done. I'll add my findings to yours. Oh, and Devereaux, no more shooting tonight. I have a breakfast date with the missus."

"Roger that, Doc."

Callie sauntered toward her car and sank into the front seat. She closed the door, and Barrows reversed. Gabe followed, hovering at a constant ten meters above their car.

"I wanted to tell you that while you were taking a leisure dip in the bay, I trailed the two beasts. It ain't good, Callie." Barrows raised his cell to ear level as a recording played.

"Did the smug bastard take the package?" A man's gruff voice came from the recording.

"Yup, with no questions asked." This man sounded younger, his tone submissive.

The gruff man barked out a manic laugh. *"He doesn't have a clue, does he?"*

The question was rhetorical, but the younger man responded. *"Not a clue. He thinks he's powerful. That we can't blindside or challenge him."*

Gabe frowned. What was the point of this conversation? Impatience had him tapping a rhythm on his thigh.

"I'm glad the fuckin' mind reader wasn't there with him. That might have thrown this plan for a loop." Gruff-man chuckled.

Gabe tilted his head, focusing his hearing. Mind reader? That had to be Leo. The only person he spent any significant time with was Syl.

The younger man cleared his throat. *"The bastard was all alone except for some crazed cop. She snatched the package."*

Silence lingered for a minute. Gabe froze as well, his breath hitching. Did he mean Callie? How many crazed female cops could there be?

"What?" the gruff man roared.

Shuffling and stomping accompanied his fury.

"Relax. We played our part as we promised the Phoenix. Besides, the vamp was furious with the woman, not us. He'll get it from her. Y'know, I almost pity her."

Gabe nodded. They were talking about the canister, Syl and Callie's involvement.

"I want you to make sure he got it! Do you hear me?" The man paused, and Gabe assumed he waited for the younger man to nod. *"Damn it. All this jeopardized by some bitch on the force. Those blood-crazed bastards need to start testing that chemical."*

"Shit!" Worry filled Callie's voice. "Send me that please, Barrows."

"You're choosing sides," Mike grumbled.

"I chose last night. You and pops raised me to be a woman of my word. It's all I have left of him, Mike."

"You're forcing me to choose too," he said.

Gabe's phone vibrated with an incoming message. Heat exploded in his chest, snatching his breath at her name on the screen warning him. She'd chosen him. Again.

He sent the message to Leo and returned his focus to Callie, wishing she was in his arms.

"That's your choice." She wiped at her cheek before forcing a smile. "If you need a wingman, I can so do that for you, Mike." She sounded determined to change the subject.

The silence thickened before Mike cleared his throat. "Are you implying I'm unable to secure my own date?"

"Crap, I must be getting rusty. Did I come across as implying?" At her aghast tone, Gabe chuckled.

"So damn sassy," Barrows grumbled.

"You say that like you're surprised. When *haven't* I been sassy?" There was curiosity in her voice.

"Every time someone shot me." His tone turned serious, as if this was something he'd kept from her—his true feelings surfaced over the events that had led to his injuries.

"You want me sassy under fire?" Shock pitched her voice. "I long for the days of old when we could deport your sorry ass." She half-meant it, but her attempt at brevity fell flat.

"Huh? I'm good, old-fashioned American. Your Irish butt would be the first to go."

She huffed. "This butt has saved your ass."

"Who's counting?" Barrows said, although, what he was trying to accomplish by pissing her off, Gabe didn't know.

"I'm done talking about this." She peered out the window, her chin raised in defiance. "Just park the damn car."

Chapter Twenty

HEART'S INVOLVEMENT

GABRIEL GRINNED AS CALLIE jumped out of the car before Barrows yanked on the handbrake. She removed the box and carried it into the precinct, ignoring her partner. Her shoulders were tense, and she was good-and-proper pissed at poor Mike.

Still shrouded, Gabriel sauntered into the precinct and sat in the closest chair, content to observe.

"Careful, it could be a bomb," Callie said to Martinez, the officer behind the desk.

"You know the procedure. Why the hell did you give it to me, Devereaux?" the man asked with his mouth pulled into a thin line.

"Because I don't like you, Martinez?" She arched a brow with a teasing smile forming on her lips. "Because my shift ends soon. Hand it over to the bomb squad, and I'll owe you."

"Damn. A favor from you? It'll be a dozen of your famous cookies, you know that, right?" Martinez said.

"Cookies?" She scowled at the young officer. "I dunno. Maybe I ought to take it to the squad myself."

"Nope, it's mine now." The man clutched the box to his chest.

"Fine, a dozen cookies, but just this once." She caved with little grace, twisting her face in a grimace.

"Yes, ma'am." Martinez flashed her a delighted smile.

"Does he know you buy them at the local bakery?" Mike asked as they strolled through the glass doors to their open-plan office.

"Nope, and I'll thank you not to share that."

"It's gonna cost you," Barrows teased, dropping his bulk behind a desk across from hers.

"Fine, I'll get you a dozen like I always do." She trailed a finger along her desk piled high with paperwork.

Gabriel grinned at the sight of it. She was not a paperwork kind of woman.

Still shrouded, he slipped into a chair beside her desk and toyed with a pen lying there. It spun, drawing her attention. She smiled and sent a lustful look in his general direction. He responded with a psychic kiss along her neck.

After sliding into her chair, she unsnoozed her laptop and started typing. He bounded out of his chair and circled her to read over her shoulder.

She was writing her report, going into excessive detail. By the twist of her lips, he realized she did so on purpose, to irritate someone up the chain of command. Warmth filled his chest, and he kissed the crown of her head. She swatted him away, released a shuddering sigh, and carried on typing.

"After I have finished with this report, I'm calling it a day." She gave a fake yawn.

"Will he know you're leaving early?" Barrows's desk was as neat as a pin. He scanned the room, peering into the corners, his gaze passing over Gabriel many times.

"Something tells me yes." Callie smiled at Gabriel, meeting his shrouded gaze before closing her laptop.

Mike wiped an imaginary speck of dirt off his desk with his large finger. "McKinney owed me a favor. I had him tail Carter when he broke with routine and disappeared one afternoon."

"Huh? How many guys do you have on this?" Her grimace implied she hadn't wanted this bandied about.

"Relax. They don't know why. I said it's for a domestic assault case."

She snorted. "We're Homicide—we don't do those cases. How dumb do you think our guys are?"

"Do you want to hear the news or what?" He didn't wait for her to answer. "Carter met with a man out in Tennet's Lake. McKinney took pictures, but they're worthless. Sun in his eyes and such. Said he couldn't describe him well either. Walked as if he was royalty was all I got."

"Did he tail the new guy?"

"He said no, not for all the cookies in this town."

"You promised him cookies from me? You said he owed *you* a favor!" At her glare, Mike shrugged. "This had better be good."

"He said the man was a suckblood, Callie. Carter meeting with a suckblood when we know he hates them? You best warn your beau."

"No one says beau anymore, Mike." She tapped her fingers on her desk, her brows crinkled in worry. "There isn't just five suckbloods in this city. There's like seven or eight. Narrowing it down is gonna be a bitch."

Mike sighed at her sass. "Just tell him, my girl. I don't get a good feeling in my knees about this."

"Holy shit! In your knees? Are you sure?" She chuckled. "Mike, I have the greatest respect for your knees. They can predict shit better than a fortune teller. So I'll tell him, but first, I'm craving bacon, eggs, pancakes covered in maple syrup, and coffee strong enough to kill a rhino."

Pancakes? Gabriel tamped down the excitement that rushed through him. He hadn't tasted syrup or honey in over three hundred years. Then again, he'd still want her if she lived on brussel sprouts.

"Oh, and those little cheese sausages?" A blissful smile formed on Barrow's face.

"Might as well." She yanked the jacket from the back of her chair and tugged it on. "Captain approved my leave, so I'll see you in about a week's time."

"Sure. Took leave as well. Maybe I ought to see how Anna's doing."

"She said she'll meet you at Branbury's at seven tonight. I sent her an email to confirm." Callie giggled as she strode toward the precinct's front doors.

"Callie," Barrows shouted, but she waved goodbye instead of staying for his rant.

"You heard that, right? The only royal suckblood I know is your brother," she said to Gabe as she lifted her collar around her neck.

"I'll have Leo look into it," he whispered from the shroud.

"Fancy some bacon?"

The sun was setting, taking its heat with it. He inched closer and surrounded her with a pocket of warm air, not liking that she shivered—a side effect of the slow conversion.

"I'd fancy anything with you." He trailed her as she turned down the sidewalk and headed for a diner a few blocks away.

"You're sexy and a sweet talker. How'd I get so lucky?" She smiled but didn't look at him, keeping a determined pace to the diner as if she was on her own.

He envisioned wrapping his arms around her, hugging her body against his.

She moaned, her cheeks flushing pink as she licked her bottom lip. "I can sense your need." Her voice sounded a little breathless.

"I need you, this is true," he said without shame.

"Yet...you don't trust me to take care of myself?" She rubbed her lips together. The leaping of her heart told him his response was important. "It's been a few days of peace, but you don't believe your fellow suckbloods have given up on me?"

"I trust you against humans and shifters. I don't trust my kind. Syl sent out a warning, and he doesn't do that lightly. Still, there are those who are stupid, fearless, desperate for something new in their mundane lives. I tried not to follow you, but I needed to know you were safe. My heart won't let me rest, Callie." The words tumbled from his lips and surprised him with how true they were.

The excited thrum of his heart sent tingles to his extremities, as if his blood raced through his veins. He studied her profile and released a slow breath. What pierced him was more potent than what Abigail had called forth within him.

This human woman had slid under his defenses with her scent alone. At first, he'd thought it her flavor and everyday lust, now, she meant far more to him than that.

"Your heart?" she asked as she paused outside the diner in the shadows of an alleyway.

"My heart's involved, Callie." Couldn't she see how much he needed her? How much she affected him and how smoothly she fit into his life as if she'd always been there?

At his confession, she stilled, her eyes widening as her heartbeat stuttered. "Come, show yourself. I can't have bacon alone." It was a command—and he obliged.

The second he formed before her, she threw herself into his arms and kissed him.

"Let's make this quick so I can show you how much *my* heart's involved." She stood on her tiptoes and kissed him again. "Why do I need you, Gabe? Why do I become giddy at the thought of seeing you, kissing you? You haven't used your pheromones on me, even though it feels like you have. I'm crazy addicted to you. You know that, right?"

"Callie," he said into her mouth, peppering her bottom lip with kisses. He liked her blend of honesty and streetwise sass, but he adored her innocence.

She placed her hands on his shoulders and gave him a gentle push. "Feed me first. Then we can do...*whatever*."

"Whatever? That's a bit disrespectful." His lips curled into a teasing smile as he laced his fingers through hers and tugged her against him.

He opened the door for her but didn't release her hand. Warm air greeted them, along with the aroma of fresh coffee, fried bacon, and sweet maple syrup. He led her to a booth, unable to contain his excitement. He was once again a young lad with his first woman. All because of syrup and the sweetness of her smile.

A waitress took Callie's order, raising her eyebrows when he only ordered coffee. She slid her pencil into her shirt pocket and went to place their order. A huge grin split his face. He couldn't remember forming it, but for now, he would let it remain.

"You can see me when I shroud. How is that possible?" he asked, adoring her features like a man obsessed, and he embraced the insanity of it. There was a delicious sinful feel to it, potent and addictive.

"You're like a reflection, a partial. I don't know why or how your shrouding doesn't work on me. It became obvious to me when a woman went down on Syl at the mayor's ball. No one else noticed. I can't believe how blatant you suckbloods are."

"Ah, yes, the ball, where you met Leo." It *still* irked him at the way Leo had looked at Callie—his expression sad yet admiring.

"You're not jealous, are you?" She gave him a worried look. "I met him on the balcony and again at the bar. He came to my apartment, but I kicked him out. That's about it. No kissing, no touching, nothing."

"He wanted to."

"Yes, he mentioned that in your hall, but I didn't know, Gabe. Honestly." She stretched her arm across the table to clasp his hand, trying to convey her sincerity.

She didn't have to. Her innocence spoke for her—her inability to milk his jealousy for her own gain or enjoyment.

"I suppose you can't help being this irresistible sex goddess," he teased.

She chuckled and shook her head. That he believed what he said was something he'd save for later when he could worship her at his leisure.

"Yeah, right, that's so me. Let's talk about the stalking." Her grin was one of teasing, understanding, and something else he couldn't recognize.

"Stalking?" He flipped his hand and caught hers, lacing their fingers. Since they'd discussed this already, he assumed she was teasing him.

"Yes, watching your girlfriend's every move? Textbook stalking."

"Girlfriend?" He repeated the word with a sigh. "Callie, you're more than my girlfriend."

"It's not yet official. Until then..." She shrugged, revealing her uncertainty.

"Fine, fiancée, at least." Would she want a wedding ceremony? He didn't like that she remained unclaimed in the eyes of her human world.

Every time, her fellow officers admired her curves, blinding fury consumed him, and he'd hated the helplessness that lingered. Two centuries ago, he'd have ripped their throats out. With no consequences. He flicked his fingers and held up a white gold ring with a large center-round cut diamond. He slid it on her trembling finger, and of course, it was a perfect fit.

"I don't want to know where you were hiding that," she said with a tremulous smile.

"Everything I need comes from within me and the elements."

Her breath hitched, and he gave her a look that communicated which emotions she summoned within him. She was his world now. He wanted to be hers, but he couldn't force it.

"You can make diamonds out of the ether?" she asked then clamped her mouth shut when the waitress slid a heavy-laden plate onto the table. Callie peered up to the server with mischief coating her features. "I'm sorry, I've received a call out. Could you pack this to-go?" She grabbed a slice of bacon before pushing the plate back across the table to the waitress.

"Yeah, of course. Anything for our girls in blue." She smiled and ran off with the meal.

He surveyed Callie's face and sparkling eyes. "What're you doing?"

"You need to taste me after every bite. You can't do that here, right?" She glanced around the busy diner with an assessing eye.

"I can if I shroud us."

"When they already know we're here? No, this is for the best. Besides," she licked her lips, "I want you inside me for every bite."

He lost his breath. His vision heightened as need pounded on the outer edges of his very being. Words eluded him. Actions, however, did not.

He projected thrusting into her, hard, and buried to the hilt. At the same time, in the projection, he claimed her mouth for a thorough kiss. She gripped the table, her knuckles going white and she released a strangled moan. Her eyes flashed heat, lust, and anger while her cheeks flushed pink.

"How fast can you get me home?" she said, through clenched lips.

"Scared of heights?" He cleared his throat, his voice hoarse.

"Not if you hold me."

She climbed out of the booth and approached the cash register to pay. Her tip was generous as she accepted the cardboard container placed in a recyclable bag. He opened the door for her, striding into the cool evening air, an excited bounce to his steps. He guided her back to the dark alley before tugging her into his arms. She tied the bag to her wrist, then clung to his upper arms—her faith in him exquisite. He wouldn't let it be in vain.

He shrouded them in darkness, lest anyone look up and see them flying overhead. While he launched them skyward, he latched onto her lips, tasting only her and not the bacon she'd eaten. It didn't matter. She was nectar, indeed. He couldn't explain the effect it had on him as if something mystical and eternal hovered on the edges of his subconscious.

"This *is* quicker, but we could take a taxi," she said as he brushed his lips along her jaw.

He ensured she wouldn't feel the cold, surrounding her with warmth while keeping her distracted with kisses. He wasn't certain how he'd react if she panicked. Not that he expected she would, yet he couldn't dismiss the possibility.

"A taxi to the middle of a field?" he said in her ear before dipping his tongue in to trace its mesmerizing pattern.

A moan of pleasure escaped from her lips. "Good point."

Chapter Twenty-One

A NEED TO TALK

GABE LAY SPRAWLED ON his back, his white sheets once more stained with blood, but Callie didn't pay it much attention. Blood had become an everyday sight in just a manner of days.

Days? Had it only been days since he had entered her life? It felt like much longer.

But blood was the least of her worries. She had other things she needed to talk to her…fiancé about. With her cheek resting over his left nipple, she twirled a pattern across his abdomen. Her engagement ring shimmered in the pale bedroom lighting.

As she recalled the last few days BG—before Gabe—she admitted she'd been lonely, with the fear of Val's impending death deepening that loneliness. A manic panic had gripped her at times, but she'd thrust it down, forcing herself to focus on surviving day-to-day. Now Val was cured, sort of, and Callie had a fiancé, one who'd implied he loved her.

She assumed he did, although he hadn't spoken the words. She studied his carved-in-stone chin, tempting her to kiss him there. Yes…she wanted to hear those words from him since this was a forever kind of relationship.

She couldn't imagine an eternity in a loveless marriage.

"Gabe…" She chewed on her lip. "Did you get my message today?"

"Yes. I sent it to Leo. This might escalate the conflict to an all-out war. The shifters know how much this canister means to vamps everywhere."

"Shit." She winced, blaming herself for the future death of thousands, not to mention the humans caught in the middle.

He tilted his head and looped his arm around her, tightening his hold. "I won't console you with platitudes, Callie. This could go either way. Not the results of the war, but whether there'll be a war."

"Fair enough, Gabe." She rubbed her cheek along his chest, marveling at his heated velvet skin, the scent of him that tantalized her. "Heard anything about this clandestine meeting with Carter?"

He frowned, lowered his gaze to hers, then nodded. "Syl hasn't seen the state senator since the ball."

Leo could unweave lies, but would he cover for Syl? Yes, he would as he'd done at the ball, but what if he wasn't? What if there was another regal suckblood terrorizing her city?

"We have a new player," she said. "Phoenix? Does that name mean anything to you?"

"No, but it might mean something to Syl."

"We need to visit him soon." She pressed a wet kiss to his skin.

His breath hitched, and she peeked at him while grazing her teeth over his nipple. He moaned, unfolding his arm from behind his head to brush a curl off her forehead.

"Yes," he said, his voice gruff. "He'll explain the purpose of the canister's contents as well."

"You asked him for me?" Her head shot up, and she smiled, tweaking her nose. She clambered up, crushing her breasts against his chest. He lowered his hands to her hips, squeezing them.

"Have I told you how incredible you are, Gabe?" She feathered her lips across his parted mouth, their breaths mingling. "How sexy you are?" Nipping at his bottom lip, she drew blood.

She ran the tip of her tongue along the length of his lip before sharing the bounty with him.

Hooking his toes on her ankles, he spread her thighs. His pelvis dipped between them as he sipped from her lips. He trailed his hands from her hips, along the indent of her waist, to between her shoulder blades, overlapping his forearms to crush her against him. Her soft breasts trapped between them hardened her nipples, spiking the lust blurring her vision. A growl shredded his throat as he crashed his mouth over hers.

She loved his animalistic grunts of appreciation, his seeking fingers, his desperate touch. He took what he needed, took her breath, demanded her heart, claimed her soul for his own.

He unraveled his arms as he lay siege to her mouth, absorbing her gasps. His palms took hold of her backside, and squeezed, yanking her upward to position her at the head of his arousal. Holy fuck, he was potent.

She tore her mouth from him. "I have to breathe. Human, remember." Her heavy pants lessened as her ragged breathing calmed. "Gabe...damn, you're a fine kisser."

He blessed her with a seductive curl of his upper lip as he thrust into her. Her just-drawn breath rushed out of her in a moan. Tingles started from her pebbled nipples before scattering down to her loins. She embedded her nails into his biceps as she followed her huffs of pleasure with a cry at his repeated thrusts. She couldn't move her legs, still looped and trapped by his.

"Please..." she begged, this time for a different and more demanding need.

She was on the cusp of a momentous orgasm, drawing her full attention. Everything else blurred against this yearning ache throbbing in her core.

"What do you want?" he teased, peppering kisses along her jaw to nibble on her earlobe.

"Claim me hard, fast...now." She made demands, not caring that her will was no longer her own. "Please, my love."

His head jerked up, and he met her eyes. He stared at her, making her worry he'd stop. Stop doing such wonderful things to her. Stop before he satiated her. With her clouded mind, she struggled to understand the look on his face. It felt important, her instincts bouncing in urgency.

She struggled to form the question on the tip of her tongue, but he dipped his head to sample her mouth, his lips gentle, with both hands grasping her cheeks to hold her still. With a predatory elegance, he rolled them over, raised her legs to rest the back of her thighs against his chest, and proceeded to give her what she asked for. He thrust into her with a force that took her breath away.

She couldn't recall feeling this good. The sheer length of him connecting with her on a cellular level inspired far more than a primal need. Every sense she had, even her so-called sixth sense, attuned to him, his every movement, the grunts and growls emitting from him as he shredded her inhibitions. He blurred the boundary where she ended and he began.

"Is this what you want, Callie?" he asked as he thrust hard and deep then withdrew, slow and methodical, before repeating the cycle.

Her mouth parted to say something, but words escaped her. Sensations bombarded her, overwhelmed her, drowning her thoughts—her very principles—leaving her weeping for him.

He bit her above her right breast, and she exploded, screaming his name as new endorphins saturated her from within and stars fluttered across her eyelids. She whimpered, shuddering at the psychic finger stroking her nub as he drank from her. Too much. Too good. Could her human body survive such pleasure? At least if she died right here, it'd be the best damn way to go.

He pounded into her, her knees touching her chest as he leaned back to look at her, her blood staining his lips.

He muttered incoherent words. "I can't get enough of you," she thought he said.

With his real finger, he parted her lips to stroke her nub and massaged her breasts with psychic hands.

She couldn't hold back, didn't know how to stem the tidal wave of burgeoning pleasure. She wrapped her legs around his waist and clamped onto the small incision he'd made once again, above his left nipple. She sucked on his skin as hard as he pounded into her, not bothered by the metallic flavor of his blood. He trembled against her, panting and grunting as he did so.

He stilled. Roaring his release—and her name—he shuddered and twitched against her glistening body. He'd thrown back his head, gripping her hips, and a beautiful, pained expression hardened his face. His strength mesmerized her, the controlled power coursing through his body. Coming to, he dipped his head, eyeing her, and a lazy smile spread across his lips.

Her breath hitched at his magnetic intensity. "You're still bleeding." She gestured to the crimson rivulet painting one pec.

He glanced down and grinned. Before her eyes, it sealed. The blood smear was the remaining evidence. She sat up and licked it off before falling back onto the bed with a satisfied sigh. He followed her down, lapping at her wound. New stirrings of lust, tendrils of desire, and decadent need made her core throb again.

But she had a burning question she needed to ask. "What will happen to my blood after you've converted me?" She gripped his biceps as he feathered kisses up her neck, his erection still buried within her.

"I don't know," he mumbled against her skin. "Regardless, I want *you*...your blood tasting like chocolate is a bonus." He leaned back to cup her cheek, brushing his thumb across her lips. "In a normal conversion, you would lose your sense of taste, but you're a legend, a myth."

"You will want me even if I taste like other suckbloods?" Her eyes burned since she refused to let them blink, needing to see every expression that crossed his face. She wanted to know this was more than hunger between them, like she wasn't a novelty. Some people married for money, prestige, or sex, and not for who their spouse was as a person.

Frustration hardened his jaw. "Woman, I want you all the time. I'm like an unschooled youngling."

"Aren't all vampires gifted with this amount of stamina?" She chuckled as she ran her nails up his sides.

He hissed, grinding his hips to remind her she was at his mercy. "Don't for one minute think what we have is just sex. You bring joy and meaning into my life, sweet Callie."

She stilled, losing herself in his gray gaze. Her stomach grumbled, and he chuckled, pulling out of her to bound off the bed. "Where are you going?"

"To get your food." He bolted for the door, flashing her an exceptionally fine ass.

"Bring the pancakes. If you promise to behave, I'll let you have a nibble."

He flashed her a cheeky smile, left within a blink and was back just as quick. He placed her un-spilled coffee on the side table and handed her the diner's unopened container. Sprawling on the bed, he rested his head on his palm and his gaze on her.

She sat up, folded her legs under her, and set the container on the nightstand. She extracted her files from the drawer, placing them on the sheet before her. Gripping a pancake between forefinger and thumb, she bit into it as she flipped through the file on Alan Hawkins, CEO of Floges. He made billions from an IT company he'd formed as a youngster, but now he employed thousands and had a generous charity department, gifting millions every year.

She sucked on her thumb before choosing another pancake, taking the time to dip it in a pool of maple syrup. She chewed the cinnamon sweetness as she opened the second file on the senator, Devlin Carter. He was charismatic and came from old wealth, so she wasn't surprised he'd won folks over. But his smile was slimy. Even though her gut screamed there was something off about him, she couldn't understand what her instincts were saying. Devlin circulated among the elite, which included the mayor and Hawkins.

There was a link between the files and the three men. What did Hawkins, Carter, and the mayor have in common?

She slumped, sucking on her thumb and forefinger again, before offering her free wrist to Gabe. He shifted closer, grazing his fingers along her inner arm with breathtaking reverence. Before he bit into her, he glanced at her spread-out files.

"Floges means *flames* in Greek," he said before pure desire coursed through her as he pierced her skin. His throaty growl drowned out her sigh. Their gazes locked, and a heated intensity poured from his stare. He fluttered his eyes closed and mumbled, "Syrup," from around his embedded fangs. He licked the wound closed and bolted forward.

She yelped at his sudden movement then laughed when he tugged her thighs apart as he planted kisses down her lower belly. His thumbs spread her sleek lips so he could drag a tongue down, then up them. He groaned, the sound rumbling through to her core.

She writhed under his ministrations, but she was unable to look away, hypnotized by his enjoyment. He pressed a palm to her stomach, pinning her down, slowing the gyration of her hips before gliding a finger into her channel while he lapped at her. Biting down into her, his tongue continued its attack. With a cry of intense pleasure, she shattered under the assault, the intensity almost unbearable for her.

He gripped her hips and spun her onto her knees, looping an arm around her to pull her up and against his groin. He buried himself in her, bending over her to bite into her shoulder as his hips pounded a demanding rhythm.

"I'm dying," she screamed as she exploded again.

This time wave after wave swept through her, extending the pleasure. Her breath caught, her world froze as if she hovered in a sea of sensation with her body, her senses. Her instincts focused on this man, *her* man. As if from far away, he roared, then collapsed onto his side, bringing her with him, his labored breathing cooling her damp nape.

"I'm never letting you go, Callie," he said.

She caught those words, loud and clear. Relief melted the remnants of doubt darkening her soul, and she allowed her heart to trust.

"And I've ruined your files."

She chuckled, wrapping his arms tighter around her. "Don't worry. It's the most action they've seen in a while."

CHAPTER TWENTY-TWO

CONTENTMENT

GABRIEL MATERIALIZED IN SYL'S chambers, not surprised to find Leo already there. He grinned a greeting to his brother, too pleased to hide his contentment. Dropping into a large leather armchair, he ran his palms along his denim-encased thighs. Excitement and satisfaction skittered along his nerve endings, and he welcomed it, embraced the change from his unemotional life.

He had no right to be this happy this quickly. He couldn't explain how or why Callie made him feel this way. Perhaps when he returned, he'd awaken her to taste her again in more ways than one. Just imagining it made him as giddy as a schoolgirl.

Then again, holding her in his arms as she slept brought him as much joy, so it wasn't about how amazing it was to fuck her or how delicious she always tasted. She filled a void in his heart, one he'd ignored as each passing year added darkness to his soul.

"Ten minutes later and you're still sitting there smiling like an idiot." Syl handed Gabriel a snifter of brandy.

"He has a right to," Leo grumbled.

Gabriel shot him a look, his joy faltering. Did Leo have access to his memories of Callie lying beneath him? He hoped not—those memories were for him alone.

Leo smiled, but it didn't quite reach his blue eyes. "I can't explain what Callie invokes in me, so don't ask, not even in your thoughts, Gabriel." Leo's eyes flashed a warning.

Gabriel sighed, not liking the situation or the implied affection Leo had for Callie.

"Don't worry. You have her, and that's the end of it." Leo folded his arms across his chest.

"How's...?" Gabriel asked, thinking of Valerie, wondering if she had the same gift in her blood. If she did, and she hadn't lost it during the conversion, he could appease Callie's curiosity.

Leo's visible shudder halted his words, having never seen the blond man this shaken.

"I can't read her. I can't scent her. It's maddening, yet...intriguing. And no, I haven't sampled her blood yet. Perhaps one day soon you'll let me ask Callie for a taste?"

Gabriel frowned, hating the burst of heat consuming his chest, tensing his muscles, and clenching his jaw. Leo's lips anywhere on her skin was out of the question. He would never let that happen.

Taking a large inhale, he opted for a subject change rather than discuss Callie with Leo in any way. "Is Val well?"

He imagined the joy on Callie's face when he organized a visit from Valerie like he'd promised. The need to please his fiancé consumed him with a single-mindedness he hadn't expected. Making her happy had become the most important goal of his life.

"Yes, I can bring Val for a visit."

"Let me finish voicing my questions. Damn it. I hate it when you read my mind." Gabriel was being unreasonable—it wasn't as if Leo could help himself. The fury boiling within him had to do with Leo reading more than his questions.

He didn't want to share Callie with his friend, not now, not ever.

"What's put a damper on your mood?" Syl sat in another leather armchair before resting his elbows on his bent knees.

"Gabriel doesn't approve of my affection for Callie," Leo said.

"Oh, ho! When did you form an attachment, Leo?" Syl chuckled.

Gabriel loved it when his brother laughed. It brought back the joyful innocence that had once been his staple expression. Just not this day. Today, he found Leo's affection an irritation, and Syl's humor salt to his wound. He didn't think any of this amusing.

"At Duhamel's ball. She saw through your shroud, by the way." Leo pursed his lips.

"What?" Syl spluttered in his brandy. He stiffened, his displeasure obvious.

This appeased Gabriel's discomfort. His lips curled upward, but he hid it from Syl by taking a good mouthful of brandy.

"I don't like surprises, Gabriel. Your woman is as unpredictable as the weather. How much longer? How many more feedings before she's converted? Where did you leave your dear one?"

"I exhausted her." Gabriel smirked and shifted in his armchair, a pointless attempt to ease his constant arousal. "Her conversion requires one or two more feedings before she's fully mine, though she has yet to mention experiencing preternatural speed or strength from the feedings she's received so far."

"Not long then. I look forward to having a sister, Gabriel. Despite my initial doubts, she has changed her affiliation, something I hadn't expected."

"Don't get excited, Syl. She tolerates you," Leo raised a graceful hand to flick a finger.

The chamber's door opened at Leo's command, and hesitating at the entrance was a human woman, her youthful blood scenting the air. She entered the room like a timid mouse.

Gabriel studied her lithe form, her clinging dark blue evening gown, and the fall of her pale blonde hair. He arched a brow at Leo, who nudged his head at Syl.

Ah, dinner had arrived.

Gabriel wasn't the slightest bit tempted. Nothing and no one tasted as delicious as his Callie. The woman kneeled in front of Syl and offered her arm as instructed.

"I offer my blood freely," she said, her voice low and throaty.

By the way she trembled, Gabriel concluded she was nervous. Her fear would have stained the air with a bitter odor. Syl encircled her wrist with his fingers, stroking her skin without glancing at her.

"What did you do with the voice clip I sent you?" Gabriel addressed Leo before settling his attention on Syl, who'd taken to grazing his fangs along the woman's wrist.

The movement mesmerized her, saturating the air with her sickly-sweet arousal and excitement.

"I've sent a few of our spies. A few human ones too," Syl said as he trailed a finger down the woman's chest, parting the silk of her gown. A pale globe popped free. He cupped it and rubbed a finger over her taut nipple.

"Before we invested, did we test the product inside the canister?" Gabriel asked, raising his glass to his lips, wishing he was sipping scotch from Callie's veins, instead.

He tamped down the rising excitement, imagining the long-forgotten tastes that awaited him—cherries and oranges, to name a few.

"You scented the test subject's fertility." Syl guided the woman's hand to his groin. "She has yet to conceive, but it's the closest we've come in centuries."

"To be able to father children..." Leo's voice hitched.

A strong, sharp need hit Gabriel, clenching his chest in a breath-snatching vise. To father children with Callie was beyond his greatest desire.

"Gabriel," Leo said.

The urgency and fear tainting his voice startled Gabriel, who raised his gaze to meet Leo's.

"Callie's gone."

Chapter Twenty-Three

FROM BLISS TO A NIGHTMARE

The bed dipped, summoning her from her light slumber, and she mumbled a welcome, throwing out an arm in supplication. She touched fabric and moaned in displeasure, rolling over to cradle his dressed form. The bed on his side was cold, but they'd warm it up soon enough.

"Naked," she said, struggling to open her eyes against her exhaustion.

She ran her hand over his hip, her fingertips brushing over studs and stitching. In an instant, it went from denim to velvet skin.

"Better."

His naked heat drew her, and she spread her body across his, shivering from his warmth. Rubbing her cheek against his chest, she threw an arm around his waist, sighing with contentment.

"Drink, Callie," he whispered, and she obeyed, latching her mouth onto his skin yet finding no blood.

Licking her way across, she lapped at the droplets above his left nipple.

It tasted funny, different, not Gabe's sweet, addictive flavor.

Come to think of it, he didn't smell the same either. When the last tendrils of lassitude dissipated, she didn't change her posture. Forcing herself to remain relaxed, she pretended to drink the blood of this unknown suckblood. Cold tendrils of fear fought against her control, wanting to stiffen her muscles, to send shivers down her spine as adrenaline pumped through her veins. Her only option was to distract her rising panic by trying to come up with solutions, but she couldn't pretend much longer.

Gritting her teeth, she faked a lustful groan even as her heartbeat climbed to a deafening roar. Damn it, where had she left her arsenal? On the bookshelf?

Too far away to help her. Her instincts roared their unhappiness, and she snorted at their sudden revival. Where were they before she'd drunk a stranger's blood? Her stomach roiled, not liking what it now held. It twisted, and a sharp pain speared through her. At the unexpected agony, she couldn't swallow the cry that tore from her, lacerating her throat, revealing her pretense.

"What have you done?" She rolled away from the intruder, taking the sheet with her in an attempt at modesty. Gathering it to her chest, she sat up and gasped. She recognized the stranger who would dare to force her, to violate Gabe's sanctuary.

Darius.

She had to admit, his audacity didn't surprise her.

"Hello, my pet." He rose from the bed as he grinned in that irritating way of his, his arrogance palpable. "You're mine now."

She blinked in disbelief, wondering if he was stupid or deaf. Gabe had claimed her in front of his people and received Syl's blessing. Where the hell did Darius think he could go after tonight? Because if Gabe didn't hunt him down, she sure would.

Backing away from him, she bumped into the headboard behind her. "I'll never be yours, asshole."

"You won't call me that again, youngling." His voice dropped a few degrees on the chill factor as he appeared before her, so quick he blurred.

Red stained her vision, with her blood pounding in her ears, drowning out her instincts, whispering a warning that her usual sass wouldn't help the situation. She ignored it. "Wanna bet, asshat? Or do you prefer asswipe?"

"Your lack of appropriate fear and respect will change, my sweet."

He clothed himself, for which she was grateful. She hadn't liked his looming nudity nor his apparent arousal.

She trembled, praying Gabe would return, hoping she could clothe herself as well. Her gaze darted around the room, searching for any discarded garment. For once, she wished Gabe hadn't made her clothing evaporate in the throes of their last heated embrace.

"Soon you will be, shall we say, not yourself?" Darius arched a brow. His gaze traveled the shape of her emphasized by the thin sheet. "Nausea in the pit of your stomach? Sharp pains? A strange fluttering sensation in your chest, as if your heart is palpitating?"

She *was* feeling all those things. She frowned, not liking that he was correct and had trapped her. A violent shudder racked her body as pins and needles pierced her eyes. She cried out, releasing the sheet to grab her face. It didn't ease the onslaught, only worsened it. Agony tore through her abdomen, like the many gunshot wounds she'd experienced. She screamed, coiling into a fetal position on the bed, whimpering Gabe's name, needing him.

What could she do?

Leo! She called to him, hoping to somehow reach him. She didn't know what she was doing, how to communicate with her mind, but she was desperate.

With the pain crippling her, she couldn't fight Darius. Helpless to stop him, he picked her up and threw her over his shoulder. Fresh agony lanced through her, the smell of him pooling bile in her mouth, coating her tongue. She gagged.

Leo, you damn suckblood! Help me, please! Kidnapping is a thing even in your stupid culture.

The floor rushed past, and she shut her eyes, fighting the dizziness. The swaying motion of Darius's gait had her throwing up, and she hoped it was all down his jeans.

Weakness assailed her next, and with her remaining strength, she pressed and held a button on her smartwatch to send a distress signal. Darius had fucked with the wrong woman. She was Gabe's fiancé. But more than this, she was a police detective. They protected and avenged their own. He'd pissed off Gabe and Barrows, and she almost pitied him when either one found her.

"Fuck you, Darius," she shouted.

"Oh, yes please," he chuckled. "As your sire, you'll have to obey me. You'll be sucking my cock soon, my pretty."

"If you want it bitten off, then, by all means, let me near it." She dry-heaved, ruining the effect of her words. The pain still searing her eye sockets had her squeezing them shut. "Besides, I've seen better on a human." She wasn't willing to let him win even something so insignificant as trading insults.

Cold night air greeted her, drenching her in waves of ice. Goosebumps rippled along her skin, puckering her nipples to hard points.

He patted her bare backside, his fingers dipping in where they had no right to. Fresh nausea hit her, and she dry-heaved again. She clenched her thighs together, but he only dug his fingernails in until she whimpered, forcing her to relax her muscles. He didn't stroke her, though, merely kept his intruding fingers there as if he proved his point—she was at his mercy.

He burst into a run, and the dizziness doubled in strength, making her call forth a deep moan.

"Gabe will find me," she mumbled.

As another shard of pain and a reactive scream tore through her, she hoped she was right.

She had to believe Gabe *would* find her because she couldn't handle the alternative.

Chapter Twenty-Four

DESOLATION

"What do you mean, she's gone?" Gabriel rose from his chair in one swift movement.

Leo's serious and concerned expression conveyed an urgency Gabriel could not ignore.

"I heard my name, and only when she insulted me did I realize who called to me. Like I said—the Devereaux sisters are maddening."

"I don't give a fuck about that. Are you saying someone would dare…"

Icy fear gripped his heart, and he bolted. Dissolving into a mist was out of the question with his unstable thoughts and emotions. So he ran. The wind whipped his hair, deafening his hearing, but it didn't matter. He doubted he'd ever run this fast, which was why he burst through his door instead of stopping in time. It hung in pieces off its hinges.

He drew to a halt once he reached their bedroom. It was devoid of her radiance, her life essence, the joy that migrated to him when he was in her presence. The blood-splattered sheet lay discarded on the floor, as if pointing in the direction she'd gone. Crumpling to his knees, he gathered the sheet in his trembling hands and buried his face in it. Her scent engulfed him, and he inhaled, drawing it deep within him.

"Darius," Leo said from behind him, startling Gabriel.

He hadn't sensed the man had followed since his duty was to guard Syl. He valued Leo's skills, and therefore would not protest his company.

He sniffed the air and growled, picking up Darius's unique stench.

"Can you track his thoughts?" He tried to keep the hopeful note out of his voice, but he was unsuccessful.

Leo shot him an arrogant look and frowned, closing his eyes to focus. His frown deepened into a scowl, and he opened his blue eyes to shake his head.

"Damn it! Where would he go? He's exiled from our Hold if I don't kill him for this." A buzzing sound interrupted Gabe, and he glanced around in surprise.

"I do believe that's your cell phone," Leo said.

Gabriel rushed to his living room, toward the bookshelf where he'd left his device, alongside the old text on Greek mythology. The sight of Callie's arsenal pierced him...she was unarmed and vulnerable.

"What the fuck is going on?" Mike bellowed down the line as soon as he answered. "I've got Callie's distress signal going off, and this had better not be a joke."

"Someone took her," Gabriel said, a fresh wave of hope hitting him, affecting his voice.

That she'd set off the signal made his chest swell. Although he trusted her, her sending the signal proved she'd gone unwillingly. Moreover, she thought on her feet and acted even when in distress.

That was *his* woman. His brilliant, intelligent Callie.

"What do you mean? You're fuckin' immortal, supernatural beings. How could you let someone kidnap her?" Mike's voice spiked as his anger rose.

"How the hell do you think I feel, Barrows? I left her asleep, and that Darius would dare to touch her..." Gabriel's voice hitched on the sheer audacity warring with the fear gripping him.

"Darius? Hmm. Any idea what his intentions are? In other words, how much time does she have?"

Gabriel released a long breath. At least Mike didn't think him incompetent. He knew who'd taken her, which was progress in the eyes of the detective.

"Worst case? To sire her and eventually claim her." He shuddered. He'd kill the runt.

"Shit." Mike paused. "Any idea where he's headed? I tracked her northwest of your location until the signal stagnated."

Hope shot through Gabriel like a beam of sunlight—hot, hard, and needed. "Northwest? All right, I'm heading in that direction now. If you've lost the signal, then he might have her underground. Where did it last pulse?"

"Dandelion Ridge. That ain't a nice area, Gabe."

"I'm not in a nice mood," he growled. The burning urgency in him had determination solidifying his resolve. He *would* kill for her. Violence and anger roiled through his body. "Send me the coordinates."

"I'm heading there as well. Wait for me." The line cut off.

"Humans lack the proper respect. My sire would've been most displeased," Leo said as he shifted closer to stare at the phone clasped in Gabriel's fingers.

His knuckles were white, and the device crackled under the force he applied, but he wouldn't damage it. The phone was the only lifeline he had to recovering her. As soon as he received Mike's text, he activated it and bolted outside to launch into the air.

"You go to the location. I'll stop off at Dimitri's," Leo said from beside him, having taken to the air.

Gabriel grunted since he hadn't given protocol a thought. A vamp couldn't hunt in another Hold's territory, no matter the lineage, no matter the reason. Despite Syl ruling the city's vamps, Gabriel still had to show deference.

"Thank you. I don't have it in me to be polite, Leo." His words were the closest he'd come to offering his gratitude.

"I assumed as much." A smirk played across Leo's features. He veered to the left and abandoned Gabriel, who increased his speed.

As far as he was aware, the de Winter Hold didn't own properties this far north. He wouldn't put it past Darius to oust an unsuspecting family, or to feast on them as if they were chattel. Such behavior jeopardized the vampires' position among the humans and shifters. Keeping the shifters at bay and the humans docile was a delicate balance. Nothing stopped them from nuking the Holds and Dens, and if more vampires behaved as Darius had done...Well, Gabriel wouldn't blame the humans.

He would meditate on the possibilities at a later stage, with Callie lying next to him. He would also increase his security. Not once had he considered someone would dare to intrude. His seclusion had drawn forth complacency from his fellow vamps. Time to remind them who was *the* predator in their midst. He would deal with them old-school since violence was the only language they understood.

He descended to the house, landing with softness on the tiled roof. The temptation to storm in gripped him, desperate as he was to find her. Less than an hour had passed since Darius had taken her, and it killed him he hadn't found her yet.

Drawing in a deep breath, he focused his mind, calmed his thoughts, letting nothing ripple the surface. With a slow exhale, he misted, catching a passing breeze as a diver would the dorsal fin of a dolphin. He allowed the zephyr to carry his form along the roof and down. Sliding under the door, he paused, taking stock of the interior. A fire burned in the hearth, and a poor but hopeful family sat around a dinner table. He wouldn't let the idyllic scene distract him. They might not be aware of the vamp in their home.

Moving past, he ignored the shivering mother as he located the basement door in their kitchen. He slithered through the keyhole and down the cracked steps. The basement smelled of age and disuse. For months, the air had remained undisturbed.

He escaped the house with speed since he no longer needed caution. He fought to maintain his focus, to keep the surface of his mind unmarred. As he rematerialized, the roar that tore through him shredded his throat, setting off car alarms and barking dogs. He waved his hand to silence the cars closest to him.

Callie wasn't there. She had never been there.

But the signal?

He took out his phone—his unsteady hands fumbling it—and followed the blue icon said to be accurate within ten feet. The flashing red light caught his eye...her smartwatch.

He scooped it up with trembling fingers, bringing it to his nose to sniff. Hot pain lanced through his chest at her familiar scent. He didn't detect blood, which meant Darius hadn't harmed her, for now. It was a small mercy, but he was grateful, easing the tension between his shoulders.

"Did you find her?" Barrows asked, striding toward him.

His police vehicle was just behind him, its lights flickering. He hadn't heard Mike pull up or jump out of his car, but his lack of awareness didn't bother him. His focus was where it should be.

"She's not in the house, and here..." He tossed the watch at the detective, not caring whether Mike caught it or not.

"Shit! Now what? How far could he travel with her? Or do we continue to search for her in Dandelion?"

Gabriel stared at the concerned human, knowing what the poor man was enduring since he suffered the same emotion—sheer damn panic. Adrenaline pulsed in his veins, his heart leaping without a steady rhythm in mind and desperation coated his actions. He sniffed the air, hoping to catch her scent yet knowing that was futile. He couldn't scent Darius either, though Mike smelled strongly of fear, permeating Gabriel's immediate surroundings with bitterness.

Leo? He voiced along their mental path. *She's not here.*

I'm on my way.

"Leo's on his way. We'll decide then." Not bothering to shroud himself, Gabe shot into the air, hovering above the house.

He focused his senses, taking slow and deep breaths. With his enhanced hearing, he listened, picking up and discarding sounds as soon as he cataloged them. *I can't hear her, Leo. Can you communicate with her?*

I've been trying since I left you. She's not responding or is…unconscious.

Gabriel winced, not liking the possibility that Callie would be vulnerable to Darius's ministrations. What he needed her to do was smear her blood across his mark. Then he could find her with ease, but since she had yet to do so, she was either unconscious as Leo had suggested, or she'd forgotten about it.

He descended to the sidewalk, landing on soft heels beside Mike.

"Who's this Darius? What do you plan to do with him when we find him?" Mike had removed his gun from its holster and its magazine, checking its capacity. "I'm aware you have your own justice system, which I hope is harsher and more definitive than ours."

"Yes, we do. For this infraction, I will bring Darius before our king for judgment." Gabriel glanced at Mike, meeting his gaze, which was easy to do with his superb vision. "However, he will have an unfortunate accident *en route* to my brother."

The wicked grin that split the elderly detective's face meant Gabriel had received his approval, and that he'd look away when the time came. The police didn't bother with vampire-on-vampire crime. They became involved only when the crime occurred in front of them or included innocent humans.

"Good. Taking our Callie is unacceptable, and you need to send a message stating that."

Gabriel's smile was tight and not sweet. *Our* Callie was to remain untouched, unmolested, and above all, protected.

Leo landed beside him with Dimitri, who'd brought quite a few of his hunters with him.

"Dimitri, thank you for this. You may ask a favor from me, as and when needed." Gabriel hugged the fellow vampire—one he'd known and respected for years.

The tall brooding man returned the hug with a thump on Gabriel's back.

"Gabriel. Rumors abound that you claimed a human woman. She must be remarkable, this *tsvetok*." Dimitri flashed a small smile, which was bright against his olive skin. "We will find her, your flower. Have no fear, *brat*." He nodded at his men, and they dispersed. "My *pal'tsy* will find her and the bastard who dared to do such a thing."

Dressed in a black leather jacket over dark denims, Dimitri was intimidating with his black hair and green eyes.

Gabriel glanced at Mike to determine whether he was nervous around such an ancient vampire as his Russian friend. Barrows seemed unaffected, and he smelled as fearful as when he'd first arrived.

"Dimitri, this is Callie's partner, Detective Barrows. Mike, this is Dimitri Vasiliev, head of the Northeast quarter."

"Evening." Mike thrust out his hand for a quick shake. "I assume you've dispatched your men to hunt for news of her?"

"Yes, my skilled fingers are thorough, and they know this city well." Dimitri gestured to his dispersing men.

"I appreciate any help you can provide. Please excuse me. I have my men looking as well." Mike scurried to his car. Seconds later, he spoke to Callie's captain.

"So, we wait?" Standing around and doing nothing didn't sit well with Gabriel.

"Yes, I have many fingers...*pal'tsy* in many pies. It won't be long." Dimitri turned, and within a blink of an eye, stood at Mike's opened car door. "Detective, send your men to scout the harbor. Water confuses our senses."

Mike fired commands down the line. He nodded at Gabriel, hopped into his car, and with a burn of rubber and a siren's whoop, he drove off.

"Leo, can you communicate with any brain?" Gabriel asked. "This city has millions of rats scurrying through gutters and infesting every nook. Can they not be our eyes and ears?"

"You want me to...? I've never tried, to be honest." Leo raised his face to the moonlit sky, and a painful grimace crossed his features, worrying Gabriel. It could mean many things—failure, success, but he knew better than to assume, not with Leo.

"Their minds are individual," he whispered, and if Gabriel didn't know better, with awe. "I'm scanning as many as I can. One of them must have seen something."

"Good," Dimitri said. "Tell me, Gabriel, is your woman strong enough to withstand this? Leonardo indicated you have yet to convert her?"

"My Callie is impressive, Dimitri. You will see. One or two more feedings and she'll be mine for an eternity."

"I am pleased for you, my friend. Now let us find her." Dimitri shot into the air, flying toward his fast-disappearing fingers.

That his infamous *pal'tsy* were aiding in the search for Callie had Gabriel breathing easier.

Chapter Twenty-Five

ALONE

CALLIE AWOKE WITH A start, inundated with fierce darts of discomfort when she fluttered her eyes open. This wasn't the pleasant awakening she'd become accustomed to. No warm blanket cocooned her, no pillow to rest her head upon. Most certainly no Gabe sprawled alongside her, his warmth reaching through her slumber to offer comfort.

She was lying on a dirt floor of compacted sand, each granule rubbing her skin like coarse sandpaper. The cold seeped into her bones, along with the realization of where she was—an unused cellar or basement. She shivered, rubbing her hands along her upper arms, hoping to wipe away the goosebumps that had taken up permanent residence there during her unconscious state. A horrid taste claimed her mouth, and she struggled to swallow past a swollen tongue. A sharp pain gripped her, hot and piercing, ripping at her belly as if it had realized she was awake.

She hungered.

Her blood sugar must have dropped over the last few hours. An image imprinted itself on her mind, and no matter how much she shook her head or attempted to dismiss it, it remained. Red, rare, juicy steak with a baked potato on the side, and a green salad. Her mouth watered, and at last, she could swallow.

She struggled into a sitting position, grimacing as her bare backside grated along the dirty floor. She shuddered and thrust down thoughts of uncleanliness, preferring to assess her situation and possible escape routes. Her limbs were intact. She was thirsty too, which didn't surprise her.

No light illuminated the three-by-four room, but she could see well. That was strange, as if she wore night goggles. Studying the concrete ceiling, there were no skylights through which moonlight could penetrate the room. A scratching sound to the left drew her attention. She whipped her head to look, too fast, and swirling dizziness welled nausea in the pit of her stomach.

A rat scurried toward her and sat there blinking, unafraid.

"What's up, little fellow?" she said, her voice above a rasp.

Its nose twitched, and his whiskers flickered.

"You won't be nibbling on me, so you can just scoot. Where did you come from, anyway?" She glanced at the wall, at a circular drain large enough for a mouse, but not for a rat this size.

She'd read somewhere that their flexibility was remarkable. They were able to fit through tiny spaces and narrow pipes.

"I can't fit through there. Got any other suggestions?"

He blinked and glanced at the door as if he understood her.

She rose to her feet and pressed on the solid-looking door. Pain lanced through her, and she yanked her hands away, peeling skin off in the process. The stench of burned flesh now saturated the dank air. She stared at her palms in disbelief, wincing at the scars, pink and stinging. Before her eyes, her skin healed, becoming smooth and soft. Then her knife scar healed.

"What the hell?" She'd had that scar since her first year as a detective.

"Wait a minute...*Darius*..." She slammed her fist on the wall, fury taking over her heart and squeezing.

The bastard had given her his blood, converting her. But... Her brow furrowed in confusion. Shouldn't she need more than a sip to convert?

Horror pulsed through her, paralyzing her. Gabriel had been converting her day by day, distracting her with his animal magnetism.

Yes, they discussed it, but never had he said they'd start immediately. Oh, when he found her, she'd strip the skin off his backside. She paced across the room, too furious to stand still. Why hadn't he just told her? Why hide it from her? It wasn't as if she would've said no. Before she died, she wanted to see Val one last time, and he had no right to risk her life like this.

He hadn't considered that it might kill her. The arrogance of suckbloods, doing what they wanted regardless of the consequences. So much for my-heart-is-involved nonsense.

Had he meant it, he'd have told her. Hell, at least asked her for permission.

She curled her fingers into fists, her fingernails forming crimson crescent wounds in her palms, only to fade. Staring at her healing hands, her instincts roared their unhappiness. What was wrong with this image? She scowled and studied each hand.

Shit. Her watch was missing. Panic struck her hard, snatching her breath. She spun on the spot, searching the floor of her cell, hoping it had come off here. Her heartbeat thumped in her ears competing with her ragged breathing, ramping up the adrenaline punching through her. In a surreal moment, she paused to admire her new ability to sense the change in her blood, to feel it rushing along her veins. *Holy crap!* It amazed her that Gabe could hear her voice above his rushing blood.

When the panic bombarded her tremulous control, she drew in a deep breath, searching for peace. Okay, so...trapped, check. No escape, check. No way to let Mike know where she was, check.

She glanced at the rat, which hadn't moved, silently observing her, unafraid of her antics. Was she dreaming? Having a nightmare? She squeezed her eyes shut and pinched herself hard. She winced, peeling her eyelids open, and sighed...not a dream. She was awake, naked, in a basement, and a vampire youngling. The shit had finally hit the metaphorical fan.

Think!

Mike had her signal until where she'd lost her wristband, not that she knew where that was. It could be close to her location or nowhere near here. She'd called Leo, but she wasn't sure he'd heard her, so there was no guarantee he could help her.

"Any other ideas, George? Any idea how to thwart an immortal psychopathic suckblood?" she asked the rat. Yes, she named him George. How could she not name a rat that seemed so...aware? His nose twitched, and he dipped his head.

"Thought as much. You don't happen to have a bottle of spring water hiding anywhere on your person?" She giggled and clamped her mouth shut against the rising hysteria.

She wouldn't lose her shit, not until she'd exhausted all options.

Leaning against a wall, she placed her bare backside on the dirt floor. Preferring to be comfortable rather than demure, she bent her knees. George scampered up her calve to rest on her knee.

"At some point, you'll have to leave me, George. Handsome buck like you must have a wife and pups waiting for you." George tilted his head, and she found herself smiling. "Not a single doe has snatched you up? That does surprise me."

A sob escaped her in that unguarded moment. She didn't smother it, not needing to. "Oh, George, what am I going to do?"

The rat's head shot up, then he scampered down her leg and through the hole. His abandonment hit her hard, the silence of the cell crushing her fragile control.

The sound of a wooden step creaking came from behind the solid door.

Chapter Twenty-Six

HUNTS

Blood trickled from Leo's nose. He'd been at it for hours. His skin had taken on a gray tint, but Gabriel didn't dare stop him.

Elongating his teeth, he sliced his wrist and held it to Leo's lips. "I offer freely," he said.

The male drank but didn't pause his search. When he'd had enough, he turned his head away. Gabriel licked his wound closed.

"I didn't know there were this many rats, Gabriel," Leo said, his voice hoarse from the strain. "They are well-informed. There is talk of a trapped human. A young rat has taken quite a liking to her."

Gabriel's heartbeat paused at this news, hope sparking to life where it had almost faded to nothing. "How do you know this? Is the rat with her?"

"No, he has returned from where he found her. I have mentally marked him, so when he moves, it will notify me. But..." Leo's eyes opened, and he met Gabriel's unblinking stare. "Something worried him."

"Worried? A rat worries?"

Leo shrugged. "In their own way. A sense of foreboding."

"Damn it, Leo. I don't want to know." Gabriel arched his back and roared, venting his frustration at the powerless moon. He sucked in sharp breaths, clinging with desperation to the vestiges of his control. "We're running out of time. I'm barely holding it together. Just find Callie. I give you one more hour before I start bashing down doors and storming cellars."

"She needs you focused."

Gabriel grunted. Telling him what Callie needed was futile. He wanted her found, at all costs. "Can you reach Darius yet?"

The question startled Leo, jumping at the change of subject, and he closed his eyes again. "East."

Gabriel levitated, not waiting. To restore what Leo had taken, he had to feed, but more than this, he couldn't stand idly by. He *would* find Callie. He had to. At least, Leo flew alongside him. Whether he did so out of friendship or a misplaced affection for Callie, Gabriel was grateful. "Can you command the rat to return to her, to bite her? I placed an *aeterme* on her left inner wrist."

"You did explain what she needs to do?" Leo nodded at Gabriel's pointed look. "Of course you did. I can suggest, as I would do with humans. Seems like rat brains work along similar lines." Leo paused in flight, hovering in place as he compelled the rat to return to Callie.

He opened his eyes with a snap, and shot forward, changing his direction to southeast. Gabriel followed. A surge of hope warmed his chest again, but hunger and weakness overshadowed it. "I need to feed."

Spotting one of their clubs, Elixir, he descended. He landed in front of the bouncer and entered. The club manager, Lyssa, rushed forward, her clothing leaving nothing to the imagination. He didn't take the time to note her assets so on display, having seen it all before.

"Lyssa, I need to feed. Now."

Her eyes widened then without a wasted second, held out her wrist. "I offer freely."

Gabriel snatched her wrist into his hand and bit down. He drank deeply, then closed her wounds with a flick. "More." His voice shook, impatience and despair crushing his vocal cords.

"Gabriel? What's the matter?" Lyssa traced a finger across his chest.

"I don't have time, Lyssa. Get me more, please." With his patience gone, his usual civility had been stripped from his words.

What drove him was something far more primal, harkening to the days of old, when vampires were brutal. Much had changed, and humans had stopped fearing them. There were still a few that practiced the old ways, but Syl had done much to absorb many of their members into his Holds.

Lyssa jolted, stared before raising her hand and summoning one of her girls. The young human woman ran up to her, offered her wrist, and mumbled the required words. He bit down on her wrist, drinking deeply before closing the wound. With a nod, he bolted out of Elixir and up into the air where Leo waited. Together, they moved southeast.

Leo drew to a halt to flash a bright smile. The satisfaction that crossed his face forced Gabriel to stop as well. "The rat has found her." He closed his eyes, and his brow furrowed. "But..."

Fire burst across Gabriel's wrist, and he gasped, holding his hand up to look at the pulsing orange *aeterme* symbol. Unadulterated joy burned through him, with hope blossoming to consume his heart. Tears pressed behind his eyes. He smiled, unable to prevent happiness from curling his lips.

Spinning in a circle, the *aeterme* brightened and weakened until its pulse was at its strongest. He headed in that direction, focusing on each house or building in the hopes it was the correct one.

He grunted when he spotted Dimitri's *pal'tsy* crowding the front entrance of an old brownstone. They stood tall, spaced from each other in precise intervals, as formidable as the rumors indicated. Amongst them was a man, one who had red staining Gabriel's vision, freezing the fire within his chest, hardening his muscles and his jaw.

After landing in the middle of their gathering, he threw the first punch, connecting with Darius's mouth. His nails extended as he swung again, slashing his face. The beating removed his infuriating smirk, not that this appeased Gabriel. Nothing could soothe the pain, the punishment he'd endured.

"Where is she, Darius?" he asked, his voice low enough to scare the most hardened of vampires.

The *pal'tsy* shifted, but they remained in position.

"You are too late." Darius spat blood from his mouth, as his lacerated skin sealed.

"Too late for what?" Gabriel asked, dreading the answer. Darius was smug, lacking fear as if he'd accomplished what he'd set out to do and his death mattered not.

"To sire her, of course."

Gabriel wrapped his fingers around Darius's throat, squeezing, fighting the temptation to end his life. Dark whisperings—long unheard and seductive in their influence—commanded him to kill him.

"Find Callie first," Leo said. "What does the *aeterme* say?"

"*Aeterme?*" Darius growled around the tight fist crushing his esophagus. "How did you come by this? It's an ancient forgotten magic," he said. As soon as Gabriel released him, he fell to his knees, gasping and choking.

Gabriel held up his wrist and spun on the spot, striding in the direction of the pulse. She wasn't in the house the *pal'tsy* guarded. As he walked away from them, so they followed, dragging Darius with them.

Chapter Twenty-Seven

LOSING TIME

The door opened, creaking under its weight, its impenetrable thickness now revealed.

Callie rose to her feet, standing strong despite the desire to cover her nudity. Doing so was futile, and she accepted that. The man who strode through the door was not Darius. Darkness moved with him, an evil that saturated his every pore. He smiled in a father-like fashion, but it was insincere. There was no kindness, no mercy in his eyes. He approached her, and she fought the urge to step away from his encroaching evil.

She grimaced, now realizing that Darius hadn't taken her for his selfish pleasure. He'd done so under this man's instruction. Were his posture and strides regal? She smothered a snort. Every tall, distinguished suckblood fit that description. She couldn't just assume this man was the missing key to her case. Perhaps Syl could organize a lineup.

Not wanting to ask Syl for anything, she curled her lips in distaste.

"He could have clothed you, at least," the stranger said with a sigh, flicking a hand.

In an instant, crimson leather encased her in an outfit a dominatrix would've been proud to own. Her hair fell down her back in thick waves, as if she'd visited a hair salon. A leather bustier hugged her waist, thrusting her breasts upward, promising them freedom. Crimson knee-high boots clung to her calves, and garters wrapped around her upper thighs. A suspender belt in leather and lace completed the ensemble.

Such a vampire cliché. At least she was clean and *somewhat* clothed.

"I can't thank you enough for this wonderful adventure and exquisite clothing," she said, bringing her legendary sarcasm into the conversation. "Now to what do I owe this inconvenience, and of course, your scintillating presence?"

Tasting her own blood was the only warning she received. He slapped her head to the side. Her inner cheek smashed against her teeth, and blood pooled in her mouth as the sting of the cut made itself known. He grabbed her jaw, squishing her lips open to press his mouth to hers, sucking the blood out of her.

A shiver of disgust racked through her at his warm lips on hers, at the scent of him. He didn't stink, per se, just smelled oily. It was the same smell she came across at gruesome murder scenes, usually the ones involving the mutilation of children. As if evil lingered in the shadows and gathering crowds, watching her work even as it planned its next brutality.

She jerked away, surprised that she managed to. She smeared her bleeding mouth on her hand, grimacing at the sight of the crimson streaks along her inner wrist to her palm.

"Your taste is unique, but nothing out of the ordinary. What is it about you that has Gabriel de Winter claiming you?"

"I'm fantastic in bed." She dodged his swinging palm—she wasn't a fool. "So what do you want?"

He smirked, folding his arms across his massive chest. On his designer suit's lapel was a pin—a bird on fire with a delta symbol in relief. *What the hell?* Phoenix meets delta? Could he be the Carter connection?

"Darius informs me Leo cannot read you?"

"That's why I'm here, so you can ask me a question? A phone call was beyond you? I find your hospitality lacking, and your decorator should be fired." She gestured to the empty cellar. No food, no chair? She tutted. "Perhaps send a driver next time you need to speak to me? Or a text message would do. Try it sometime."

"I can remove your tongue for you, woman." He stepped closer, his posture threatening.

Her legs locked in place, the bottom part of her not afraid of the walking-death-dealer in front of her. The rest of her trembled. "No, Leo cannot read me. Or so he says. It still doesn't explain why you went to these lengths to take me."

"Detective Callista Devereaux, you disappoint me." He tucked a curl behind her ear and caressed her jaw as he leaned back. His fingertips were smooth, as if he'd never done a day's labor in his life.

She clenched her jaw under his touch, withdrawing, but not enough to lose face.

"Tell me, as a youngling, are you not hungry? Thirsty?"

"I *am* thirsty. A bottle of water would be wonderful." She licked her dry lips, tasting her own blood, but the thought of water made her salivate.

"Water?" He chuckled, the cold sound skittering along her nerves.

His fangs dimpled his bottom lip as he raised his wrist to his mouth. He sliced his skin, and a thin ruby rivulet flowed, dripping onto the dirt floor. The scent of it made her stomach coil. In his other hand, a chilled bottle of water appeared. Without thought, she grabbed it before he vanished it. With trembling fingers, she fumbled with the lid before gulping down the cool liquid, a moan of appreciation humming along her throat.

"Water?" His surprise was clear in his voice, but she didn't look at him, intent on quenching her thirst.

When she did regard him, it was in time to catch him licking his wrist to heal his wound.

"I came here to kill you, my dear."

She blinked, amazed at his candid words. Fear spiked through her. Death by his hands would be a gruesome one, not the possible one Gabe would have offered her.

Swallowing past the new lump in her throat, she tamped down the fear before it consumed her. To stay alive meant keeping her wits about her.

"What for? You can't trust Darius to do a good job?"

"I wanted to taste your infamous blood. Rumor has it you're a myth. As usual, rumors are unreliable." He waved a hand, and the room filled with furniture, antiques, lush carpets, lined bookshelves, and candlelight. "I will keep you alive for a little longer. Your disrespect is refreshing...for now."

"Don't do me any favors." She wasn't willing to admit that the bed did look inviting.

Hesitating, she chewed on her lip, weighing her options. A sharp tug from her stomach reminded her what was important here. She didn't want any more favors from him but needed to keep her strength up. "But if you're offering, how about a steak, a baked potato, and a green salad?"

Gabe was coming—it was her duty to be alive when he did.

A plate appeared on the Queen Anne table, along with a fresh bottle of water. Char-grilled steak perfumed the air, and her mouth watered in anticipation.

"Thank you." Her words were sincere this time.

She pulled out the chair and sat, taking a deep breath. "Your name? Or should I be calling you master? Sire? Boss man? Oh-captain-my-captain?" She sliced a chunk of steak off and shoved it into her mouth, not caring that her manners were not at their finest. She was starving due to this idiot's shenanigans. The steak was soft, done to perfection, and melted on her tongue. She moaned and fluttered her eyes closed in bliss.

"Stavros." He flashed her a—surprisingly—genuine smile.

And she could envision the young attractive man he'd been before he'd sold his soul to an evil she hunted daily. He'd given his name with arrogance, as if revealing it would cost him nothing. Identifying him was all she needed to investigate further.

"So you're not going to share why you took me? None of what you've said makes sense. Vendetta with the de Winters? Or with Gabe?" She needed to get this man talking, to gain clues, anything to help her escape.

"Gabe?"

"My fiancé." She wrapped her lips around a forkful of steak.

Out of the corner of her eye, she caught his head jerking up, and he scowled. The terrifying man who had entered her cell was back. Darkness reformed around him, and she nodded. As per her initial assessment, he was evil personified. They said Satan could be charming, charismatic, and if Stavros was his emissary, she'd believe it.

"How did they...?" He glared and advanced toward her. His head jerked again, and this time she heard it too. Footsteps on wood. "I've placed an ancient containment rune on this cell. They cannot find you." He dissolved into mist and left through the door's keyhole.

She gaped at the spot where he'd been a second ago. What the fuck? She hadn't known suckbloods could do that...whatever that was.

George scampered from under the bed and up onto the table.

"Oh, so now you show yourself?" She cut pieces from her steak and potato and placed it on the polished wooden surface for George to nibble on. "Welcome back, buddy."

As they ate, she listened for movement. The earlier footsteps had faded. She scooped up the second bottle of water, pressed her palm onto the wood so George could climb on, and moved to the bed. She placed him on the pillow and sprawled alongside him, not caring that her boots might ruin the covers.

"It seems my death is imminent, George." Her eyelids drooped now that her stomach was full. Lassitude called to her.

As she drifted on the edge, she sent another plea, hoping Leo could hear her.

It's about damn time, Callie. Gabe's gone insane. It's taking all my power to keep him calm. Where the fuck are you? His voice penetrated her mind, loud and angry.

She winced at his sharp piercing words, even though concern saturated his tone.

In a cellar, Leo. I can't say where exactly, or what's above me. How...how long has it been?

A day, at the most. Can you hear or smell anything that could guide us?

At his question, she squeezed her eyes shut and focused her hearing, having not thought to do so. She didn't castigate herself for not knowing, since she'd been a human until yesterday. *I can hear church bells and a play school.* She paused to listen. *A nightclub and a mosque.*

Smear your blood across the symbol to strengthen it. I'll let Gabe know.

Warm tears welled in her eyes. *Don't leave me, please, Leo.*

Keep your mind open, sweetheart. You're shutting me out.

She groaned. *I'm sorry, I don't know how...*

Imagine a door with my name written on it. Open it.

She drew in a deep breath and focused. It would be an ancient imbuia door carved with strange runes. Three letters burned into the wood. L. E. O., and in her handwriting. Grabbing the ornate brass handle, she yanked it open.

Shit! Leo voiced. *Just a little, not all the way.*

Sorry. She closed the door until a sliver remained.

We'll find you, sweetheart.

She held her inner wrist to her lips and waited. Her pulse pattered, her senses alert to the sound, the scent of her blood pumping through her body. *Argh.* She didn't know how to make her new teeth extend, but the sharp tug on her upper gums had her sighing.

Two incisors pierced her bottom lip, drawing blood—salt, spice, and iron coated her tongue. She smeared it across her wrist where she'd streaked her blood earlier. That was fortuitous.

The orange symbol glowed. She whispered Gabe's name across it and spun in a circle. When there was a pulse, she froze. He was in the direction of the mosque. Excitement skittered through her, and she cried out, unable to contain her renewed hope.

He'd find her soon.

She ran the tip of her tongue over her lip, healing the tiny tear. Instant healing was a neat trick. Being on the opposite side of the playing field was strange. Cytotoxin-tipped daggers would harm *her* now.

She clambered onto the bed again. George scurried up and curled into a ball on her chest, content to wait and rest as well. She smiled, stroked his little forehead with a fingertip, and allowed sleep to claim her.

Her eyes flew open at the first wooden creak. She doubted she'd slept for more than ten minutes. Exhaustion dogged her, along with a demanding thirst. She frowned at its persistence, accepting that it wasn't a good sign.

George jumped up and down on her chest in eagerness, summoning a smile. He didn't scurry away as he'd done with Stavros.

"So no one bad is coming, hey, buddy?" she teased, and he paused, twitching his nose. "Okay, off you get."

He bounded off as she pushed herself into a sitting position. Her crimson boots and garters caught her eye, and she grimaced. It wasn't the best outfit in which to entertain guests, but neither was her nudity. The sheets could be made into a toga. She pushed off the bed to fashion one when the door opened.

The tall man who strode in had hope spiking through her. Except the shape of him was wrong, drooping her shoulders in despair. She didn't drop her guard, assessing whether he was friend or foe. Her instincts weren't screaming, and George wasn't hiding.

No man should look this good. Ebony curls cascaded over a face carved by angels. Strong square jaw, firm lips, and molded cheekbones to piercing green eyes. As she analyzed him, he studied her. Warmth swept her body, trailing the path of his emerald gaze. She drew in a deep breath and scented an ancient vampire. The power flowing off him was almost visible. Where that knowledge came from, she couldn't say. His long hair, in various shades of black, brushed his shoulders as he entered her cell.

"Ah, *tsvetok*. I can see why Gabriel claimed you," he said, his voice rough, she suspected due to an interwoven scar that ran up his throat.

A scarred vampire? Interesting.

He lifted his nose and scented the air, scowling as if he recognized it. "Stavros was here?"

"Yes, he implied he was curious, but I doubt you could go to the bank with anything he said." She kept a set distance between them.

When he stalked forward, she scampered back. After all, he could be a friend of Darius, which would make him her enemy. Her instincts could be wrong or delayed in their warnings. They'd been lax of late.

"Stavros's involvement complicates things. I thought I would ensure you were well, clothed, and fed before Gabriel descends those steps." He admired the length of her again, pausing for a while on her garters. "I need not have bothered."

"Gabe's here?" She gasped, taking a step toward the open door before halting.

It could be a trap. Wariness was an unexpected gift from her forced confinement. For all she knew, he had a similar gift to Leo.

"Ah, you don't trust me. It's understandable. I'm a stranger. My name's Dimitri Vasiliev, head of the Vasiliev Hold. It's a pleasure to meet the woman who has inspired loyalty within two of the most powerful vamps I know."

"Leo's here?" Joy hit her, for if Leo was here then she could easily verify this man's identity. *Leo?*

Yes, Callie?

Can I trust Dimitri?

Yes, though I'd advise you to stay below. Gabe's dealing out justice, and it's not pretty. Mike approves.

Mike's here too? She flashed a huge smile at Dimitri, unable to contain it.

"Do you wish to feed?" He offered her his wrist. "I give freely."

"No...thank you. The only suckblood I wish to drink from is Gabe."

"Suckblood?" He chuckled. "So not starving?"

"Stavros summoned a steak for me. I'm super thirsty, though. Could I have another bottle of water?"

"Water?" Confusion furrowed his brow and narrowed his eyes, but he created a bottle out of the ether for her.

She took it, giving him a nod of thanks before opening it to drain it. She tossed the empty bottle on the bed and reached for George. He scurried up her arm to find a seat on her shoulder. Despite Leo's warning, she climbed the narrow stairs, finding the steel-heeled boots easy to move in. She stepped into the moonlight, inhaling the fresh air deep into her lungs, picking up a myriad of other scents she couldn't identify.

With a contented smile, she scanned her surroundings until she found Gabe with his fingernails embedded in Darius's throat, drawing rivulets of blood as he lifted the man off his feet.

"Callie's mine. *My* woman," Gabe roared, his knuckles whitening as he squeezed harder, enough to silence the murmurs escaping Darius. "I will not allow this to go unpunished."

Every curve and line of his face was visible to her, and she paused to memorize him, imprinting his furious yet handsome image into her mind.

"He'll always be her sire," Leo said.

Gabe grunted, ripped his fingers out, and severed Darius's head with one smooth slash. He raised his bloody hand to the heavens, and a bolt of lightning struck Darius's healing corpse, incinerating him in seconds. "Not anymore."

She stumbled back, bouncing off Dimitri's chest. "Holy shit."

She had never seen the like. Gabe had said they had power over the elements, so that didn't surprise her. What took her breath away was the beauty of her man seeking vengeance on her behalf. Desire made her core throb just as a white heat dropped her to her knees. She cried out under the sheer agony coursing through her veins. Wave after wave swept through her body. Tremors and spasms followed.

Gabe called her name like a whisper in the wind, but she couldn't gather the strength to look for him. Dimitri scooped her into his arms as the blessed relief of darkness claimed her.

Chapter Twenty-Eight

AT LAST

Gabriel stared at the scorched concrete, at the black charred marks in the shape of Darius's headless body. The lightning strike was final, but he couldn't regret his actions. He'd have to answer to the Drimari and the council, not that he gave a damn now.

He glanced at Mike who nodded, a primal pleasure in the old detective's eyes. The man approved, and for that, Gabriel was grateful. As much as he warned Syl not to, Gabriel didn't want to bring the police down on the de Winter Hold either.

For Callie, he didn't give a shit about the Hold.

The cry that pierced the nocturnal silence was one he'd recognize anywhere. He spun as her scent reached him. The vision of her crumpling into Dimitri's arms was bittersweet. She'd never looked as beautiful, the clothing she wore arousing more than relief within him. Dimitri's hands on her skin made Gabriel's vision tinge a crimson to match her bustier. He bolted forward and snatched her out of his friend's arms, extending a warning with his pheromones, as well as his posture. His Callie was to remain untouched. He hunched over her in a protective embrace.

"Relax, Gabriel. I didn't want her hurting herself on the concrete." Dimitri held up his hands in a submissive manner. "She's yours, *brat*."

"Why did you dress her so?" Gabriel roared, not liking that the *pal'tsy* were ogling her. He glared at each one, forcing them to look away.

Dimitri raised his hand, and his men dispersed. "I did not. Stavros did. His scent lingers in her cellar, and Callie confirmed his presence."

"Stavros? That can't be. I killed him in Paris." At Dimitri's wince, Gabriel sighed. "I'm sorry, Dimitri. I didn't mean to imply you scented wrong. I can't imagine how he escaped my death trap."

"You didn't bolt him?" Dimitri's green gaze darted to all that remained of Darius.

"I wish I had. Then this wouldn't have happened. I wouldn't have endangered her. My arrogance has cost me, us. Dimitri, I...can't live without her."

"Stavros has targeted her, but he hasn't harmed her yet."

Gabriel cuddled her closer, only then noticing the eyes peering from the depth of her curls. *A rat?* The one that had formed a fondness for Callie? He eyed Leo, nudging his head at the observer.

"Leo, is this our rat?" A smile curled his upper lip. Many aspects had united to locate Callie, including this little rodent.

"Yes, and I'm sorry to say, he's here to stay. She even named him, Gabriel."

"Of course she did." Warmth blossomed in his chest—bright, overwhelming, snatching his breath. Most women wouldn't have befriended a feral rat.

"When she awakens from the power burn, you will need to aid her." Dimitri maintained eye contact, as if to convey the severity of his warning.

Gabriel scowled, having not considered what Darius's death might mean to Callie. All his powers had transferred to her, and the unexpectedness of it must have overwhelmed her. "Aid her how?"

"She refused my blood, asking for water, instead. This is not the norm." Dimitri ran a knuckle along his scar. "The youngling sickness hasn't hit her yet, and I've never seen it this delayed."

"Thank you for your concern, Dimitri, and for your *pal'tsy*. Any sense on Stavros's location? I'd like a word or two with him."

"As would I. I understand why you bolted Darius. I just wished you'd waited. He might have provided some much-needed information." Dimitri shrugged before flashing his ne'er-do-well smile. "What we have here is a mystery. One I'm eager to solve."

"Do come by for a drink. I'm certain Callie would like to thank you in person."

"Tomorrow evening I shall be there." With that said, Dimitri burst across to Mike, shook the man's hand, then launched skyward.

Leo lowered a hand onto Gabriel's shoulder. "I'll bring Valerie tomorrow evening as well."

"Thank you, Leo. Without you, I'd be..." Gabriel's voice faltered. A sharp pain in the region of his heart reminded him of what he'd almost lost.

He lowered his gaze to Callie's face, and he allowed it full rein to memorize every nuance he'd come to treasure.

Leo chuckled. "Claiming a woman seems like effort, Gabriel. It weakens you, You're vulnerable now."

Gabriel shook his head. He hadn't regretted the Rite of *Adsumo,* and he doubted he ever would. "Callie calls herself my kryptonite, and she's right, Leo. I'd rather face my enemies than live without her."

"I wish you the fortitude for victory. Once Callie is ready, I suggest we train her. If she's as strong as you, then you need not fear your enemies." Leo gestured to Dimitri's disappearing back, volunteering his services.

Gabriel allowed a small smile to form. He was grateful for any aid his friends could offer. "I agree. We'll be a united front, and they'll regret ever trifling with us."

"Us? I like that. Perhaps I *should* claim a woman. It's been a while since I was an *us.*" Leo assessed Callie's prone form.

Gabriel scowled. He didn't like the intrigued and calculating expression on his friend's handsome yet exhausted face.

"Leonardo," he warned, his voice lowering to a growl.

"Not Callie, Gabriel. Valerie." Leo's focus turned inward, determination hardening his features.

Gabriel grunted. "Good because Callie's mine."

"Yes, yes, so you've said, demonstrated, and whined about. Can we go home now, because damn, I'm drained." Leo launched into the sky, but Gabriel hesitated. He faced Mike, still waiting at his opened car door.

"Thank you," he said the second Gabriel was close enough. "In a way, it's your fault this happened. But you also found her. So in my book, that cancels each other out. Just don't let it happen again. I'm old, Gabe. I can't lose her...the heart, y'know. I promised her father I'd take care of them both, and to fail now..." He rubbed his hand over his face. He'd aged ten years in the last day.

Gabriel listened to the man's faltering heartbeat and nodded. His heart *was* failing him, and it wouldn't be long. Losing Mike would devastate Callie.

"I could convert you," he said.

Mike jerked back as if punched, and he gaped, intrigued yet horrified. "I'll think about it. Tell Callie I'll call her tomorrow." He lowered himself into his car, shut the door with finality, and drove off.

Gabriel glanced at Callie and sighed. He surged into the cool night air, his attention remaining on her face, searching for any discomfort. He surrounded her with warm air, but her unending unconsciousness alarmed him. Had the power burn been unbearable?

He tried to remember Darius's lineage, but it was vague, as was his reason for acceptance into the de Winter Hold. Someone prominent had vouched for him, which would gain him entrance into the Hold. Obedience and verification of his lineage earned him membership.

Maybe she had a low pain threshold? Which also made no sense since she was a convert. Younglings could endure so much, survive many obstacles. Or was Darius's lineage ancient? Which meant all the power from his deceased sires had flown into her veins upon his death.

Gabriel would find out more in the next few days. For now, he needed her home, in his bed, and in his arms for as long as she'd allow it.

CHAPTER TWENTY-NINE

NEEDS

CALLIE AWOKE TO PITCH darkness, leaving her wondering what had disturbed her. She shut her eyes, drawing in a deep breath as she assessed her body and her surroundings. Exhaustion saturated her limbs, her mind, dragging her will to the depths of no return. She couldn't muster the energy to raise her hand. Just thinking of doing it had her yawning.

From the bed beneath her, sun-drenched sheets and a spicy scent engulfed her. She could smell Gabe, and she wondered how Stavros had managed that detail. She rolled onto her back and groaned as every muscle protested. She remembered suffering like this once when Captain had enrolled her detectives for martial arts training. Her calves had taken the brunt of it despite the muscle relaxants prescribed.

"George?" she whispered with her throat grated. The pattering of tiny feet along her arm and onto her chest had her opening her eyes to focus on her friendly rodent. "There you are, sweetheart."

His coat gleamed, and an aura of happiness strobed off him.

"What has you in such good spirits?" She smiled, wishing she could lift a finger to stroke his tiny head. He scampered closer to rub his cheek along her chin. "Love you too, buddy." She chuckled.

Raising an aching hand to cup him, she struggled into a sitting position.

"Do you think Gabe's still searching for us?" She asked the question aloud but her voice dwindled as the room's features penetrated her mind.

It looked like Gabe's room. Had Stavros been there before, and knew it well enough to replicate it to this extent? A shiver rippled through her, reminding her she was in pain. The thought of that man staring at them while they slept wasn't a pleasant one. It would explain a lot, though, like how he had perfected Gabe's scent. Even the door was in the correct spot. It opened on silent hinges, and her breath hitched. She clutched George to her chest as she bit down on her lip to smother any reaction on her part.

The bare-chested man who stepped through the door had disbelief, hope, and bright joy warring for supremacy in her heart.

"Gabe?" She silently begged the Lord to let this man be him and not a Stavros-illusion.

He flicked his fingers, and the room brightened, slow enough to allow her eyes to adjust. Gabe stood there in nothing but black silk yoga pants hanging low on his hips, revealing his Adonis belt to her hungry gaze. Golden light played across his torso and pebbled nipples. She admired the bared length of him, skimming over the dazzling smile curling his sensual lips. Arresting her attention was the expression in his gray eyes. Joy, gratitude, and affection were easy to discern, for they echoed within her.

"I wanted to be here when you awoke." His voice thickened with emotion.

"I wasn't alone." She stroked George's neck.

"I can see that." He chuckled before clambering onto the bed to tug her into his arms. His embrace tightened as he buried his nose in the crook of her neck. She burrowed into him, relief draining her tension, pouring lethargy through her limbs. She was grateful he was careful not to crush George, but being in his arms meant she was safe, home.

"I can't express how happy I am to have you home." His muffled words echoed her thoughts. "How are you feeling? Hungry? Thirsty? Whatever you need, Callie."

She lifted George to her shoulder, then rested her palms on Gabe's chest, relishing the velvet heat of him. "I'm thirsty, and I could do with a rare steak."

"Callie." He leaned away to cup her cheek. "As a youngling, you need blood."

"I know, it's just that I'm craving steak. Besides, the only blood I'd drink is yours. Oh, and about that..." She sat up and glared at him. "When were you planning on revealing your deceit?"

"What deceit?" His expression was one of innocence.

The consummate actor, the freaking suckblood.

"That you've been converting me every time we fucked? It's my decision, Gabriel. Mine!" She shoved him back so she could scramble away from him. Sitting still and berating him trembled her body with pent-up energy.

"I didn't decide on a date or time. Sharing of blood is part of a vamp's sexuality, and I hoped doing it this way would be the least painful for you." He rested against the headboard, folding his arms behind his head, and crossed his ankles, as if her furious tirade wasn't justifiable.

"Right, you deceived me to help me. How noble of you." She paused her pacing to glower.

"Callie, what truly upsets you?"

"Every time you do something like this, it shakes my trust in you. What if I died during the conversion? You tell me Val is fine, but I haven't seen her in a while. If I died, it would be without bidding her goodbye."

"The slower the conversion, the higher the success. I'd never jeopardize your life. You must know that, otherwise, why claim you? Besides, Leo's bringing Val over tomorrow."

"Tomorrow?" she squeaked, gulping past the lump in her throat.

Gabe sighed, uncrossed his ankles to slide off the bed. He circled his arms around her as if she wasn't furious with him.

"Promise?" She dipped her head to assess him, determining whether he deceived her again. Regardless, her anger dissipated. She wanted to stomp her foot, to rage, but he dangled Val like a carrot. "Don't lie to me again, Gabe. I'm a big girl, I can handle harsh truths."

He lifted her gaze to meet his with a finger under her chin. His lips curled in that familiar smile, the one that broke the rhythm of her heart. "Let's get you fed, then we'll see to your *other* needs."

He led her back to bed as a tray appeared before her. Steam rose from the steak, and a seared-beef aroma greeted her. She gathered her utensils, ignoring her shaking hands. George scampered down her arm and onto the tray, so she set a piece aside before taking her first bite. She groaned as garlic and rosemary coated her tongue.

"Good?" Gabe teased her.

She nodded. "It tastes chargrilled. I thought you said I'd lose my taste buds," she said between mouthfuls.

"You have."

"No. Rosemary, garlic, pepper." She grabbed her water bottle and downed it after serving George a capful. "Right, buddy? You taste it too?"

His nose twitched, and she laughed, stroking the curve of his back while he drank.

"Your conversion was unusual. I don't know if keeping your taste buds should be alarming. Mind if I borrow her for a while, George?" Gabe scooped up the rodent and placed him on Callie's pillow.

He vanished the tray and the dirty dishes before lifting her into his arms. She was content to let him carry her. In the bathroom, a steaming tub awaited her with petals floating on its surface. Exotic fragrances rose to welcome her as he lowered her into the water. Her protesting muscles relaxed, drawing a moan from her.

He pampered her, washing her hair a few times, massaging the knots in her shoulders from police work before running a soapy hand all over her body. His tented pants, his shallow breathing and trembling hands made his arousal evident.

She had never been so treasured. Vibrating through her was the feathering of his fingers, his breath skittering along her skin, his thundering heartbeat, and the blood rushing through his veins.

She watched him under heavy-lidded lashes, poking at her reactions to him. Her core throbbed with an aching need, and her nipples stiffened in anticipation. Her own blood rushed through her, sending shivers and excitement to the tips of her toes.

Gabriel admired Callie soaking in the tub he'd prepared for her. That the effort it cost him was a flick of a finger wasn't the point. He'd thought to do it for her and had done it. What drew his repeated focus wasn't her blissful and beautiful smile. The water's soapy and petalled surface played peekaboo with her nipples.

He'd knelt beside the tub to soap every delicious inch of her, had ignored her grumbled protests, and listened to her sighs, instead. Yes, his arousal throbbed, demanding attention, but nothing mattered more than his Callie.

"I'm clean, Gabe." She sat up to cup his cheek.

He paused at the sight of her breasts rising from the water. Glancing at her face, he clasped her hand with his.

"How about you show me how much you missed me?" Her lips curled into a breath-taking smile. Her green eyes glowed with heat and raw need. Black circled her irises, telling him she would need to feed soon.

He pictured her hair pinned at her crown and watched as it did so. The soap and petals cleared from the water to reveal her delectable nudity for him. She was so beautiful, so vibrant. With a slow inhalation expanding his lungs to the fullest degree, he vanished his pants and stepped into the water, standing before her with his erection proud and eager. She gripped him on each thigh to run her tongue along the length of him. His knees trembled, and he released a deep groan.

"Callie, please, I'm not strong enough."

She tilted back, blessed him with a sultry smile, and opened her arms. He grunted, lowering himself into the water to press his body against hers. She looped her legs around his hips, and the head of his erection nestled at her entrance. He squeezed his eyes shut to gain control. He wanted to thrust into her, to have her surround him. She was his home, his sanctuary.

"I've missed you." She kissed his chin before she plucked at his lips with hers.

He opened his mouth for a deep kiss, his tongue mimicking what he wanted to do to her.

Clinging to him, she arched her hips, begging him to take her. "Gabe." She gasped, breaking away from their kiss. "Please don't go slow. I need you. This...*you* are tormenting me."

After launching them into the air, he floated her down, feet landing on the tiled floor, then pinned her against the wall. "Remember, you asked for it."

"Begged for it." She tightened her legs around him.

He dipped the tip of his erection in, finding her more than ready. With a thrust, he growled. The soft, tight heat of her engulfed him. Moon above, she felt incredible. As did the kisses she feathered along his shoulder. He withdrew to thrust into her again. She arched, crushing her breasts against his chest, a keening sound tearing from her.

"So good," she said between pants. "Again, do it again." She kissed him with a passion he'd missed.

As he pistoned into her, increasing his pace, fiery tingles burned from his balls to the tip of his erection. She feathered kisses and nips along his throat to his shoulder. Then she bit him, her teeth sinking into his flesh. Heat—bright, sweet, and intoxicating—hit him, hiking his arousal. As she drank from him, the euphoria bolstered him. With a roar, he orgasmed, unable to fight the flood of pleasure, nor control his thrusting hips. Her pulsating channel didn't help, causing mini orgasms as she climaxed around him. She licked the bite wound, the rasp of her tongue searing his very soul.

"Have I told you I missed you too?" He brushed her damp hair from her face, using his hips and the wall to hold her up.

"No, not that I can remember. But even if you did, you're more than welcome to tell me again." Her sassy mouth curled into that joyful smile he adored.

"Moon above, Callie, don't ever leave me again."

"You say that as if I had a choice, Gabe?" With a quick kiss to his mouth, she lowered her legs.

He stepped back but kept his hands on her hips, not quite ready to release her.

"Tomorrow, you train me. If any asshole wants a piece of me, I'm going to give him a fight he'll remember." She paused to trace her bare toe over the shiny marble tile. "What happened to Darius? I have a vague recollection of him headless?"

"I killed him," Gabriel said, his voice devoid of emotion. He searched her face. She was law enforcement, after all, but he couldn't keep it a secret, not with an eternal bond. None knew of its origin, but the strength of such a telepathic bond meant no memories or thoughts remained hidden. He would share his centuries of existence, as she would share her life's adventures with him.

"How? Suckbloods are immortal." She rested her hands on his forearms, her thumbs stroking his hair there.

He loved her doing that, as if she needed to touch him.

"It's called bolting. I sliced off his head and summoned lightning to disintegrate his body."

"Summoned lightning?" Her mouth gaped, and the tempting dark pink called to him.

He dipped his head for a kiss, inhaling her breath as if he could merge their souls.

"A vampire can summon any form of nature. If not lightning, then fire will do. It was nighttime and in the middle of a street, so creating a storm was more appropriate." He feathered kisses to her earlobe before nipping at it.

"There was a man named Dimitri? He found me first?" Her voice was throaty and arousing.

Gabriel adored her flushed face, trailing caresses along her jaw. Confusion flitted across her eyes, and he nodded, understanding that her recollection of last night might not be clear. He could take the time to assuage her doubts or concerns. Not for long, though. He couldn't resist the temptation of her parted thighs and soft skin pressed against him.

"Yes, it's forbidden to hunt in another Hold's territory, even for a de Winter. Leo asked his permission, and he decided to help with his *pal'tsy*. They are excellent at hunting. He'll visit tonight, along with your sister, Mike, and Leo."

"Do you know Stavros?"

She scraped her nails over his nipples, and he growled, yanking up her leg to nestle his arousal, wanting...no, needing to bury himself in her again.

"Stavros is a thorn in mine and Dimitri's side. I should've killed him when I had the chance." Regret, a bitter pill to swallow and one that could linger for centuries.

"Why didn't you?"

A question he had asked himself too many times in the last day. "He's Abigail's brother. She was a woman I loved. It's my fault she died, and my fault Stavros plagues me."

Chapter Thirty

OLD LOVE, NEW LOVE

"What?" Callie gasped. "The woman you loved?"

She jerked back. Jealousy was swift, lancing through her before her pragmatic mind had a chance to warn her. She wanted to push him away, but the desire pooling in her core wouldn't tolerate that. Torn between her heart and her body, with the latter winning, she kept him close. She'd give him a chance to explain. Then he'd better finish what he'd started.

"Many years ago, I fell in love with a human. When I revealed what I was, she ran from me. Stavros confronted me, and we fought. It wasn't my proudest moment. I was stronger than him, but the need to take the arrogant upstart down a peg drove me. Neither of us knows who killed her. She tried to come between us, but one of us threw her back. She smacked her head on a rock when she fell." He grimaced, his eyes shrouding in shadow as he remembered. "Stavros begged me to convert her, to save her, but she drew her last breath before the conversion took hold."

"He blames you." Callie's heart broke at the sorrow in Gabe's eyes. "You blame yourself."

He nodded, his lips pinching white. He pulled away from her, but she tightened her legs, trapping him. Cupping his face, she kept his focus on her. His intense gray eyes shimmered with sadness, self-recrimination, and unforgiveness.

"Gabe, this was years ago. You can't let it beat you up like this. Abigail's death wasn't your fault. Don't assume the blame for Darius's actions either. Stop. Analyze it from all angles before you accept accountability. From my perspective, as an ex-victim, I don't blame you at all. I doubt Abigail would have. You did try to save her." She feathered a kiss across his lips. "You're my hero, Gabriel de Winter." Her voice cracked under the potent emotions that claimed her chest, but she didn't care to analyze them.

"I am?" A hesitant smile formed. "But I failed you."

"Did you? You claimed me when you could've left me to die. You found me and killed Darius. Or am I dreaming I'm in your arms, enjoying your touch? How much you've pampered me in the last hour?" She drew in a shuddering sigh, gyrating her hips to enhance the sensations of his erection against her.

He pressed his mouth over hers. She savored his soft lips, inhaled his scent, and tasted his heat, then moaned as he did as she had silently asked. He lifted her other leg, and with one thrust, buried himself to the hilt. She cried out, her thoughts drowning in pleasure. Within minutes, with their breathing erratic, he carried her back to their room. When he opened the door, he stilled. He remained there, staring at their bed.

"Callie," he whispered, then lowered her feet to the floor, and twisted her toward the bed.

Her breath hitched at the girl curled up on the pillow. She was asleep, her bare body shivering.

"Is that...George?" Callie asked Gabe, stepping farther into the room, careful to make as little sound as possible. "Dress her please, Gabe." With a flick of his wrist, pink pajamas covered the child. Her long black hair, minutes ago a bird's nest, was now braided. Tiny bunny slippers adorned her feet. "How is this possible?"

"She's a shifter, Callie. Though, how she changes from a rat into a girl, I can't say. Many vampires have yearned to understand the genetics of our mortal enemies. It's therefore understandable why the shifters choose not to reveal their...magic."

"Magic?" She mouthed, arching her brow. Disbelief consumed her mind, but she brushed it aside. It was a human reaction, which she wasn't anymore. The evidence of the glowing orange symbol on her wrist should have proved she knew nothing of his...their world.

She sat on the side of the bed. A diaphanous negligee with a deep-V neckline appeared, hugging her curves. She shot a look at Gabe despite smiling. A matching gown appeared, and she sighed, accepting she was lucky to get that. Soon, he would show her how to conjure items as he did. If she relied on him for her wardrobe, who knew what he'd dress her in.

"Gabe? I have to save her." She brushed a curl off the little girl's forehead.

"I understand, but she's a shifter in a vampire Hold. Her life won't be safe here either."

"What if she has no one?" She raised wide eyes, pleading with him.

"If she chooses to stay with us, Callie, then she's welcome. You take care of George. I'll create a bedroom for her." Gabe kissed her temple and left.

She stared after him, her heart swelling to overflowing, seizing her breath. He was such a wonderful man. Somehow he'd known chasing George away would tear Callie apart.

"George?" She stroked the girl's cheek, trying to wake her without frightening her.

Her long eyelashes fluttered against her caramel skin, and big black eyes peered up at Callie.

"It's Tara, but I like George better." She scrambled to sit up, all thin limbs and clumsiness. She rubbed an eye with her small hand, and Callie's heart softened.

Offering George a gentle smile, she climbed on the bed to lean against the headboard and tugged the girl onto her lap. "George it is, then."

"Did Gabe dress me?" She snuggled against Callie, who kept her arms wrapped around her.

"Yes. Do you like it?"

"I do, though I shouldn't. Pink's easy to spot." Her words hinted at a sad history, one where George had to linger in the shadows to survive.

Callie scowled. "There's no need to hide anymore. You're with me now. I've got you, little one."

"Gabe's a vampire," George whispered.

"So am I. Are you scared of me too?"

"I'm not scared," she said, despite the squeak in her voice.

"Of course you're not. You're fearless, George. So spill it. You're a shifter?" she asked, and George nodded. "Right. Where are your parents?"

"It's just my mama, and she couldn't keep me, not when I'm a poly."

"Poly?"

"My brothers are wolf cubs. I should've been one."

The way she said that had Callie frowning. There was longing in her voice, as if being a werewolf meant she belonged. Callie could relate to the need for a family. It must be a universal need, across all species.

"We have to find your mom," Callie said, but George trembled in her arms.

A sharp unpleasant smell followed. She shifted to face the little girl, connecting the child's gaping mouth and wide eyes to the acrid stench.

"N-no, please. Mama said to never come back." Her stilted cry broke something in Callie.

"What about your alpha?" Beasts have those, right? Like in her romance novels.

"He's mean. Mama said he hates poly-shifters, so staying home would make him angry."

"I'd love to keep you, sweetheart. We just need to make sure we can."

"You'd keep me?" The hope on George's face was painful to witness.

Callie crushed her in her arms, kissing her temple.

"I'd love you like a daughter." She stroked her black hair, hoping George could remain with her, and that there were no other obstacles to hinder adoption.

She'd been there for Callie when she needed help. There was nothing in the world that would force her to abandon George who needed her now. Even if she couldn't keep her, Callie wouldn't abandon her.

"You will?" There was a sniffle then a sob.

Callie let her cry, but rubbed her hair and back, hoping to convey how safe she was.

"Gabe's readying your bedroom. I've no idea where it is, but it's yours if you want it."

"My own room?" George hiccupped.

"Yes, it's all yours. You're kind of stuck with me, whether you stay or not. I'm in your life for good."

"As am I," Gabe said from the doorway.

George jerked back, her head popping up to meet his gaze.

He bounded over and landed on the bed, shaking it. "I hope you like pink...tons of it, because it's my favorite color. Everyone knows vampires can't like pink. We *have* to wear blacks and grays. That's more fitting."

George giggled, shaking her head. "I like pink too. It's not a shifter color either."

"We'll make it our family color." Gabe flashed a charming smile. "Are you hungry? You had a nibble of Callie's steak, but I can get you anything you want, princess."

"You can?" She gasped, lifting wide eyes to Callie. "Like pizza? Hotdogs? Ice cream?" Her voice rose with excitement, squealing with delight.

"Sure," Gabe said.

"Don't you want to see your room first? We can eat in the kitchen afterward." Callie was curious where George's bedroom was.

"Like a family?" George asked in a soft voice, hope, excitement, and joy splitting her cheeks with a bright smile.

"Yes." Gabe scooped George into his arms, spinning her as he carried her out of the room.

She squealed in delight but clung to him, just in case. Her fear had lessened but hadn't left her completely. That would take time.

Callie followed, wiping away a stray tear.

Chapter Thirty-One

ENTERTAINING

Gabriel forced himself to glance at his ancient Greek texts. He would read a line, then find himself watching Callie. She sat on the Persian carpet with her files strewn around her, a frown furrowing her brow. She'd shuffle papers, scribble a note, and sigh. The lighting caressed her auburn hair, the shape of her cheek, the pink of her lips. He was as fascinated by her as the day he'd met her.

Every fifteen minutes or so, George would rush out of her room, having discovered a new toy or book or to parade a clothing item. His heart swelled when Callie's face softened, and she'd tug George onto her lap for a cuddle. The little girl would jump up to show Gabriel her discovery with excitement and pure joy in her eyes. Such innocence was a rare gift.

He'd receive castigation for bringing a shifter into his home, perhaps even mocked for his decision. Surrounded by vampires wouldn't make her life easier. They would bully and demean her, but not if he was near, or so help them. He'd already contacted the alphas to locate the one he should murder. Tossing a child out into the streets to survive on her own was unacceptable.

She belonged to the Knights Ridge Pack, but their new alpha, Rhys Whitaker, hadn't known anything about this. The fury pouring across the connection meant this alpha planned to mete out a justice of his own. Gabriel had stated his intention to adopt the girl, leaving no opening for Rhys to argue otherwise. That he'd used Dimitri's and Syl's Holds as a threat was neither here nor there.

Callie tilted her head, listening. Gabriel smiled at this development since it meant her vampire traits were, at last, manifesting. Leo and Valerie were at the door, but he'd wanted her to use her senses. She jumped up and rushed there, swinging it open with a cry. Hugs and tears followed, interspersed with blurred chatter. The growing joy on her face was all he needed to confirm she was happy.

"Gabe, come meet my sister." She turned to him; her fingers laced with Val's.

She had the same red flowing hair and green eyes, but to him, no woman was more beautiful than Callie.

He strode toward them, holding out a hand. "Welcome to our home, sister of mine." He clasped Val's hand with his before releasing it.

Her eyes widened, and she glanced at Callie.

"Yes, you heard him. Gabe's my future husband." Callie looped her free hand around his waist and squeezed, lifting her shining eyes to meet his.

Something tight gripped his heart, but now wasn't the time for declarations.

"I'll have a brother-in-law?" Val asked then hugged Gabe, surprising him.

He gave her an awkward pat on the back.

"You have to meet George. She's your niece!" Callie bounced away, then returned to give Gabe a quick kiss. "It's time for girl talk, so no eavesdropping, both of you." She wagged a finger at Leo, who thumbed through Callie's files strewn on the carpet.

Gabriel stared at George's closed door. Giggling and squealing came from behind it. He winced, silently agreeing not to eavesdrop if that was what he'd overhear.

"A recent addition to our Hold is a woman named Monique. Her father is Senator Carter." Leo tapped the senator's picture. "Had I known Callie investigated the man, I might have mentioned that tidbit." He scrolled his fingertip along a line of text. "It says here she died in a motor vehicle accident. I saw her just this morning drinking from a feeder."

"I don't know if it has any bearing on Callie's investigation." Gabriel shrugged. "Tell me, Leo, is it possible for a youngling to taste rosemary or garlic?"

"No. There have been a few instances where other senses have been sluggish to convert but never taste. Why do you ask?"

"No reason." Gabriel grinned.

Leo could pluck his thoughts out of his head, so he waited and watched. His friend's face grew serious, then he arched a brow. "Most senses transform within a week of conversion. I am interested to see if Callie falls in line." He took the nearest chair and sipped from the snifter of brandy he'd materialized.

"Thank you for bringing Val. I'll owe you," Gabriel said.

Leo met his gaze and nodded. "Adopting a shifter? I'm not sure Syl will allow it."

"I don't see why not. Her mother tossed her out like she was garbage, Leo." A wave of protectiveness swept through Gabriel, and he grimaced. How could he already feel as if George was his own child? He did admire the little girl for helping a stranger. That said more about her character than anything else could have. "I'd like you to spend time with her. See for yourself she means us no harm."

"I intend to. Syl will demand it. That's not what concerns me, Gabriel. There are many with prejudice, or downright hatred, for all things shifter. We need to train Callie and Val as soon as possible. They must be able to defend themselves."

Gabriel had intended to start her training tomorrow. "Dimitri said the same thing. Between the three of us, their training will include various skill sets."

"Can you scent Val?" Leo asked, a frown marring his features.

Gabriel lifted his nose and inhaled, picking up Callie's addictive essence and George's sweetness mixed with puppy. Val had no scent, no indication of her presence.

"No. I've never encountered that before," Gabriel said.

"Neither have I."

"It might be their bloodline. Callie, do you have other sisters?" Gabriel asked, loud enough for her to hear him above their chatting.

"No, Gabe, just Val and me." She popped her head around the door.

"We do have female cousins in the Devereaux line," Valerie said. The door opened, and she appeared with a coffee in hand. She seated herself in the empty chair and winked at Callie, who'd climbed onto Gabe's lap. He wrapped his arms around her, tugging her against his chest.

"Thank you for saving my sister."

He nodded before planting a kiss on Callie's head. George dropped onto the rug, content to play with her doll.

"Leo, did you do this?" Callie gestured to Valerie's appearance.

"No, your sister did that all by herself."

"Val, it looks like the dress I got you for Christmas. Those are the Prada pumps you spent a fortune on and only wore once."

Valerie glanced at herself, and pink stained her cheeks. "I did wear it more than once," she whispered, and shyness leaked into her expression, softening her features.

With a flick of Gabe's fingers, Callie's outfit changed from jeans and a T-shirt to a form-hugging red velvet gown, her feet covered in decadent red peep-toe pumps, her hair he'd pinned up in a chignon. She squealed her surprise, bringing forth an answering chuckle from him. With another flick, she was back in her jeans.

"Keep the shoes," she said, planting a quick kiss on his chin.

Valerie's eyes opened wide. Then she laughed.

"The conversion healed you," Gabriel said when her laughter dwindled into a smile.

"Yes, with blood as my new addiction." She grimaced.

A few younglings retained their human distaste for blood, so that wasn't unusual.

"What happens to my sister now, Leo?" Callie's directness had Leo's gaze meeting Valerie's.

"I asked to be her sire. She's under my protection and guidance."

"Like a slave?" Callie asked, anger crisping her voice.

"Like a student." Leo evaporated his glass and stood. "On that note, come, Valerie, let's not overstay our welcome."

She rose to her feet, placing her empty mug on the side table. Callie stiffened. "But—"

"Callista, if you want to see her, open your mental door and talk to me," Leo said, his tone abrasive. "That goes for you too," he grumbled at Valerie.

She didn't respond, just wrapped her arms around his neck.

"Ready," she said, and with that, they dissolved.

"Intriguing," Gabriel flashed Callie a smile.

"Yes. It looks like Leo has developed a fascination with my sister. So what did you two discuss?"

"Could you scent your sister?" Gabriel asked.

Callie frowned and tilted her head. "She smells like she used to before the chemo."

He sent the information to Leo and received a grunt for his trouble. "Leo said something about Carter's daughter, Monique, being a recent recruit."

"Then she faked her death to become a suckblood?" Callie darted off his lap and rifled through her files, eagerness cementing her features.

He leaned forward and scooped George onto his lap, wrapping his arms around her tiny body.

"What do you want for lunch today, princess?" he asked, considering going grocery shopping for items she could help herself to. Fruit, snacks, juice? He was uncertain what products she liked.

"Hot dogs!" She bounced on his lap.

"Again?" he teased. "How about you and I sneak off to do grocery shopping?"

She jumped off his lap with a squeal and disappeared into her room with a singsong. "Getting my shoes!"

He rose to circle his arms around Callie, burying his face in her neck.

She patted his arm, distracted.

Grinning, he nuzzled her hair. "You should talk to Leo. It looks like he might have information to share." She blinked, twisting to kiss his cheek. "I'm taking George shopping. See you later?"

"Have fun."

She jolted and spun in his arms to bless him with a hot and spicy kiss. "Hurry back," she said, a little breathless. "But enjoy this time with George."

Chapter Thirty-Two

A THEORY

Gabriel and George arrived home carrying many packages. Some held food items, but most were things that had brought a bright smile to George's face. Was he spoiling her? Yes, he was, and loving every minute of it. He did explain she received leniencies now because he and Callie had never had a daughter. That they would learn how to be a family together.

George was silent for the trip home.

He shot glances at her, trying to assess her mood from her stern expressions. After she clambered out of the parked car, she wrapped her arms around his legs. "Thank you, Gabriel."

The little minx had wheedled her way into his hardened heart without trying. He chuckled, bending to press a kiss on her head.

The scene that greeted him arched his brow. Sprawled on the rug, along with Callie's files, was Dimitri, Leo, and Mike. George darted around, bouncing with joy and laughter, blessing everyone with hugs.

"What did you get?" Callie asked as she walked through the kitchen door with a coffee in hand. It held cream and sugar, the way she liked it.

Their daughter burst across the room to throw her arms around Callie's legs.

"Gabe is wonderful!" George squealed, her enthusiasm drawing a smile from Callie, who ruffled her hair, even as she dragged a lustful gaze over Gabe's body.

"I know." She flashed him a meaningful look.

He huffed, scanning their guests and George's happy smile. It still wasn't the time for declarations. He needed to reveal how he felt, but circumstances thwarted his every attempt.

"Why don't you show me what you bought, George?" Callie leaned against his chest and brushed her lips across his. Then with a deep sigh, gathered the bags out of his hands and disappeared into the kitchen with a chattering George.

He rubbed the warm spot on his chest, gazing at the closed door with longing. Mike rose to speak with him, hovering at his side until he faced him. He gestured to outside. Gabriel led the way, curious as to why they needed privacy.

"It's a yes, if the offer still stands." Mike cleared his throat, awaiting Gabriel's response.

He nodded, having anticipated his choice. "I'll have Leo organize a suitable sire. You'd better not die on me. She'll kill me if she finds out that I offered."

"I'll try." Mike's chuckle sounded forced, but Gabriel ignored it as they slipped back inside.

Whatever led Mike to choose a life of a vampire must have torn the detective apart. It wasn't an easy decision to make, but his conversion would be more enjoyable than Gabriel's had been. They used civilized techniques, blurring the pain with lust. Not like the violence he'd endured for decades until he could stand on his own.

After dropping into a leather chair, he studied the strewn files with unseeing eyes. Mike took the chair alongside him, his stubby fingers plucking at the stitched leather.

"Anything new?" Gabriel gestured to the scribblings marring Callie's case files.

"Yes." Mike beamed with excitement. Gone was his earlier reticence. "We've linked Duhamel and Carter, but more than this—"

"Stavros is behind the cure." Dimitri's Russian accent sliced through Mike's enthusiasm, and he quieted, leaning forward in the chair lest he miss a word.

"Stavros?" Gabriel frowned, once again wishing he'd killed the man. This and all the death staining his hands were on Gabriel's shoulders. He thought he'd loved Abigail, that sparing Stavros's life was what she would have wanted.

"Stavros owns Floges, a silent partner, but the CEO, Hawkins, is clean. We haven't told Callie yet," Mike whispered.

Gabriel chuckled, then whispered back, "She can hear you."

Color mottled Mike's cheeks, and he released a resigned sigh.

"Floges sponsored the mayor and Carter's campaign through various shadow organizations. The link isn't easy to find, not if you don't know what to look for," Leo said. "Floges has a department known as Delta, created to research vaccines."

"This note," Dimitri tapped Callie's scribble of Stavros's lapel pin, "was the key. Flames, a delta symbol, and a Phoenix. Such a blatant connection hidden in plain sight would appeal to his sense of humor. He's on a mission to destroy you, Gabriel, and the de Winter Hold." He sipped his materialized vodka.

"Including the shifters in his plan was genius." Leo pinched the bridge of his nose, his voice strained. "From Syl's memories, I have determined they played it from a human-hates-vampire perspective, claiming humans were about to destroy the chemical. The shifters pretended to save our species. Syl's a better judge of character than this, which implies the shifters didn't know they were part of the plan."

"I wouldn't put it past Carter or Stavros to play both sides," Gabriel said. What amazed him was that the plan unraveled with such ease, and it had gone unnoticed by all. "If Stavros tampered with the cure and deceived the shifters, wouldn't it kill on both sides if an all-out war erupted between us? We are on the cusp. A spark is all it would take."

"*Der'mo!*" Dimitri cursed. "Where's the cure now?" He shifted on his backside as nervous energy coursed through him.

His heart pounded loud enough for Gabriel to discern without focusing his hearing.

They faced Leo, who had fallen silent, now deep in thought.

"In our labs, Syl says. He didn't trust their altruism." Leo flashed a smile. "I'm pleased to say our king isn't as easy to dupe as they'd hoped."

"We still need to deal with the shifters," Dimitri said, raising his glass as if in salute.

"How?" Gabriel frowned at Dimitri's simple statement. "That's an ongoing battle for territory, resources, humans. Stavros has kept his side clean. Carter and Duhamel are human politicians, so untouchable."

"We can't kill them?" Dimitri flashed a look at Mike, who held up his hands in surrender.

Mike shrugged. "I wasn't here."

"That's a strange attitude for law enforcement to have," Dimitri teased.

"Dragging Callie into the middle of this made it personal." Mike folded his arms across his chest, appearing uncomfortable with the topic. "She's had files on these idiots for ages. That makes them dirty in my eyes, and if need be, I'll shoot to kill."

"Syl's on his way," Leo said. "Alone."

Gabriel offered Mike a whisky, who blinked at the materialized glass but accepted it. After taking a tentative sip, he smacked his lips in appreciation.

"You have been busy," Syl said to Gabriel as he appeared in his lounge. "Your taste in company has deteriorated." He looked at Mike who nodded a greeting but didn't get up to leave or appear offended by Syl's statement. "I hear you scoured the slums to adopt a daughter. I'm not sure how I feel about this, Gabriel." He raised his nose and sniffed, scrunching his face as if George's scent was unbearable.

Gabriel growled, his nostrils flaring. He drew in a calming breath before facing his brother. "I love you, Syl, you know that, but mess with my family and you force me to challenge you for the throne."

Syl jerked as if punched. "Is that a threat?" His posture stiffened as he squared his shoulders and curled his fingers into fists, but sorrow lingered in his eyes.

"No, of course not. It's a plea, little brother. I will blood vow that I won't contest your rule if you bless my daughter."

"Bless her?" Syl grumbled under his breath, which was more for effect. "Let me meet her first. If I accept her place here in your home, she may never set foot in the Hold. For her safety, of course."

Dimitri glared at Syl. "She's welcome in mine."

Gabriel placed a hand over his heart, grateful for his support.

"You have your *pal'tsy* to keep your members in line, Dimitri." Ice chilled Syl's voice, his full authority clipping each syllable. "I have long considered the need for our own enforcement, something I was hoping to discuss with Callista. Regardless, I cannot claim your daughter as my niece, Gabriel, no matter how much I might want to."

"I'll assess her and the danger she brings." Leo closed his eyes and nodded as if he had a private word with Syl.

"Good. Now that we've dealt with this, let's discuss the canister." Syl huffed a resigned sigh.

The kitchen door opened, and George darted across the room to throw herself into Dimitri's arms, startling him, but he recovered, tickling her until she squealed and giggled. Callie trailed, a strange, conflicted expression on her face. She must have overheard Syl's words, or George's unexpected affection for Dimitri alarmed her.

Gabriel gritted his teeth against his frustration and the need for their bond to be complete. How was he expected to know her needs without it?

"George, come meet Lord de Winter." Callie held out her hand.

Dimitri rose, bringing George with him. He lowered her to her feet but remained standing behind her, his warning clear.

"Hello, Lord," George said in a small voice as she cowered behind Callie's leg.

"I hear you saved Callista," Syl said in a gentle tone. "You have the heart of a mighty warrior."

Gabriel hid his surprise by glancing away. He hadn't known his brother remembered how to talk to children. Centuries had passed since they'd last encountered anything younger than teenagers, and no one, not even humans, could talk to teens.

George shook her head, tossing her curls. "It's not nice being alone. When I felt that man coming, I ran...I'm sorry." She faltered, her eyes growing wide before she buried her face in shame. "He scared me."

"Which man?" Syl knelt to tuck a curl behind her ear.

"He gave us food, but he wasn't a nice man. He's not coming here, is he?" She raised a large fear-filled gaze to Syl, her body trembling.

Gabriel gripped the chair, the urge to gather her in his arms and protect her sweeping through him. He didn't want to dwell on how much his solitary life had changed.

"Gabriel and Callie wouldn't let any harm befall you, *malen'kiy*," Dimitri said.

She released Callie's leg to leap into his arms. Snuggling against him, she settled with a contented sigh. Their bond was disturbing despite its beauty. Perhaps the trust had formed when Dimitri had rescued Callie?

Gabriel shot a look at Leo and arched a brow. *Investigate this, will you?* he asked, tossing the request in thought.

I plan to, Leo said.

Gabriel waved a hand, and a mahogany table appeared with Callie's files now strewn across its polished surface.

"Start at the beginning," he said to Syl.

Dimitri slid into a chair with George still clinging to him. Her eyes drooped, and after the day she had, Gabriel wasn't surprised.

Callie chose the seat next to Gabriel, her warmth spreading to his palm when she laced her fingers with his. She left the farthest chair for Syl.

He sat, his brow furrowing with concern. "Alrik, the previous alpha of the Knights Ridge, approached me saying they'd discovered, through various sources, the cure to vampire infertility."

Callie gasped before breaking into a relieved and delighted smile. Her shoulders relaxed, but she squeezed Gabriel's hand with her excitement barely contained.

Syl materialized a snifter of brandy, staring at its amber liquid before swirling it. "Of course, I didn't trust him. So, I played along and agreed to test a sample. The results were promising. The women smelled fertile, so I purchased the canister. It's in our lab now. The chemical breakdown is different, though, as if they have added something since the sample. We have yet to test it on women for obvious reasons."

"What if you say you tested it?" Mike asked. "Hear me out." He raised his hands in supplication. "They're watching, waiting. I know I would. React as if the cure is killing your women. Start gathering your forces as if you plan to attack the beasts...I mean, shifters."

"Yes...that could work. I would chat first to the new alpha, Rhys. Find out if he's in on Stavros's plan." Gabriel gestured with his head to Leo, suggesting Syl take him with to the meeting.

"If he is oblivious, we can deceive Stavros with a fake war." Dimitri grinned, revealing how eager he was to best Stavros.

"No one likes to be played," Callie said.

"Monique, Carter's daughter, must reveal her existence to her father to end his vendetta, and if he cannot accept what she's become, then we'll destroy him." Syl gave Leo a make-it-happen look.

"Carter won't go down alone. He'll take Duhamel with him," Mike said.

"That leaves Stavros." Dimitri grinned, his eyes sparkling.

"This ruse should flush him out," Leo said, sipping his cognac.

"He's after Gabriel. We'll use him as bait." Dimitri rubbed his palms together. The full details as to why he hated Stavros were still unknown.

"Keep my family safe." Gabriel shot a glance at Callie's pinched lips.

"No." She slammed her fist on the armrest. "I'm with you."

"I need you safe." He tried to keep the pleading from his voice. After her abduction, he wouldn't survive it if she was in danger again.

"As I need you to be. We do this together, Gabe." She folded her arms across her chest.

He shook his head, his heart racing. The idea of Callie in danger... "You're no match for Stavros. I have yet to train you."

"I don't care." She raised her chin and glowered. "I've taken down suckbloods before."

"We can escalate her training," Dimitri said.

Gabriel clenched his fists and stared him down for his suggestion, his glare lethal and long, until Dimitri at last glanced away. "I planned to, but even if we had months to train her, Stavros has had centuries to hone his skills." He threw a pointed look at Callie, conveying his decision was final.

Typical of her to ignore his command. "I'm a detective, Gabe. Danger I can deal with. Losing you or George? Not so much."

Silence descended then Syl said, "I see the bond is not complete yet."

"Everything with Callie's conversion is unusual. It's as if she's still human." Leo's expression deepened in thought.

"Are you reading my mind?" Her body stiffened as she challenged him.

Gabriel hid a smirk.

"Parts of it." Leo's honest response drew forth a head shake from Mike. The man didn't realize how much danger he was in. "As I understand, you've walled your inner sanctum. I can't penetrate it, which means neither can the bond."

"Leo, get out of my head or so help me," she threatened, placing a white-knuckled fist on the table's surface.

"But—" He flinched, his skin paling.

Pain marred his features, but Gabriel didn't care what she had done to him. All that mattered was the sudden influx of emotions, thoughts, and memories that were not his own. Whatever she'd done had opened herself to the *Adsumo*.

He gasped, shuddering at the sweet, intense overload. Every one of his senses sparked to life. Goosebumps skittered across his skin, and his nipples responded in kind.

"Out," he growled, unable to regulate his voice.

Dimitri rose, taking Mike and George with him, while Leo and Syl evaporated.

"George?" Callie squeaked. She twisted in her chair to stare at Gabriel, waiting for an answer.

"Dimitri will care for her." His voice deepened as he relished their connection.

Closing his eyes, he drew her into his arms. Concern was her core emotion, at the unexpected exodus, nervous about George, worried about Gabriel's strange behavior. With one bold and joyful decision, she placed her trust in him, as she'd done from the day they'd met.

"Do you feel it?" He kissed her temple.

Her gasp was her answer, along with the tightening of her arms around him. "What is that? Are those your memories?"

"And my emotions." His voice was husky. "All that I feel for you, Callista."

"You love me?" Her voice filled with hope and surprise.

"As you love me." He wallowed in the core of her mind.

The glowing warm depths shone for him, saturating the dark recesses of his soul. He stopped breathing, not that it was a necessity, but it was indicative of how much her opinion of him mattered. Now she'd know how much she meant to him.

"You loved me from the start." Her lips curled into a delicious smile. "You *knew* what you were doing when you spoke the Rite of *Adsumo* over me. You had every intention of keeping me forever, regardless of my permission."

"But you did agree—your honor demanded you keep your word. That, and your hatred for Syl." He laughed, unable to contain the blissful happiness inside him. *I never thought I'd be grateful to Syl.*

"Did you just...?" *Speak to me telepathically?* Awe graced her features, along with doubt and fear.

Yes, it's what claiming can do. A bond forms that surpasses all boundaries. With this complete, we are married, Callie. You are mine, at last.

Have I told you I love you, Mr. de Winter? She trailed her fingertips along his collarbone.

His heartbeat pounded out a new rhythm. She loved him. He'd suspected, had wanted to ask her many times, but to have her tell him, of her own free will...it was precious to him.

No, you haven't, Mrs. de Winter. "You *have* shown me though."

She leaned closer to feather her lips along his neck. "There's power in the spoken word."

He agreed, then again, she had power over him, by word and deed.

"It changes hope to reality." He plucked the words from her mind. "Tonight, I have other plans for your lips and for your tongue."

She giggled, lifting her sparkling emerald gaze to meet his. *Show me.*

Chapter Thirty-Three

To Be a Suck-Blood

"To make something from within yourself, you need to imagine every aspect of it, every detail. Hold it in your mind and will it to appear." A ruby-red rose formed in Gabe's fingers, close enough for its fragrance to tickle Callie's nose. "As much detail as you can think of will solidify the conjure. Weak vampires create illusions. Ancients and masters create substance."

"I'm exhausted, Gabe. We've been at this for hours, and I'm lucky if I get pixie dust." She stomped her foot in frustration, and hell, even that drained her.

"If a talentless youngling can conjure, so can you." He stood before her and crossed his arms over his muscular chest. "Besides, if you don't master these skills, you're staying home."

She glared, hating that she agreed with his threat. He was right to demand she learn because without these skills, she'd be a liability.

She took a deep breath, focusing on an image of a rose. She imagined the velvet petals, the light playing on them, the sweet, intoxicating scent, and a thornless stem. After five minutes of willing it to appear in her hand, all she got was another shimmer of pixie dust—a swirl of peach light. A vague outline of a rose appeared, but she filed that under an overactive imagination and a desperate need to conquer this skill.

Try something you are familiar with.

She huffed at his thoughts. It implied she hadn't received many roses in her life to imagine the delicate flowers well enough. He was right, of course.

His continued patience and calm acceptance of her failures encouraged yet saddened her. She didn't want to disappoint him. Warmth and energy flowed through their link, strengthening it the more they used it.

An image of a berretta formulated in her mind, complete with a personalized engraving on the grip and a telescopic lens. She imagined its internal mechanisms, the sound of it cocking, and the peach glow came sooner. She held her breath, tense with hope and excitement. Within seconds she held a loaded handgun.

"Awesome." She bounced on her toes as she tested its scope. Her grin cracked her cheeks in half. The euphoria saturating her chest had her giggling.

"Good." He gave a mouthwatering smile. "Now make it vanish. Imagine it dissolving into molecules, and draw the energy back into yourself."

The gun turned into ash, which coated her palm like a thick layer of paint before fading into her skin.

Unusual but it worked.

"Unusual good, or unusual bad?" She studied her palm.

"Just different. You can do that for your body as well. Imagine it fading into microscopic molecules, then reforming. Though, that requires extensive practice. How we see ourselves isn't always reality. Now try clothes. Evaporate your shirt and don another."

With a slow wave of her hand, her T-shirt dissolved, and another wave had her in a black bustier with satin ribbons. His breath hitched, and judging by the images fluttering through their connection, she had his full attention.

A flamboyant wave later, she completed the ensemble with knee-high boots plucked from his mind. The stockings and garters with micro-panties were her idea. His desire, the strength of it, bombarded her through their link, and she couldn't halt the heat rippling through her body at his vivid fantasies.

"Is that all it takes?" she teased, albeit with a breathless tremor in her voice.

Yes.

An hour later they were back in the exercise room he had constructed for training. She wore her gym leggings and a sports bra, which suited the current lesson—learning how to burst with speed. When the room went black, her instincts kicked in. She didn't need them. The panic that pumped adrenaline through her veins subsided. She could see Gabe in the dark even as her hearing sharpened and the steady rhythm of his heartbeat called to her.

He'd yet to drink from her, and she wondered about that. Was he concerned she was still weak?

Yes, I'm concerned.

"I thought it's because I'm not delicious anymore."

"Never, my love. I long to sate my thirst, to feel you orgasm around me when I do."

"I am well enough, Gabe. Drink from me tonight." The promise of pleasure swirled low in her belly. She cleared her throat. "Now, why do I see you in night-goggle-green, and you see me in infrared?" She shifted between her own vision and his shared one, undecided on which one she preferred.

"You were human, sweet Callie. It's logical for your mind to grasp familiar explanations. I'm an ancient predator. We didn't have technology when I was human. This is how I see in the dark."

"Shit. I was so naïve." Her last stakeout came to mind. She was lying on top of the container with her pistol in hand. No wonder suckbloods had never taken humans seriously.

He chuckled, circling an arm around her waist to kiss her temple. *Ready to try running?*

Within seconds, brand-new sneakers adorned her feet. She stared at them with her green-tinted vision and sighed. That she could conjure them amazed her. How long would she find that talent incredible before the novelty wore off? She suspected never.

You don't need sneakers. Your feet won't touch the ground.

As soon as they stepped outside under a full moon, she burst into a run, pumping her legs as hard as she could. Sweat beaded her forehead and upper lip as she struggled to breathe. She wasn't unfit by any stretch of the imagination, but this was ridiculous.

"You are running like a human." He chuckled as he jogged alongside her sprinting self.

"Running is running." She panted between words. "Pump legs, move forward. It's physics."

"Can you feel the wind's touch?"

She gulped, fighting for breaths, but shook her head.

A wind picked up, tossing her hair around her. It cooled her flushed face and neck, summoning a blissful sigh from her. "I feel it now." She flashed him a smile.

"Call to the wind and allow it to carry you," he said.

"What?" She stumbled to a halt and bent over, gripping her knees while sucking in air.

"Imagine you weigh no more than a feather adrift. Direct the wind and manage its speed."

"Holy shit." She straightened to rest her hands on her hips. "Are you freaking kidding me?"

He gathered her hand in his, palm upward, then swirled his fingers over it. Gray smoke twirled in a gentle tornado, tickling her. "Now you try."

She raised her fingers above the mini-vortex only for it to fall flat. He grinned, flicked his fingers again, and it spun upward. She glared at it, determined to win. She twirled her fingers in the opposite direction, and with a gasp, the micro-tornado halted mid-spiral and spun counterclockwise.

"Now call on the air around us, have it press against your back."

She did, whipping her hair forward to blind her. With a wave of her hand, her hair braided itself. She drew in a deep breath, still winded from her sprint, and imagined her feet lifting off the ground. With a yelp, she tilted forward, losing her balance. He grabbed her shoulders, and she formed a fist to smother the gray smoke still spiraling on her palm. He looped an arm around her waist and pressed his lips to her ear.

"Light as a feather," he said, his warm breath sending tingles along her neck.

She closed her eyes. The wind pushed at her back, and she twisted so it caressed her face.

You're so sexy. His masculine voice floated through her mind.

I am? An excitement of another sort set her insides on fire.

Your strength of will, your stubbornness. Lord of the moon, Callie. I love you. Love everything about you.

She giggled. *What brought this on?*

You're flying, my love.

"What?" she squeaked, opening her eyes to see the ground several feet below them. "Holy…"

Gabe released her to hover beside her. *It's not me doing this. It's you.* "Now propel yourself forward."

Joy—hot, intense, and overwhelming—gripped her, and she laughed, spinning in the air before darting forward. *Running's the same?*

Yes, just inches off the ground.

"Am I ready for Stavros?"

"Not yet. You *are* ready to train with Dimitri and his *pal'tsy*, though. They'll hone your skills."

"Okay. Gabe?" She held out her hand, asking for his. "Show me your world."

He laced his fingers through hers and shared the beauty of the night—the moon's pale silver caressing the ocean waves. The predators on the hunt. By the time they returned home, she had realized one important thing about herself. She was where she belonged.

She spun into his arms and scraped her fangs along his neck. His answering shiver rippled through her. She envisioned sliding her hands along his inner thighs as she nipped at the pulse in his neck. She projected latching her mouth on a certain part of his anatomy, and his breath caught, his fingers flexing on her hips.

"You play dirty," he said, his voice hoarse, flashing visions of his own, his psychic touch making her tremble with need.

By the time they made it to their home, they'd vanished each other's clothing. He pinned her to the wall with his arousal teasing her. With one thrust, he bit into her shoulder. Across their link, his orgasm mingled with hers, along with the chocolate flavor of her blood. She arched her back, bombarded with sensations on all sides, and shattered again, feeling as if the sheer pleasure would kill her.

She drifted back to reality, now nestled in his arms in their bed. He feathered kisses along her shoulder, spooning her from behind. The emotions coming from him were too intense, overpowering, and breathtaking for her to comment. Instead, she snuggled deeper into his embrace and kissed his forearm gripping her against him.

Gabe?

Yes, my love?

I love you too.

Callie didn't know how she felt about their plan or that they'd conceived it without her input. Sure, she'd eavesdropped to stay informed. She hadn't realized that as soon as they'd decided on a strategy, it would fall into place with immediate effect. Turns out, the beast's alpha, Rhys, hadn't known about Stavros's plan. In an unheard-of move, Rhys agreed to a truce and to play the role of a conniving beast. As she waited outside Metcalfe's open office, the suckbloods and beasts were mobilizing their forces and spreading rumors of an impending war.

Judging by her captain's expression, she'd just received the word. There was something to be said for suckblood hearing, because without any effort on her part, Callie could hear the mayor breathe through the phone line.

Metcalfe placed the phone down, stunned. A wince of guilt pierced Callie, and she sighed, accepting that what she was about to do would place Metcalfe under pressure. Warmth flooded through her, and an image of her hesitating formed in her mind—a projection from Gabe to show he was there for her. She flashed him an intimate image, something like yesterday's sensual endeavors, and his teasing, tormenting bombardment of his sexual fantasies ceased.

"Captain, do you have a minute?" She poked her head through the door.

Johanna had pulled her graying hair into a tight bun at the back of her head, and her pantsuit was crisp. It dared not crease, even after many hours of office work. She wouldn't have stood for it. "What do you want, Devereaux?" She gestured for Callie to enter her office.

She did, closing the door behind her. She faced her captain, who frowned at the door. Had Callie's need for privacy startled her, or did she see a shrouded Gabe leaning against the glass?

"This must be unwelcome news."

"You did task me to liaise with suckbloods, and despite everything going on, I managed..." Callie tried to smother a grin. Yup, liaison as in wife? That could work.

"No need to explain. There's time. I can't expect immediate results, Devereaux."

"Good, because I'm resigning." Callie said the words in a rush, taking the leap over the roiling emotion clambering inside her for supremacy.

Metcalfe blinked. "What? This is your life, your dream."

"I met a man, and he needs me to be something else. This job's no longer feasible." Callie smiled.

Choosing sides had changed her life for the better.

And my life too. Gabe wrapped psychic arms around her, his appreciation of her blossoming warmth inside her, as always.

"A man makes you give up your dream, and you agreed to it?" Metcalfe shoved back from her chair before striding around the desk to lean her backside on the front of it. "I never thought you'd be an idiot over a man."

"I'm a suckblood, Johanna." Callie raised her top lip to reveal her fangs.

Metcalfe's eyes widened, then she pursed her lips.

Yes, this was more like it. Her captain had an unholy dislike of suckbloods. Having gotten to know them better, Callie could argue their merits, but not when it came to Syl. He still rubbed her the wrong way. Whenever she saw him, the urge to spank his backside persisted, and not in a sexual way.

Gabe chuckled. *I used to feel the same way.*

"What the hell happened?" Metcalfe asked. "I said liaise not fucking join them."

"I got claimed. It's their version of marriage, just for eternity, with no possibility of divorce."

"Shit." Her shoulders slumped.

"I must build a suckblood police force. Y'know, to bridge the gap between our two species."

"Our?" Metcalfe asked with an arched brow. Her lips curled in a half-smile, which had Callie's breathing a sigh of relief.

"You know what I mean. I would suggest you and I brainstorm the hell out of this. It would look good on your resume, and I get to practice law enforcement, just for the other team this time."

"Intriguing." Metcalfe tapped her fingers on the edge of her desk. "Go on."

"Suckbloods have their own way of dealing with disobedience, and it's far more lethal than our...your justice system. Minor infractions receive a reprimand, a slap on the wrist. There's no documentation, and their...our way relies on memory." Callie darted her gaze at Gabe, who hovered by the door.

He flashed her an image of taking her on Metcalfe's desk, over the scattered documents, and she couldn't fight the flush on her cheeks. Didn't even bother trying.

"Want to meet him?" she asked, her gaze lingering on the width of his shoulders, the curve of his neck. Just one glimpse and her heartbeat thumped loud enough to deafen her. He flashed her a knowing smile that pooled desire in her core.

"No." Metcalfe shook her head.

"Suit yourself. He's with me all the time, shrouded."

"What?" Metcalfe's eyes widened in horror before she cleared her throat, collecting herself. "I didn't know they can do that."

"Now do you want to meet him?"

"Do I have a choice if he's in my damn office?" Metcalfe slapped her desk.

Callie shrugged at the outburst. Metcalfe always yelled and demanded, but Callie doubted she knew any other way to behave.

"Can you shroud?"

Callie frowned. "Not yet, still learning."

"I will teach her," Gabe said as he revealed his presence, having strolled to the window. "Hello, Captain Metcalfe. It's a pleasure to meet you, face to face." He strode forward to offer his hand.

Metcalfe accepted it, a little in awe and a lot in shock. Her hazel gaze traveled Gabe's body in disbelief.

"A pleasure to meet you too, Mr. de Winter."

Oh, shit. She recognized him. What the hell?

Callie quickly understood why, and she wanted to facepalm. Gabe was Syl's brother, and since Syl liked tuxedoes, it made sense that he schmoozed with the city's elite. Hell, Gabe might even know the mayor. Once again, her superpower of deduction had failed her.

"I apologize for stealing Callie from you, but one look at her and I knew." Images flashed across their bond, memories of when he met her, held her, first kissed her, all saturated with the emotions he'd felt at the time. Gabe wasn't kidding when he said he'd known from the start.

"I'm stunned at this turn of events. She's one of my warriors, determined to mete out justice no matter the species," Metcalfe said, surprising Callie.

She'd always assumed she was a burr on her captain's backside.

"She'll continue as a justice warrior. The only difference is that she's *mine* now."

"You had a suckblood on the force for over a week, Captain. I'm more than willing to do interviews if it will help your image." Callie looped an arm around Gabe's waist.

"Since the vampire is you, that makes it tolerable, Callie."

"That's the nicest thing you've ever said to me," Callie teased.

Metcalfe blushed, and at her dismissive gesture, Callie dragged Gabe out the door.

That went better than I expected. Gabe laced his fingers through hers.

Metcalfe isn't stupid. She sees the benefits of working closely with the Crimson Corps.

The what? He arched a brow.

She flashed him a smile. *Thinking of names for the new police. How about Suckblood Squad?*

He shook his head.

Blood Battalion?

He chuckled, drawing her against him for a sideways hug.

Vamp Force?

Better.

He kissed her then and there, in front of her ex-colleagues. They whooped and whistled, so she introduced Gabe as her husband. That shut them up before they crowded her to pound her back in congratulations.

Chapter Thirty-Four

THE STRATEGY OF ANCIENTS

Callie added extra sugar to her coffee, needing the sweetness after a trying day. Spending hours with Syl and Metcalfe yelling at each other had drained her. Typical of her ex-boss not to fear the king of suckbloods. Many a time, she'd thought this was the end for Metcalfe, but Syl had reined in his temper and the negotiations had continued. Leo, the coward, had disappeared an hour into the planning session. Callie wished she could've done the same.

With the claim bond between them, Gabe shared any conversations on the pseudo-battle planned, often asking her opinion. She was redundant, like a fifth wheel. Even though they all tried to include her in the decisions, the plan evolved and steamed ahead without her.

Dimitri had whisked George away at Rhys's suggestion. Surrounded by Dimitri's fingers, she was in no danger while she played with the Knights Ridge's children. Her home was empty, but she shoved the loneliness aside knowing George needed the interaction with other children, and Gabe needed to feel as if he protected his family. Still, twiddling her thumbs was a new experience for her.

A hot bath sounded enticing, and she giggled, a mischievous idea forming. She meandered to the bathroom and filled the tub with a wave of her hand before placing her coffee cup down. She projected teasing images of her undressing. Gabe rewarded her with sensual thoughts for her efforts.

Woman! He flashed a suitable punishment, but it didn't deter her.

I'm just having a bath. Little old me, all alone. What's an aroused girl supposed to do? She released an overdramatic sigh. *Play with myself?*

Callie, please. The plea in his voice gripped her with sadness, longing, and acceptance. *Wait for me.*

She climbed into the bath and sipped her coffee, no longer tormenting her husband. The bath had lost its appeal, and as soon as she'd finished her coffee, she stepped out of the water. With another swipe of her hand, her hair was dry and braided, her body in boring pajamas.

"Damn it." She stamped a slippered foot. "I've got to find a hobby."

The all-consuming burn of anger came next, and she stomped to the exercise room. There she worked through the stances Dimitri had taught her. When had her life become so dull? She married and lost who she was? What bullshit. She learned something new though—don't wear silk pajamas when exercising.

With sweat drenching her body and the silk clinging to her, she strode toward the kitchen in search of bottled water. Yes, she could make it appear out of the ether, or wherever, but it made no sense to do so when she was thirsty. Wouldn't it dehydrate her further? A question for another time. She grabbed a bottle out of the fridge and drained it.

Gabe stacked the fridge with the usual sachets of blood, but alongside those were snacks, juice, milk, fresh fruit, and vegetables for George. It was a visual sign of how things had changed for him.

After flicking her fingers, she was clean again, but hungry. Within minutes, she had pasta on the boil with the sauce simmering in a pan. She made enough for George for when Dimitri brought her home. The adage was true—a watched pot never boils. Even though she could make this also appear out of wherever, she had time to spare and boredom to kill.

Halfway through a bowl, there was a knock at the front door.

Bounding over to the door, she flung it open, expecting to see her sister, Leo, or Mike. The dark visage of Stavros shocked her, and she thought her twisted mind had conjured him. He stepped toward her, and she stumbled backward, uncertain what to do.

Mayday! Gabe, we have a visitor. She sent him the picture of Stavros standing in their entrance foyer.

Keep him occupied.

Gabe's command had her snorting. What tricks did he expect her to do? Dance the hula hoop? Do the fandango? Make a rabbit appear out of Stavros's backside? Popcorn and a movie?

I can hear your thoughts. Gabe's humor crossed the link.

Yes, well, what do you expect me to do? Recite Shakespeare?

"This is a surprise." She forced a tight smile and gestured to the couches, inviting Stavros to make himself comfortable. He'd do so anyway, regardless of her permission. She couldn't help but sense there was something less intimidating between this man and the one who had her kidnapped. This Stavros appeared broken.

"Since the Holds monitor my every move in the city, your home was a logical choice." He chose the chair facing the door.

Strategic of him, but expected.

"Your plan is working. Why aren't you elated?" She slid onto a chair and curled her leg under her backside. She might as well be comfortable.

"Carter's plan is working—mine was a failure." Stavros ran a frustrated hand over his face, mussing his hair. "Did Gabriel mention our history?"

"Yes," she said but refused to say more. This wasn't Christmas where he could hope she would gift him with information. The bastard would use it against her and her family.

She schooled her features, hiding how delighted she was he'd confirmed his connection to Carter.

"Did he say he killed my sister?" His eyes darkened, as did the skin under them. Contrasting with his serene expression was his stiff body and clenched knuckles.

"No, he said he didn't know who threw her back, and that she died before the conversion took hold."

Stavros grunted as his broad shoulders slumped. "Perhaps Gabriel was wise to move on, to find another love."

"It's tough to move on after losing a loved one."

It took her years to return to some sort of normal after Dad died. When Val received the fatal news, Callie had cleansed her home of any reminders of him. She couldn't deal with both and still be the rock her sister needed.

"I imagine it's harder for humans with their shorter lifespans," Stavros said.

I am almost there. Gabe's voice snatched her breath, and she released it in a slow exhale of relief.

No rush. She punched sarcasm behind her thoughts, to which she sensed his head shake.

"Do you blame Gabe, or yourself, for your sister's death?" she asked.

Stavros gasped, and he jerked back as if she slapped him. "How dare you?" His voice rose as anger mottled his features.

"Survivor's guilt is crippling, believe me." She didn't know what calmed him—her tone of voice or the sorrow that squeezed out a tear. He settled back in his chair, but his fingers gripped the leather armrests.

Seeing she was getting through to him, she decided to open up, keep him occupied. "Dad's death was *my* fault. Something no one wants to mention. He died saving me when I rushed in like a hothead. Outliving my older sister would've brought me to my knees." She drew in a shuddering breath, wiping at the tears with trembling fingers. "I can understand your hatred, your unforgiveness. I hunted Dad's killers and brought them to justice. With Val, how could I kill cancer? What could I do to save her? Hopelessness was the hardest thing to fight. It has no form, no source, and is indestructible. It forces you to face how pointless your existence is."

"Gabriel has chosen wisely," Stavros said, his voice above a rasp. "It has been too many years for me to relinquish the battle. Revenge was my focus, what drove me. How do I replace something that is part of me?" He dipped his head, sorrow slumping his shoulders.

"Forgive yourself. Only from there can you start anew. Find what brings you joy, and surround yourself with that. Find what gives you purpose. Without it, life fails to have meaning." She shook her head. "I struggled. I won't lie, Stavros. One day you will wake up, and all you will remember is how Abigail made you laugh, the sunlight dancing in her hair, and her teasing blue eyes." She had snatched the image of her from Gabe's memories.

"Blue eyes?" He shook his head. "You were a formidable foe. Many times, you almost thwarted my plans." He rose to his feet, and as he lifted his gaze to meet hers, his fake sorrow slipped from his smug smirk. "Your honorable heart is your weakness, Devereaux. But you are a fool to welcome me into your home, and hope I will change my wicked ways." He chuckled—cold, maniacal, sending trickles of ice down her spine. "Bid your husband farewell, Callista."

She gasped, her heartbeat roaring in her ears as a wave of heat flushed her face. His earnest tone had her hoping she could soften his resolve. She had never succumbed to a criminal's sweet talk and an evil bastard like Stavros would be the exception.

Honestly, where the hell are you? She jumped up, not liking Stavros looming over her.

"What do you want, Stavros?" she asked, stalling for time.

"I smell your fear, young one, and your anger. Your *beloved* cannot save you. Not this time." He looped his arm around her waist and yanked her against him.

"What are you doing?" Raising her chin with a glare, she pressed her palms against his chest. "Release me now!" She pushed, and despite a youngling's supposed strength, she couldn't budge him.

"Gabriel and the de Winter Hold will spend all their resources hunting for you. This will ensure the shifters win this war. You could say I'm doing my part for humanity."

Gabe!

Seconds later, Stavros dissolved her into a mist. Her mind clouded, enshrouded by gray walls of fog—unbreakable, impenetrable. She tested the boundaries, bouncing off them with each attempt. At the center of it was the loss of her connection with Gabe. A cold and dark void draining her hope, her strength.

Had Stavros killed him? Is that what the hollowness meant? Or was Stavros playing with her mind?

No, no. This can't be happening again.

You're a naïve little girl, my sweet. Stavros's voice echoed through the shroud. *I can keep you like this indefinitely. To choose another when he claimed to love my sister? I cannot condone such disloyalty.*

You are a psychopathic bastard, Callie screamed as she ran her fingers over the fog, searching for weaknesses. *You didn't want him to love Abigail. Now you're pissed off he loves me? I might not be a psychologist by profession, but I know batshit crazy when I see it.*

Converting you hasn't taught you respect. His tone was colder.

This delighted her. At least she was drawing a reaction from him.

You earn *respect, idiot. Any respect you ever had, you lost when your sister died.*

The fog pulsed, the edges shimmering with black. Lightning bursts of white sparked across its surface, so she grabbed for one, shoving her fist through it. The shroud quivered, encouraging her to force her other fist through the same crack. The energy and strength it took from her to widen the hole had her whimpering. Agony throbbed in her skull, shooting shards of glass through her body, and left sweat dripping off her chin. Her arms trembled as she fought the force of the closing hole.

Gabe! She sobbed his name, tears streaking down her cheeks unhindered. She hoped the crack was wide enough to reach him. If he was alive, he'd answer her. She pleaded with him to say something.

There was no response. Just soul-destroying silence.

Images, memories flashed in her mind. Of Mike shaking his head at something she'd said. A smiling Val standing alongside a perplexed Leo. George in Dimitri's arms, crying. Tears misting Gabe's gray eyes, and the abject sorrow dragging his mouth down. She wailed, crying out as her soul ripped from her.

She couldn't lose them…him.

There was no way in hell she'd let Stavros win. She had to find a way to end this cycle of revenge, or they'd never be safe. Callie kept her arms in the crack and closed her eyes, sucking in slow calming breaths, willing her tears to fade. She listened to her heart thumping a steady rhythm, ignoring the sensation of a thousand ants crawling across her skin as the shroud shrank, threatening to swallow her.

She always knew where the criminals were, where to fire when they attacked, and when to duck when they fired. Fey blood ran along her veins. As a legend, she could save herself.

Detective Callista Devereaux needed no one to help her, to free her.

That wasn't true. She needed Gabe.

She tugged on the core of molten steel that simmered in the very depths of her being. One strand released, and the crack widened. She thrust in until her elbows brushed the edges of the hole. The twang of electricity spiking her heart rate was bearable, but when many strands released, clawing their way to her limbs, an animalistic scream tore from her. The white burning power pulverized her senses, overwhelmed her nerve endings, and just like that, she was standing on a rocky outcrop with a kneeling Stavros before her.

She couldn't sense Gabe's presence. A breath rushed out of her, and she dashed at the fresh wave of tears drenching her cheeks.

Behind her was a sheer drop into a ravine, the gurgling and bubbling of the flowing river far below. Teasing zephyrs danced with tendrils of her hair, cooling the sweat still beading her skin. A clicking sound drew her attention, and she focused her vision on a spider working its web. The wind whispered its news: a deer a mile east, an old man chopping wood outside his cabin southeast of her—his blood aged but no less tantalizing. Her mind shot from eagle to cougar to deer, seeing their worlds through their vision.

"What have you done to Gabe?" she asked as Stavros clambered to his feet.

His skin had paled to an ashen color, his eyes darkening to solid black.

"You are strong for a youngling." He ignored her question, gripped her wrist and yanked her toward him.

As he opened his mouth to bite her, his teeth elongated. Anger vibrated through her, and she envisioned a long sword, sharp enough to slice through wood. It formed in her other hand. Curiosity won out, and she kept it hidden from him. He'd tasted her blood before, so what would a second sample reveal to him?

His purple-pink tongue—reminiscent of rotting meat—slid out and lapped at her bleeding wrist. The sight of it disgusted her. She shuddered and smothered her gag reflex. Stavros groaned and squeezed her wrist until she thought he'd snap it. The pain was excruciating, a vise so tight she fought the urge to whimper, to tug her arm free. She bit her lip to silence any sound escaping her.

"I taste garlic, cilantro, tomato." He stared at her, unblinking. "He guards a myth. Oh, how heroic of Gabriel. A heady mixture of power beneath that. I expected Gabriel's, but Darius's power flows through your veins." Stavros's eyebrows arched upward, and he scowled. "It appears he deceived me. How surprising. It's small but there, the blood of an original—Antistia." His smirk was back. "Or did Darius not know?"

She didn't understand why her blood mattered or who this Antistia was. Callie gripped the hilt of the sword, the leather binding biting into her palm. The weight of it was comforting. Why had she imagined a sword instead of a gun? Did she have time to debate this?

Stavros was still talking, calling her back to the present. "...to have such power in your veins, with the knowledge of a child is a waste."

Shit. He'd said something important, and she'd missed it. She doubted he'd repeat himself if she asked him to. Although, the expression on his face would've been priceless.

"Blood aside, Stavros, explain yourself. Where the hell were you taking me?" She shot another broad-sweeping glance around her and frowned.

Forests surrounded her. Sounds, undisturbed by humans, ebbed and flowed with discordant life—except for the old man.

She studied Stavros, assessing whether he knew about the sword. Could she slice off his head and summon lightning? She doubted the latter.

She was utterly alone. The darkness in her heart surprised her. Where Gabe had once been, now was cold silence, a vacuum of emotion as if he and their connection had never existed. The devastation of it decimated her, and she whimpered, fighting the wall of depression that threatened to overwhelm her. A fresh wave of tears stung her eyes, and she blinked them away, willing them to wait.

"Does it matter? You broke my mental hold, Callista. You chose this location for our final encounter."

"Our what?" she asked, then a gun formed in his hand like she should have chosen. "You do know bullets can't kill me, right?" She kept her focus on his face.

Any nuance would reveal his impending attack. As a threat, he was minor. What crippled her was the crushing weight on her chest. It was a familiar one—of mourning. Fear and despair were swift, numbing her limbs and affecting her ability to breathe.

"Kill you?" Stavros laughed, the gun bobbing as his shoulders shook. "Incapacitate you long enough, yes. One shot to the head, then I'll toss your body into the ravine."

"Ah, thanks for sharing, evil villain." She hoped her sass would ground her. She would try to dissolve—a skill Gabe said required practice. Fuck, she hadn't tried to do it once! She was stubborn, ofttimes reckless, so what better opportunity to test this out than in a life-or-death situation? Idiot.

The corner of his mouth twitched, and she dissolved a second before the burn of a bullet bored through her. Thankfully, it didn't harm her in her current form. She hoped she could envision herself well enough to reform and prayed she didn't materialize deformed with duck lips or a sagging ass.

She solidified, swiping the sword. Stavros jerked back, the blade slicing a thin red line across his throat. She dissolved again and shifted behind him, reforming to swing the sword. He spun to meet her attack with a blade of his own. The kiss of steel rang loud in the now-silent forest.

"A sword? You are a constant surprise, Callista."

"I'm happy I entertain you, Stavros." She jumped back to avoid his thrust. She smacked his blade away with hers and lunged forward expecting him to dodge her attack but not the new sword in her left hand. She sliced across his throat, drawing a steady stream of blood.

His face morphed into disbelief. He stumbled backward, falling to his hands and knees to watch his blood pool on the rock beneath him.

"Twice you drew my blood." His words gurgled, then his shoulders shook as he chuckled. "It's not enough for one as old as I am, my dear."

Wait. He'd said, *"He guards a myth,"* not *guarded*. Saturating joy roared as it rejuvenated her soul, deafening her.

Gabe's alive!

Gabriel de Winter! If you don't answer me this instant, so help me.

As threats go, color me unimpressed. His teasing voice had relief flooding her, and she sucked in a shuddering breath.

Where the hell have you been, you damn suckblood?

A groan called her back to Stavros. She dissolved and reformed in front of him to cross her blades, pinching his throat between them. He stilled, his eyes widening. This time she smelled his fear, an acrid stench.

"Who's afraid now, Stavros?"

"You won't kill me, Callista. It isn't in your genetics." The bleeding stopped, with the gurgle no longer affecting his voice. He was healing.

Gabe, do you want to kill him, or should I?

I'm here.

He appeared beside her, placing his hand on one of hers. The sight of him pierced her with hope, love, and a sense of safety. Joy enflamed her insides.

Many suckbloods popped into existence around her. She recognized their clothing as *pal'tsy* uniforms, black and minimalist. Dimitri took a position behind Stavros. A cold pleasure skewered his handsome features. He raised his gaze to meet hers, and the corners crinkled with laughter.

"Callie, you're a huntress, *tsvetok.* I've never seen a vampire partially form during fights." The awe in his voice was surreal.

"What?" She glanced down. Only her arms were visible. "Shit!" Her cheeks burned, and she forced her body to solidify.

Gabe shared images of her battling Stavros—dissolve, sword strikes, dissolve again, never fully solid—and she moved with such speed that she blurred.

You saw the entire fight? "How long have you watched me?"

"We had to test your skills." Dimitri shrugged.

"You were never alone, my love," Gabe said, as if that eased the bonfire of fury that set her belly alight. *Why are you angry?*

She ignored him.

"You used me as bait?" She gaped at them, but a sense of betrayal twanged through her heart. "Gabriel de Winter, you said you'd never endanger my life." She absorbed her blades and kicked Stavros on the chest so he sprawled at Dimitri's feet. "Fuck you both!"

She dissolved into mist, taking to the heavens. Anywhere was better than fighting the temptation to skewer Gabe with a rematerialized sword.

Callie, love.

No! You don't get to charm your way out of this. I must calm down first, and for that, you're not welcome.

She threw up her wall, not willing to listen to his uber-sexy voice or his strategic reasons. She wasn't angry that he'd used her as bait. That was a customary practice for law enforcement. She was furious he hadn't thought to include her in the plan, hadn't trusted her to know, had scared her into believing he'd forsaken her. Or worse, died.

Trust was critical, and he'd already violated it with the secret conversion. And now this had her believing there was a pattern of deceit. Without trust, there was no foundation to their relationship, their marriage.

Without it there was no *us*.

Chapter Thirty-Five

CLOSURE

When Callie first let Gabriel know of their visitor, he'd dashed over, Leo trailing him. Moments before bursting inside his home, Leo had asked him to wait, to listen. Perhaps she would reach through Stavros's grief. The longer they spoke, and the more Leo held him back, it made him realize they'd planned this, to use Callie as bait. Dimitri and his fingers dropping down around him confirmed this.

Stavros muffled their connection, and the only way to do that was to force a dematerialization. Gabriel saw red, an angry fire burning through him as he fought Leo's attempts at restraining him.

She must pass this on her own, Gabriel.

He'd grunted, knowing the test was crucial, yet hating that they'd denied him time to prepare for it. They trailed Stavros until she broke free of his hold. Her pleas for aid almost killed Gabe. Leo had to exert some sort of control on his mind, as if the scene played out from far away. This dampened his senses, his emotions, making him malleable, stealing his will.

Her strength of will, her sassiness, and her remarkable skills called forth a pride he couldn't recall ever feeling for a woman. Dimitri had the right of it. She was a huntress, and her sense of justice would ensure she remained a true protector.

Her emotional turbulence before she shut him out haunted him. His knees trembled as the darkness consumed his soul with alarming greediness. He wanted to fall to the ground and wail his despair. Thoughts circled his mind, destructive and addictive, the pain coating each word with a malevolence that drowned reason.

"Gabriel," Dimitri's bellow yanked him back to reality. "Focus. We need to deal with him, once and for all." He had pressed his blade to Stavros's neck, keeping him there.

Leo's expression hardened, and sweat beaded his forehead, a clear sign of an internal struggle. "He's trying to mist. Will you two hurry the fuck up?" he said from between clenched teeth.

Gabriel waved his hand, carving a rune inches above Stavros's chest. The light sizzled, shooting out on either side, forming a trellis of sorts before fading to a shimmer.

"I didn't know you could do a *vincula*," Dimitri said, awe softening his raspy voice.

"You can release him now," Gabriel said.

Both men stepped back on tentative heels. Dimitri held his blade out, ready to strike the killing blow. Gabriel stared at Stavros, who lay immobile, fear sliding into his eyes. He'd spared him because of Abigail, and now he wouldn't spare him because of Callie. The way Dimitri gripped his sword told Gabriel who needed to end this the most.

"The plan was brilliant," Stavros said, sweat glistening on his body as he fought the rune. "One I toyed with for decades, Gabriel. A way to end our era of weakness, hiding from the humans and bowing to the shifters."

"Involving Callie made it personal for us both. I don't want to hear your excuses, your reasons. It makes no difference to your fate." Gabriel ran a hand over his face, needing to be with Callie and not here, hating losing more time to a pointless vendetta. "None of what you've done would have pleased Abigail."

"What the hell do you know?" Spittle flew as Stavros's face mottled. "She was my sister. My only family."

"*We* killed her. I'm tired of rehashing this. I don't live in the past anymore, and I longed for you to be free of it all." Gabriel looked to the sky, not taking a second to appreciate its vibrancy but needing its magnitude for clarity. "I am over this, Stavros. You no longer influence my thoughts nor summon any form of guilt. You don't exist. Your death isn't on my conscience, and whether this would displease Abigail, I don't give a shit." He tapped Dimitri on the shoulder. "He's all yours, *brat*."

"Wait!" Stavros's shoulders straightened, his ancient power testing the strength of the rune. "Don't you want to know what Carter has planned for your precious Callie?"

Gabriel stilled, tempted to listen to the poison he would spew, but his dwindling logic whispered not to...perhaps there was a twist in the tail, something Carter *had* planned. He shot a glance at Leo, and at his slight nod, Gabriel allowed a sad smile to form.

"This is farewell, Stavros. Dimitri, Leo, and I will leave him to you. The rune won't protect him from harm nor a bolting," Gabriel said.

"My gratitude. Let me know if you need my *pal'tsy* to find your beloved. I sense she will not return to your home."

Gabriel couldn't answer. Longing, despair choked him and swallowed his voice. He launched into the air, trusting Leo to follow.

He's right. Gabriel, I've never felt this much pain from her. She believed you died, but upon finding you're alive, she thinks you abandoned her to die. I'm sorry. I can't track her. When she shut you out, she became unreadable to me.

"You return to the Hold. I'll search everywhere else she might go. Please let me know if she shows herself to you."

Ah, you believe she'll want to see Valerie. Very well. Leo veered off, and the cold silence descended.

Gabriel shivered as the silence traveled along his veins, the destination his heart. Everything Carter had planned now lay with Leo, who'd read Stavros's mind. None of that mattered if Gabriel couldn't find Callie.

Mike was undergoing a slow conversion, so he wasn't available to her. Which left Val or Callie's old apartment.

Since Leo guarded Val, Gabriel headed for George. Callie would go nowhere without her.

Chapter Thirty-Six

An Undead Life

Callie debated with herself where to go.

Mike wasn't home or answering her calls. Val was with Leo, which meant a mindfuck and many questions. Metcalfe would say I told you so. That left her old apartment and sulking in Dad's brown recliner.

As she climbed up the stairs, her front door ajar had her reaching for her gun. She didn't have one, so she summoned one, gripping it in both hands. Toeing her door open, she crept in. Nothing was taken or disturbed but something had shattered all her windows and splintered her doors.

Everything drained out of her, as if this was the last straw.

Trudging down the stairs, she knocked on the landlord's door. Her husband answered, and Callie explained the problem. She'd pay for the damages if the repairs could be done as soon as possible.

Back in her apartment, she sank her backside into her chair's molded depths, the rich scent of aged leather and Dad's tobacco assaulting her. The familiarity of it ripped through her, misting her eyes as nothing else could have. It didn't help that Gabe's cologne rose to greet her, reminding her of the clusterfuck she found herself in. She blinked away the tears, summoning her anger to blanket her heart.

She drew in a shuddering breath, flipped the lever, and relaxed, staring at the ceiling as if it held all the answers.

Perhaps she overreacted?

Recalling the fear coursing through her, paralyzing her, had her rebelling against the suggestion. She could've been emotionally prepared, armed to the teeth, and content with the knowledge that her *husband* hadn't abandoned her to *his* enemy.

She believed they were a team. She shook her head. He'd shoved her out of *her* investigation, pacified her with his supposed progress, and used her as bait. What else awaited her?

Did he love her, or had that been a lie too? They had gifts—perhaps revealing a fake inner self was one of them? Damned suckbloods. Sexy, lying, pieces of nasty evolution! Pain lanced through their connection, and she coated Gabe's mental door with sealant. Was she being unfair? Damn right she was.

She chose to wallow in her anger, disappointment, and heartache. No matter how deep her pool of self-pity was, the problem remained: she loved him, and she had trapped herself and, like a child, mourned her decisions when the consequences weren't favorable.

"Miss you, Dad," she said to the silence coating the stale air. She pushed herself out of the chair and slipped onto the balcony through the shattered sliding door. The pseudo-battle loomed, and with it an opportunity to mold her suckblood life into something worthwhile.

She vaulted into the air, seducing the wind into carrying her to the de Winter Hold. Blood ruled a suckblood, death or life. It was the only thing they understood. If any of them hindered her, they'd find out what a killer she could be.

As expected, the fools denied her entrance. Why? What was Syl hiding from her? Didn't he think of her as family? Or had the guards simply reacted to her stiff posture and bared teeth? Her deliciously wicked laughter skirted the edges of insanity as she'd darted between them, snapping a neck, ripping out two hearts, and smashing a face into a wall.

She giggled, throwing the Hold's wooden doors open with enough force to rip them off their hinges.

"The first day of freedom, my true self gave to me, one broken neck, two beating hearts, and a face in a stone wall," she sang as she skipped across Syl's throne room. "I still haven't found what I'm searching for." She twirled, arching her back to echo her voice off the high ceiling.

A young man stormed across to her, his nostrils flaring, no doubt smelling the blood dribbling off her chin and fingers. She dragged her forearm across her mouth. She stared at the bright crimson streaks staining her arm before licking the blood off her lips. It wasn't as appetizing as Gabe's, but it would do.

She bolted forward, morphing between physical and mist, but as she stretched her arm to yank out this one's heart too, he jerked back. With a familiar snap, he collapsed.

Leo was here.

Growling, she scanned the hall.

"Callie, what are you doing?" He leaned his bulk against a wall as if she hadn't forced her way into the Hold and injured three suckbloods with plans to harm more if need be.

"I want Carter's daughter. Be a dear and summon her for me or get out of my way."

"What are you planning?" He pushed off the wall to approach her.

"Read my mind and you'll bleed, *my friend*." She grimaced, fighting the growing red haze tainting her vision. Seductive voices whispered, demanding she rip her so-called friend's heart out. Oh, the temptation was delicious.

"Relax." He held up his hands in supplication. "I see you mean business."

He stilled, with his focus far away, she assumed to summon the woman then he gestured to her to take a seat. She did so on Syl's throne, testing out the soft leather with her backside.

"I've questioned her already." Leo eyed Callie. "She's prepared to confront her father and reveal her existence."

"How magnanimous of her," she said, looping a leg over the throne's arm to swing her foot. "It's not as if her deception didn't force her father down this path."

"What happened, sweetheart?" Leo conjured a chair to drop his bulk into.

"Betrayal." That one word said it all, widening the fissure in her heart.

She expected some sort of reaction. There was nothing, which meant he'd known about it. That confirmed everything her rabid mind had come up with. The pain consuming her was breathtaking. Shards of white heat filled her where once she'd held hope, love, and acceptance.

"I was a fool to trust you, Gabe, or Dimitri. I should've listened to Mike, should've remained neutral." She ran a hand over her face as if it could rid herself of the stench of blood, of the tears stinging her eyes. "Now I need to make the best of this situation. I'll meet Carter and Duhamel tonight. Have done with this investigation so I can move on with my undead life."

"Undead?" His lips twitched, irritating her frayed nerves.

"My rant." She burst to her feet, ready to hunt this woman down. If she didn't show soon, Callie would face Carter without her. That was acceptable to her. A dead senator and her file on him made public would cause chaos in the suckblood *and* human worlds. She could live with having attained a justice of sorts.

"When you say move on, do you mean without Gabriel?"

"Don't be obtuse, Leo, that's exactly what I fucking mean." She shoved aside her heart, wailing its displeasure.

He sucked in a sharp breath, and sadness emanated from him. Like she should care? "*Adsumo* couples cannot be apart for extended periods."

"They cannot harm each other either, Leo. But pain comes in many forms."

He stilled, as if he spoke to the bastard. "Gabriel says you're overreacting."

She jerked as if Leo had slapped her. She released her breath in a rush, and tears cascaded down her cheeks, unheeded. "I thought he *died* today, Leo. I *believed* Stavros would kill me. I had no weapons, no warning, just a desperate need to escape to see if my *oh-so-loving* worthless piece-of-shit husband was still alive. I could kill him for what he put me through, but I won't. You played me." She clapped her hands in sarcasm. "Well done to you both."

She glanced around the silent throne room and conjured a sword as a realization dawned on her. She half-misted as she pressed the blade against Leo's throat. "You're stalling me?" Her laughter was hoarse and cold as the need to pursue this investigation, to fight for justice, drained from her.

Removing the sword, she stepped back, accepting that what she had once treasured and valued no longer mattered. "Goodbye, Leo. Tell Val I'll be in touch."

"Callie, wait!"

She ignored him, leaving the Hold as fast as she could with one destination in mind—Knights Ridge, to find George.

Chapter Thirty-Seven

RESTORATION

Using George as bait was low, even for suckbloods. Gabe sat cross-legged opposite her little girl, drinking imaginary tea from tiny pink plastic cups. The sight of him shredded her resolve and the wall she'd built around her heart since yesterday. He was attentive, handsome, and charming.

All *lies!*

He raised agony-filled eyes, piercing through her anger. Her instant reaction was to ease his pain, to soothe him. Part of her ached to do so. The detective in her, however, marveled at his acting abilities.

He spoke to George—too low for Callie to hear the words despite her new skills—then flicked a finger and rose to his full height. Dimitri materialized and sat. He gathered a cup in his massive hand, throwing a carefree smile at George.

Gabe's strides were strong, determined, and the need to flee gripped her. Her heart faltered as fear shivered through her. She didn't want to hear his excuses and his husky voice or stand close enough to smell him. Tears pressed against her eyes, and she shook her head, denying them the right to fall. She couldn't leave, no matter how much her instincts screamed at her to do so. George *had* to come with her.

He halted in front of Callie, forcing her to raise her gaze to maintain eye contact. Heat poured off him, and she shivered, curling her fingers into fists until her nails drew blood. Her fingertips had memorized the feel of his skin and yearned to relive the experience.

"We test all vamps, and passing it earns our respect." His voice grated along her sensitive nerves like gravel on tarmac. "As your husband, they didn't tell me until it was too late." His hand trembled as he tucked her hair behind an ear. "I endured all your terror, Callie, your desperation and misery before you locked me out." His breath escaped in a rush. e pinched his lips. "I don't want you in such a situation again. Not helping you devastated me."

Doubts furrowed her brow and pierced the blanket of sorrow enshrouding her. She knew nothing about this *Adsumo* bond, hadn't thought to ask him, to read his mind. Was there something magical involved, because standing here and not touching him was driving her insane. The divided parts of her mind screamed demands, and she couldn't decide which one to listen to.

"Who planned it?" She glanced at Dimitri, imagining ripping out his spine if he was behind this. "Dimitri? Leo? Syl?"

"Does it matter?" Gabe asked, his voice still coarse, but hope crawled across his features, crushing her chest in a vise.

She *had* suspected he hadn't known or that she may have overreacted. Now the guilt, agony, and hope pouring off him had her, at last, admitting she'd blamed him without evidence, without granting him an opportunity to defend himself.

"Yes, it matters." Because if this cost her Gabe, she needed a name, someone to kill. She rolled her shoulders as a power, potent and addictive, sang along her nerve endings.

"Rhys suggested we test you. He plans to combine his enforcement with ours to form a paranormal unit."

Her head shot up with excitement of another kind gripping her. The smile spreading her cheeks clashed with the dark emotions roiling inside her.

"Suckbloods and beasts policing each other?" She bounced on her toes as the possibilities formed in her mind.

This would blow Metcalfe's career sky-high. Callie chose to forget she'd decided she no longer wanted anything to do with Carter, Duhamel, or Stavros. She was a woman and had the right to change her mind.

"He didn't believe you could handle his betas." Gabe captured her wrist to slide his hand up to her elbow.

She shivered at his touch.

"How did you get Stavros to play along?" she asked, doubts once more creeping through her chaotic thoughts.

"That was Dimitri's idea, to use you as bait in the hopes Stavros would fall for it." He caught her other wrist, stroking his fingers to her elbow and gripping her there. His touch alone sent excitement tingling down her spine.

"Lucky me. Did you kill him?" she asked, traveling his features with a lustful appraisal. The swelling of her heart and her breathlessness had her realizing she would always love this man.

"Fuck Stavros!" Gabe burst forward, releasing her hands to grip her upper arms, pinning her to the length of him.

She shuddered under the sensory onslaught despite the volatile emotions pouring off him.

"I'm your husband, your *Adsumo*, your eternity, I love you. Please, Callie, I'm...*dying* here."

His pain touched her despite the plug hindering their connection. It contorted his face, and he trembled against her, his breathing coming in great gasps. With a deep breath, she peeled open his mental door. Agony, abject misery, deep isolation flooded their connection, and his memories followed. He spoke the truth, if she could believe him.

What convinced her this was real was the cessation of the dark whisperings in her own mind, the seductive lures to kill, to destroy those who opposed her. He built a solid mental wall around them, encapsulating her until his love engulfed her, protecting her. His understanding and forgiveness drowned her regret.

She didn't realize she was crying until he wiped her tears away with the pads of his thumbs. She whispered words she hadn't thought to, mutterings and pleas for forgiveness, of her devotion. All unnecessary with their connection restored. The kiss he bestowed on her soared her soul above the stars.

"I love you," she said across his parted lips.

"I never stopped loving you," he said, and she believed him. "Now would you like some tea?" He laced his fingers through hers to tug her toward George. Dimitri handed her a cup. Callie accepted it and sat on the blanket beside him.

"Are you feeling better, Callie?" George asked, her small hand extended for Callie's cup.

"I've missed you, sweetheart. Has Dimitri treated you well?" Hot tea filled her cup, and she grinned, accepting it from George with a smile.

"Dimitri says I'll always be his princess," George said with a giggle as if it was the finest thing.

Callie shot a warning glance at Dimitri, hoping to convey that she'd kill him if he ever hurt her daughter.

He loves her like a sister. You have nothing to worry about, mama bear. Gabe teased her through their link.

With a deep sigh, Callie admitted she'd missed this.

Chapter Thirty-Eight

THE EVE OF BATTLE

They say that war was waged not just on a battlefield. Whoever *they* are. Judging by the tense silence in the room, Callie believed it.

The inclusion of the beast's armed forces—their words—had delighted Metcalfe, transforming her into an almost-pleasant person to be around. Once she'd met the alpha, Rhys, of the Knights Ridge pack, sparks had flown, and not the good kind. That might have been creepy to witness. Callie didn't want to imagine her ex-captain in a romantic lead, though she'd often joked with Mike that she needed a good swing from the chandeliers.

Rhys was a bear of man, in size and persona. He growled or rumbled his words, and his meaty hands flicked his shoulder-length, golden-streaked brown hair away from his baby-blue eyes. When they met, she could've sworn the blue glowed. A neat beard adorned a sharp jawline, and his narrow lips never smiled.

Syl showed his mettle, calming the two with firm words—a language both combatants valued. They'd gathered in the formal sitting room at the de Winter Hold, resplendent with Baroque influence merging with high-tech gadgetry. The carved gold paneling parted to reveal a glass wall, giving a wide view of a smaller lounge where Monique awaited her father. Syl had lured him with a promise of a senatorial campaign contribution.

"Stavros is dead. Why do we still need this fake fight?" Callie asked the room in general. "Wasn't this ruse meant to lure him out?"

"Yes, among other reasons," Syl said. "We needed to force Duhamel and Carter to reveal their involvement, to bring them to your enforcement's attention." He blessed Metcalfe with a formal nod as if to say *mission accomplished.*

"Though you kept meticulous files, Callie, your allegations held insufficient evidence. Discovering the wider plot was a stroke of luck," Metcalfe said. "I couldn't have genocide in *my* Inner City, now could I?"

Callie frowned. *Luck? It was hard work, you old bat.* She didn't say that, biting her lip in case her tongue ran away with her.

Gabe looped his arm around her waist and tugged her against him. His touch, both mental and physical, calmed her, otherwise, she might have gone verbal on her ex-boss.

"With all due respect, Johanna, Callie was the first to investigate. Without those files, we would not have discovered the extent of Carter's involvement." Syl's defense of her had her gaping, disbelief flushing her cheeks.

Damn it. She now owed the bastard.

"Neither side was aware of Stavros's duplicity, nor his reasons behind it. I'm eager to see how Carter handles this reunion, how he reacts when he realizes he's a pawn in a game greater than he imagined." Rhys prowled closer to the one-way mirror, his great bulk dominating the room. The fact his voice was like gravel added to his intimidation factor, and if she'd met him in an alley, she'd have been the loser. Her precious silver bullets and poisoned daggers would have merely annoyed him.

Monique sat in a chair, tapping her fingernails on the brocade fabric. She alternated between sitting, standing, and pacing—her agitation clear. According to Leo, she hadn't wanted her father to discover her conversion. He abhorred all things non-human. She'd formed an obsession with vampires when she'd been a feeder and hid this from him. Callie could empathize.

Monique flicked her black curls out of her eyes as the door opened. She drew in a deep breath and squared her shoulders when her father entered the room. The scene played out as expected. Carter wavered between shock, delight, and anger.

"You see, Daddy, Stavros played you, and now your revenge will harm me," Monique said.

"We're all a part of someone else's agenda." He lowered himself into the chair, his long legs folding in half. "I have my reasons, my girl." His shoulders squared, mimicking his daughter's earlier mannerism.

"Have?" Her pout was pretty. "You're determined to go ahead with this?"

"You know how I feel, Nicky." He slammed his fist into his palm, the slap reverberating through the room. "They're unnatural and a blight on this planet."

"Humans are better?" She flicked a dismissive hand. "You destroy everything you touch." She folded her arms across her chest and glared at her father. "You're the idiot, Daddy. Killing one Hold, one pack, won't rid the city of them, never mind the world."

"War begets war," he said as he rose to his full height. "You'll understand why I won't tell your mother about you. She doesn't need to see what you've become."

"Mama knows," Monique smirked. "I sent an extensive list of your nocturnal activities to her divorce lawyer. You didn't raise a fool, Daddy. Are you proud of me now?" Without waiting for a response, she sauntered out of the room.

"I didn't expect that," Leo chuckled. "Sad thing is, he *is* proud of her." He shook his head. "The pseudo-battle plays out. His thoughts circle the rumors of our impending war."

"So be it," Syl said, finality hardening his voice.

"Can't we just arrest him now?" Callie asked. They were so close to ending this vendetta, it had her trembling with nervous energy. She curled and unfurled her fingers, squeezing the fists until her nails dented her palms.

"Confession first," Syl said. "The audio we have on him reveals he's eager for tomorrow but not the reasons why. They also mention he's reserved a motel room overlooking the abandoned loading dock. We've bugged said room with audio and video equipment."

"With healers on standby, should our people become overzealous," Rhys said. "Once bodies litter the ground, and I fake-kill Syl, that should garner an unrehearsed reaction from Carter."

"Duhamel has accepted an invitation to attend Carter's culmination. He will be present and reacting to our performances," Leo said. "I will be in the room alongside them, conveying what they're hoping will happen."

"Where will I need to be?" Callie asked, stiffening her shoulders and meeting everyone's gazes without fear. She wouldn't accept an exclusion from this battle.

Syl smirked like the arrogant idiot she believed him to be. "We're tying you up." He'd said it with much eagerness.

"What?" she asked, her voice ending on a squeak.

"It keeps you away from Carter and his goons. As a huntress, your skills could accidentally harm someone. It will also convince Carter that we don't want an ex-detective to garner peace between us," Leo said.

"We'll need you yelling at either side, so we won't gag you," Rhys grinned. The unexpected warmth softened his features, painting him handsome. He gave her a slight nod. What the hell that meant she didn't know.

"In the initial stages, there will be no police presence, other than you, Callie." Metcalfe scowled. "Our involvement might lead to allegations of entrapment."

"There's no way I'm allowing Carter and Duhamel to go free on a technicality." Callie slammed her fist into her palm. "I'll be the best damn restrained peacekeeper you've ever seen."

"You know your roles. We'll meet at the docks an hour before sunrise." Syl flicked his fingers, and everyone dispersed before he slipped into the room to speak to Carter.

Callie stayed latched to Gabe's side with a promise of an amorous evening in her near future. Shifter girls had invited George to a sleepover, babysat by one of Dimitri's *pal'tsy*, of course. Which left only one more question for her to ask.

"Where's Mike?" Images of her ex-partner's rather sensual conversion with a vampire woman, Clarissa, flitted across their connection, and she spun on Gabe with a gasp.

"He asked, Callie," Gabe said.

"If the conversion had killed him, then what?" She stomped her foot instead of hitting him. If Mike was there, she'd smack him.

"Clarissa did a slow conversion, a little blood every night."

"I don't care how cautious you were. Neither of you took my feelings into account or my opinion. Again. You'd think you'd have learned from the last slow conversion you did, Gabe."

To have lost Mike would have devastated her. Since Dad's death, Mike had taken on a fatherly role. Not that she'd ever tell him this. Knowing the old curmudgeon, he'd use it against her.

"He was dying, Callie." *Heart failure.*

She stilled and raised her wide-eyed gaze to Gabe's face to measure his sincerity. *Dying?* Tears welled, stinging as she blinked them away. *I'm going to kill him for hiding this from me.*

With Val battling cancer, he didn't want to burden you further. Gabe cupped her cheek, rubbing his thumb across it.

How did you manage to hide this from me?

You don't intrude in my memories, even though you have the right to. He flashed a loving smile.

"I'm damn well going to start." She ground her teeth. "Please stop trying to protect me. I know I'm a youngling and new to suckblood life, but I can't learn if you don't let me."

You're precious to me, my love. I've had nothing in my life worth guarding until now.

We're a team, deciding on things together. She met his gaze, willing him to take her words to heart.

I'll try. That's all I can promise you.

That's all I ask. She scanned his thoughts, searching for sincerity, and found it.

He spun her, capturing her against his warm chest to brush his lips across hers. She hummed her eagerness when he nibbled on her earlobe.

Home? he asked.

Oh, yes, please.

CHAPTER THIRTY-NINE

AN EPIC CLUSTER-FUCK

THE GATHERING MASSES SQUARED off, underlining animosity tainting the air enough to fragrance it. Callie shot nervous glances at the beasts throwing angry growls at the smirking suckbloods. She was certain Syl and Rhys had made it clear no one was to shed blood, and only accidents would be tolerated. The day was going to hell in a plaid-lined handbasket.

Tension rippled along Gabe's shoulders, visible under his tight T-shirt.

She nudged him and shook her head. *Keep calm.*

I can scent their anger and resentment. It feels centuries old.

Gabe, remember why we're here.

He snatched her against him for a kiss. *I must keep the huntress in check.*

She snorted before pursing her lips. Syl striding across the chaos drew her attention from Gabe's lust-filled stare. Rhys met him halfway and rumbled a greeting.

"Your kind lacks honor. To tempt us with offspring is crueler than usual, Alpha." Syl thrust his furious face in Rhys's.

That wasn't an easy feat, with the werebear over six feet in height.

"Your kind is fickle. We no longer tolerate your killing sprees and disregard for family."

"Ah, so we're at an impasse?" Syl folded his arms across his chest with an irritating smirk claiming his face again.

"A life for a life, vamp," Rhys roared but didn't transform yet.

They'd decided he'd blend in better if he remained in human form.

"Last one standing wins Inner City." Syl offered his hand for a shake. Rhys slapped it away and lunged.

Bodies flew across her vision—beasts contorting into various animal forms, suckbloods darting across the docks. It looked good. A well-choreographed dance as each cog in the wheel performed its role to perfection. Until a pain-filled cry wrenched the air. Real claws and fangs emerged. Beasts roared and suckbloods leaped into the air before descending to strike. Blood splattered the concrete floor. Unmoving bodies littered the battlefield with moans of agony underlying the sounds of flesh ripping and punches connecting with skin.

Shit! She shot glances at Gabe who trembled, the need to fight blurring the edges of their connection. The tantalizing scent of blood permeated the air, and her fangs slid out to dimple her bottom lip. *Untie me. I won't stay out of this, Gabe.*

He fumbled with the ropes, tearing them away and setting her free.

She grimaced, rubbing her stinging wrists. *We need to save as many as we can.*

Save many. He curled his fingers into fists.

She slipped in front of him and slapped him across his face. He turned his gray-eyed gaze to her, a hiss escaping through his clenched jaw. *Are you with me, Gabriel de Winter?*

Yes. He forced a smile, and she raised her hand to slap him again. He caught her wrist and yanked her in his arms for a knee-weakening kiss. *I'm with you, always.*

They spun to battle the writhing masses, swinging uppercuts, hooks, and kicks, leaving a trail of bodies behind them even as she screamed at them to cease fighting. She was a poor peacemaker. She blurred from combatant to berserker, neutralizing as she moved. She'd drawn her daggers, not to kill, but to poison. Her instincts demanded she come prepared.

The beasts and suckbloods collapsed to their knees, and over one head, she tossed Gabe a dagger or two. Her arms should've grown heavy, but she wasn't human anymore. Amazement made her stare at them, at their automatic actions, nicking beasts and suckbloods with speeds almost beyond her ability to see. Words tumbled from her mouth, as if she bargained for peace. In a way she did, but they didn't listen, and now she performed the action for the senator's eyes. She snorted at Syl and Rhys's demand she remain neutral. Fools!

Bring them to me, and I'll throw them into the bay, Gabe said.

She scrambled backward as if to imply weakness. They followed, unaware that as enemies they stood alongside each other with the common goal to kill her. She sighed, holding out her hands as if to placate them. When they lunged, she leaped, sending kicks and jabs, dropping them one by one. Gabe tugged each one off the pier, tossing her daggers back at her when she'd lost her last one. She mourned the loss. Those weapons had been with her for years and had helped her escape many situations, not unlike her current one.

Where are they coming from? I didn't know we had so many participating today. She threw a glance at Syl and Rhys who fought alongside each other, trying to keep their alliance intact. Neither killed, but later, there would be quite a few in agony on both sides.

Almost done, my love. Gabe's mental voice was calm, and a scan of his mind revealed it wasn't a ruse. Gone was the red haze of battle lust from earlier.

I'd like to finish this before the sun rises. Fighting at a disadvantage doesn't sit well with me. As it was, her energy leaked from her with the first rays of the sun touching the bay's water.

If Syl or Rhys endanger you in any way, they will not be happy with my retaliation. Red tinged their connection again, and she sent her love in waves, calming him.

Black-uniformed suckbloods cut a path through the masses and bowed before her. They gave her their backs and formed a circle around her, even as more of the *pal'tsy* swirled outward, neutralizing as they moved.

Dimitri sent his fingers. I could kiss him! She lowered her arms to watch his men work.

Swift and effective, with their usual lethality missing. Any deaths from today would cement the feud between the suckbloods and the beasts. It would be a shame if that happened. She'd come to respect Rhys as an alpha.

No, you won't kiss Dimitri. Gabe said, conveying an image of him scowling.

There's only one grumpy ass suckblood I want to put my lips on. She slid her remaining daggers into her boots and stepped over the strewn bodies to reach him.

The circle of *pal'tsy* shifted with her.

I can't decide if I'm delighted or offended by Dimitri's need to protect me. Does he not trust me?

Since he has an attachment to our daughter, I'd say you're delighted. Gabe brushed his lips across her temple, and she sighed with contentment.

Remind me to thank him later. She tugged his arms around her, nuzzling her nose across his blood-stained sleeve.

There better be no kisses.

Chapter Forty

PSEUDO-BATTLE

Leo scanned the battlefield from the hotel window, seeing every detail, planned or otherwise. The docks had been Callie's suggestion. Her suckblood journey had involved witnessing the canister pass hands, and it seemed symbolic that the conclusion should occur here. The full moon cast light and shadows, but they'd repaired the floodlights so the officers and Carter could see the show. The sun teased the horizon, kissing the ocean's edge with a splash of color.

This was a bad idea. There had been too much hatred for the pseudo-battle to play out without casualties. It was a full-out blood bath, trickles of it staining the tarred ground. The enticing scent of it reached him in his room, extending his teeth as if he hungered. Callie had gone from damsel-in-distress to huntress, knocking out shifters and vampires to spare their lives. Gabe protected her with more lethality, no matter the species.

Leo tuned out the gleeful reactions from Carter, which he could hear through the thin walls. The recordings would capture his incriminating words. Dimitri's *pal'tsy* followed Callie's example and neutralized large swathes of combatants. Blood had been spilled, and it was sacrosanct to both sides—sustenance versus lineage.

Syl and Rhys battled alongside each other as they fought to keep the new alliance strong. Metcalfe's officers had arrived, but they hovered on the outskirts with weapons drawn, indecisive since this free-for-all wasn't part of the plan. Their choice to remain on the sidelines was wise, for many a human would have died this night.

Leo conveyed his panoramic view to the key members, sharing where the chaotic nuclei were. Even including an absent Dimitri in the communication. The man had chosen to remain with George, trusting his *pal'tsy* to do as trained.

Dripping blood from their fingers or claws, and with their chests heaving, Syl faced Rhys. Callie leaned against Gabe, seeming content to remain so. Around them, bodies sprawled outward, resembling the petals of a flower.

"That didn't go as planned," Syl said to Rhys, who grunted in response. The sound was animalistic but its meaning understood. "Take your wounded and go."

"I need to kill you first," Rhys said. The words were discernible in his coarse voice, but Leo had read the thought before Rhys spoke it. "We can salvage this."

"Ready," Syl said.

Rhys roared, his jaw extending amid the bellow of a grizzly bear. His body contorted in jerks and spasms. The alpha's pain lancing through Leo's mind had him shutting off the connection. The massive brown bear stood on its hind legs, towering over Syl, who looked frail in comparison. It was an impressive sight.

Syl darted around the bear, his movements swift, blurring as he plunged a fake knife into the shifter's thick fur. Rhys roared, twisting and turning until, with a swipe of a paw, he threw Syl back. He vaulted to his feet and faced the bear. With one sweep of his massive claws, Rhys 'sliced' Syl's throat, and Syl instantly dissolved. A triumphant roar from the room next door told Leo that Carter had believed the deathblow. He followed this with a string of words dripping in hatred—how he'd deceived and sold his soul for this victory.

"Well done, my kings." Leo sent the memory of Carter's cheer to Rhys and Syl. One by one, vampires limped off the battleground, their performances believable as they forged a path through the stunned police.

Leo was grateful they'd at least remembered the instruction not to fly. They didn't need to reveal all their abilities to the spectators. Shifters helping their wounded was symbolic of how they cared for each other. The 'fallen' vampires remained unattended and dissolved, mimicking Syl's death.

Callie consoled a grieving Gabriel, his face switching between despair and fury. Rhys moved around his wounded, offering aid where needed. He was once again human but naked since shifters couldn't manipulate the ether. His broad shoulders glimmered in the morning light, an easy target to follow.

The room's door clicked open, and on silent feet, a *pal'tsy* approached Leo. Dressed as a waiter, his young face held deceptive innocence, which was why Dimitri had chosen him for this task.

"The audio files." He placed the memory stick on the glass table.

Leo lowered himself into the leather chair he'd conjured. It was a replica of Callie's, right down to the indented seat cushion. For Carter, the evening wasn't over. The man intended to celebrate into the small hours of the night, no matter the state of his liver. Leo would keep him company, albeit separated by a wall. The information on the memory stick was enough to send the human to prison for a long time, but Leo wanted to continue recording, just to make sure they hadn't missed something. Carter, in his drunken stupor, might reveal more of his nefarious deeds. Leo knew what lay in the man's thoughts, but he needed Carter to reveal it in his own voice.

"The extended audios, I will deliver tomorrow," the *pal'tsy* said.

"Thank you." Leo summoned a snifter of cognac. The heady fragrance scented the air, and he pressed the glass to his lips. The *pal'tsy* slid out of the room, careful to close the door without making a sound.

I sense boredom.

Leo's heart leaped into his throat, causing him to choke on the fiery, bitter liquid as it slid down.

Valerie. He thought no more. Her voice alone had such an effect on him, one he couldn't fathom.

How did the ruse go? Even in his mind, her words were in her usual huskiness.

Well. But with bloodshed.

You cannot anticipate everything, Leonardo. Her insight had a frown forming on his lips. *No wonder you're bored. A life without surprises is a dull one.*

His frown morphed into a smile. He loved it when she used his full name. She did so because he used hers, and that irritated her.

Coming home soon?

His breath hitched, and a tremor laid siege to his limbs. Home? The way his heart pounded made him realize she was correct. Anywhere with her was home.

In a while. He managed to convey this without the tumultuous emotions roiling within him.

Be careful.

Worried about me, princess?

She snorted, then silence smothered their connection, but not the smile still spreading his cheeks. He forced her out of his mind, not willing to distract himself with how their relationship could play out. He needed to sit her down and tell her how he felt, but he feared ruining their friendship, one he'd come to cherish.

Laughter pierced the walls—a bombastic bark from Carter and a woman's trill. He scowled, not appreciating the time wasted as the senator got his kicks off. Leo would give them an hour, force them into a sleep, then fly home. He imagined sliding between Valerie's sheets and curling his body around hers.

The idea consumed him many times during a day, but she hadn't invited him to her bed, not by word, thought, or deed. He played out various scenarios, and all returned to one fact. He couldn't wait any longer. Perhaps this was the night he revealed his intentions to the beautiful, enchanting Valerie.

Chapter Forty-One

BREAKING NEWS

"In an unbelievable turn of events, vampires and shifters united to uncover corruption and possible genocide on a state senatorial level. Senator Carter and Mayor Duhamel declined to comment as the Inner City police arrested both on numerous charges. Captain Johanna Metcalfe is confident that justice will be swift and satisfactory." The camera panned from the reporter to Metcalfe, the city's courthouse a backdrop to her crisp pantsuit.

"The evidence brought to our attention by the de Winter Hold and the Knights Ridge pack is irrefutable." Johanna looked years younger as she smiled into the camera.

Callie snorted, snuggling into Gabe's embrace. They'd gathered at the Hold to watch the news and discuss any unexpected fallout from the battle. Rhys engulfed a leather wingback chair farthest from the fireplace. Val and Leo were on opposite sides of the room, sneaking glances at each other. Callie didn't know what the hell that was about, but she'd find out soon enough. Syl stood in front of the hearth, a hand on the mantle as he sipped his brandy.

A young man entered the room. There was something familiar about his overall shape, the color of his hair, and his large feet plowing him forward, regardless of the obstacles in his path.

Mike.

At Gabe's thought, she twisted in his arms to shoot him a disbelieving look. His lips curled into a sensual smile before snatching a kiss from her.

No. It can't be. I didn't lose years when I converted.

You were young to begin with. A conversion removes decades, returning the person to the prime of their lives.

She focused on the young man's face. The jawline was the same, as were the hook-like nose and his deep brown eyes. But the smirk teasing his upper lip was what convinced her.

Wow. I can see now that the rumors were true. I'd have let him bend me over a water cooler. She chuckled. *Not now, of course.*

I'd bend over you right here. Gabe stroked the curve of her backside, his mental touch devastating her senses.

She gasped and spun to throw her arms around him. Peering into his eyes, she kissed his chin. *I'd let you. Behave. No more psychic touches tonight. Mike's coming over, and I can't be a quivering mess when I speak to him. He's practically my father.*

Gabe's laugh warmed her heart, and she found herself sighing, drowning in the gray of his eyes. She sensed Mike staring at her and flashed him a smile.

"I ought to box your ears, converting without saying goodbye. Since you had your reasons, and you turned into something candylicious, I suppose I could be the magnanimous one and forgive you." She raised her nose into the air and sniffed, then ruined it with a chuckle.

She tugged out of Gabe's arms to hug Mike. He smelled the same, though with loads less cologne. She pulled away, studying his face. "How do you feel?"

"What kind of question is that? I'm twenty years younger. Forever."

His grin had her bouncing on her toes. She loved seeing him happy. "A valid question, since you're still my partner. There's no way Metcalfe's letting you back on the force. You're a walking poster boy. Suckblood conversion is the new fountain of youth." She waved her hand in the air as if she laid out the headlines. "I'm thinking Anna McCarthy is a no-no. Not to mention that you won't be needing me as your wingman anymore."

"I didn't need a wingman. I kept telling you that." Mike shoved his hands deep into the pockets of his denims and shook his head. "You're on your own, my girl. I'm spending time with Dimitri and his *pal'tsy*. Could do with a few more skills in my repertoire."

"I can't break in another partner. I'll get him killed." She chewed on her lip and wondered if she still needed backup. As a suckblood, she had skills galore. The thought of not seeing Mike for a while was too devastating for her to form words.

"You don't need a new one. You've been on your own all this time," he said.

"He learned years ago to stay back. Trailing you closely meant you'd have to worry about him." Leo offered Mike a handshake. "Welcome to the Hold, Mike."

"Is that true?" The sting behind her eyes forced her to squeeze them shut for a second to deny the tears. "You kept back for my sake?" Her voice was soft, unable to speak through the pain seizing her lungs and burning her throat.

"Yes. Your father said you had a talent to survive, that it was almost supernatural. Since your birth, he said. Despite all odds, you didn't die alongside your mother." Mike drew her into his arms for another hug.

She went willingly, needing his familiar comfort.

"He saw your training scores, videos, and instructor's comments. It's why you went through so many partners. They refused to listen to your old man and tried to be the frontrunner."

"See, my love, you've always been a huntress," Gabe said. "Now, come here, release poor Mike."

"I don't want to." She pouted, but she let him go, laced her fingers through Gabe's, and allowed him to tug her back.

"I'm keeping my smartwatch, so you can talk to me anytime." Mike showed her his wrist.

"You'll always be my father of sorts, no matter how young you look." She was tempted to wag her finger in his face.

"I wouldn't expect anything else from you, my girl." His eyes were misty, and the sight of it broke her heart.

"Now, for the good news." Syl muted the television with a flick of his hand. "Hawkins has made amends for Delta's involvement by supplying all the research material for the original sample." The grin he bestowed on them was wide, brimming with excitement and satisfaction. "Rhys has offered his laboratories and staff to assist, for which I am grateful." Syl drew in a deep breath. "We have no idea how the babies will turn out, whether immortal at birth or fully human. It's trial and error, as horrifying as that is." His gaze settled on Callie. "Perhaps I'll soon be bouncing a nephew or niece on my knee." He winked, conveying who knew what.

Was he mocking her? Was she to be the guinea pig for the new formula? The asshat didn't even know if she wanted children or not. Her cheeks stung with heat but not from embarrassment. George was Syl's niece, and he damn well knew it.

Small steps, sweetheart. He wants to acknowledge her, but doing so without jumping through political hoops places George in danger.

Callie huffed. *That doesn't mean I have to like his treatment of her. Why can't he sneak in to see her?*

Because he's under surveillance. Leo suspects a few spies from the Drimari are within our Hold.

The suckblood council? She read Gabe's thoughts.

At the snail's rate he fed her information, she was ready to smack him. The council's involvement was due to her, George, the infertility sample, and the death of Stavros. The de Winter Hold and the Knights Ridge alliance had added to their interest.

This development drained her. The exhaustion consuming her was soul-deep, and she exhaled a shuddering breath, wishing they could escape it all.

Why don't we go on a vacation? Somewhere tropical. I haven't had a break in years. Let Rhys deal with Metcalfe for a while. She will rope poor Mike in, anyway.

Gabe's excitement streaming across their connection inspired the same within her. She could see herself lounging on the beach under a large umbrella, with George building sandcastles in the sand. In her imagination, a cocktail appeared before her, and a glance at the bearer revealed Gabe in nothing but a pair of swimming trunks.

"Done," Gabe said, his voice hoarse. *I'd love nothing more than to spend such a time with you, my love, and it's just what George needs.*

I'll get George. You break the news to Dimitri and Mike.

Coward. Gabe chuckled.

Telling Dimitri they were taking George away for a while wasn't going to be fun.

I'll make it up to you. Callie kissed him, brushing her lips across his, meaning to tantalize and not satiate.

"I'll hold you to that promise." The look Gabe bestowed upon her, the love overflowing his heart into hers, completed her, and for the first time since Dad's death, she was at peace.

Epilogue

HONOR AMONGST BEASTS

Rhys trudged through the forest, choosing his steps with care. He wasn't in his werebear form, despite his inner bear nagging him to change. The sweet scent of pine teased his need to roam free, to hunt, to breathe in unpolluted air. His thoughts spun like a dervish. Within this month he had made an alliance with the vamps, found out that his former alpha had failed the pack twice, and on top of it, met the woman of his dreams.

Callista Devereaux.

Glorious molten hair, green eyes, and an attitude to match.

His bear grumbled, still furious at him for not taking her and saving her from a vamp. Rhys released a long sigh. He'd explained over and over that she wasn't their mate. She was Gabriel's. Blood doesn't lie. Her blood called to his bear. Yet hers and Gabriel's bond had formed on a telepathic level. They'd conversed, expressions crossing their faces even as words remained unspoken.

Missing a chance at her had doomed him to a life of loneliness, unmated and unloved, and because of this, many would challenge him for the role as alpha. He needed a mate to solidify his reign. There was still time before his pack would demand he choose anyone. Until then, he'd enjoy spending time with Callie as they built the paranormal unit.

He suspected she'd fall for that—asking the vamps to test her was necessary to prove her strength and his neutrality. He was far from impartial though when it came to her. Rhys had considered Valerie as a possible wife since she had the same blood in her veins, but she was more reserved than he liked. His pack needed a huntress or someone with a similar disposition. Now he'd have to choose from the surrounding packs and perhaps form alliances to strengthen his position.

Drawing in a deep breath, he squared his shoulders and focused on the task at hand. He was here, in the middle of the forest, on pack soil, to deal with the old alpha's first failure. The canister had been the second failure—forcing him to make amends with the vamps by breaking with tradition and centuries of animosity.

There was no aroma of cooked food to greet him as he entered the clearing. Broken chairs littered the unkempt yard, and the stench of garbage wrinkled his nose. It had his bear grumbling, but that wasn't what shot iced fury through his veins. The roar that tore from him was animalistic, his bear's voice shredding his human vocal cords.

Four wolf cubs whined from within an iron cage, their own feces staining their paws. No one had taught them how to shift into human form, and the condition of their coats revealed they lacked nourishment.

He ripped the door off the cage, tossing it to the side. It scarred the hardpacked dirt with deep grooves and narrowly missed his beta, Noah. Since he shifted into a wolf, Rhys gestured to the frightened cubs, instructing him to take care of the little ones.

He stormed the dilapidated house, his steps vibrating the porch's rotten floorboards. Rhys slammed the door open, breaking it off its hinges, then shielded his nose and entered, uninvited. Unwashed bodies, decayed food, and stale air assaulted him. What kind of a person lived like this? Raised children in this filth and tossed out little George to survive on her own?

Along with the disgust was the self-directed anger. How had he not known of this? Noah's face held shock, so this was as much a surprise to him. How many other pack members lived like this? The scowl that tugged Rhys's lips cramped his jaw. He clenched his teeth until they ached. Make that three failures he needed to attend to. No one, especially not a pack member, should live like this.

He walked down the narrow passage, his shoulders brushing the thin walls. Mold grew on sections under the peeling wallpaper, but the cold dampness didn't make him shiver. The squalid desperation did. He peered into each room, finding the same conditions—a few unlivable—until he broke into the kitchen.

A woman—in nothing but a tattered dressing gown—sprawled on the floor. Discarded needles littered the filth around her. He raised his nose to the ceiling and sniffed, picking up the tell-tale scent of narcotics. Empty bottles of beer painted a larger picture. He didn't see food anywhere, which meant she hunted, and only for herself if he judged the state of her children.

Rhys spun on his heel, exiting the lopsided house with a determination stiffening his shoulders. Noah arched a brow as he tried to hold onto the four scrambling cubs. Fear echoed in their yelps. Their distrust of anyone was clear.

"Burn it to the ground and if she manages to survive that, kill her." Rhys scooped two cubs into his arms, and with a low growl, they quieted. "I want all houses documented—their location, condition, and occupants. This shit ends now."

"As you command," Noah said, handing him another cub, then pulling out his phone to make a call. Once done, he took back the cub and they stood there, waiting for his pack members.

The first to arrive was Jase. After one look, he carried the cubs to his truck. He was on his phone when he returned. Rhys nodded. He had good men, and many were friends he'd grown up with. They were like brothers, having endured much under the former alpha Alrik's reign. Never had Rhys imagined that things were this bad.

His pack arrived; some having run here in their were forms. They helped pour gasoline on the house, and minutes later the blaze had him sweating. As a bear, he ran at a hotter temperature and didn't need fireplaces or heaters to keep warm. Despite the discomfort, he didn't move away.

Other men kept the ground around the house wet to ensure that the fire didn't spread to the surrounding wilderness. As a pack, they watched it burn to the ground. Smoldering embers glowed into the darkness of night, but no one left.

"I will take the cubs," Reade said. "We lost our child. The little ones might ease Miriam's pain." The agony lingering in his gaze meant he suffered.

"Thank you, Reade," Rhys said, acknowledging his offer with a nod. He faced his men, a few disgusted or horrified at this discovery. "Spread the word. If you hunger, ask. If you need diapers, ask, but if I find you abusing a child, your life ends."

They grunted their agreement, and thus formed a new law.

About the Author

Sevannah Storm is a fiction writer who immerses herself in fantastical worlds both magical and science fiction. She has a flare for the creative, having studied art and interior architecture, and spends her time drawing, oil painting, and writing. An avid reader from an early age, Sevannah finds her inspiration from various sources: games, novels, music, and the land of make-believe. The unique versus the practical has brought on numerous debates.

In her spare time, she does CrossFit and Krav Maga and rereads novels that snatch her breath away. Having embraced the social media world, you can find her on most platforms.

Her home is a land south of Wakanda, where animals roam free. Born in Zimbabwe, she grew up in South Africa. The crisp blue skies with cotton-candy sunsets expand her heart and soul, encapsulating a sense of freedom.

Words she lives by: "Know your pothole and dodge it. Don't work in a pencil factory if you're a vampire."

Sevannah loves to hear from her readers. You can find and connect with her at the links below.

Website/Newsletter:

https://www.sevannahstorm.com/

Facebook:

https://www.facebook.com/sevannah.storm

Instagram:

https://www.instagram.com/sevannah.storm/

Twitter:

https://twitter.com/sevannah_storm

Thank you for taking the time to read *The Huntress*. If you enjoyed the story, please tell your friends and leave a review. Reviews support authors and ensure they continue to bring readers books to love and enjoy.

Stay tuned for sample chapters.

THE HEALER

DOES HE LOVE HER or the blood of legends in her veins?

Becoming a doctor is all Ilona ever dreamed of, especially with her parents being the best in their medical fields until a car accident forces her to re-evaluate her choices. Scarred and alone, she finds herself in a small town buried in snow, but worse, she's forced to use her medical skills to heal shifters.

One shifter has her knees trembling, but when she discovers he likes her because she looks like the woman he's crushing on, Ilona flees, unwilling to risk her fragile heart.

Rhys pines for a woman he can never have, believing he lost his mate to a vampire. But on a visit with his brother, when he discovers a doctor with the same last name as his crush, he prays her blood will trigger the mating urge and free him from unrequited love.

The problem is, Ilona's blood does summon his primal urges, but she won't believe his interest is sincere. Now he needs to find her and prove he loves her, and only her.

Chapter One

A MEAN BASTARD

When Rhys stepped onto the splintered wooden porch, the familiar stench of blood hit him—salty, tangy, but with a wealth of wet fur and fish. He stilled and sniffed, allowing the miasma of colors to saturate his nose. The sharper the odor or emotion the brighter the color.

A sunlight yellow 'smoke' trail slipped under the door. Blood laced with bear meant one thing. Roaring, he burst into the cabin he shared with his brother, tearing the door off the hinges.

"Aiden!" Bounding up the stairs leading to their bedrooms, he jerked on the balustrade, almost ripping it from its base.

"He's fine." Noah, Rhys's best friend and beta, filled Aiden's bedroom doorway, blocking the path.

"Move, Noah." Rhys tried to shove past, but Noah stood firm. Short of shoving him against the wall and injuring a brother-in-pack, Rhys spun away to pace. His bear snarled, threatening to take over and bowl Noah out of the way.

"Calm your bear, Rhys. He'll agitate Aiden, and we just got him to relax."

His vision tinged with red, focused, blurred, then sharpened. "What the fuck happened?"

"We think Alrik sent you out on a food run for this reason." His brother-in-pack Jase peered over Noah's shoulder, his dirty-blond hair disheveled, with blood smeared across his temple. "Aiden's usual disrespect didn't help the situation."

"Might have been the trigger." Noah dipped his head. "With a little tact, he might have avoided this."

"Fuck." Rhys yanked his bun loose to run his fingers through his hair, hoping to calm his bear and ease the tension tightening the muscles in his neck. "Go on. Tell me what happened."

"It wasn't a fair fight, but Aiden should have seen this coming. You know how much he wants you to lead." Noah held out his hands, palms out to prevent Rhys from barreling him over. "Alrik and his sycophants cornered Aiden in the gym."

Rhys's breath caught and seared his lungs. Gym equipment could kill if used with brute force. "Is he...?" The lump in his throat strangled his voice. Ice drenched his scalp, sliding down his spine to his fingertips. He shoved them into his pockets, hoping to hide their trembling. "Can I see him now?"

Noah studied him for a long-drawn-out moment. "Don't mention his face."

Rhys halted mid-stride. "Why?" He gripped the door frame and splintered the wood beneath his fingers, fear and fury pummeling his thoughts, his senses. "I'm going to fucking kill Alrik."

"You *could* take him on, Rhys, but winning means becoming the alpha."

Rhys shot Jase a sharp glare. "Like I don't fucking know that."

"It's just a reminder, brother-in-pack." Noah thumped his back, trying to calm Rhys.

He was far from it. His bear paced inside him, whining for release. Rhys snorted and flicked his head side-to-side, cracking his neck.

"I'll see Aiden first. Alrik's death can wait." One step into the room petrified his muscles. His bones locked, and his bear clawed at the walls, roaring in despair. The stench of antiseptic, blood, and the burned ozone of pain hit him.

The man in the bed wasn't the Aiden Rhys had seen at breakfast. The youthful skin molded over his features was blue, black, swollen, and mottled. Both eyes were sealed shut, his eyelashes like the legs of a squashed spider. His nose was broken, and his lips split and bleeding.

Sure, shifters healed fast, but in the meantime, he would be in fiery agony while his muscles and bones reknitted. Aiden lay like an ironing board, his arms bandaged in place, and one leg in a worn orthopedic boot.

"Sans was here?"

" He *is* our doctor." Jase nudged his chin at Aiden. "Sans snuck in to tend to Aiden. Said he saw it go down. I asked my brother to escort him home."

"Good." Rhys grunted. Jase and his brother Sawyer were the best trackers in the pack.

At least, Rhys had one ally from Alrik's camp. Taking their alpha on wouldn't be easy, and despite knowing it was the right decision, Rhys didn't like the risks if he failed. The Knights Ridge pack would continue to suffer without him to shield them. Cast out, exiled, he would have to head north to Dane's pack. That wasn't fair on his old college friend. An alpha shouldn't have to tolerate another alpha in his pack, and Rhys wasn't designed to be a beta.

He slumped. "Alrik has to know what this means."

Noah spun a chair and squatted on it, folding his arms across the back. "He was tired of waiting for you to make your move, Rhys."

"Well, by attacking the 'last' member of my family, he made sure I would react." He smiled, but it was nothing more than a tightness across his mouth. There was no mirth, no eagerness behind it. "I won't give in to him."

Jase gaped, but after a glance at Noah's knowing smirk, he quit looking like a fish out of water. "What do you intend to do?"

"I'll wait, bide my time, gather the elders and the strongest pack members eager for new leadership. Let Alrik stew, raise his paranoia to a new level."

"We must bow but not shy from him." Noah grinned. "Spur on rumors of attacks, of allies outside of Knights Ridge. Giving Colt a call might be wise. Might as well do the same for Travis. Having Fenneg's Rabidhide and Suddale's Dawnguard packs on your side would bolster your authority. Dane's already on your side, but Coedwig is smallish and won't hold any sway against Alrik."

Rhys smirked. "I'll tell Dane you said so."

Noah chuckled and flicked a dismissive hand.

"Everything must fail. We'll create a leak in the water towers, cut the power supply, drain the food stores, and cut off the pack's finances." Jase ticked these off on his fingers. "Not so bad we can't repair them when you're in power, of course."

"A battle strategy," Rhys said while brushing Aiden's hair off his temple.

"I love that idea, except we need to challenge him soon." Noah dipped his head. "I can't keep silent for much longer."

Rhys studied Noah's face, familiar with the sadness in his eyes. They had all suffered at Alrik's hands as expected of a cruel alpha. "All right. How much can we organize by sunset?"

Jase's whoop startled Aiden awake who tried to rise, groaned, then slumped.

"Rhys?" His hoarse voice tore through Rhys who had vowed to protect his brother when their parents were killed and Uncle Sean left the pack. Finding Aiden sprawled, bloodied, and bandaged, lashed at the guilt encasing Rhys's heart.

"I'm here, baby bear." He patted Aiden's bicep.

Aiden's brow furrowed. "Argh, quit calling me that."

"Quit trying to get me killed. I'll take on Alrik when I'm ready. Your shit-stirring is to blame for this."

Aiden fell silent before he mumbled, "You're right. I'm sorry."

"Rest, Aiden, heal." Rhys pushed off the bed. "If you're a good little patient, I'll take you for ice cream in the morning."

"Ass." Aiden chuckled, then coughed. Blood dewed on his split lip.

Rhys nudged his head at the door. Striding out, he didn't check whether Jase and Noah followed. Their boots thumping on the wooden floor and their wolf and tiger scents were all he needed. "Make it happen."

Noah jerked, then beamed. "Are you sure?"

"Now you doubt me?" Rhys harrumphed. "I'll set up a barbecue closest to the club-house. I want you two, and any of our pack mates, to come and go. Spend some time with me laughing and drinking beer. If I can't have Jase's sweet strategy, then let's go for the element of surprise."

Jase bounded down the stairs, banging cupboard doors as he gathered the makings of a barbecue. "The meat you brought from town hasn't frozen yet. I'll grab a few steaks."

Noah yanked the door off its one hinge and leaned it against a wall. "I'll round up who I can, then tag Jase. A crowd will gather before sunset."

An impromptu barbecue wasn't unheard of, and it would lead Alrik into a false sense of security. "Send someone to gather the elders. This can't go down without their attendance."

Rhys sighed at the reminder of how old and neglected their elders were. Anyone strong enough to challenge Alrik's reign found a swift death. Their eldest was Sans, and that old lion wouldn't last many more winters.

Gritting his teeth, Rhys swept up a pile of logs and carried it to the firepit. He didn't choose the one closest to the clubhouse, but the largest. Tonight, there would be a show for everyone, with minimum damage to the dilapidated clubhouse and surrounding cabins.

With a hand in his pocket, he nursed the fire, sipping on his beer. Noah arrived with his arm across Willow's shoulder. His younger sister was adorable with her blonde hair in pigtails. Her wide-eyed gaze darting to Rhys's cabin hinted that she would rather be with Aiden.

He offered her a soda. "Drink half of this, then stroll to my cabin." What would happen between him and Alrik wouldn't be pretty, and casualties were possible. Willow out of sight with Aiden meant one less soul for Rhys to worry about.

She forced a smile. "Kick ass tonight."

"Language." Noah chuckled at her glare. "The elders are on their way. They'll trickle in along with their kin."

"Sawyer is rounding up the others." Jase rocked on his heels, cradling a beer can to his chest.

Rhys released a slow breath. Adrenaline pumped through his veins while the excitement and a healthy dose of fear raised the hairs on the back of his neck.

"He's watching from his lofty perch." Noah tipped his beer to his lips.

"Wondering why he wasn't invited?" Jase laughed, a little too loudly. "Let him hear how much fun we're having, how much we care for his brutality."

The urge to look tugged at Rhys. His bear roared, willing him to give Alrik the middle finger. Rhys grinned at the idea. No, he wanted him to join the party. The older male would do so unafraid, bringing Dyl and Vik as his only protection.

Rhys snorted. An alpha shouldn't need bodyguards, and Alrik's security detail said it all. The challenge match would be between Rhys and Alrik. Taking down his bodyguards would weaken Rhys, and that was exactly how it would play out, breaking the challenge laws.

Folks trickled in, each stopping by to offer their support. Fear lingered in their eyes, in their broken spirits, yet they had ventured out with hope the driving force. The weight of their suffering settled on his chest like an anchor, bolstering his determination.

They feasted. The aroma of charred meat added to the pseudo joy in the air. While he nursed one beer and was desperate for another, the chill of midnight approaching tested his patience.

"What are we celebrating?" Alrik's bombastic voice grated on Rhys's last nerve.

The fool smirked, as if everyone's silence was a mark of respect. In an expensive jacket and a crisp white shirt, he had the air of a gentleman at leisure.

Behind him stood Vik, all muscle with no hair. Rhys had never liked the kid growing up. His bullying of others less fortunate or weaker than him wasn't an admirable trait. No matter what Rhys said to him, it had ended in brawling. To be fair, Rhys had Vik to thank for his fighting skills.

Dyl hovered farther away, his gaze vigilant. Not originally from the Knights Ridge pack meant no blood ties to the folks there, no history. A stranger was easier to manipulate, easier to pay off.

The temptation to lunge, to snap Alrik's neck was strong. Eager for a fight, Rhys's bear banged against the restraints. Yet, to assume the alpha role, he had to challenge and win.

"No reason." Shrugging, he met Alrik's gaze, not backing down, not glancing away in submission.

The older male bristled, squaring his shoulders. "Where's Aiden?" He chuckled, but his focus didn't shift from Rhys's face.

He didn't rise to the bait. "I believe he and Willow asked for alone time."

Alrik's attempts to keep the bloodlines pure was pointless. Species with species was his motto despite the mix each pack sported. Rhys hadn't heard of pure bear packs or wolf packs except from fables told around the campfires. Those days were long gone. And besides, love didn't care about blood, gender, age, or status, and Alrik thinking he could control or deny it was proof the old male was an idiot.

He whipped his head to stare at Noah, a pulse ticking at the base of his jaw. "And you condone the dilution of your bloodline?" Alrik growled. "Impure blood weakens our connection to the Lunar goddess."

"Maybe, but from where I'm standing, I'd say the goddess has long abandoned you."

Alrik roared, his face mottling. "You challenge me?"

Noah laughed. "No, not I, old cat."

"I suggest you remove that jacket. When we're done, I'll sell it to pay for repairs. And you better pray I kill you before we find out what you've wasted our money on." Rhys peeled off his T-shirt, draping it across a tree stump.

The problem was the moment he bent to undo his boots Alrik would charge. It was in his nature, and a tiger never changed their stripes.

Rhys loved these jeans, and releasing his bear would shred the well-worn denim. Sighing, he rested his hands on his hips as he studied his alpha.

Surprising him, Jase kneeled and undid Rhys's laces. Fuck, right then, he loved his brother-in-pack. Alrik growled, lunging forward to nudge Jase aside, but Sawyer and Noah leaped in front to shield him.

Vik loomed behind Alrik, attempting to warn them off without shifting into his bear. Made sense, since his hairless bear was a laughable sight. He had the claws and teeth of a polar bear, just not the intimidation factor. Vik was evidence Alrik's "beliefs" were subjective. The last person to mention that had died.

During their posturing, Rhys removed his boots and shimmied out of his jeans. "Thanks, Jase." He nudged his head to the crowd, asking him to guard the innocent.

Noah and Sawyer settled behind Rhys, mimicking Vik and Dyl.

"You have a choice before you." Rhys folded his arms across his chest and met Vik and Dyl's gazes. "Stay, and you die for this male. I sure as fuck think that would be a waste of life."

Without eyebrows, the only way to measure Vik's surprise was by the furrowing of his forehead.

"You know me, Vik, you know my history, my stance, my honor."

The male nodded.

"We may not have seen eye-to-eye, but you're welcome at Knights Ridge, no judgment, a free bear."

Vik settled his gaze on Alrik, before bowing his head. "I prefer to walk away with my life."

Relief flooded Rhys at not having to kill someone he had known for so long.

Alrik spat and faced Vik. "You piece of shit."

Before Rhys could stop him, Alrik swung out a clawed hand, slicing across Vik's face. Rhys took Alrik down, releasing his bear just as they hit the compacted ground. They rolled, scrambling for dominance, claws and teeth connecting when Alrik assumed his ragged tiger form.

Rhys roared as Alrik bit into his shoulder, his incisors sinking deep. Unable to shake the old tiger off, he flipped onto his back and threw Alrik over his head, tossing him far. Ignoring the throbbing numbness working its way down his front limb, Rhys lumbered over to the tiger, tackling him again. The crowds scattered, then regathered like a shifting shoal of sardines.

A wolf pounced on Rhys's back and clenched his teeth around Rhys's fur-lined bicep. As the pain registered, the wolf flew off, sliding along the ground and into the tree stump. Noah's wolf growled, keeping Dyl at bay. He broke the challenge laws by interfering, but then again, so had Dyl.

Rhys settled his bear's full weight onto the tiger, hoping to force him to submit. It took all his control not to slice his claws across Alrik's throat. His bear roared for blood and justice.

"Submit," Rhys grated, the words barely audible when spoken through his bear.

"Never." Alrik's tongue lolled out as he fought for air.

"Submit," Rhys roared, baring his teeth an inch from Alrik's cheek. Rhys didn't want the other's death on his hands, even though the certainty of it pierced his jagged thoughts.

When Alrik met Rhys's gaze with blatant challenge, he leaned back to swipe his claws.

Seconds before he sliced the soft flesh of Alrik's throat, the crowd sucked in a collective breath. Clambering to his feet, Rhys receded his bear to stare at Alrik's lifeless human body. The pooling blood glowed in the flickering light of the dying fire. The stench was as sharp and as yellow as Aiden's. The purer the lineage didn't alter the smell.

Rhys's sweat-drenched chest rose and fell as the sounds of night settled on him, and his aches registered. Flicking off the blood dripping from his fingertips, he stumbled back then faced his...pack.

He met each person's gaze. "Any challenger?" As part of the law, he had to ask.

In a wave of obeisance, they dipped their heads, submitting to their new alpha. Noah and Jase holding Dyl in place, also bowed, despite the grins morphing their faces. They released Dyl who took off into the night. Sawyer broke away to chase after him—the determined set of his jaw assured Rhys this loose end would be settled this night.

Rhys threw his arms wide and laughed, success melting the tension from his body. "I need a beer."